wanted

By J. Kenner

wanted

A
Most
Wanted
Novel

J. KENNER

Bantam Books Trade Paperbacks *New York*

2014 Bantam Books Trade Paperback Original

Copyright © 2014 by Julie Kenner
Excerpt from *Heated* by J. Kenner copyright © 2014 by Julie Kenner

Published in the United States by Bantam Books, an imprint of Random House, a division of Random House LLC, a Penguin Random House Company, New York.

BANTAM BOOKS and the HOUSE colophon are registered trademarks of Random House LLC.

This book contains an excerpt from the forthcoming book *Heated* by J. Kenner. This excerpt has been set for this edition only and may not reflect the final content of the forthcoming edition.

Library of Congress Cataloging-in-Publication Data
Kenner, Julie, author.
Wanted : a most wanted novel / J. Kenner.
pages   cm
ISBN 978-0-8041-7666-8 (acid-free paper)
ebook ISBN 978-0-8041-7667-5
1. Erotic fiction.   I. Title.
PS3611.E665W36 2014
813'.6—dc23   2013043694

Printed in the United States of America on acid-free paper

randomhousebooks.com

10 9 8 7 6 5 4

acknowledgments

Special thanks to Elle, Christie, and Dana. I so appreciate you taking the time to read and comment, especially when the turnaround was so dang fast! Hugs, kisses, and buckets of emojis to you!

A big shout-out to my former boss, Steve, for letting me have the use of his Chicago condo so I could get the feel of the city, and to Jim at In Chicago Sedan and Limousine for being such an incredible and informative tour guide.

To my daughter Catherine (even though it'll be years before she can read this book!), for being a great travel companion, and for not complaining when Mom insisted on walking everywhere in order to enjoy the city's vibe!

To my awesome agent, Kim, and to Shauna and Gina and all the wonderful folks at Bantam whose support and enthusiasm thrills me to my toes and beyond.

Most of all, to all the incredible readers who've reached out to me through my website, social media, snail mail, conferences, and book signings. Y'all are truly amazing.

XXOO,
J.K.

wanted

one

I know exactly when my life shifted. That precise instant when his eyes met mine and I no longer saw the bland look of familiarity, but danger and fire, lust and hunger.

Perhaps I should have turned away. Perhaps I should have run.

I didn't. I wanted him. More, I needed him. The man, and the fire that he ignited inside of me.

And in his eyes, I saw that he needed me, too.

That was the moment that everything changed. Me, most of all.

But whether it changed for good or for ill . . . well, that remains to be seen.

Even dead, my Uncle Jahn knew how to throw one hell of a party.

His Chicago lakeside penthouse was bursting at the seams with an eclectic collection of mourners, most of whom had imbibed so much wine from the famous Howard Jahn cellar that whatever melancholy they'd brought with them had been sweetly erased, and now this wake or reception or whatever the hell you wanted to call it wasn't the least bit somber. Politicians mingled with financiers mingled with artists and academics, and everyone was smiling and laughing and toasting the deceased.

At his request, there'd been no formal funeral. Just this gathering of friends and family, food and drink, music and mirth. Jahn—he hated the name Howard—had lived a vibrant life, and that was never more obvious than now in his death.

I missed him so damn much, but I hadn't cried. Hadn't screamed and ranted. Hadn't done anything, really, except move through the days and nights lost in a haze of emotions, my mind numb. My body anesthetized.

I sighed and fingered the charm on my silver bracelet. He'd presented me with the tiny motorcycle just over a month ago, and the gift had made me smile. I hadn't talked about wanting to ride a motorcycle since before I turned sixteen. And it had been years since I'd ridden behind a boy, my arms tight around his waist and my hair blowing in the wind.

But Uncle Jahn knew me better than anyone. He saw past the princess to the girl hidden inside. A girl who'd built up walls out of necessity, but still desperately wanted to break free. Who longed to slip on a pair of well-worn jeans, grab a battered leather jacket, and go a little wild.

Sometimes, she even did. And sometimes it didn't end right at all.

I tightened my grip on the charm as the memory of Jahn holding my hand—of him promising to keep my secrets—swept over me, finally bringing tears to my eyes. He should be beside me, dammit, and the swell of laughter and conversation that filled the room was making me a little sick.

Despite the fact that I knew Jahn wanted it that way, it was all I could do not to smack all the people who'd hugged me and murmured softly that he was in a better place and wasn't it wonderful that he'd lived such a full life. That was such bullshit—he hadn't even turned sixty yet. Vibrant men in their fifties shouldn't drop dead from aneurysms, and there weren't enough pithy Hallmark quotes in the universe to make me think otherwise.

Antsy, I shifted my weight from foot to foot. There was a bar set up on the other side of the room, and I'd positioned myself as far away as physically possible because right then I wanted the burn of tequila. Wanted to let go, to explode through the numbness that clung to me like a cocoon. To run. To *feel*.

But that wasn't going to happen. No alcohol was passing these lips tonight. I was Jahn's niece, after all, and that made me some kind of hostess-by-default, which meant I was stuck in the penthouse. Four thousand square feet, but I swear I could feel the art-covered walls pressing in around me.

I wanted to race up the spiral staircase to the rooftop patio, then leap over the balcony into the darkening sky. I wanted to take flight over Lake Michigan and the whole world. I wanted to break things and scream and rant and curse this damned universe that took away a good man.

Shit. I sucked in a breath and looked down at the exquisite ancient-looking notebook inside the glass and chrome display case I'd been leaning against. The leather-bound book was an exceptionally well-done copy of a recently discovered Da Vinci notebook. Dubbed the Creature Notebook, it had sixteen pages of animal studies and was open to the center, revealing a stunning sketch the young master had drawn—his study for the famous, but never located, dragon shield. Jahn had attempted to acquire the notebook, and I remember just how angry he'd been when he'd lost out to Victor Neely, another Chicago businessman with a private collection that rivaled my uncle's.

At the time, I'd just started at Northwestern with a major in poli sci and a minor in art history. I'm not particularly talented, but I've sketched my whole life, and I've been fascinated with art—and in particular with Leonardo da Vinci—since my parents took me to my first museum at the age of three.

I thought the Creature Notebook was beyond cool, and I'd been irritated on Jahn's behalf when he not only lost out on it, but when the press had poured salt in the wound by prattling on about Neely's amazing new acquisition.

About a year later, Jahn showed me the facsimile, bright and shiny in the custom-made display case. As a general rule, my uncle never owned a copy. If he couldn't have the original—be it a Rembrandt or a Rauschenberg or a Da Vinci—he simply moved on. When I'd asked why he'd made an exception for the Creature Notebook, he shrugged and told me that the images were at least as interesting as the provenance. "Besides, anyone who can successfully copy a Da Vinci has created a masterpiece himself."

Despite the fact that it wasn't authentic, the notebook was my favorite of Jahn's many manuscripts and artifacts, and now, standing with my hands pressed to the glass, I felt as if he was, in some small way, beside me.

I drew in a breath, knowing I had to get my act together, if for no other reason than the more wrecked I looked, the more guests would try to cheer me. Not that I looked particularly wrecked. When you grow up as Angelina Hayden Raine, with a United States senator for a father and a mother who served on the board of over a dozen international nonprofit organizations, you learn the difference between a public and a private face very early on. Especially when you have your own secrets to keep.

"This is so goddamn fucked up it makes me want to scream."

I felt a whisper of a smile touch my lips and turned around to find myself looking into Kat's bloodshot eyes.

"Oh, hell, Angie," she said. "He shouldn't be dead."

"He'd be pissed if he knew you'd been crying," I said, blinking away the last of my own tears.

"Fuck that."

I almost laughed. Katrina Laron had a talent for cutting straight through the bullshit.

I'm not sure which one of us leaned in first, but we caught each other in a bone-crushing hug. With a sniffle, I finally pulled away. Perverse, maybe, but just knowing that someone else was acknowledging the utter horror of the situation made me feel infinitesimally better.

"Every time I turn a corner, I feel like I'm going to see him," I said. "I almost wish I'd stayed in my old place."

I'd moved in four months ago when Uncle Jahn's aneurysm was discovered. I'd taken time off from work—easy when you work for your uncle. For two weeks I'd played nurse after he came home from the hospital, and when he'd been given the all-clear by the doctors—yeah, like *that* was a good call—I'd accepted his invitation to move in permanently. Why not? The tiny apartment I'd shared with my lifelong friend Flynn wasn't exactly the lap of luxury. And although I loved Flynn, he wasn't the easiest person to cohabitate with. He knew me too well, and it always made me uneasy when people saw what I wanted to keep hidden.

Now, though, I craved both the cocoon-like comfort of my tiny room and Flynn's steady presence. As much as I loved the condo, without my uncle, it was cold and hollow, and just being in it made me feel brittle. As if at any moment I would shatter into a million pieces.

Kat's eyes were warm and understanding. "I know. But he loved having you here. God knows why," she added with a quirky grin. "You're nothing but trouble."

I rolled my eyes. At twenty-seven, Katrina Laron was only four years older than me, but that didn't stop her from pulling the older-and-wiser card whenever she got the chance. The fact that we'd become friends under decidedly dodgy circumstances probably played a role, too.

She'd been working at one of the coffee shops in Evanston where I used to mainline caffeine during my first year at Northwestern. We'd chatted a couple of times in an "extra cream please, it's been a bitch of a day" kind of way, but we were hardly on a first-name basis.

All that changed when we bumped into each other on a day when extra cream wasn't going to cut it for me—not by a long shot. It was in the Michigan Avenue Neiman Marcus and I'd been surfing on adrenaline, using it to soothe the rough edges of a particularly crappy day. Specifically, I'd just succumbed to my personal demons and surreptitiously dropped a pair of fifteen-dollar clearance earrings into my purse. But, apparently, not as surreptitiously as I'd thought.

"Well, aren't you the stumbling amateur?" she'd whispered, as she steered me toward women's shoes. "With a shit technique like that, it's a wonder you haven't been arrested yet."

"Arrested!" I squeaked, as if that word would carry all the way to Washington and to my father's all-hearing ears. The *fear* of getting caught might be part of the excitement. *Actually* getting caught wasn't a good thing at all. "No, I didn't—I mean—"

She cut off my protests with a casual flip of her hand. "All I'm saying is be smart. If you're going to take a risk, at least make it worth the trouble. Those earrings? Really not the bomb."

"It's not about the earrings," I'd snapped, then immediately cringed. The words had been a knee-jerk response, but they were also true. It *wasn't* about the earrings. It was about my dad, and the grad school lectures and the career-planning talks, and the never-spoken certainty that no matter what I did, my sister would have done it better.

It was about the oppressive, overwhelming weight of my life and my future that was bearing down on me, harder and harder until I was certain that if I didn't do something to break out a little I'd spontaneously combust.

Kat had glanced at my purse as if she could see through the soft Coach leather to the contraband inside. Then she slowly lifted her eyes back to my face. The silence hung between us for a full minute. Then she nodded. "Don't worry. I get it." She cocked her head toward the exit. "Come on."

Relief flooded through me, and my limbs that had frozen in both fear and mortification began to thaw. She steered me to her car, a cherry-red Mustang that she drove at more or less the speed of light. She careened down Michigan Avenue, maneuvered her way onto Lake Shore Drive, and came so close to the other cars as she zipped in and out of traffic that I'm surprised her convertible didn't lose a layer of paint. In other words, it was freaking awesome. The top was down, the wind was whipping my hair into my face and mouth, and all I could do was tilt my head back and laugh.

Kat risked our lives long enough to shoot me one sideways glance. "Yeah," she said. "We're going to get along just fine."

From that moment on, I'd adored Kat. Now, with Jahn's death sending my universe reeling, I realized that I not only loved her—I relied on her.

"I'm really glad you're here," I said.

"Where else would I be?" She scanned the room. "Are your mom and dad around somewhere?"

"They can't make it. They're stuck overseas." The familiar numbness settled over me again as I remembered my mother's hysterical sobs and the deep well of sorrow that had filled my father's voice when he'd learned about his half-brother. "I hated calling them," I whispered. "It felt like Gracie all over again."

"I'm so sorry." Kat had never met my sister, but she'd heard the story. The public version, anyway, and I knew her sympathy was real.

I managed a wavering smile. "I know. That means a lot to me."

"The whole thing sucks," Kat said. "It's so unfair. Your uncle was too damn cool to die."

"I guess the universe doesn't give a shit about coolness."

"The universe can be a raving bitch sometimes," Kat said. She exhaled loudly. "Want me to crash here tonight so you won't be alone? We could stay up late getting so wasted that there's no way in hell either one of us will dream."

"Thanks, but I think I'll be okay."

She eyed me uncertainly. She was one of the few people I'd confided in about my nightmares, and while I appreciated the sympathy, sometimes I wished I'd kept my mouth shut.

"Really," I said earnestly. "Kevin's here."

"Oh, yeah? And how's that going? Engaged yet?"

"Not quite," I said wryly. I supposed we were dating since I'd slept with him twice, but so far I'd dodged the let's-be-exclusive conversation. I wasn't sure why I was so reticent. The sex wasn't mind-blowing, but it did the job. And I did genuinely like the guy. But I'd spent the last few months holding him at arm's length, telling him I needed to keep my attention on Jahn's surgery, then his recovery.

Obviously, I hadn't planned on his sudden death.

How horrible was it of me to think that now Jahn was gone, I had no more excuses to hand Kevin?

Beside me, Kat craned her neck and scoped out the crowd. "So where is he?"

"He had to go take a call. Technically, he's working today."

"What are you going to do now?" Kat asked.

"About Kevin?" Honestly, I was hoping to avoid doing anything on that front for the foreseeable future.

"About your job," she countered. "About the roof over your head. About your life. Have you thought about what you're going to do?"

"Oh." My shoulders sagged. "No. Not really." My job in the PR department of Jahn's company might pay my bills, but it was hardly my life's ambition, and Kat was one of the few people to whom I'd confessed that deep, dark secret. Right then, however, that wasn't a conversation I wanted to have. Fortunately, something across the room had caught Kat's attention, effectively erasing my lack of direction and purpose from her mind.

She stood slightly straighter and the corners of her mouth tilted a bit, almost hinting at a smile. Curious, I turned to look in that direction, but saw nothing but suits and dresses and a sea of black. "What is it? Kevin?" I asked, praying he wasn't heading our direction.

"Cole August," she said. "At least I thought I saw him."

"Oh." I licked my lips. My mouth had gone suddenly dry. "Is Evan with him?" I forced my voice to sound casual, but my pulse was racing. If Cole was around, it was always a good bet that Evan was, too.

Then I remembered what day it was and my pulse slowed as disappointment weighed down on me. "Isn't tonight the ribbon-cutting for the hospital wing Evan funded?"

Kat didn't even spare me a glance, her eyes still searching the crowd. "Not sure." She shot me a quick look. "Yeah, it was. You invited me before, you know, all of this happened."

I blinked back the sudden prick of tears. "Evan's going to hate missing this. Jahn was like a dad to him."

Beside me, Kat took a quick step backward, startling me.

"What is it?"

She dragged her gaze away from the crowd, then frowned at me. "I . . . Oh, shit. I have to go make a call. I'll be right back, okay?"

"Um, okay." Who the hell did she need to call right now? That wasn't a question I pondered for long, though, because I'd caught a glimpse of Cole. And right beside him—looking like he owned the world and everything in it—was Evan.

Immediately, my chest tightened and a current of electricity zinged across my skin. Technically, I saw him first, but it was my body's reaction that caught my attention. Only after I felt him did I truly see him.

And what a sight he was.

Whereas Cole might be sex on wheels, Evan Black was the slow burn of sin and seduction—and tonight he was in rare form. He must have come straight from the hospital, because he was still in a tux, and although he was clearly overdressed, he appeared perfectly at ease. Whether in a tux or jeans, where Evan was concerned, it was the man that mattered, not the garment.

He had the kind of chiseled good looks that would have gotten him plucked from obscurity in the Golden Age of Hollywood, and the kind of confidence and bearing that would have made him a box-office draw. A small scar intersected his left brow, giving the angel's face a hint of the devil.

He both came from money and had made his own fortune, and it showed in the way he held himself, the way he looked around a room, managing to take control of it with nothing more than a glance.

His eyes were as gray as a wolf's and his hair was the color of cherrywood, a deep brown that hinted at golds and reds when the light hit it just right. He wore it long in the back so that it brushed his collar, and the natural waves gave it the quality of a mane—which only enhanced the impression that there was a wildness clinging to the man.

Wild or not, I wanted to get close. I wanted to thrust my fingers into his hair and feel the locks on my skin. I imagined his hair was soft, but that's the only part of him that was. Everything else was edged with steel, the hard planes of his face and body hinting at a dangerous core beneath that beauty.

I didn't know whether the danger was real or an illusion. And right then, I didn't care.

I wanted the touch, the thrill.

That desperate need to fly I'd been feeling all night? So help me, I wanted to fly right into Evan's arms.

I needed the rush. I craved the thrill.

I wanted the man.

And it was just too damn bad that he didn't want me, too.

two

I'd known Evan Black for almost eight years, and yet I didn't really know the man at all.

I'd just turned sixteen when I first saw him during the sweltering heat of a summer that marked so many firsts in my life. The first summer I spent entirely in Chicago. The first summer away from my parents. The first time I fucked a guy. Because that's what it was. Not a sweet teenage romance. It was release, pure and simple. Release and escape and oblivion.

And damned if I hadn't needed oblivion, because that was also the first summer without my sister, who was back in California, six feet beneath the sun-soaked earth.

I'd been lost after her death. My parents—wracked with their own grief—had tried to pull me close, to help and soothe me. But I wriggled away, too burdened with loss to cleave to them the way I wanted. Too heavy with guilt to believe I had any right to their help or affection.

It was Jahn who'd rescued me from that small corner of hell. He'd appeared at the front door of our La Jolla house the first Friday of summer break, and immediately steered my mother into the dark-paneled office that was forbidden to me. When they'd emerged twenty minutes later there were fresh tears in my mother's eyes, but she'd managed a cheery smile for me. "Go pack your carry-on," she'd said. "You're going to Chicago with Uncle Jahn."

I'd taken three tank tops, my swimsuit, a dress, a pair of jeans, and the shorts I'd worn on the plane. I'd expected to stay a weekend. Instead, I'd stayed the entire summer.

At the time, Jahn was living primarily in his waterfront house in Kenilworth, a jaw-droppingly affluent Chicago suburb. For two solid weeks, I'd done nothing but sit under the gazebo and stare out at Lake Michigan. Not my usual M.O.—during past visits, I'd taken out the Jet Ski or skateboarded in the street or taken off on a borrowed bike down Sheridan Road with Flynn, the boy I would later fuck who lived two doors down and had as much of a wild streak as I did. When I was twelve, I'd even rigged a zip line from the attic bedroom all the way to the far side of the pool, and I'd eagerly tested it out, much to the consternation of my mother who had screamed and cursed once she saw me whipping through the air to land, cannonball style, in the water.

Grace had squealed at me from her chaise lounge throne, accusing me of ruining her hardback copy of *Pride and Prejudice*. My mother had ordered me to spend the rest of the day in my room. And Uncle Jahn had remained completely silent, but as I passed him, I thought I saw the twinkle of amusement in his eyes, along with something that might have been respect.

I saw none of that the summer of my sixteenth year. Instead, all I saw was worry.

"We all miss her," he said to me one afternoon. "But you can't mourn forever. She wouldn't want you to. Take the bike. Go into the village. Go to the park. Drag Flynn to a movie." He cupped my chin and tilted my face up to look at him. "I lost one niece, Lina. Not two."

"Angie," I corrected, making up my mind right then and there to kick Lina soundly to the curb. Lina was the girl I used to be. The one who'd always felt larger than life, and who'd needed to feel the rush of the world around her all the time. Who'd been too alive to be calm or careful. Who'd been a damn stupid fool who smoked cigarettes behind the school and snuck out to dance clubs. A little idiot who made out with boys because she wanted the thrill, and who rode on the back of their motorcycles for the exact same reason. Lina was the girl who'd almost been suspended from high school just one week into her freshman year.

And Lina was the reason that my sister was dead.

I'd lived in Lina's skin all my life, but I didn't want to be that girl anymore.

"Angie," I repeated, firmly cementing the first brick of the wall I was building around myself. Then I'd stood up and gone inside.

Uncle Jahn hadn't bothered me for the rest of that day or the next, though I knew he was worried and confused. When Saturday morning came, he told me that he was having some students from the graduate-level finance seminar he taught as an adjunct over for burgers by the pool, and I was welcome to join them. My call.

I'm not sure what compelled me to emerge from the dark cave of my room that afternoon, all I know is that I came down in my ratty cutoffs with Uncle Jahn's ancient Rolling Stones T-shirt over my bikini top. I thought I'd stay for an hour. Have a burger. Remind myself not to sneak a beer, because that was the kind of thing Lina would do, not Angie.

But when I actually got down to the pool deck, all thoughts of beer and burgers evaporated, replaced by pure, decadent, desperate lust. And not the teenage-crush kind, either. No, I saw Evan Black shirtless and in swim trunks that clung in a way that made my sixteen-year-old hormones light up. His wet hair was swept back from his face, and he was brandishing a metal spatula as he stood by the grill, laughing with two other guys, who I later learned were his best friends, Cole August and Tyler Sharp.

All three seemed younger than the other four students who also populated the lush backyard. I later learned that I was right. The others were in their last year of grad school, whereas Evan was still an undergrad who'd been given special dispensation to take the class. And Tyler and Cole weren't even enrolled at Northwestern. Tyler was a freshman at Loyola. Cole was a year older than Tyler, and had just come back from some sort of art internship in Rome. They'd come with Evan who, along with the others, made up the whole of that summer's seminar class in finance.

Together, Cole, Tyler, and Evan were a smorgasbord of hotness that even my reasonably inexperienced eyes were more than capable of appreciating. But Evan was the only one that I wanted to take a bite out of.

I heard my uncle call my name, and the three of them turned to look in my direction. I stopped breathing as Evan's gaze swept toward me, his expression never changing as he looked me over and then, oh-so casually, went back to flipping burgers.

I'm not sure what sort of movie I'd had running subliminally in my head. Something wild and romantic, I guess, because the moment he turned away, I felt a hot wave of disappointment wash over me. And that, of course, was immediately replaced by mortification. *Could he tell what I was thinking? Was he going to think of me now as Jahn's gawkish niece? The one with the schoolgirl crush?*

Holy crap, the idea was horrifying.

"Hey, Angie," Jahn called, his words jerking my posture straight as effectively as a string pulling a marionette. "You joining us for burgers?"

"I—" My words had stuck in my throat, and I knew I couldn't stay there. I needed space. Hell, I needed air. "I—I think I'm coming down with something." I blurted the words, then turned and ran back into the house, certain that my burning cheeks were a fire hazard.

I tried to concentrate on television. On a book. On screwing around on the Internet. But nothing held my attention. My mind was too full of Evan, and in the end I went to bed early. Not because I was truly sick, but because I wanted the pleasure of the dark. The thrill of sliding my hand down my belly and under the band of my underwear, then touching myself with my eyes closed as I imagined that it was Evan's fingers upon me. His fingers, his tongue, every decadent inch of him.

It was a bedtime fantasy that became a personal favorite, and one I repeated many nights over the next few years. Fortunately, I didn't repeat the squealing and running like a twit every time Evan came around. Fortunate because Jahn took a fatherly liking to them, and those three guys became a fixture at the house. And since I wasn't inclined to spend my summer hiding inside, I began to venture out. By August, I thought of Tyler and Cole like big brothers. As for Evan—no way would I ever feel brotherly toward him, but at least I could carry on a conversation without imagining his lips on mine.

Jahn called them the Three Dog Knights, because the Three Musketeers wasn't original enough for guys as unique as them. "Besides," he'd joked one evening as he hooked an arm around my shoulder and grinned at the guys, "this way I have my knights and my princess."

Evan focused those hypnotic gray eyes on me, obviously considering the comment. "Is that what you are?"

I froze, stunned by the question. Grace had always been the princess to my jester. But now that she was dead, I'd slipped on the mantle even though it was an awkward, uncomfortable fit.

He was watching me—his gaze holding steady on my face as I floundered for a reply, and for a moment I thought that he saw the girl beneath the facade and the family name. I thought that he saw *me*.

Then he smiled, all casual and false, and the spell was broken. "It's just that in the stories, the princess is always dragon-bait."

I had no idea how I was supposed to respond to that, and my discomfort made my temper flare—and then explode when Tyler and Cole both guffawed and Evan shot them a cocky *I've won this round* grin.

"Don't worry about me," I said coldly. "I won't ever be dragonbait."

"No?" He looked me up and down, and it took every ounce of my self-control to stand still as his eyes raked over me. "I guess we'll see," he finally said, and then without another word, he turned around and walked away.

I watched him leave, feeling itchy and unsatisfied. I wanted something—something big and wild. Something like the sizzle and pop that Evan's slow, heated gaze had made bubble up inside me.

Something? Oh, please. How much bullshit was that? I knew exactly what I wanted—or more accurately, I knew *who* I wanted. And he'd just flat-out left, as uninterested in me as I was enraptured by him.

As I bit back a frown, I saw my uncle watching me with an odd expression, and for the first time I feared that he knew my secret: I had more than an innocent schoolgirl crush on Evan Black. And somehow, someway, I was going to do something about it.

* * *

I released a long-suffering sigh, my eyes still fixed on the almost-magical image of Evan in his tux. I didn't know if I was charmingly optimistic or sadly pathetic. All I knew was that despite the years that had passed—and despite the lack of any interest on his part whatsoever—my fascination with Evan Black never waned.

For just a moment, I allowed myself the luxury of a fantasy. His finger crooked under my chin. The slight pressure as he lifted my face to look into his eyes. His touch would be gentle but firm. His scent masculine and heady. "Angie," he'd say. "Why the hell haven't we done this before?"

I'd open my mouth to answer, but he'd cut me off with a kiss, hot and open and so desperately demanding that I would melt against him, our bodies fusing from the electricity zinging through me, all of it focused between my thighs, making me squirm. Making me *need*.

"And there she is."

I flinched, yanked from my reverie by the caramel masculine tones. I turned to smile at the two-hundred-plus pounds of perfectly proportioned male that made up Cole August. At first glance, he was intimidating as shit, despite being empirically gorgeous. All muscle and power and hard edges, with the kind of air that warned away anyone who might want to fuck with him. He'd been born and raised on Chicago's rather scary South Side, and the rawness of his heritage still clung to him despite the tailored suit and other trappings of success.

His mixed-race background had blessed him with creamy dark skin that boasted a golden undertone, and his eyes flashed a deep ebony. It was in those eyes that you really saw the man. Massive and intense and just a bit menacing. But also fiercely loyal.

He held out his arms and I went willingly into them. "How are you holding up there, Dragonbait?"

"Not great." I sighed, his scent reminding me of Uncle Jahn, a musky male scent that probably came in a bottle but seemed to me to be part and parcel of those men I adored. "I'm glad you're here. I thought you were out of town."

"We came back, of course." By *we,* I knew he meant himself and Tyler Sharp. "We had to be here for Jahn," Cole added. He pressed a chaste kiss to my forehead. "And for you."

"Is Tyler hiding in the crowd somewhere?" I didn't mention that I'd already honed in on Evan.

"He was right behind me. But he was snagged by a limber blond thing who looked like she wanted to wrap herself around him."

I had to laugh. Even at a funeral, Tyler was a girl-magnet.

Cole grinned. "Yeah, well, don't hold it against her. I got the feeling she's been self-medicating her grief for hours."

"I know how she feels."

He looked hard at me, the humor all but erased from his face. "You need anything, you ask."

I nodded, but stayed silent. The only thing I needed was to let myself go a little wild. To shake off the weight of my grief, cut loose, and get lost in an adrenaline haze. It would work—I knew damn well that was the best way to take the edge off the pain and loss I was feeling. But no matter what, I wasn't going to go there.

Beside me, Cole called out a greeting to Tyler. I inched away from Cole and watched as the third of Jahn's knights approached. Where Cole was burly, Tyler was lean and athletic. He had the kind of good looks that could sneak up on a person, and the kind of charm that could make people do whatever Tyler wanted, and be absolutely certain it was their own idea all along.

He reached out for my hand and gave it a squeeze. "Tell us what you need."

"Nothing," I lied. "Just you two." I lifted a shoulder. "Really. It's better just having you guys here."

"Where's Evan?" Tyler asked, and though the question was directed at Cole, I turned to look, too. But Evan had disappeared.

"Well, shit. He was right beside me a minute ago." Cole glanced around. "Should be easy enough to spot. He's still in that damn monkey suit."

"He didn't want to take the time to go change." Tyler's attention turned to me. "You've seen him, though, right?"

"I—no," I responded. "I mean, I've seen him across the room, but I haven't talked to him. Not yet."

"Yeah?" Tyler's mouth curved down in a frown. "He texted me as he was leaving the dedication. Said he was coming straight here to make sure you were okay."

"He did?" A lazy little ripple of pleasure crept up my back.

"Yeah, he—wait. There he is. *Evan.*" His voice carried across the room, and several heads turned toward us. I, however, saw only his face. His eyes. And I swear they were looking at me with the kind of wicked heat I'd fantasized about.

I gasped, that sweet ripple of pleasure now moving to decidedly more interesting parts of my body. I glanced down at the floor, telling myself to get a grip. When I looked up, Evan was moving toward us in response to Tyler's insistent gesture. This time, however, I saw nothing in his eyes, leaving me to wonder if the ripples of heat existed only in my imagination.

He came toward us with long, confident strides. The crowd shifted automatically as he walked, as if it was as natural to clear a path for this man as it was to defer to royalty.

When he reached us, he didn't look at me. Not even a glance. Instead his attention was focused entirely on Tyler and Cole. His manner was brusque, his tone all business. "Everything okay in California?"

"We'll talk later," Tyler said, "but it's all good, man."

"Good," Evan said. He shifted his weight, as if he was about to drift away from our group.

"I hear all those movie stars are raving about your burritos,"

I blurted. I didn't know about all the various business ventures that the three had their hands in, but I'd paid attention when they'd bought the California-based fast-food chain that I used to frequent during high school. The place had been in violation of so many health codes it's a wonder I survived my teenage years without succumbing to hepatitis, but the guys managed to not only clean the place up but actually expand it into a half dozen other states.

Not that I gave a flip about burritos or California—I just wanted the warmth of Evan's eyes on me. Hell, I would have settled for the quick flash of a smile—I mean, both Cole and Tyler managed as much. But it wasn't their reaction I craved—it was Evan's. And all I got there was the chill of his indifference.

It made no sense. My secret lust notwithstanding, I'd known Evan my entire adult life, and the conversation had always flowed easily. After all, I'd had a lot of practice at hiding my secrets.

I told myself that he had business on his mind, but I didn't really believe it. His silence felt like a slight. Like he was intentionally avoiding looking at me. And, frankly, on this of all days, that kind of ticked me off.

I was so intent on being irritated with Evan, that I didn't realize Kevin had approached until he stepped up next to me and tugged me firmly into his embrace.

"Hey." I flashed a quick smile, hoping I didn't look disappointed to see him.

"Hey, yourself."

I leaned in to receive his sweet kiss. And, damn me all to hell, all I could think as my lips brushed this man's was whether or not Evan was watching.

I pulled away and forced myself to focus entirely on the man I'd just kissed. "Everything okay? Do you have to go in?"

"No crises," he said. "Truth, justice, and the American way can continue on without me."

He gently kissed my temple, and as I glanced between him and Evan, I had to wonder why the hell I was stalling. This was an incredibly kind and thoughtful man who had made it perfectly clear that he wanted to move past casual dating into a more serious relationship, and yet I was still caught up in lingering teenage fantasies? Honestly, did men get more upstanding and eligible than FBI agents? And considering my father had introduced us, he already had the parental seal of approval.

Purposefully, I moved closer, hooking my arms around his waist, then tilting my head up to look at his face. His wavy blond hair was neatly trimmed and his blue eyes held charm and humor. All in all, he had nice-guy good looks, like the cute quarterback who's not as sexy as the guy in leather with the low-slung car, but still totally hot. "I really appreciate you being here with me."

"I told SAC Burnett that I needed to be here for you today," he said, referring to the special agent in charge to whom he reported. His gaze flicked in turn over Cole and Tyler and Evan. "I'll get back to kicking criminal butt tomorrow."

"Who are you hounding now, Agent Warner?" Evan asked. There was a hint of humor in his voice, but also the tightness of control. Both Tyler and Cole must have heard it, too, because they each cut a sharp glance Evan's way. I had the impression that Cole was going to say something but thought better of it.

"Whoever the evidence points to," Kevin said. "Follow the trail long enough, and you find the asshole at the end."

"Evidence," Evan said, his tone musing. "I thought you boys stopped worrying about evidence years ago. Isn't the method now to fling shit and see what sticks?"

"If you're suggesting that we go to whatever lengths are necessary to gather the evidence that we need," Kevin said smoothly, "then you're absolutely right."

Any pretense of humor in the conversation had now been firmly erased. I winced, remembering too late that the FBI had

been all in the trio's face about five years ago. I'd seen the news-
paper articles and had asked Jahn about it. He told me not to
worry—that a business rival had made some nasty accusations,
but that his knights would have their names cleared soon
enough. I'd been deep into finals, and so I'd taken my uncle at
his word. And, since nothing else popped up in the news, I forgot all about it.

Clearly Evan hadn't forgotten, and the air around us crackled with an uncomfortable, prickly kind of tension.

I cleared my throat, determined to change the subject. "How
was the hospital dedication?"

"Inconvenient," Evan snapped. He shoved his hands in his
pockets, then drew in a breath, and it didn't take superhuman
observational skills to see he was making an effort to rein in his
temper. "Sorry," he said, his voice now gentle.

He turned slightly, and for the first time since he joined our
group, he looked in my direction. "The dedication—hell, the
entire wing—means a lot to me and even more to the kids we're
going to be helping, but I needed to be here." For the briefest of
moments, he looked directly into my eyes and I felt my breath
catch in my throat. "He was a good man," Evan said, and the
pain I heard in his voice reflected my own. "He'll be missed."

"He will," Kevin said. His voice sounded stiff and stilted,
and I had to fight the urge to pull out of his arms, because he
didn't get it. How could he? He didn't really know my uncle; he
didn't really understand what I'd lost.

I tried to swallow, but my throat was suddenly thick with
tears. I clenched my fists, as if mere force of will could keep the
grief at bay.

It didn't help. I felt suddenly lost. There was nowhere to
turn, nowhere to anchor, and any moment now I knew I would
spin out of control.

Damn.

I'd been doing so well—missing Jahn, yes, but not crossing

the line into self-pity. I'd been surviving, and the fact that I was coping had made me proud.

I wasn't coping anymore. Evan's coldness had thrown me off my game, and without warning, I'd become antsy and all sorts of fucked up. I wanted to step out of this weird triangle made up of me and Evan and Kevin, but I couldn't seem to move.

All I knew was that Uncle Jahn had always been my way in. He'd always understood me. He'd always been there to rescue me.

But he wasn't there right then—and to my total mortification, the tears began to flow.

"Angie," Evan murmured. "Oh, baby, it's okay."

I have no idea how it happened, but suddenly my face was pressed to Evan's chest and he was holding me and his hand was stroking my back and his voice was soothing me, telling me that I should let it out. That it would be okay. That *I* would be okay.

I clung to him, soaking up the solace that he was offering. His body was hard and firm and strong, and I didn't want to let go. I wanted to draw in his strength and claim it as my very own.

But then my nose started to run, and I pulled back, afraid of mucking up his gazillion-dollar tux. "Thanks," I said, or at least I tried to. I don't think the word actually left my mouth, because when I looked up at him, it wasn't friendly concern that I saw. No, it was heat. It was desire. Vibrant and pure and absolutely unmistakable.

And it was wild enough to burn a hole right through me.

I gasped, and the sound seemed to flip a switch in him. Then—as quickly as it appeared—that fire was gone, and I was left feeling cold and bereft and desperately confused.

"She needs you," Evan said, passing me off to Kevin, who took me into his arms even as a shadow crossed his face.

"Didn't you want to say something to the crowd?" Cole asked, his voice reminding me that he and Tyler were standing just inches away, their penetrating eyes taking in everything.

"I did," Evan said, his expression now bland and his tone businesslike, as if that could erase those last few seconds. But it was too late, and everything had changed. I'd seen it. Seen? Hell, what I'd seen in his face had just about knocked me over.

But he was walking away from me now, and as I watched him go—as I stood there clinging tightly to Kevin's hand—I knew that if I wanted him, I was going to have to go after him.

Because where Evan Black and I were concerned, he would always walk away.

And in a moment of sudden clarity, I goddamn knew the reason why.

three

I started my freshman year at Northwestern right about the time that Evan was dropping out, too successful in all of his various ventures to bother with anything as mundane as grad school.

The air seemed scented with lilac that fall, and Jahn had thrown one of his famous parties. Evan was there, of course, flanked as usual by Tyler and Cole. I'd sat with them by the pool, my bare feet dangling in the water as I answered their questions about how I was surviving my first weeks.

The conversation was casual and easy, and I was proud of myself for playing it cool. Or I was until Jahn asked me to go inside with him to pick out a bottle of wine.

"You know that you're like a daughter to me," he said, once we were standing in the bright and airy kitchen, looking out at the pool through the huge bay window.

"Sure," I said happily. Then I caught sight of his face and frowned. "Is something wrong?"

He shook his head, just the tiniest of motions. But the shadow in his eyes suggested something else entirely. "I just hope you know that I would do anything for you. That I'll protect you from anything and anyone."

My chest tightened and I felt the beads of perspiration rise on my lip. "What's going on?" My mind filled with images of knives and threats, of assault and rape. Oh, god, no. Surely—

"*No.*" Jahn's voice was as forceful as his hand clutched around my wrist. "No," he repeated, but this time more gently. "That's not what I'm talking about. Nothing like that."

Slowly, my fear ebbed. "Then what is it?"

"I've seen the way you look at them, Angie."

"Them?" For the briefest of moments, I was genuinely confused. Then I got it—and my cheeks flamed with embarrassment.

"Those boys will always look out for you," he said, ignoring my discomfiture. "They'll watch over you until the end of time because you're important to me. But it can't ever go further than that. Not with any one of them." His voice had hardened, taking on a commanding and serious tone that I rarely heard from him. "I said I'd protect you," he said. "Even if that means protecting you from yourself."

"I don't know what you—" I began, but he cut me off sharply.

"They're not the men for you," he said firmly. He faced me straight on, his expression deadly serious. "And they know that you're off-limits to them."

I opened my mouth to say something, then shut it again, because what the hell was I supposed to say? This was totally freaking surreal.

My instinct was to deny, deny, deny. But curiosity got the better of me. "What's wrong with them?" I asked.

"Not a goddamn thing."

"Then why are we having this conversation?"

He turned his back to the window and leaned against the granite counter, his arms crossed over his chest. His eyes narrowed, and I felt my posture straightening automatically under his appraising gaze.

He glanced quickly away. "They're too old for you."

I almost spit out my laugh. "Seriously? *That's* the problem? Daddy's thirteen years older than Mom, and no one thought that was a big deal."

When he looked at me, there was something almost wistful in his eyes. "Sarah is special," he said.

"And I'm not?" I was teasing, sure, but I was also serious. "Evan's barely six years older than me, and he's the oldest of all three of them. Come on, Uncle J. What's really going on here?"

Instead of answering, he grabbed a corkscrew from where it sat on the counter, and went to work on one of the bottles he'd pulled out for the evening. I watched silently, both amused and frustrated, as he poured a glass, took a sip, and then poured another. When he handed the second to me, I had to bite back an insolent smirk. Technically, I was under the drinking age.

When he finally spoke, his voice was low and even and tinged with a hint of regret. "When was the last time you've seen me with my wife?"

The question was so unexpected that I answered right away. "Not for years." I hadn't seen his most recent wife, or any of the parade of previous ones, in ages. I knew they'd all left him, but I'd never known why. And since I'd never gotten close to any of them, I hadn't ever asked.

"Too many secrets will destroy a relationship," he said.

"I don't have any secrets." Except, of course, I did.

Jahn paused, and for a moment I thought he was going to call me on my lie. But then he nodded, almost casually, as if my words were a given. "Maybe not. But he does. His own, and those he holds for others."

He.

That one simple word rattled around in my head, making me a little dizzy. Because I knew what it meant. It meant that we weren't really talking about the trio, but about Evan. About the fact that I wanted him—and that Jahn knew it.

I swallowed, embarrassed but also relieved in a weird way. Jahn *knew* me—possibly better than anyone else ever did or ever would.

But he was wrong about one thing—secrets didn't bother me. How could they when I held so many of my own?

Now, as I stood in the open living room of Jahn's condo and listened to Evan speak to the crowd, it was as if Jahn's ghost had drawn me, Scrooge-like, back to the past, to see that afternoon all over again. I'd been unsure before, believing that, like his best friends, Evan thought of me like a sister.

I no longer believed that.

Jahn's lecture that night hadn't just been about warning me to stay away. He'd been telling me that he'd ordered Evan and Tyler and Cole away, too. And while Cole and Tyler might not find that request to be a burden, I'd seen the heat in Evan's eyes.

He wanted me, dammit.

He wanted me, and he was too goddamned loyal to my uncle to do anything about it.

"Howard Jahn was a man who loved his life."

The deep tones of Evan's voice filled the room, mesmerizing and clear. "In the short time that he was on this earth, he not only lived that life to the fullest, but taught others how to do the same. He changed the lives of so many people, many of whom are standing here tonight. I should know. I'm one of the lucky people that he took under his wing."

I took my eyes off Evan long enough to examine the crowd. They were as enthralled as I was, caught up in both Evan's charisma and the words that he was speaking. I watched him—this man who'd made a fortune for himself at such a young age—and understood in that moment how he'd risen to be one of the most influential men in Chicago. Hell, if he were a tent preacher, he could have swindled millions from that crowd.

The only one who didn't look impressed, in fact, was Kevin. I wasn't sure if he was still stinging from his smack-down with Evan earlier or if he was picking up on my Evan-lust vibes. But since the latter was enough of a possibility to make my highly tuned guilt antennae hum, I reached over and took his hand—then felt even more guilty because of my own hypocrisy.

"Howard Jahn taught me a different way of looking at the world. In so many ways, he rescued me, and he never once gave up on me." He had been looking out over the crowd as he spoke, but now his eyes found mine. "We're here today to honor his memory," he continued, with an odd kind of ferocity in his voice. "His memory. His requests. His legacy."

He paused and the air was so thick between us that it took all my strength just to draw a breath. I'm surprised that every eye in the room wasn't turned to us, watching the spectacle of the fire that blazed between us. Because it was there. I felt it—I felt it and I wanted to burn in it.

I have no idea what he said next. He must have continued talking, because before I knew it, people were raising glasses in a toast and wiping damp eyes.

The spell that had captured me dissipated, and I watched, breathless, as Evan melted into the crowd. He shook hands with people and accepted consoling pats on his shoulder. He ruled the room, commanding and calm. A steady presence for the mourners to rely on.

And never did he take his eyes off me.

Then he was coming toward me, his gait firm and even, his

expression determined. I was only half-aware of Kevin beside me, his fingers still twined with mine. Right then, Evan Black was my entire world. I wanted to feel his touch again. Wanted him to pull me close. To murmur that he knew what I'd lost when Jahn had died.

I wanted him to brush his lips sweetly over mine in consolation, and then to throw all decorum aside and kiss me so wild and hard that grief and regret withered under the heat of our passion.

And it pissed me off royally that it wasn't going to happen because of a promise he made to a dead man.

I'm not sure what I was trying to prove, but I spun around and folded myself into Kevin's arms.

"What—"

I cut him off with a kiss that started out awkward and weird, but then Kevin must have decided I needed this. That my grief had sent me over the wall and into the land of rampant public displays of affection.

His hand cupped the back of my head as his mouth claimed mine. As far as kissing was concerned, Kevin definitely got an A. Empirically, he was everything a girl should want, and yet I wasn't satisfied. I wasn't even close. There was no heat, no burn. No butterflies in my stomach, no longing for more. On the contrary, all Kevin's kiss did was make me more aware of the void inside me. A hunger—a craving—that I couldn't seem to satisfy no matter how much I wanted to.

Evan, I thought, and was shocked by the desperate longing that went along with those two small syllables. Somehow the tight grip I'd kept on my desire all these years had come loose. It was as if my grief had shoved me over the cliff, and for the first time in forever, I wished I could just erase Evan Black from my mind. I felt out of control. Frenzied and reckless.

And for a girl like me, that's never a good place to be.

When Kevin broke our kiss and pulled away from me, all I

wanted to do was pull him back again. To kiss him until we broke through my resolve. Until we created a fire out of friction if nothing else. Because I needed that. I needed to get clear. I needed to lose myself in him until the blazing heat that was Evan Black was reduced to nothing more substantial than a burn across my heart.

But that, I knew, was never going to happen.

Kevin's palm cupped my cheek, his smile gentle. "Sweetheart, you look ripped to pieces."

I nodded. I was. Just not for the reason Kevin thought.

I glanced around the room, searching out Evan. Wanting to know that he'd seen. Wanting him to be as twisted and tied up in knots as I was.

But he wasn't even there.

"Angelina, my dear, the young waitress said I might find you in here. It's so good to see you again, even under such sad circumstances."

The Southern-smooth voice rolled over me, and I grimaced. I'd escaped to the kitchen—which was technically off limits to guests—with the hope of squeezing out just one tiny little moment alone. Apparently, that wasn't going to happen.

Forcing a political-daughter smile onto my face, I turned away from the counter and greeted Edwin Mulberry, a congressman from either Alabama or Mississippi or some other state that most definitely wasn't the Midwest.

"Congressman Mulberry. What a pleasure," I lied. I willed my smile wider. "I didn't realize you knew my uncle."

He had silver hair and an audience-ready smile that I only half-believed was genuine. "Your uncle was an amazing man," he said. "Very well connected. When I spoke to your father yesterday and he told me he couldn't be here, I knew I had to come by."

"I appreciate that," I said. Mulberry was a representative

with an eye on the Senate, and though my father was still on his first six-year term, he had forged powerful allies, including several who had started tossing his name around as a potential vice presidential candidate. I didn't need to rely on my poli sci degree to realize that Mulberry was more interested in getting in good with the flavor of the month than he was in paying his respects to my uncle.

"It's been what? Almost five years since I've seen you? I have to say, you've grown into quite the lovely young woman."

"Thank you," I said, managing to keep my smile bright though it had become significantly harder. "It's been almost eight," I added, unable to help myself. I'd seen Mulberry last at my sister's funeral, and the memory of that day bumped up against the one I was currently living in a way that made me feel cold and hollow.

I hugged myself tight, trying to remember all my various bits of social training, but now feeling too lost to make small talk. "Well," I said, and then just let the word hang there, suddenly unable to come up with a single thing to say.

It was Evan who rescued me.

"Congressman Mulberry?" The older man turned to Evan, who stood in the doorway looking as dark and mysterious as still water at midnight. "There's a young woman out there looking for you. She seems very anxious to speak to you."

"Is there?" The congressman perked up, his hand rising to straighten his tie as I bit back a grin.

"Long blond hair, short black dress." He moved into the kitchen to stand near us. "She was heading into the library as I left her."

"Well," Mulberry said. He turned to me. "My dear, it's been a pleasure, but if this young woman is a constituent, I should go see what she has on her mind."

"Of course," I said. "It was lovely seeing you again. Thank you for coming."

As soon as he was out the door, I turned to Evan. "You are a very smooth liar."

"Apparently not as smooth as I thought if you found me out so easily."

"Maybe I just know you too well," I quipped.

He looked at me for a moment, then took a single step closer. My breath hitched and my pulse began to pick up tempo, and when he reached out an arm toward me I stood perfectly still, anticipating a touch that never came—it wasn't me he was reaching for, but a bottle of wine.

Idiot, idiot, idiot. But at least I could breathe easy again.

"Too well?" he said, as he poured a glass of pinot noir and passed it to me. "Does that mean you've figured out all my secrets?"

Our fingers brushed as I took the wine from him, and I shivered from the spark of connection that seemed to shoot through me, all the way from my fingers to the very tips of my toes.

I saw the quick flash of awareness in his eyes and wanted to kick myself. Because it wasn't me that knew his secrets—it was the other way around. And damned if I didn't feel confused and exposed and vulnerable.

"Secrets?" I repeated. I stood up straighter, determined to snatch back some measure of control. "Like the mystery behind why you've barely said two words to me all night? Why you've looked everywhere but at me?"

He tilted his head as if considering my words, then he poured his own glass of wine and took a long, slow sip. "I'm looking at you now."

I swallowed. He damn sure was. His cloudy gray eyes were fixed on my face, and I saw the tension in his body, as if he were fighting the coming violence of a storm.

Against my better judgment, I took a drink of my own wine. Yes, I needed a clear head for tonight, but right then I needed courage more. "You are," I agreed. "What do you see?"

"A beautiful woman," he said, his tone making my heart flutter as much as his words. "A beautiful woman," he continued, "who needs to take a step back and think about what the hell she's doing and why she's doing it."

"Excuse me?" His tone had shifted only slightly, but it was enough to totally erase that flutter. "Excuse me?" I repeated, because he had so completely flummoxed me that I couldn't seem to conjure any other words.

"You've had a hard time of it, Angie," he said. "You deserve to be happy."

I twirled the stem of my wineglass between my fingers as I tried to figure out his angle. Was he about to tell me that he could make me happy? The thought sent a small tingle of anticipation running through me, but I didn't believe it. He was too hot and cold, too confusing. And I wasn't going to figure out what the hell he was thinking unless I flat-out asked.

"What makes you think I'm not happy?"

He lifted one shoulder in a small shrug. "I get why you're dating Warner," he said. "Political father. FBI agent boyfriend. It all fits. It all makes sense. The perfect daughter piece in the picture-perfect puzzle that makes up your life."

I'd gone completely tense, my throat tight, my chest heavy. I felt like a walking target that he'd just skewered with a dead-on bull's-eye.

"Not that it's any of your business, but Kevin's wonderful," I said tightly, determined not to let him see that his barb had hit home.

"No," Evan said. We were still standing next to the counter in the kitchen, completely alone except for the few waiters who wandered in to refill their trays. Now he moved a step closer, and I swore I could feel the thrum of the air molecules buzzing between us. "For someone, maybe. But he's not for you."

"What would you know about it?" I'd intended to sound indignant. I didn't even come close.

"I know enough," he said, closing the distance between us even more. "I know you need a man who's strong enough to anchor you. A man who understands what you need, in bed and out of it." A deliciously sexy smile eased across his mouth. "You need a man who can just look at you and get you hot. And, Angie," he said, "I also know that Kevin Warner isn't that man."

Oh, my. Perspiration beaded on the back of my neck. My breathing was shallow, my pulse fast. I felt hyperaware of my body. Of the tiny hairs standing up on my arms. Of the needful, demanding feeling between my legs. I was wet—I was certain of it. And all I wanted right then was Evan's hands upon me.

It took a massive force of will to manage words, and even more strength to look him in the eyes. "If not Kevin, then who?" I asked, but the question that remained unspoken was "You?"

He reached out and tucked a loose lock of hair behind my ear, the soft brush of his finger against my skin just about melting me. "I guess that's something you'll have to figure out."

four

I spent the next hour circulating through the condo, chatting with the guests, and reminiscing about Jahn. I caught sight of Cole twice and Tyler once. I didn't see Evan at all, and I wasn't sure if that was a good thing or a bad thing. On the one hand, I'd liked the way he'd looked at me. I'd liked the frisson of awareness that tingled through me simply from his proximity.

On the other hand, our conversation in the kitchen had been so surreal that I wanted to avoid him until I could wrap my head around what had happened. And I sure as hell didn't want another lecture about Kevin. Especially since everything Evan had said was so damn right.

As for Kevin, he'd been my almost-constant companion since the moment I'd left the kitchen. He played the role of the supportive boyfriend with such gusto that I barely had a moment to myself. I finally escaped, claiming that I was going to the bathroom when all I really wanted was a moment when I could stand by myself and simply breathe.

Rather than slip away to one of the restrooms, I hurried up to Jahn's rooftop patio. It's my favorite place in the condo, accessed by a stunning spiral staircase on the north side of the living room. Jahn decorated it with as much detail as the interior of the condo, so the covered and uncovered areas were full of comfortable chairs and lounges, conversation areas, and beautiful plants that made this oasis in the sky feel like a park. Or at the very least, like the best rooftop lounge of a five-star European hotel.

While most of the guests were lounging on the couches and sipping drinks by the outdoor kitchen, I moved away from the crowd. I stood alone between the tiny potted firs that lined the perimeter, my hands pressed to the glass that provided that extra bit of protection against the urge to spread your arms and leap, proving once and for all that though you might appear human, you really weren't. You were just air and breath and the thrill of motion, and nothing bad could happen to you in the night sky because the wind would always catch you.

"I hope you're not thinking about jumping."

Ironically, I did exactly that, practically leaping out of my skin as my hand rose to my throat. My heart beat double-time, but whether that was because of the surprise or because of the man who'd so stealthily approached, I didn't know.

I drew in what I hoped was a calming breath, gathered myself, and then turned to face Evan.

"I was," I admitted. "But don't worry. I'm not suicidal."

"No," he said simply, his eyes flat as they assessed me. "You're too strong for that."

"That is such bullshit." I bit out the retort automatically, irritated that he'd so easily pushed my buttons. People had said the same thing after Gracie died, every word like fingernails on a chalkboard. *You're so strong, you're handling it all so well.* And it was all crap, because I wasn't handling it at all.

I'd moved like a zombie through the days, barely managing to function. The days were bad enough. The nights pretty much fucking killed me.

I sucked in a shaky breath. "There's nothing strong about surviving," I said. "All it means is that one more time, death passed you up."

I winced, because the second the words were out of my mouth, I knew I'd said too much. *Shit.*

I turned back to the glass and looked out over the world. I didn't turn when I heard him move up beside me, taking his own position at the barrier. For the first time I could remember, in fact, I wanted Evan Black to just go away.

"I'm sorry," he said. His voice was low and level, and I liked the way it felt inside my head. I didn't turn, though. I wasn't sure if he was sorry for my loss or apologizing for his words, and if it was the former, I really didn't want to know.

"So why are you here?" I finally asked, my back still toward him. "Did you track me down to give me more grief about the guy I'm dating?"

"Believe it or not, I don't spend that much time thinking about Kevin Warner."

I turned, my brow raised in question. "No? Because in the kitchen earlier he sure seemed to be on your mind."

"Not Kevin," he said simply. "You."

"Oh." I swallowed, liking the sound of that word on his lips. *You.*

For a moment, silence hung between us. I didn't know what to say. I didn't know what he wanted. I didn't know what he was doing there or what was going on between us, or if anything even *was* going on between us. I waited for him to speak, but he seemed content to let the silence continue. He was doing nothing more than standing there, and yet I felt suddenly trapped, as if he'd captured me in that firm and unwavering gaze.

In desperation, I finally managed to form a sentence. "You're wrong," I said, looking down at my fingernails so that I wouldn't have to see his face. "I'm not strong at all." I thought of how much I wanted to escape this day. Of how much I wanted my uncle back. Of how desperately I wanted to cry, and of how hard I was having to work to keep all that grief bottled up inside.

Mostly, I thought of how certain I was that I wouldn't make it through the night. That no matter how hard I tried, in the end the explosion would come and somehow, someway, everything I'd wrapped up tight would come completely unraveled.

"You are. I've watched you," he said firmly. "Over the years, I mean. You keep yourself under tight control, Angie. That takes a lot of strength."

I fervently wished that what he saw was true. It wasn't, of course. I'd been trying for years to keep myself under control, but the tighter I grasped, the more pieces of me seemed to break free.

Stifling a sigh, I turned away again to look out at Lake Michigan and the boats that were now nothing more than tiny points of lights in the distance. "You must not have been watching too closely," I said.

"On the contrary," he said, his voice low and even and so intense it seemed to erase all my protests even before I could voice them. "I paid a great deal of attention. I always do when something matters to me."

"Oh." My voice felt small and breathy.

From his position beside me, he hooked a finger under my chin and turned my head to meet his eyes. Heat from the contact shot through me, and I half-wondered if I'd see a burn mark there the next time I looked in the mirror.

He moved his hand away, and I wanted to cry out in protest. "Trust me on this, Lina. I know all about control."

I swallowed. I wasn't entirely sure I knew what we were talking about. And I sure as hell didn't know why he called me by my old nickname, but to my surprise, I found myself liking it. I liked even more the way that he was looking at me. I think I could have stood there forever, the city and lake below and the night sky above and this enigmatic man only inches from me.

His lips began to move, and I thought that he had a beautiful mouth. "It's not a weakness to want to let go," he said. "To want the thrill of taking a risk. The pleasure of feeling the rush."

I blinked. "How did you—"

"Shhhh." His smile was slow and easy, revealing a rarely seen dimple in his cheek. "You need it. You've been pent up all night, going crazy. Locked inside your grief. Go ahead, now. Close your eyes and turn around."

"But, I—"

That finger rose and pressed gently to my lips. "Don't argue. Just do."

Unquestioning obedience isn't usually my modus operandi, but to my surprise, I complied. I closed my eyes, letting the dark take me, and then I shifted, so that I was facing the glass again. If I had opened my eyes, I would have seen the night sky spread wide in front of me. Instead I saw only Evan, larger than life inside my head.

"That's a good girl."

I'd worn my shoulder-length hair loose, and I held my breath as he gently pushed the thick waves aside, then pressed his hand to the back of my neck. I shivered from the contact, then cringed with embarrassment because I know he must have noticed. His thumb moved ever so slightly, lightly stroking my skin. I had no way of telling if he was doing it on purpose or if it was simply a reflex. Either way, it was driving me crazy, and I bit my lower lip, thankful that he was behind me and couldn't see that additional break in my composure.

When he spoke again, his voice was husky. "Now put your hands on the glass."

I was confused and nervous. But, damn me, I was also turned on, and I hoped he couldn't tell that my nipples had peaked beneath my bra, and that he couldn't see the flush of my skin in the dark.

Before I could do what he asked, he moved behind me, taking my hands in his and guiding them to the pane. The connection was shocking, powerful, and a raging heat stormed through me as I let myself go, reveling in the incredible sensation of submitting to this man.

"Do you feel it, Angie? The pressure of the glass? It's pushing back on you. It's holding you up. It's keeping you here, safe with me."

His words barely registered. All I knew was the way his voice caressed me, like a trail of kisses down my body. All I could feel was the pressure of his hands over mine, and the whisper of his breath on my skin, as tantalizing as a ray of summer sun.

"What if the glass were to tumble away?" His voice was soft and gentle, as if that was the most natural thing in the world to think about. "You wouldn't fall, Angie. You'd soar."

I squeezed my eyes tighter. He'd already captured the attention of my body, but now he'd captured my imagination, too.

"Maybe you wouldn't purposefully push the glass out of the way, but if that barrier disappeared, you'd experience it to the fullest. You'd spread your arms, you'd embrace the tumble. You'd breathe in the air and feel the wind rushing around you, gathering you up. Lifting you up. Because that's what you were thinking about, wasn't it? Not jumping. Not falling—"

I drew in a breath, gasping as I leaned back against him, my ass against his crotch. He was hard, and so help me, I was wet.

"You want to fly, Angie," he whispered, and then brushed his lips over the top of my ear. I trembled, and oh, dear god, if he touched me again I knew I'd come, my body exploding out to greet the stars.

And all I could do was stand there, the heat of our connection burning through me, and silently beg for him to never leave. For this moment to never end.

He moved his hands to my shoulders, then eased them around to place his palms against my ribs. His thumbs rested on my back and his fingertips brushed the swell of my breasts. I bit my lower lip, determined not to cry out, not to move. Not to do anything that might make him stop. That might end this wondrous fantasy.

His hands eased lower, encircling my waist. I'm not particularly small, but I felt petite and fragile right then, because I knew in that moment that he had the power to break me. To utterly and sweetly destroy me.

"Angie," he said and began to turn me in his arms. I closed my eyes, savoring the moment. But before I could shift—before I could even absorb the possibility that he was going to kiss me—the moment shattered, torn apart by the high-pitched chirp of my cell phone.

He drew his hands away, and as he did, I heard another sound. A whimper.

I'm pretty sure it came from me.

I opened my eyes just in time to see Evan's face shift into a stony, unreadable expression. I didn't know what it looked like before, but I imagined there'd been lust in his eyes.

I felt something tight squeeze at my heart, because we'd just lost this moment. And I knew damn well that we could never, ever get it back.

"You should answer it," he said.

"What?"

He glanced down at the tiny purse that I'd decided to carry tonight only because I had no pocket for my phone.

"Oh." I'd already forgotten. "It's a text." I fumbled to retrieve it, then glanced at the display.

"Kevin?"

"Flynn," I said quickly, not wanting to bring Kevin anywhere near this conversation. "Remember? The boy who lived down the street from Uncle Jahn in Kenilworth."

"Probably not so much a boy anymore," Evan said, in a tone that made the gooey feminine side of me shimmy with joy.

"No," I said casually. "Not so much."

I kept my focus on his face, and for a moment I thought that he was going to reach out for me. That he was going to pull me to him and press his lips to mine, and send us both soaring past that damn glass partition.

But the moment passed, and he turned away to look out over the darkened lake.

For a moment, we stood in silence. Then he spoke, low and steady. "I think about jumping, too."

"Suicidal?" I quipped.

"No." He turned back to me, and what I saw on his face wasn't heat or lust but bald determination. "Arrogant."

My brows puckered with confusion.

"I'm arrogant enough to think I can control my own fall," he clarified.

"But you can't," I said, thinking of my sister. Of my life. Of my uncle. "Nobody can."

His grin was wide, achingly sexy, and desperately sad. He reached out, then lightly stroked my cheek. "Watch me."

I did, but only in the sense that I watched him leave. I stayed there, alone on the patio. Just me and my confusion and mortification. Not to mention two dozen people I barely knew. All of us on this Chicago rooftop, hurtling through space and time and the universe.

I stared after him, not moving. Not really even thinking. Behind me, the fireworks over the Navy Pier began to explode and suddenly the night sky was alive with color. I barely noticed. The only color I saw was Evan, his hue standing out against the backdrop of gray that had consumed me.

It took a full five minutes before I realized that I was still holding my phone.

I pulled up the message and, despite my confusion, I smiled.

Just landed. You okay?

I typed my answer—Surviving, I think—then hesitated. I wanted to edit it before hitting send. To tell Flynn about what just happened with Evan, whom he'd heard about ad nauseam since we were both sixteen. About how I was seeing Jahn's ghost around every corner. About how much I hated death and funerals and I wished that I were a runner because then I could shove my feet into some Nikes and just go.

I didn't type any of that, though. Instead, I just hit send.

I'll be there in 10.

I couldn't help but smile. He really did know me well.

It's okay. People leaving.

Don't want you alone.

Kevin's taking me home w/ him.

There was a pause before the next text came through, and I understood why. I've spent far too many nights boring him with my rants about how Kevin is empirically perfect and I'm an idiot to even contemplate blowing him off.

Is that what you want?

It wasn't, of course. What I wanted was Evan. His voice in my ear. His hand on my back. I wanted to return to that place in the sky, and I was suddenly terribly afraid that he was the only one who could get me there.

Violently, I jabbed my finger on the keypad. I really wasn't going to do self-analysis by text. Just not happening.

Gotta go. TTYL

I set the phone on Do Not Disturb and shoved it back in my purse. If he texted me back, I didn't want to know about it. I looked up in time to see that Kevin had entered the patio and was looking right at me, his expression quizzical. I wasn't terribly surprised. I was feeling ripped to pieces, not to mention confused and unsatisfied and more than a little bit guilty about my pleasant, odd, and totally unexpected encounter with Evan. Unfortunately, I didn't have the chance to adjust my expression before he zeroed in on me.

"You're looking tired," he said, smiling gently as he took my hand. "Let's go."

" 'Tired' being a euphemism for 'destroyed'?"

"What can I say? I minored in English."

My laugh was completely genuine. "You're a good man, Agent Warner," I said. "You deserve more than a wreck like me."

"Maybe I like a fixer-upper." He lifted our joined hands and kissed my fingertips. "You need distance. Come on. I already told Peterson I was whisking you away," he added, referring to Jahn's ever-present but usually invisible butler. "He'll make sure the rest of the guests get on their way."

I let him tug me toward the door. The guests were already leaving, and a few pulled me aside, giving me a hug and an encouraging word. Kat hurried over as we neared the entrance hall. "You're heading out?"

"She needs to get away for the night," Kevin said. "I'm taking her to my place."

"Great," Kat said, her voice bland, but a question in her eyes. I wished I could answer it. A cliché, maybe, but I could have used a night of nail polish and ice cream and talking about men.

"It's gonna get easier," Kat said, then pulled me into a tight hug.

"So they tell me."

"Tomorrow," she said. "We'll meet for cupcakes, okay?"

"Definitely," I said, because who turns down cupcakes or sympathy from her best friend?

I didn't see Tyler or Cole, and since I agreed that I needed to get out of there sooner rather than later, I continued willingly toward the door, figuring I'd see them in a couple of days at the attorney's office. I still had the trauma of the will to look forward to. Maybe after that, I could start to heal.

I heard Evan before I saw him, that low, whiskey-smooth voice unmistakable. I was overcome by the desire to take a detour. Unfortunately, he was right by the front door.

"I understand," he was saying. "But this isn't the place."

"It's just without the damn liquor license, I can't get enough traffic to turn the profit we need, and I can't get the license without—"

I could see him now, and I watched as he cut off a stout, weasel-faced man with a hand to the shoulder. "Now's not the time. But I promise you I'll take care of it."

"Seriously?"

I saw a muscle twitch in Evan's cheek. "Are you doubting my word?"

The weasel looked a little bit terrified that he might have offended Evan. "Oh, no. I didn't mean that you—"

"It's not a problem." Evan's voice was a blanket of calm against the hyper backpedaling. "I've got a few favors I can call in. We'll get it worked out."

The weasel nodded. "I'll owe you. I know I'll owe you."

I saw the moment Evan noticed me. Just the slightest shift of his gaze from the weasel to my face, and then back again. "Tomorrow," Evan said. "We'll talk." Then he turned to me, effectively dismissing the weasel, who slipped through the door, shoulders sagging in what looked like relief.

"Angie." His voice stroked me like a strong, firm hand, and I felt my body heat in memory of his touch. His eyes flicked to Kevin. "Agent Warner."

"Nice speech," Kevin said. He held his hand out to shake. "You're an articulate man."

"It pays to be able to persuade people in my line of work," Evan said.

For a moment, I thought he was going to ignore Kevin's out-stretched hand. Then he reached out—and as he did, I saw the raw, red knuckles. I couldn't believe I hadn't noticed them before, and I had to blame my lack of attention on the dark. And on the fact that I'd been somewhat preoccupied by his general proximity, his touch, and my raging hormones.

"Evan! What happened?"

"Street fighting, Mr. Black?" Kevin said, in what must have been a joke but just sounded rude to me.

"If I was," Evan said smoothly, "the other guy must be pretty fucked up." He held the hand up for inspection. "I'd say I got off easy."

For a moment, the two just stared at each other, a sticky, uncomfortable tension filling the space between them. Forget the War of the Roses, that historic battle was nothing compared to this War of the Alphas, and I had a sick feeling that I was the root of the trouble.

"It's hardly a joke," I snapped. "Seriously, Evan, you should clean that up. And for Christ's sake, Kevin. Could you be any more of a jerk?"

He angled a glance at me. "Sorry."

"It's fine," Evan said. "Really. I was helping a friend with her car. My hand slipped, and the engine was still pretty hot. It wasn't pleasant, but I'll survive."

"You should be more careful," Kevin said.

"I'm always careful," Evan countered smoothly. "But sometimes shit happens."

He was right. Jahn's death was about as shitty as it got.

For a moment, the silence hung awkwardly between the three of us. Then Kevin hooked his arm around my shoulder. "She's had a hell of a day. We're going to get out of here."

I waited for Evan to say goodbye, some tiny part of me hoping that he'd step in and insist I stay in the condo, because how could he just let me leave with Kevin? But he only stood there.

There was no sign—no hint—of the man who'd evoked such sensuality on the patio. The man whose voice had told me to fly and whose touch had burst through me with at least as much color and flare as tonight's fireworks.

I was too tired and too slashed to try to understand it or even to think about it. All I felt was sad.

"Will you tell Tyler and Cole goodbye for me?"

"Sure," he said, and though his voice was more gentle than I'd expected, I noticed that he didn't say that he'd talk to me soon or that I'd be seeing the guys in a day or so. Once again I was struck by the awful reality: Everything had changed. Jahn had been our intersection point, and now that he was gone, I felt adrift.

I grabbed Kevin's hand and hurried out of the condo before the tears I'd been fighting all night began to flow.

As soon as we were on the elevator, Kevin repeatedly jabbed his finger on the lobby button as if he couldn't get out of there quickly enough. "At least that's one good thing that will come of your uncle's death," he said darkly.

"Excuse me?"

"I just mean that you won't be seeing those three anymore."

"What the hell?" My voice lashed out like a whip, but I didn't care. As far as I was concerned, there was nothing—*nothing*—good that could come out of Jahn's death, and that most especially included losing three men I counted as friends.

"I'm sorry," he said simply.

"Good. You should be. Now tell me why you'd say something like that."

"Dammit, Angie, I can't. I shouldn't have said anything in the first place."

"No, you shouldn't have. But you did. And now you're going to explain."

"Angie . . ." He trailed off.

I crossed my arms over my chest. No way was he getting off

the hook that easily. "Is this about that bullshit investigation a few years ago? I mean, honestly, Kevin, you were a shit to them earlier tonight."

"Bullshit investigation? Do you even know what we were talking about?"

"Do you?" I countered. He'd been in the Bureau for only four years. That whole fiasco that Jahn had told me about with his knights was a full year before Kevin's time.

"Burnett was, and he's told me enough. I know you grew up around them, but that doesn't make them good guys. They were fencing stolen merchandise, Angie."

I gaped at him. "That's insane. They're businessmen, just like my uncle."

"They have their fingers in a lot of businesses, I won't argue that."

I narrowed my eyes, irritated by the smirky tone of his voice. "If what you're saying is true, they'd be behind bars instead of being the toast of Chicago. I mean, come on, Kevin. They're three of the most prominent—not to mention public—men in this city. They aren't holed up in some lame-ass pawn shop buying stolen stereos." I mean, seriously, what the hell kind of game was Kevin playing?

"You say they're businessmen?" Kevin said. "I'm not disagreeing. But not all businesses are legit, and you damn well know it."

I started to reply, but held my tongue, because as much as I didn't want to concede any point to Kevin, I had to silently admit that on the surface what he said was true. My father had helped draft dozens of crime-prevention bills and oversaw at least as many task forces at the state level over the years. And since he wasn't a man to leave his work at the office, I couldn't help but pick up some salient points here and there. And one thing I knew was that legitimate businesses often stood as fronts for criminal enterprises. But Evan's businesses? Tyler's and Cole's?

I wanted to stamp my foot and tell Kevin he was being ab-
surd. That there was nothing about their businesses that would
make the government even look twice. But my foot stayed firmly
on the ground. Because now that he'd shined a spotlight, I
couldn't help but notice one or two red flags.

The biggest one was Destiny, of course, the high-end gentleman's club they owned together, and which had been a bone of
contention between them and my uncle, who thought they were
wasting their money and tarnishing their reputations. The guys,
apparently, either hadn't agreed or cared.

Other than the anomaly of the club, the guys were in the
business of businesses. They'd founded Knight Enterprises,
which bought and sold companies, and its exceptional performance had rocketed the guys into multimillionaire status. I'd
asked Jahn to explain to me what they did, and he'd run me
through the basics. Essentially, they acquired all sorts of businesses, everything from car washes to liquor stores to temp
agencies to I don't know what else. Some, like the burrito place,
they kept, hiring managers for the day-to-day stuff, and folding
the business in under the umbrella of their holding company.
Others they sold, making money off the various assets and real
estate.

In other words, they were gambling, making their fortune by
betting on the acquisitions doing well. Apparently, they made a
lot of really good bets.

Ten minutes before, all of that seemed perfectly legit. Now
Kevin's suspicions had me hearing words like fencing and smuggling and money laundering. Had I been blind? Or was Kevin
being an ass?

Both possibilities pissed me off, and my words came out
sharper than I'd intended. "If there was any evidence, then the
case wouldn't have been dropped. Five years, Kevin. You're all
ruffled about some blip on the radar from five years ago."

"It wasn't a blip," he said. "And I never said that was the only reason I wanted you to stay away from them. Dammit, Angie, I care about you. I don't want you around men like them."

The elevator slid to a stop, the doors opened, and we stepped out. He headed toward the exit, but I wasn't even close to being done with this conversation. I grabbed his sleeve and tugged him into a small alcove near the wall of mailboxes. "No way are you leaving me hanging," I said. "You say they're bad news, you tell me why."

"You know I can't talk specifics, Angie."

"*Shit.*" I snapped out the curse, because I understood the unspoken message. The allegations from five years ago may have disappeared, but Jahn's knights were still in the FBI's sights. "If they're such badasses why hasn't the FBI or the cops or whoever swooped down and carted them away?"

Kevin just looked at me, his expression suggesting I was being naive. For that matter, I probably was. "There's evidence," he said. "There's strategy. And I'm not talking about this anymore. I've already said more than is prudent, but you're important to me, Angie."

"What is this about, really? You don't like that I have male friends? That I was talking to Evan?"

"Talking to him? You cried on his shoulder, Angie."

I tried to protest that Evan was just a friend, but the words felt bitter on my tongue, and I couldn't seem to get them out.

Kevin took a step closer, closing the distance between us, and for the first time I realized that despite his lanky physique, there was an innate power to Kevin. "And no, I didn't like it. I don't like the way he looks at you, either. I don't trust him. And I don't want you getting mixed up with him or his friends. And honestly, Angie, I don't think your uncle would like it, either."

His last words ripped a sharp breath from me. He was right, of course. Jahn didn't want me to be with Evan. Was this why? Was Evan—were all three of the guys—dangerous? Were they really criminals?

Holy shit, the possibility that the allegations five years ago had been true had never even occurred to me. And assuming it was true, had Jahn known? Had he simply discounted the possibility that men he loved like sons ran a criminal enterprise?

Or had my uncle, in some small way, admired the ingenuity that must go along with staying one step ahead of the law? Had he been just a little bit jealous of the rush those three must have experienced every time they crossed a line and got away with it?

Dangerous, yes. Edgy, absolutely.

But pretty damned exhilarating, too.

I shivered, and saw that Kevin was looking at me with a kind of fierce protectiveness. "I know," he said. "Those guys are scary. Stay away from them. From all of them."

I nodded mutely, but only because I knew I had to.

My shiver wasn't from fear, but from excitement. From the possibility of finding that rush that I craved embodied in a man I wanted in my bed. A man that I already knew fired my senses.

I didn't know what that said about me and, honestly, I wasn't inclined to dive into a pool of introspection. After all, the bottom line remained the same. I wanted Evan Black. Wanted his touch, his kiss. I wanted to be swallowed up whole, swept away.

Hell, I wanted to fly.

It would never happen, though. Maybe I didn't know all of Evan's secrets, but I knew damn well that he was loyal. He'd made a promise to Uncle Jahn, and nothing could make him break it. I may not have understood what kind of game he'd been playing with me on the balcony, but I was absolutely certain that it wouldn't end with me in Evan Black's bed.

And as much as I hated to admit it, that was probably a good thing. I might crave the thrill, but I knew better than anyone that my wild urges had teeth—and I'd been bitten too many times already.

five

"Wait," I said, as Kevin started to climb out of his Prius. "Let's not go up just yet." We were in the parking garage of Kevin's condo, just a few blocks from Michigan Avenue. As parking garages go, it wasn't bad, but neither was it a particularly comfortable or pleasant destination, which is probably why Kevin looked at me so curiously.

"Are you okay?" He reached over to take my hand. "It's been one hell of a day."

"It has," I said. "Please, can't we go out?"

"Out?"

"A drive, maybe." Although honestly, if we were just going to drive I wanted a convertible and some serious speed. "Or the Ledge. Is it open this late?" Despite the crowds, the Ledge at Skydeck was my favorite destination in the city. Even though I knew it was as safe as houses, I still got a rush from standing

103 stories above the city on the clear platform, my mind unable to comprehend how it could be that I wasn't falling.

Kevin's expression reflected both concern and bafflement. "Honey, are you okay?"

"No," I said plaintively. "I haven't been okay for days." I'd been pulling it in. Playing the part I was supposed to play because I was the grieving niece. The senator's daughter. The face of my family in Chicago. I'd made statements to the press twice—albeit coached by my immediate boss who ran Jahn's PR department—and I'd made it a point to accompany his secretary through the halls of HJH&A for no reason other than to give the employees a sense of continuity. An exercise that was wholly ridiculous since I couldn't have run Howard Jahn Holdings & Acquisitions if my life depended on it.

Still, I'd played a role and I'd played it well. But now I just needed to breathe.

"Just tell me what you need," he said.

"I'm trying to tell you." I could hear the frustration in my voice and tried to rein it in. I reminded myself that Kevin didn't know me—despite having slept together twice and having my father's seal of approval. He didn't know how hard I worked to be the girl that I was. Didn't know how I always kept a tight check on myself. How could he, when I'd never told him?

But I'd never told Evan, either. And yet he'd understood me. I recalled the feel of his words washing over me, the heat of his body beside me. He'd given me everything I'd needed right then. The heat, the words, the understanding. He'd given me a taste, but damned if I didn't want the whole meal.

"Hey," Kevin said, shifting our hands so that he could twine his fingers with mine. "I'm listening."

I drew in a breath, feeling chastised. Because he *was* listening. He was trying. And I was sitting there having fantasies that he could read my mind.

"Haven't you ever felt like everything is too much?" I asked.

"Like you keep everything bottled up so tight, but sometimes you have to let off steam. Because if you don't, you'll explode, and that would be so much worse."

"A release valve," he said, and the band around my chest loosened a bit.

"Yes. Yes, exactly." I couldn't quite believe that he got it.

"Honey," he said, then released my hand so he could stroke my cheek. "Just let me take you inside."

"I—" I started to argue, but then cut myself off. Because, really, wasn't this exactly what I wanted? It wasn't about going dancing, it was about losing control. Hell, it was about relinquishing control.

I closed my eyes, imagining the moment we walked into the apartment. He wouldn't even shut the door before he'd have me up against the wall, my hands above my head, his body hard against mine. I'd close my eyes, letting the sensations roll over me as he gripped my wrists with one hand, his other hand hard upon my breast. I'd arch into his touch, but not much. He had me trapped there, able to take only what he was willing to give. Lost in sensation, floating away in the decadent arms of surrender until I opened my eyes, so desperate to see the heat reflected back at me that I had no choice.

And when I did, it wasn't Kevin's face that I saw—it was Evan's.

I gasped, my eyes flying open for real this time, and I saw Kevin peering at me, concern cutting across those perfect features.

"Angie? Hey, are you okay?"

I nodded. "Tired. Just tired."

"All the more reason to go inside."

Again, I nodded. I didn't want to talk, didn't want to think. Guilt and grief were screwing with my head, and I wasn't at all sure what to do about it.

We took the elevator from the parking level to his eighth-floor studio, and as we stepped through the door, I realized I was holding my breath—but whether that was because I was craving or dreading his touch, I really didn't know.

It didn't matter, though, because all he did was turn around and shut the door. "How does a cup of hot tea sound?" he asked, after he'd locked both dead bolts and put on the chain.

It sounded horrible, but I nodded anyway. Tea sounded soothing. It sounded calm. But I didn't want calm. I wanted hands on my body. I wanted electricity. I wanted to be consumed in a lightning storm, destroyed by passion. I wanted to get lost in pleasure so intense it burned away everything until I was a blank slate, the horror of the last few days all but forgotten.

But this—I didn't want this.

More, I didn't want Kevin.

"I'm sorry," I whispered.

"Don't be silly. It's no trouble." He started to turn toward the tiny kitchen, but must have seen something in my eyes, because he stopped. "Angie?"

Would everything have changed if he'd kissed me right then? If I'd seen fire brimming in his eyes, would I have stayed? Would I have lost myself in his touch, gotten high on the drug of sex? Would I have let him take me where I wanted to go—and would I have stayed there with him?

I don't know. I don't think so. I didn't doubt that Kevin was a good man, but he wasn't the man I wanted, and I deserved more than the runner-up. So, for that matter, did Kevin.

"I'm sorry," I repeated. "I shouldn't have come here tonight. I shouldn't have—" I shook my head, as if shaking off the thread of my words. "I *am* a wreck tonight. But I really just want to be alone."

"No." My words spurred him to action, and he reached out, his hand closing around my wrist. "You're distraught, I get that. Stay. I'll take care of you."

I shivered, because that's what I wanted. For someone to take care of me so that I really could slip away and lose myself in that ultimate thrill of surrender. But not with tea and cookies and a warm bubble bath. That was never going to take my edge off.

"We'll talk tomorrow," I promised, already moving away, trying to avoid the walls that were squeezing in around me. "Right now, I have to go."

I was tugging open the front door locks when he gripped my elbow. "I'm not letting you go back there. Not tonight. Not when you're like this. Grief messes with people, honey. I see it all the time."

"I'm just going to crash," I lied. "I want to sleep in my own bed. And this isn't your decision," I added when he looked ready to argue. "I know you want to help, but I need the space."

He just stood there, his fingers digging into my bare arm, exposed in the sleeveless black sheath I still wore.

"Kevin . . ." I heard the apology in my voice, along with the plea.

"Dammit—fine." He released me and held up his hands, fingers spread, and in that moment I imagined him talking to a suspect, patronizing them. Telling them to just be calm and everything would be okay.

Unfair, maybe, but the direction of my thoughts only made me more determined to get out of there.

"Now," I said. "I'm going now."

"I'll drive you."

"No." I drew in a breath, tried to calm the panic that seemed to want to spring out of me. Couldn't he see that I needed to run—needed to go. "I just—I want to be alone. Please."

He should have yelled at me and called me a liar and told me to get the hell out. Instead, his eyes softened and he nodded. "Fine. But I'm putting you in the cab. Tomorrow," he said as he gently stroked my cheek. "Tomorrow, we talk."

It took a solid seven minutes for the cab to arrive. I know because I looked at my watch seven times during the period. I shifted my weight from foot to foot. I glanced around the darkened neighborhood. The lights were out at Yolk, one of my favorite breakfast places, and just looking that direction made my stomach growl. I'd eaten nothing since that morning, I realized, and had to acknowledge that hunger might be contributing to my moodiness.

A black Lexus with tinted windows turned onto McClurg, slid to a stop in front of Fox & Obel, a high-end grocery store one block down, and idled there. Because I am always—*always*—aware of my surroundings when I'm outside, I noticed. But since there's nothing inherently wrong about a car waiting at a curb, and because I had Kevin right beside me, I paid it little attention. Then I erased it from my thoughts entirely when the bright yellow cab turned off East Grand and came to a stop right in front of us.

Kevin opened the door for me, and I slid in, feeling as though a weight had been lifted off my shoulders. He leaned in to kiss my cheek, then firmly shut the door. I expected that would be that, so I was surprised when he tugged open the front passenger door. I held my breath, not wanting to argue, but damn sure ready to do just that if he was planning to break his word and come with me. But all he was doing was giving the driver the address—and paying the fare in advance.

"I have cash," I said.

"I've got it," he said firmly, and because I'd turned down the tea, I acquiesced on the cab fare.

The moment the cab pulled away from the curb, I breathed easier. Kevin was sweet, of course, and I knew that he genuinely cared about me. But he didn't give me what I needed. Then again, I wasn't entirely sure what I needed, though the possibility of continuing what Evan had started on the roof was certainly on my list.

For a moment, I entertained the fantasy of knocking on Evan's door, throwing myself in his arms, and kissing away his protests. But there is a huge gap between fantasy and reality.

Besides, I had no clue where he lived.

Fuck.

Antsy, I shifted on the seat. We were on Lake Shore Drive now, getting close to the condo, but that wasn't where I wanted to be. I wanted someplace so loud I didn't have to think. Someplace I could go and be someone other than Angelina Raine, the good girl. The senator's daughter. The entrepreneur's niece.

Stop it, already.

I drew in a breath and forced myself to just lean back, close my eyes, and enjoy the ride. I knew damn well that I needed to not be that girl. I needed to be Angie, not give in and be Lina, who would let her grief and her frustration and need just take over.

To my credit, I got as far as the condo. But when the cab pulled up in front, I couldn't do it. I couldn't go back in there. Not while I felt so frayed and at loose ends.

"Drive," I said, my voice raw. "Just keep driving."

He glanced at me in his rearview mirror. "You sure about that, sugar? Because that man of yours was adamant, and I have the C-note to prove it."

I exhaled loudly through my nose. I should have figured Kevin wasn't just giving him the address.

I pulled out another hundred and handed it to him. "Drive," I repeated.

He did. And as he pulled back into traffic, I noticed a black Lexus by the curb across the street. The same one? I shifted in my seat, intending to get a better look, but the cabbie's demand to know where we were heading pulled my attention away.

"Someplace loud," I said. "With a dance floor. And tequila. And not one single person I know."

"Gotta be more specific than that, sugar."

I pulled out my phone. "Give me a second," I said, wondering how the hell folks survived in the Dark Ages before smart-phones.

The Poodle Dog Lounge seemed like the best of a ragtag collection of possible clubs. It was located on a relatively run-down block right on the edge of Wrigleyville, but was well-lit enough to reassure me that I'd be safe getting from the cab to the door. I wanted an adrenaline rush, yes, but not the kind that came from avoiding thugs in dark alleys or drug deals in shadowed corners.

And, just in case the club wasn't set up to hail taxis, I tucked the cabbie's card in my purse. "My friend got your card, too, didn't he?"

"Sure did, sugar."

I held out a twenty. "This is to buy me a message. If he calls you, you tell him you dropped me at home, and the last time you saw me, I was heading into the lobby."

"Not too sure I feel right about that, little girl."

I managed not to roll my eyes, then pulled out yet another twenty. "Feel better now?"

He plucked the bills from my fingers. "Honey, I'm feeling just fine."

I stood on the sidewalk to get my bearings and was a little surprised when the burly bouncer at the head of the line waved me over. To be honest, I was even more surprised there was a line, especially on a Wednesday. I hadn't exactly selected a high-class club in a high-class neighborhood. Then again, any club that wanted a shot at being thought of as cool needed to at least go through the motions of being exclusive. And apparently this one had killer drink specials on Wednesdays and live music from some legitimately up-and-coming bands.

"You on your own, beautiful?"

I raised a brow. "So what if I am?"

The bouncer waved a hand, indicating the door. "No cover for single ladies with an ass as sweet as yours."

I wavered between rolling my eyes and thanking him, and ended up doing neither. I did, however, accept his invitation and headed inside as the eyes of the still-waiting women—some conspicuously single—burned a hole in my apparently fine ass.

The inside of the club was exactly what I'd hoped for. Dark and loud and semi-sleazy, with a crowd congregated around the bar and a mass of bodies on the dance floor. I stood out a bit in my funeral-black sheath and pumps, but I didn't much care. I wanted a drink. I wanted the music. And I wanted to lose myself on the dance floor, eyes closed, body moving, and my imagination running wild.

I wanted escape, dammit. And right then, this place was the best that I could do.

I sucked in my stomach and turned sideways to squeeze through the crowd toward the bar, a journey that was at least as treacherous as crossing Lake Shore Drive against the light. When I finally reached the polished-but-sticky oak bar, I held up my finger to get the bartender's attention, and quickly learned that while my sweet ass may have gained me admittance to this den of iniquity, after that, the perks fell off considerably.

"Fuck," I cursed, after the bartender hurried by in front of me for a third time without even sparing me a glance. The word held more venom than the situation probably called for, and I realized that not only was I irritated by my utter lack of alcohol, but I was also just generally angry. At my uncle for dying. At the universe for taking him. At Evan for getting me worked up, and at myself for fantasizing about a man I couldn't have and shouldn't want. And at Kevin, for not actually being the man I wanted.

"Fuck it," I repeated, then pushed away from the bar. I didn't need the drink, all I needed was the buzz, and I weaved my way onto the dance floor and edged in next to a drunk blonde who was on the verge of a wardrobe malfunction. She was dancing with two guys—or, more accurately, they were dancing with her. Her eyes were shut, her head back. As far as I could tell, she was entirely oblivious to their attention.

I let my body absorb the music, channeling my roiling emotions into the pounding thrum, letting the beat blast through me as I eased in, only inches from a bruiser of a guy with a buzz cut and bare arms that sported some of the most impressive snake-and-dagger tattoos I'd ever seen. His eyes caught mine, and he grinned, a familiar, hungry expression on his face. Because I was in that kind of mood, I danced closer, arms above my head, hips swaying. Getting close, but not touching. Teasing and playing.

Apparently, Bruiser wanted more than a tease, because he moved in. He smelled of alcohol and tobacco and lust, and though I wasn't the least bit interested in getting naked with him, I was more than happy to dance-flirt, feeling my blood pumping in my veins. Feeling *alive*. Because I was tired, so damn tired, of feeling numb, and when he put his hands on my waist and tugged me close, I closed my eyes and gyrated to the music. I wasn't there with this guy. I was somewhere else. With someone else.

Hell, maybe I even *was* someone else.

Because that was the trick, wasn't it? When I let myself go, I was getting out of my skin. Shedding the guilt and the pain and all the damn secrets and—*fuck it*.

With desperate abandon, I pressed my body hard against his. He let out a low moan of pleasure and cupped my ass, pulling me tight against him so that there was no mistaking his arousal.

I drew in a breath and tilted my head back. I saw the lust in his eyes. Saw the way his lips curved. He was bending close, either to claim my mouth or to whisper that we needed to get the hell out of there. I didn't want him, this stranger. I wanted everything I'd lost and everything I couldn't have, and I just wanted to run away.

But how can you run from yourself?

I stiffened, anticipating his words, and knowing damn well that I'd say yes to whatever he suggested—and then hate myself tomorrow.

And then it all shattered.

I heard myself cry out as the bruiser was shoved roughly aside—and then heard my gasp of surprise when I saw the man who'd so cavalierly tossed him away. *Evan.*

I stood there, completely frozen, as Evan stepped closer to me, his expression thunderous. But beneath the anger in his eyes I saw a heat that shot through my belly to settle between my thighs. Holy shit. This was it, my fantasy, and while part of me leaped with celebration, another part wondered when the hell I'd started hallucinating. Because this couldn't be real. How the hell could this possibly be real?

"What the fuck, friend?" Bruiser snarled, giving Evan's shoulder a shove and soundly destroying my theory that I was living in some sort of dream state. "You wanna get away from my girl?"

I started to say that I was most definitely not his girl, but the brimstone rose in Evan's eyes and I opted for the wiser course and stayed quiet.

"She's not your girl," Evan said mildly. "And I'm not your friend."

Bruiser's eyes narrowed and I saw the fingers of his right hand curl into a fist. "I think you need a lesson in manners, pretty boy."

Evan glanced down at the now-fisted hand, then back up to the man. "I'd think twice if I were you."

"Fuck you," Bruiser retorted, sending the fist flying as fast as the words.

In a move worthy of James Bond, Evan shifted, blocking the punch entirely. "I wouldn't try that again." He appeared casual and cool—and yet there was something in his manner that announced that he was the biggest badass in the room. And that he'd prove it to anyone who crossed him.

Bruiser's balance had been thrown off and he stumbled a bit, eyeing the nearby dancers who'd finally clued in that there was trouble. He licked his lips, and I could see common sense warring with bravado. Finally, his face went slack and he carelessly rolled a shoulder. "Whatever, man. Bitch isn't worth the trouble, anyway."

Faster than I would have imagined possible, Evan reached out, snagged the guy's collar, and hauled him close. "Apologize to the lady," he said, his words like ice. "And maybe you'll get to walk out of here on your own power."

As I watched, the blood drained from Bruiser's face, giving him a gaunt, half-dead appearance. "Sure. Sure, shit. I didn't mean anything by it. Just being an asshole. Sorry, babe."

His pleading eyes shifted back to Evan who, with a look of total contempt, gave him one quick shake and turned him loose. "Get the hell out of here."

As soon as Bruiser disappeared into the wash of bodies, I rounded on Evan. "What the fuck?"

Evan stood as calm as if he were standing in a lecture hall giving a presentation. "He's an asshole."

"So?" I mean, I was hardly going to argue the point. "I was dancing with him, not marrying him."

He took a step closer to me, and despite my irritation, my pulse kicked into high gear. "And now you're not doing either," he said.

"Oh." The word escaped my lips, more breath than sound. It wasn't even the sound I wanted to make. What I wanted, was to ask *why*. Why was he there? Why had he shoved the guy away? He'd followed me here, of course. The odds that this was a coincidence were simply too astronomical to fathom. But why? Did he regret walking away from me on the roof? Was he jealous of Kevin? Or, for that matter, of Bruiser?

Or was he simply watching over me? Looking out for me the way that Jahn had said he always would?

"He was dangerous, Angie," Evan said, leading me to the edge of the dance floor. "And what the fuck are you doing here, anyway?"

My eyes snapped to his face, and the words were out before I could think better of them. "Maybe I like dangerous men."

He hesitated only a heartbeat before replying, but even if he'd planned the words for a year, he couldn't have cut me deeper. "Maybe you shouldn't."

Without thinking, I lashed out, intending to slap his face. I didn't make it. He caught my wrist and pulled me close until I was mere millimeters from him, the heat from our bodies so intense I feared I might spontaneously combust.

He stood a full head taller than me, and he had me so close that my lips were almost pressed to the indentation at the base of his neck. He smelled like sin and despite how riled up I was, I had to fight the urge to sneak my tongue out and taste him.

He bent his head, his breath brushing over the top of my ear as he whispered to me. "I get it," he said simply.

I went completely stiff. "What exactly do you get?"

"That you're still crying for him."

I felt frozen and my breath caught in my throat. Somehow, I managed to force my words out. "What do you mean?"

Something brushed my hair, and though I couldn't know for certain, I imagined it was his lips. For a moment he didn't answer, just held me. The thrum of the music pounding through me had nothing on the surge of blood through my veins. I wanted to stay like that forever. Lost in a forest of the senses. Lost in his arms.

This was what I'd craved—why I'd come out tonight. Not the club or the music or the alcohol, but *this*. The numbness vanquished, my senses on overdrive.

I'd known that the music and the dancing would get me there. That I'd be able to thrust my hand through the curtain and draw in at least a moment or two of real, solid sensation, even if most of it slipped through my fingers like trying to clutch sand.

But I'd never imagined this. Never imagined that I even had it in me to feel so much all at once. To know—to really and truly *know*—that I was alive.

I swallowed again. Part of me was afraid to speak for fear of breaking this spell. But another part of me had to know. "Evan?" I finally whispered, not at all certain he'd be able to hear me over the roar of the club around us. "What do you get?"

"You," he said simply, and though it couldn't possibly be true, right then it was the best thing he could have said to me.

"I miss him," I said hoarsely, as if that explained why I was going wild in a sleazy club instead of curled up under a blanket sipping hot cocoa and crying.

"I know," he said, and I felt a shiver run through me because I knew it was true. He *knew*. Not about the numbness. Not about the times I couldn't take it anymore and had to fight through the fog. But about tonight and my grief and everything that I'd lost. About the fact that being here in this anonymous crowd with music pumping through my veins took the edge off just a little. It filled up the black hole of grief and loss. Made it bearable.

I didn't understand how, but he got it. Everything that Kevin couldn't see in me, Evan did.

I eased back so that I could tilt my head up, and found those gray eyes on me. *Wolf's eyes,* I'd thought earlier, and the analogy was even more apt now. I saw danger there. Hunger. As if he would gleefully eat me alive.

And oh, dear god, I wanted him to. "Why are you here?" I whispered.

"You wanted to fly. I wanted to make sure you didn't crash."

"So you're just looking out for me?" I held his eyes, drawing courage from the need I saw reflected back at me. "Or are you interested in helping with liftoff?"

His words were slow and measured. "It's never wise for a princess to tease a dragon."

"Who says I'm teasing?"

"It's not wise to tempt one, either."

"Why not?" My voice was breathy and full of need.

"Dragons burn. And the wounds leave scars."

"What if I don't care?"

He didn't answer, but his eyes darkened and I knew damn well that he wanted this, too.

"Evan." I didn't realize that I'd spoken his name aloud until I heard my own voice, soft and low like a plea.

He shook his head slowly. "No."

The word was firm and insistent—and I didn't believe it for a second. This was my chance. My one shining, sparkling moment. I shouldn't push—I knew that. Hadn't I already told myself that this was a line I shouldn't cross? That I needed to keep myself in check. That I needed to not push that envelope.

But dammit all, when I looked at his face, I knew without a doubt that I could fall with Evan. If he would make the jump with me, I was absolutely certain that he wouldn't let me get hurt. He'd said it himself—he knew how to keep control. And I so desperately wanted to let go of it.

Fear and desire and an odd unwelcome shyness twisted inside of me. I was risking everything but I couldn't stop. I had to have him. At the very least, I had to try. "Please," I said simply.

"I stopped being reckless years ago," Evan said, his tone firm and determined. "That shit gets you in trouble."

I swallowed. Every ounce of reason told me that he was right, that I needed to take a step back. That I needed to stop, to go home, to count to ten. To calm the fuck down.

I didn't do any of that. Instead, I took a step closer. "So now you're all about control?"

A muscle in his cheek twitched. "Yes," he said simply, but I knew that he was fighting to hold it together. I could see the tension in him, and a surge of feminine satisfaction cut through me because I knew with absolute certainty that if I pushed him, he would break.

I reached out, then gently pressed my palm to his chest. I felt wild. Hell, I felt reckless—and the irony really wasn't lost on me. "All right," I said, tilting my head up to meet his hard, heated gaze. "In that case, control me."

"Holy fuck, Angie," he growled, and I knew that I had won.

"Evan." That one soft word was like taking a match to dynamite, and I saw the fire ignite inside him. His hand slid around to my lower back and he yanked me close. I pressed against him, so hot with need it was a wonder I wasn't reduced to ashes. I felt the hard length of his erection press against me and thought I might cry, simply from the knowledge that he was as desperate for me as I was for him.

I'd truly never felt anything like this. As if each vein, each hair, each atom inside me existed for no purpose other than to spread pleasure through me. So much pleasure that I wasn't sure I could withstand the force of it. This was everything I'd wanted. Everything I'd imagined I would feel when Evan finally touched me. But it was so fast and so hard and so overwhelming that I was on the verge of exploding.

Either that or stripping off my clothes and pulling him down to the floor right then and there.

And that probably wasn't the most prudent of plans.

Breathing hard, I backed away, increasing the space between our bodies. I saw the question on his face, the dark disapproval at our broken connection, and before that could shift to regret, or prudence or responsibility, I moved back to him, pressing my body against his torso and my hands over his ass. For the first time, it registered with me that he'd changed clothes. The tuxedo was gone. The man in front of me wore simple Levis and an even simpler white T-shirt that exposed the vine tattoo that encircled his upper arm.

He looked young and hot and completely fuckable, and once again I was blown away by the fact that he was here. With me. A very literal fantasy come true.

I felt the quick rhythm of his heartbeat and knew that he was real. I swayed against him, moving in time with the music—and then realized that Evan wasn't doing the same. "Dance with me," I pleaded, edging toward the dance floor.

His gaze raked slowly over me, leaving me feeling fully exposed and very needy. "I don't dance."

"Oh." My chest tightened, and suddenly I was afraid that all this—whatever "this" was—was going away.

Then his mouth curved up into a slow, sensual grin and he slid his hands along my waist and over my hips, the friction making a flurry of sparks between us. "But I think you're doing a good enough job for the both of us."

"Yeah?"

"Dance for me, Angie." His voice was low and firm, and the command I heard was undeniable.

I'd been doing exactly that, but now my moves seemed more sensual, more erotic.

I was aware of Evan's eyes on me, the heat of his gaze burning through me, giving me confidence to flirt, to beg, to tease in time with the music. Never had I been more aware of my body—or of the effect I was having on a man.

Damn Jahn for what he'd wanted or feared or forbidden. Right then I didn't care. There was no way in hell I was letting Evan Black get away from me tonight. I needed this. Hell, I needed him.

And if the way he was watching me was any indication, I was pretty sure he needed me, too.

I danced even closer, my breasts brushing his chest, one arm going around his neck. I eased myself up on my tiptoes and pressed my lips to his ear. "There are all sorts of ways to dance," I murmured, as I cupped my free hand over his crotch and felt the hard steel of his erection straining against his jeans. "So tell me, Evan. Are you sure you don't want to dance with me?"

six

His eyes went dark, and I was afraid that I'd pushed him too far. That he was going to blink, and then we'd suddenly be just two people on a dance floor in a sleazy bar without this heat, this tug, pulling us together.

Then his hands cupped the back of my neck and he pulled me in closer. I gasped, breathing in the scent of arousal, his and my own. He bent his head and a shudder cut through me as he nipped, just a little too hard, at my earlobe.

"I swear to god, Angie, you're like Kryptonite—you fucking break me." He pulled back, moving his hands to either side of my head, his fingers twining through my hair as he held me just a little too tight, keeping me completely locked in his grasp.

I was breathing hard, my body primed. My lips parted ever so slightly and I tried to lean in, drawn like a magnet to the energy of this man. He held me fast, though, and I knew in that moment that whatever edge I thought I held over Evan Black was a tenuous thing. He could turn the tables on me whenever he wanted to. Hell yes, he was dangerous. And right then, he was mine.

"I've done a lot of fucked up shit," he said. "But this—right here, right now—this may be the worst."

I tried to shake my head, but he still held firm. "I don't believe that," I said.

"I do." He slid one hand around to cup the back of my head, keeping me steady as he moved his other hand so that his thumb could brush gently over my lower lip. Automatically, I opened my mouth, my breath coming in soft, shuddering gasps even as a shiver ran through my entire body. There was no hiding anything from him now, and I didn't want to. The air between us was thick with heat and lust, and though I stood fully clothed in front of him, I'd never felt more exposed in my life than I did in that moment.

The edge of his thumb continued to torment my lip. He eased it inside my mouth, just barely, and though some tiny, rebellious part of me wanted to play it cool, there was no way that was going to happen. I closed my lips around him, my tongue tasting, my lips sucking.

I shut my eyes, hyperaware of the heaviness in my breasts and the demanding throbbing in my cunt. I moaned, not quite able to believe that I could be this turned on when the only physical contact between us was his thumb in my mouth and his hand in my hair.

"If you knew what I wanted to do with you right now, you'd run." His voice was low and edgy and as sharp as a blade, and it cut right through me, leaving me wide open and vulnerable.

I tried to respond but couldn't seem to make sounds. With supreme willpower, I tried again, and somehow managed to form words. "I'm not running."

His eyes were dark. Stormy. And I could see the battle raging across his features. His face was cast in shadows, giving him an even more dangerous appearance, and for just a moment I wasn't certain if I wanted him to win the battle, or lose it.

Then it didn't matter, because his fingers tightened in my hair, pulling me roughly to him in the split second before his mouth captured mine. Around us, other dancers hooted and whistled, but I barely heard them over the rush of blood pounding in my ears.

I parted my lips, and his tongue swept into my mouth, claiming me. He tasted decadent, like the finest of chocolates, the headiest of liquors. I clutched tight to him, my fingers lost in the silky waves of his hair, my body pressed against him. I felt lighter than air, and it was a good thing he held me so tight, because if he had let go I would probably have floated all the way up to the ceiling.

Our kiss was hard and wild, nipping and teasing. I tasted blood and didn't care. I wanted to feel everything, to give everything. To take everything. I felt frantic, as if I needed it all— every bit of his touch, his emotion, his being—because if I stopped or blinked or backed off, it might all go away. This might turn out to be a dream. A mistake. A fantasy.

I didn't think that I could handle that. He was like a drug, and now that I'd tasted him, I knew that I could never give him up.

He pulled away from me then, his breath hard and shallow. I whimpered in protest, terrified that this was it. But my fear dissipated when I looked into his eyes. We weren't stopping. Hell, if I went by the fire I saw burning in his eyes, I didn't think we'd ever stop.

For a breathless eternity we just stared at each other, and I imagined getting drawn into him, lost in his eyes. Melding and merging and never doing without this feeling again. My heart was pounding so hard I was certain that everyone could see the movement of my dress in time with my pulse. I wanted to beg for him to touch me again, to kiss me again, but at the same time I didn't want him to stop looking at me, because under Evan's gaze I felt more alive and real and solid than I had in years.

I didn't know if we stood like that for hours or seconds. I was deaf to the music, blind to the crowd. There was only Evan, watching me. Wanting me.

He broke first, taking my hand and tugging me impatiently across the dance floor. I went willingly, following him down a dark hallway to a propped-open fire door. He kicked it all the way open, then tugged me outside into a dimly lit alley. Immediately, I was accosted by the stench of stale beer and french fries, but I really didn't care. Alley or five-star hotel, it didn't matter to me. All I wanted was this man. This moment. All I wanted was to surrender.

I remembered my frustration with Kevin, but that wasn't a problem with Evan. He took what he wanted, giving what I needed. Power, control, intensity.

In one motion, he had me back against the alley wall, his arms caging me.

"Dear god, Angie. You're beautiful."

"Evan." That single word was all I could manage. The only sound I could push out past the swarm of emotions clogging my throat.

"Do you have any idea how long I—"

"What?" I demanded when he cut himself short. My word was a whisper, a plea. Hell, it was a prayer.

"I'm sorry," he said, and fear shot through me, making me cold. "Christ, I'm so damn sorry."

I reached out and clutched his T-shirt, refusing to let him walk away. It was only when I did that I realized that he wasn't walking and the apology wasn't meant for me. Or maybe it was. I didn't know, and I didn't care, because whatever he was doing or apologizing for or thinking about, it had nothing to do with leaving. I figured that out from the hard and fast way his mouth came down on mine, the way his knee edged between my legs. The way his proximity thickened the air between us, making it warm and liquid and sensual and safe.

He broke the kiss long enough to meet my eyes. His were dark with passion. Mine, I'm sure, were wide with wonder and delight.

I opened my mouth to speak, though I didn't know what I intended to say.

He shook his head, then brushed a soft kiss over my lips. "Don't talk. Don't even think."

I shook my head, then nodded, then shook it again. Don't think? Hell, I *couldn't* think. Not then, and certainly not when his lips brushed my temple and his hand closed over my breast. Then, all I could do was gasp.

His thumb grazed my nipple, now hard behind my bra. What the hell had I been thinking? I should have burned the thing. Worn lace. Worn nothing at all.

"Damn clothes," he murmured, and I almost laughed with delight at how in sync our thoughts were. That bubble of laughter, however, soon faded in the wake of the words that followed. That smooth masculine voice telling me he wanted to touch me, to drag his teeth over my nipples, to tug my skirt up and my panties down so that his fingers could cup and stroke me.

No, it wasn't laughter that bubbled inside me anymore. It was molten lava. Hot. Thick. I wanted to bathe in it. To melt under his touch. To let him take me wherever he wanted to go.

I sighed with pleasure, my hips shifting in response to his words. My back arching in silent demand for more of his touch. More of *him*.

"Evan," I said again, only this time it wasn't a name, it was a plea. Hell, it was a command.

His fingers twined in my hair, and he tugged, forcing me to tilt my head back and look at his face. I felt drugged and woozy, all the more so when I looked at the deep gray of his eyes, soft with lust.

"Angie," he said, his voice flat and almost sad. I saw the lust fade from his eyes, replaced by something hot and hard. Before I even had time to fully process this change in him, he released my hair and smacked the brick wall behind me. I jumped, surprised and confused by this change in him.

"God*dammit*," he said. And then, more gently, "God, I'm an asshole."

I shook my head, denying his words and his actions. I didn't want him to stop, and I didn't understand why he had.

No, that's not true. I understood it—but I just wanted it to go away. The world around us. Promises. Loyalties. They had no place between us. Not now. How could they, when the fire that burned between us would render everything else to ashes?

"Tell me." My voice was low. Breathy, but determined. "You said if I knew what you wanted, I'd run. So tell me, dammit, because I'm not running yet."

"Tell you?" he repeated, his voice rough and uneven, as if he wanted to hold back but couldn't. "Tell you how I want to strip you bare? How I want your breasts to fill my hands, your nipples pinched between my fingertips until you cry out in pleasure and in pain?"

I shuddered, my nipples tightening simply from the promise of his words.

"Or should I tell you how I want to feel the sting of my bare hand on your naked ass until your cheeks are red and your cunt glistens." He leaned in closer, his whisper ragged at my ear. "I want you naked, Angie. Naked and bound and wet for me. I want your legs wide and your body exposed. I want to see you. Hell, I want to feast on you. I want my mouth on you, my tongue driving you mad. I don't want you to know a goddamn thing except me and the pleasure I bring you. And I want to watch the way your eyes go bright when I finally let you come."

I was breathing hard, my panties soaked, my thighs damp and trembling. His words shocked me, yes. But they also turned me on.

I leaned back, increasing the distance between us infinitesimally, but only because I had no choice. It was either find support against the rough brick wall or collapse to the ground, my body no longer quite able to hold me upright.

The second I edged back, though, a shadow crossed his face. "Like I said, I'm an asshole."

Despite the fact that he'd completely undone me—despite the fact that every bone, muscle, and tendon in my body had turned to jelly—I somehow managed the smallest shake of my head and the tiniest noise. "No."

I drew in a gasping breath, then said more forcefully, "*No.* I'm not running. I'm not going anywhere." I licked my suddenly dry lips and glanced down at the ground, embarrassment overtaking me. But not enough to cripple me. Not even close.

Traffic rushed by at the end of the alley and the pulse of music filtered through the thick walls of the club. None of that noise penetrated, though. The alley seemed still and quiet, as if the world had quit turning and everything—my existence, Evan's, the whole damn universe—was stuck in limbo until I spoke again.

I steeled my shoulders. "Everything you just said . . . I—I want it, too."

My cheeks were so hot I was certain they must have been flashing as red as neon, and I kept my eyes down, afraid that if I looked up and saw him I might spontaneously combust.

"Angie. Oh, Jesus, Angie." He took my head in his hands, his fingers sliding into my thick tangle of hair as he tilted my face up to see his. "You completely unwind me." There was such intensity in his voice that it sounded almost painful, and the tenor of his desire shook me to the core. "Tell me you want me. Tell me you want this." The words were rough and urgent. "I need to hear you say it."

"I want you," I said, the words sounding inadequate against the complexity of the emotions behind them.

For a moment, he held my gaze, as if he was searching my face for some sort of deception. I didn't flinch. I knew what he saw in me—himself, reflected right back.

He stroked my cheek with the pad of his thumb, the sweetness of the gesture in stark contrast to the rawness of all the things he'd said he wanted to do with me. But somehow, that simple touch made me melt even more.

He was everything I'd ever wanted. Everything I needed. Hell, he was more than I could have imagined. And in that moment, I knew I would do anything to keep him there with me.

"I want you," I repeated. "I want this."

"This?" he repeated, then leaned in to brush a trail of feather-soft kisses down my neck, then along my collarbone. His touch was lighter than air, and yet it pounded through me like the steady, rhythmic thrum of a bass drum building to a crescendo.

"Or maybe this?" He ran his hands down my arms, then twined our fingers together. He pressed his body tight against me as his mouth sought mine, his tongue demanding entrance as he thrust our arms out to the side as if readying to take flight. He deepened the kiss, exploring with his tongue, delighting me with his teeth, nibbling on my lips. And as he did, he slowly maneuvered our arms up until mine were completely above my head and he gently released his fingers from mine. "Or maybe this is what you want," he said, manipulating my hands so that I was clutching my own wrist above my head.

"Evan, I—"

"No." He brushed his lips over my ear, his voice so low I had to strain to hear him. "No talking. No moving. The arms stay up, the hands together. Nod if you understand me."

I licked my lips.

"Nod," he repeated.

I nodded, so lost in him that if he'd told me to strip naked and spread my legs right then, I think I would have done it, and eagerly. I was that much in thrall to him.

Yeah, he was dangerous all right—but damn me, it was that danger that I craved.

"Good girl," he said, then brushed the gentlest of kisses over my lips. "And I think we've found what you want," he added, closing his hands over mine.

I drew in a shuddering breath, because he was right. He had me trapped—maybe not by reality, but by the promise of my own obedience. The result was the same. I was desperately, hopelessly turned on.

"You like this," he said. "You're open to me—open to the world. Down and dirty with me in an alley where anything could happen." Once again, he leaned in to whisper. Once again, I was struck by how well he knew me. "This excites you, doesn't it? Not knowing where we're going next. What's going to happen. Who might turn that corner. Not knowing if I'm going to kiss you or fuck you." He paused, and his next words made me moan aloud. "I'll give you a hint, Angie. I'm going to do both."

I hadn't noticed when he'd removed one of his hands from where he gripped mine, but I noticed now that he was trailing his fingers up my thigh, slowly lifting the hem of my skirt as his hand rose higher and higher.

I whimpered a little, but the hand on mine held fast, and he shook his head. One tiny motion. *No.*

I closed my eyes and surrendered to both the unspoken command and to my own overpowering need to revel in the exhilaration of this moment. He had me pinned against the wall, held in place by his large hand cupped around my wrists. His body was so close to mine I could feel his heat. And his hand was rising higher and higher toward my now-soaked panties, my throbbing clit, and my cunt that was slick with arousal.

Every scrap of reason inside me was screaming that I needed

to open my eyes and tell him no. That I needed to walk away. That this was a bad idea and that I knew better and hadn't I told myself over and over that it was a bad idea to let myself go wild? That nothing good ever came of it.

That I would regret it in the morning.

But I didn't regret it then. Not one little bit.

I shifted my stance and spread my legs wider—and I was rewarded by his low, sensual growl of approval. Slowly, his fingertip traced the edge of my panties, easing down the side of the V that covered my pubic bone. I whimpered as he teased me mercilessly, his finger grazing over silk and elastic, the edge of his skin barely brushing the sensitive skin of my inner thigh.

"Frustrated, beautiful?" he murmured.

My head was back, my breathing fast. "Are you insane?" In my head, I was screaming. In real life, I could barely formulate words. "Jesus, Evan. *Please.*"

He spread his fingers so that now he was teasing the indentation at the juncture of both my thighs, his strokes light but firm. And never, ever touching the soft flesh beneath the silk or brushing over my tight, demanding clit.

I struggled to pull my hands free, desperate to finish what he had started. But he held me fast, and I wanted to shout curses, to make demands, to drop down on my knees and beg. But it was all I could do to draw breath as my body shuddered, every nerve, every sensation pooled between my legs in anticipation of a touch that he seemed determined not to give me.

"Please, what?" he asked, as I dragged my teeth over my lower lip.

"Please," I repeated. "Please everything."

His low, satisfied chuckle washed over me, teasing my skin with as much sensuality as if he were trailing a feather over me.

"Touch me," I demanded.

He bent closer so that his breath tickled my cheek. "I am touching you."

I wiggled my hips in unspoken demand. "You know what I mean."

"I do," he said. "But I want to hear you say it." He drew his tongue up the edge of my ear, and I bit down on my lip for fear that if I didn't I would cry out in both pleasure and frustration.

"I want—" I swallowed and tried again. "I want you inside my panties."

To his credit, he complied, and I sighed with pleasure as his fingers stroked my slick, swollen flesh. I was completely bare, having recently discovered Brazilian waxes, and the way his finger slid over my wet flesh was driving me completely insane.

He didn't, however, touch my clit, and so I had no relief for the desperate, pounding, growing need that was building inside me.

I moved my hips, trying without words to let him know exactly what I wanted.

"Demanding thing, aren't you?" he teased.

"Dammit, Evan, you're being exceptionally mean."

"Maybe." He stroked his finger lightly over my clit, and my entire body lit up. "But I'm damn sure enjoying myself." He slipped his fingers inside me, and I gasped as my muscles tightened around him, drawing him in. "That's it, baby. That's what you want, isn't it? You want to be fucked."

I clenched my hands into fists, managing to gather enough self-possession to say, "You're just figuring that out?"

He laughed softly, but whatever amusement I'd felt in the wake of my comment faded under the slow, rhythmic assault of his hands upon my body, sliding deeper and deeper, leaving me breathless and anxious and so very, very close.

When he drew his hand free, I actually whimpered, and when he slid his fingertip—wet with my arousal—between my lips, I moaned and took him in, closing my eyes as I sucked and teased, imagining it was his cock in my mouth.

"Dear god, that's hot," he whispered. He moved closer, and I felt the press of his erection against my belly, tight and hard beneath the denim of his jeans. "I want you, Angie. I want to yank your skirt up and rip these damn panties off. I want to bury myself inside you and watch your face while you come."

I said nothing, only drew him in deeper and relished the soft sound of his own, responsive groan.

"But not here—not in an alley." He drew his finger from my mouth, and my eyes fluttered open. "I'm taking you home. I'm going to fuck you, Angie, but I'm going to do it properly. Say yes, baby."

I nodded.

"I want to hear it."

Stupidly, I nodded again. "Yes," I said, after fighting to regain the power of thought.

"Good girl." He gave me a moment to recover the ability to walk, then led me toward the street where, I presumed, he'd parked.

We'd only taken two steps toward the intersection of the alley and the street when a shadow fell across the sidewalk, followed quickly by a form that I recognized. Bruiser.

A second guy flanked him, tall and lean, with the kind of sauntering walk that told the world he could beat the crap out of just about anyone.

A shock of panic—hard and fast and cold—shot through me. How could this have happened? I never take my guard down when I'm outside, and sure as hell not in a dark alley. And yet I'd been totally unaware of everything. I'd seen nothing, heard nothing, noticed nothing. From the moment we exited the club, there had been only Evan. I'd let myself go with him—I'd let myself fly—and everything had gone to hell. *Fuck*.

"He the one that horned in on your girl?" the lean guy asked.

"My girl? More like my slut." Bruiser aimed his beady eyes at me. "What would your mamma say about you doing the nasty in a dark alley with that son of a bitch?"

"Fuck you," I snapped. Or, at least, I tried to. Instead, the words stuck in my throat, trapped there when I spied the glint of the knife in Bruiser's hand. A chill crept over my entire body, icy fingers trailing up my spine. I sucked in air, and tasted salt water. I closed my eyes, and saw blood.

This wasn't happening. This couldn't be happening.

I didn't realize that I'd taken a step backward until I felt Evan's hand closing tight around mine, locking me in place. I froze, taking shallow breaths, trying to concentrate only on the reassuring feel of his hold upon me.

He was order to my chaos, calm to my storm. Fear might have me tight in its grip, but Evan slipped out of its fist like butter. The alley—hell, the whole damn situation—was his to command.

"I think you owe the lady an apology," he said smoothly.

"Fuck you."

"I'd really rather not," Evan said. "Now get the hell out of my way." His voice was hard, his manner equally so. He took a single step toward them, forcing me to take a corresponding one. I bit my lower lip, then tasted blood. I saw Bruiser's mouth moving, but I couldn't make out the words. Though I knew I was looking at this dark Chicago alley, what I saw was the barnacled posts beneath the pier. What I heard was the crash of the ocean against the beach. It was as if I'd fallen into one of my dreams, and I couldn't fight my way out of the nightmare.

Then Bruiser lunged, leading with the knife, and the sharp pierce of a scream ripped me back into reality. It took a second before I realized that it was my scream, and that in that minuscule amount of time, Evan had released my hand, raised his arm, and managed to block the oncoming knife.

"Shit, Chris!" the lean guy shouted as Evan twisted Chris-the-Bruiser's arm behind his back and wrested the knife free.

"Motherfucker!" Chris snarled, but he didn't struggle, and from where I stood I could see why—considering Evan's grip, if Chris even breathed wrong, his arm was going to snap.

"You fucked up bad, pretty boy," the lean guy spat, already in motion with his own knife tight in his hand.

In the kind of move that Hollywood directors probably spent weeks choreographing, Evan shoved Chris aside, spun toward the lean guy, knocked his knife arm out of the way, then thrust the tip of the knife he'd taken off Chris into the flesh at the base of the lean guy's throat. Chris cursed and sprinted down the alley, leaving his buddy to Evan's mercy.

Evan didn't even spare him a glance, his attention focused entirely on the lean guy with the knife still twitching in his hand. "Give me a reason," Evan said. "Give me just one reason, and I'll slice through you like butter."

"Fuck you."

"Wrong reason." In a move too fast for me to see how it happened, Evan yanked the guy into a clench, his face a wash of rage. Now the length of his blade was pressed to the lean guy's throat. I saw a single drop of blood trail down his neck. "All I have to do is flick my wrist," Evan whispered, the voice so soft and menacing it seemed to be inside my head instead of spoken.

The guy's eyes were squeezed tight, and the knife he still held clattered to the pavement. I caught the pungent scent of urine and knew that he'd wet himself.

I heard a soft noise, like the cry of a child. At first I thought it came from the man in Evan's arms. Then I realized it came from me.

I saw Evan's muscles stiffen, saw the shift of expressions on his face, the way he brought the rage down. The way his chest rose and fell as he looked at me and gathered himself. Slowly—very slowly—he drew the knife away, and I couldn't help but wonder what would have happened if I'd stayed quiet. The thought should have terrified me. It didn't. This was Evan, and like Jahn, he'd do whatever it took to protect me.

"Get the fuck out of here," Evan said, his voice like the low roll of thunder.

The guy didn't waste any time. He took off down the alley, practically tripping over himself in the process.

Slowly, Evan moved to the trash bin and tossed the knife in. Then he came toward me, moving gingerly, as if I were a wounded animal. I didn't understand the reason for his tentative approach until he crouched in front of me. Only then did I realize that I'd slid to the ground, my knees pulled tight to my chest.

"Hey," he said, his voice as gentle as I'd ever heard it. "It's okay. You're okay." He reached out and stroked my hair. "They've gone. They're not going to hurt me, and I'd kill them before I'd let them hurt you."

I nodded, thankful for his touch. The pitching, tossing waves inside me began to settle into soft, undulating swells.

I reached out a hand for him to help me up, but he shook his head. "No. I've got you."

Before I could protest, he had his arms under my legs and behind my back. I thought I should protest, but I couldn't quite work up the desire. Instead, I curled against him, letting his steady strength soothe the rawness of my memories.

I have no idea where it came from, but the moment we emerged from the alley onto the street, a familiar-looking black Lexus pulled to the curb. A burly man with arms as thick as my thighs hurried out and opened the back door for Evan, who moved gingerly as he placed me on the soft leather.

"Don't go," I whispered, as the icy prickles and hard knots of fear began to return.

"Never," he said, as he slid in beside me. And then I was in his arms again, safe and warm. I curled up next to him, my eyes closed. I heard the door slam, then the sound of Evan's palm against the back of the front seat. A signal to go, I realized, because the next thing I felt was motion and power as the Lexus pulled out onto the street.

Evan said nothing, and for that I was grateful. I didn't want to talk. Didn't want to explain. I didn't even want to be reassured. All I wanted was for him to hold me, and he did that, his arm around me, his fingers idly stroking my upper arm. My head rested on his shoulder, and though I thought I felt his lips brush over my hair, I couldn't be sure, as I didn't have the strength to lift my head and look at him.

I was tired. My body drained, my muscles limp. Everything was coming at me too damn fast. I didn't want anything but the feel of Evan's arms around me, and if I had my way, I would have stayed like that, held tight in the warmth of his embrace, forever.

seven

Forever ended all too soon.

The next thing I knew, the engine had stopped and we were parked in front of Jahn's building. As I blinked groggily, I saw Tony the doorman hurry over. He pulled open the door and Evan slid out, then bent back in to give me a hand.

"I'm fine." The breath I drew in was shaky, and I knew that my voice was going to sound petulant, but I couldn't help myself. "You brought me to the condo."

His gray eyes were clear and full of understanding. "I thought you needed someplace familiar."

I nodded, even though he was wrong. I didn't want familiar. Hell, *I* was familiar, and wasn't that the whole point? To get as far away from myself as I could? I'm not sure I knew anymore. All I knew was that for years, I'd felt lost. Until tonight, that is. Until I felt Evan's touch and knew that I'd finally come home.

That, however, wasn't something I was going to tell him. I might be feeling ripped and scared and sentimental and a million other emotions, but I knew better than to dump the heavy shit on a guy I wanted to stay. So, wisely, I stayed silent as he led me through the polished lobby to the sleek elevator bank.

The car arrived and we got on. I started to dig in my purse for the card key that would access the penthouse, but Evan already had one. I'm not sure why I was surprised. He was as close to Jahn as I'd been. Maybe closer. For years, Evan had been around full-time, while I'd only been able to visit during the summers and then, later, when my college load permitted jaunts into town.

Only silence greeted us as we entered the condo, a sharp contrast to the noisy hum of the guests that had filled these walls earlier in the evening. Not even Peterson was around. Though he was ostensibly Jahn's live-in help, he actually lived in a separate apartment one floor below the penthouse that could be accessed by a private set of security stairs.

In other words, Evan and I were alone. And while I could still recall with vivid, delicious clarity the way that his body had felt against mine in the alley, right then it wasn't the press of skin against skin that I craved. It was simply the man, beside me, telling me that everything was going to be just fine.

As if he could read my mind, he led me to the comfy leather couch, then pulled a soft afghan over me. "Shoes off," he said. "Then I need you to tell me the truth."

I looked at him sharply, not sure I was ready to talk about the way I'd flipped out.

"Hot chocolate, wine, or something one hell of a lot stronger?"

I actually smiled, the expression feeling foreign. "Cocoa, please." I narrowed my eyes. "But only if it's good. I have my standards, after all."

His smile was casual, but I could see the spark of relief in his eyes. If I was making quips, maybe I wasn't quite the wreck he'd feared. "Sweetheart, I'm always good."

My smile widened and a genuine laugh escaped.

"That's what I like to hear." He reached for my hand, then brushed his fingers over mine before he moved off toward the kitchen.

The moment he was out of sight, the weight of the air in the room seemed to bear down on me. I'd done this before. Curled up beneath a blanket. Hot cocoa. Only Evan wasn't in the kitchen that time, my mother had been. And my father had been beside me, holding tight to my hand. I'd had my back pressed against the sofa, but as much as I'd hoped and wished, the cushions refused to open up and swallow me.

The detectives and uniformed officers had been gentle, their questions respectful, their voices soft. But that hadn't stopped the walls from closing in or the tears from flowing.

And it sure as hell hadn't brought my sister back.

"Angie."

Evan's voice was feather soft, but even so it ripped me violently from my memories. I jerked my head around to see him standing in the doorway, a steaming mug held tight in his hands.

"I'm okay."

He cocked his head as if considering my words, and I gave him bonus points for not calling me a damn liar. He crossed to me without another word, then held the mug out for me. I took it, my fingers brushing over his as I closed my hands around the warm ceramic. Our eyes met, and I felt the flash of a connection shoot through me. Real and solid and unmistakable.

And nothing more now than a missed opportunity.

The heat I'd seen in his eyes was banked now, replaced instead by affection and concern. But I didn't want affection. I wanted the fire back, and I wanted it hot enough to burn away my memories—of tonight, and of eight years ago.

"Tell me," he said, settling down on the couch next to me.

I was sitting cross-legged with a pillow in my lap and the afghan draped loosely over me. His thigh brushed against my knee, and that single point of contact was the only part of my entire body of which I was aware. It was hard to concentrate on his question, and I knew that I needed to. I had a feeling that despite my usual reticence, I would say things around Evan that I shouldn't, and just because I wanted to fuck him didn't mean that I wanted to trust him. Not with everything. Not with that.

I took a sip of the cocoa, then looked up at him in delighted pleasure. "You added peppermint schnapps."

"You once said you like it that way."

I blinked, surprised. I'd spent one Christmas at Jahn's house with my parents. Evan and Cole and Tyler had come over one evening, along with the students who were in Jahn's seminar that year and a few of the neighbors. Jahn had served cocoa with peppermint schnapps. It was the first time I'd ever tasted it, and I'd thought that if heaven had specialty drinks, that would certainly be on the list. "You remember that?"

His eyes never left my face. "I remember a lot of things."

"Oh." I looked down, suddenly self-conscious, and took a long sip of the drink, relishing the way it eased down my throat, warming me from the inside out.

"Angie," he said gently. "Who hurt you?"

I looked back up sharply as I realized what he thought. That I'd been the victim. That I was having flashbacks of some horrible attack.

I laughed, but there was no humor in the sound. "I did."

If I'd been trying to shock him, I'd failed. He didn't move or flinch. There was no surprise on his face. Only compassion.

"Tell me," he ordered. "I can help."

"I'm not asking for help."

"No, you're not." He twisted a lock of my hair around his

finger. I waited for him to say something else, but no words came. He just sat there with me until I couldn't take the weight of the silence any longer.

"You never met Gracie," I said, the words sounding almost like an accusation.

"No, but Jahn told me about her."

"That she died?" I said, with more venom than I intended.

"That she was a wonderful girl that he loved very much. That he missed her. That you all missed her."

I nodded, fighting the knot of tears that was forming in my throat. "I miss her every day." I drew in a breath to steel myself. "Did he tell you how she died?"

"No. And we never asked. Angie," he said. "I'm asking now. Was she attacked? Was it in an alley?"

He reached over and carefully took the cup out of my hands. Only then did I realize it had been shaking, the cocoa sloshing over the sides to land on the silk of my dress, leaving it dotted with puckered wet spots.

"It's okay," Evan said, and I knew he wasn't talking about the dress.

"It wasn't an alley," I finally managed. "They attacked her under the pier. At least three of them and they had knives. They dragged her to a van. They raped her. They sliced her. And three days later they dumped her." A tear trickled down my cheek. "They didn't kill her. They left her to bleed out. She died all alone in a ditch near Miramar."

"Goddamn bastards." His voice was deceptively calm, but I could hear the steel beneath it. "Who? Did they catch who did it?"

I did. Me. It was me. I wanted to shout the answer, because that was the truth, wasn't it? If it weren't for me, Grace would still be alive, and nothing I could say or do or hope or beg could ever change that.

I tried to imagine telling him the whole truth. Leaning my

head against his chest and feeling his hands on my back as I told him the story that I'd only ever told one person. Not my father. Not my mother. Not even the police. Just my uncle Jahn, and now he was dead, too, and my secret was mine once more.

I could imagine it, but I couldn't do it.

"Was it political? Aimed against your father?"

"I don't know who did it," I said, looking at my hands, now fisted in the blanket. "But the police called it gang-related. My dad was still in the California legislature back then, but there didn't seem to be anything political about it. There was no ransom note. No demand. They never arrested anyone. My dad even hired a PI, but he never got anywhere, either."

"You were with her?"

I shook my head, expecting him to look at me like I was a little bit crazy.

"I should never have gone out tonight," I said. If he thought the change in subject was strange, he didn't comment.

"There's nothing wrong with needing to let go sometimes."

I wiped my hand under my nose and sniffled, feeling small and young and terribly lost. "Even when people get hurt?"

He slid off the couch and knelt right in front of me, then gently pressed his hands on my knees. "No one got hurt, Angie."

I shrugged. "You almost did."

His mouth twitched a little, making the dimple flash. "I'm not sure if I should be flattered you care, or insulted that you think so little of my skill."

"Flattered," I said, managing a smile.

He met my smile, and this time his own went all the way to his eyes. He leaned over and retrieved my cup from the floor, then handed it back to me. "Drink your cocoa."

I actually grinned, and it felt nice.

"What?"

"It feels like you're babysitting me."

His scarred brow lifted, making him look sexy and arrogant

all at the same time. He shifted his weight forward, and before I knew what to expect, he'd caught me in a kiss, hard and deep. I moaned, my body softening with need and thrumming with desire. We touched in only two places—lips and knees—and yet every inch of skin on my body crackled with banked electricity, as if Evan were a storm and I'd been caught unawares.

As swiftly as he'd moved in, he released me and settled back, leaving me gaping breathlessly at him. "You're not a child, Angie. I'm not sure you were ever a child. And I damn sure know that I wasn't."

Since I didn't have a clue what to say to that, I remained silent, holding my mug and wondering if my mouth was tingling because of the schnapps or because of his kiss.

After a moment, he rose, then held out his hand to me. I left the mug on the floor, put my hand in his, and stood.

Without a word, he led me to my bedroom. He turned me around, then slowly unzipped my dress. Whatever chill had lingered from the evening and the onslaught of memory disappeared, vanquished by the heat of his proximity. I soaked in his warmth, letting it soothe my rough edges even as tiny sparks bounced and fizzed inside me. And yet this simple touch was enough. So much, in fact, that he'd filled me up completely.

Gently, his hands stroked my shoulders. "Slip it off," he said. "Get under the covers."

"I—"

"Don't argue. Just do." He moved toward the connecting bathroom, and while he was gone, I complied, letting the dress slide off my body to pool around my ankles. I hesitated a moment, then unclasped my bra and let it fall, as well. I still wore the panties, silk and lace that were one of my many wardrobe indulgences.

I drew in a breath, lifted the covers, and slid into bed.

He returned momentarily with a glass of water. He handed it to me and I took it. I drank a long swallow, wondering if I should be sad that he'd manufactured this reason to leave the room while I undressed, or impressed that he was a gentleman at heart.

I landed on the side of gentleman. "Thank you," I said.

"It's just water," he answered, but he smiled in what I thought was understanding. He nodded toward the bed. "Sleep now."

"I—" I stumbled on my words. "I don't want to be alone."

He bent and gently stroked my forehead. "I'll be right here." I watched as he settled himself in the floral print armchair near the wall of windows, the dark expanse of the lake behind him with just a few scattered boat lights glittering like stars. "Sleep," he repeated, and I nodded, suddenly aware of how heavy my eyelids felt.

I snuggled under the covers, then let myself drift off.

I felt warm. I felt safe. I felt protected.

At least until the shadows came.

The scream cut through the air, so loud and sharp and painful that it wrenched me awake.

Strong arms surrounded me, and I drew in a breath, terrified, and only then realizing that I'd been the one doing the screaming.

"Deep breaths, baby. I've got you. Just take some deep breaths. You're safe. You're with me and you're safe." Evan's voice washed over me, warm and commanding, as if simply by saying that I was safe he could make it so. I was sitting upright, clutching tight to him. My arms were around him, my hands fisted in the back of his T-shirt.

The sheet had tumbled away to gather at my waist, and my breasts were pressed against him. His hands, big and warm and strong, gently stroked my bare back as I gulped in air, trying to shake free of the tendrils of fear that still clung to me, cold and menacing.

"You're safe," he repeated gently. "You're okay."

I nodded, realizing as I did that I was starting to believe it. I was awake. I was safe. I was warm in the security of Evan's arms.

I'm not sure how long he held me like that. All I know is that by the time I finally did pull away, he'd given me enough of his strength so that I could make it the rest of the way on my own.

"Better now?"

I nodded, then sat upright on the bed, one leg tucked under me. I took the tissue he handed me and blew my nose.

"Was it about Gracie?"

I closed my eyes in silent acknowledgment. "It was like I was there. The men. They were attacking her. They had knives. They were coming at her. But I couldn't do anything. I couldn't move. I wasn't there—not really. But I had to watch. I had to watch, because it shouldn't have been her at all. It should have been me."

Once again, the tears burst forth, and he gathered me into his arms. I thought that I should pull away or curl up into a ball or tell him to leave me be for just a little while until I managed to get my act together. But I didn't. I didn't have the strength, but more than that, I didn't have the desire.

For so long, I'd been fighting the nightmares by myself. To have Evan beside me now, giving me both strength and comfort was like opening the biggest present on Christmas morning.

He stroked my back slowly, but I could feel the tension in his touch. "I should have just walked away."

I didn't have a clue what he was talking about, and I pulled away only long enough to look at him with curiosity.

"In the alley," he explained. "I should have taken you back inside the club. I should have walked away from those assholes. Gone inside. Called a bouncer. Just gotten clear. Anything to get you away from there." He cupped my cheek with his palm. "I didn't think. I wanted you—goddammit, I wanted you so fucking much—and I just didn't think about what you'd see. What you'd think."

My eyes were wide. "No, oh, god, Evan, no. You were brilliant. You were perfect."

"I didn't feel perfect when I saw you cowering on the asphalt. Or now, when you wake screaming from a nightmare."

I could see the emotion in his face, along with the frustration. This was a man prone to action—but how do you fight fear and nightmares? He would have, though. If there was a way, I was certain he would have gone into battle for me, just like any proper knight.

The thought was almost enough to make me smile.

I didn't, though. Instead, I said, "I have them every night. They cling to me. You didn't bring the nightmares, Evan. Not even close." I shifted position, pulled into motion by the need to make him understand. "But what you did in the alley—I wish someone like you had been at Gracie's side that night. Someone who could have protected her. Who could have—" My voice hitched in my throat, and I felt a single tear snake down my cheek.

Evan brushed it away with the pad of his thumb. "I would end those bastards right now, if I could." His voice was so tight I thought it might break. "For what they did to your sister. For what they took from you. And for the fear they left behind."

I swallowed, undone by the ferocity that he was barely holding in. A feral determination that was so raw, so primal, it took my breath away. Our eyes locked, and for a moment I thought I would fall inside of him, both of us tumbling away from reality into some world that was uniquely ours.

Then he pulled me roughly against him, and I knew that we had to stay here. This world. This reality. But with Evan beside me, maybe I could stand it.

"Angie," he said, then caught my mouth with his. His kiss was rough, in sharp contrast to the tenderness of his touch. I matched him, my need frantic. Intense. I was desperate to get lost in him, to go to that place where reason and memory and fear and regret evaporated. To leave everything behind except the reality of Evan and Angie and heat and need.

This was what I'd wanted. What I'd fantasized about. This man in my bed. His body hard against mine. His hands upon me, his tongue tasting me.

We were wild. Frenzied. As if we'd both exploded into supernovas of passion. One of his hands clutched my head, holding me in place as we devoured each other with kisses. The other roamed my back, palm flat, each bit of skin that he caressed lighting up in the wake of his touch until I was sure that I glowed as bright as the sun.

I was wide open to him in so many ways, and when I felt his hand cup my breast, I gasped from the sweet pleasure of the inevitable. "Yes," I murmured. "Oh, please, yes."

His hands moved to my shoulders, then stroked down my arms even as his gaze roamed down my body, making my nipples tighten as his eyes dipped toward my chest. "God, Angie, do you have any idea—"

I didn't know what idea I was supposed to have because his words were cut off when he thrust me backward onto the bed, then moved to straddle me. I was trapped beneath him with his groin right over mine. I was naked but for the panties, so wet now that I was certain they clung to my body like a second skin.

I was completely exposed to him—completely open to him. He could do anything to me in that moment. Take me any way he wanted. I was completely and utterly his, and that knowledge made my pulse skitter and my skin tingle. I held my breath, not knowing what would come next, but only that I craved it. Craved *him*.

His lips skimmed the curve of my ear, then down the soft skin of my neck, the feather-soft contact designed to drive me wild. Slowly, he traced my collarbone with the tip of his tongue before moving lower still.

I groaned with delighted abandon as he closed his mouth over my breast, his teeth teasing my nipple as he suckled me, sending threads of fire to shoot from my breasts all the way to my throbbing, needy sex.

"Evan." I'm not sure I even spoke his name. It was a plea, a prayer. And as his hot mouth continued lower down my abdomen, his tongue teasing my navel before moving on to my panty line, I had to acknowledge that it was also a thank-you. I may have awakened in a nightmare, but I could barely remember it now. All I knew was Evan. All I understood was his touch. All I wanted was the man.

"Off," he growled, his fingers tugging at the lace of my panties.

I wriggled my hips as he yanked them down. I have no idea if he tossed them aside or if they ended up tangled in the sheets. I was too preoccupied with the way he clutched my thighs, his thumbs grazing teasingly close to my sex. He pushed my legs apart, spreading me wide as he bent lower, then licked every intimate inch of me.

He was the first man to touch me like that since I'd been waxed, and the sensation of his tongue against my bare flesh came damn close to pushing me over the edge, the glorious sensation matched only by the teasing way that his tongue danced over my clit in sweet little motions designed to send me spiraling into the heavens.

I wanted to cry out—to scream in pleasure—but I also didn't want him to stop, and so I bit down on the pad of my thumb until I couldn't take it anymore. Until the sweet, decadent pressure inside me became too much to bear and I had to cry out as my body shuddered and exploded, only to be drawn back to earth again, tethered to Evan, just as he had promised.

"Evan—oh my god, Evan."

"Shhh." He moved up beside me, then pulled me close until he was spooned against me. He was still in his jeans and T-shirt, but I could feel his erection straining against my ass as he hooked an arm over my waist to anchor me against him.

"Don't you want—?"

"I want to hold you. I want to fall asleep with the taste of you on my lips and the scent of you all around me. And I want you to drift off with nothing in your head but the pleasure I gave you. Do you understand, baby?"

I remembered everything he'd said in the alley. I wanted that—I wanted it desperately.

But I didn't want it right then. All I wanted was the safety of his arms.

I nodded, and if I weren't so tired, I would have smiled. Once again, Evan Black understood what I needed.

"Good girl. Now close your eyes." His voice was soft, almost sing-song, and I complied.

I never fell asleep easily, but with Evan beside me, I felt myself drifting off. Falling away in the arms of this dangerous man.

And never in my life had I felt more safe.

eight

The rest of the night passed easily, and I woke up feeling so alive and refreshed and alert that I actually laughed out loud. I never slept without the nightmares. Not ever. Even when they snuck in under the radar, so small and quiet that I didn't remember them in the morning, I always knew that they'd been there, creeping around the edges of my subconscious like vermin.

And yet in Evan's arms they'd stayed away, as if he'd stood sentry against the dragons, slaying them as a proper knight would.

Slowly, I rolled over, careful not to wake Evan, who still had his arm over me. His face was calm, at peace, and yet I could still see the dark hints of the man who had protected me in the alley. The sharp contours of his face. The shadow of beard stubble. That scar that stood out as a reminder of what he was capable of. I'd seen it, hadn't I? If those men had taken it further—if they'd tried to hurt me—Evan would have killed them with no thought and no regret. He was, I thought, an avenging angel. *My* avenging angel.

And all I wanted right then was to finish what he'd started. To give him the same pleasure that he'd given me.

Gently, I shifted on the bed, hooking my leg over until I was straddling him, my knees pressed into the mattress on either side of him. The covers slid down my body and the cool air brushed over my back and my bare breasts. I was naked now, my panties having been flung aside last night like an afterthought.

I stayed like that for a moment, my eyes on his face. My breasts felt heavy, my nipples tight. My breathing was ragged and wild, and I slid my hand down my belly, then closed my eyes as my fingers found my sex, hot and slick. I drew in a shattered breath as the remnants of a dream returned. He'd banished the nightmares, yes. And the dreams that had replaced them had been sweetly, desperately arousing.

I pulled my hand away. My body might have been on the edge, but I had no interest in being the one who pushed me over. I wanted Evan and only Evan. I bent forward at the waist and lowered my hips until I was brushing against his crotch. Just that one point of connection, and yet every atom in my body was reacting, swirling and bouncing and dancing in glorious anticipation.

My hands were on the bed, palms flat, on either side of his head. I was low enough now that my breasts brushed the cotton of his T-shirt, my nipples so tight and hard that the friction was almost painful. My breath was ragged, my body nothing more than need.

I brushed a soft kiss over his lips and watched as his eyes fluttered. I held my breath, exhaling only when his eyes fluttered open to reveal the smoky depths of those enigmatic gray eyes.

"Angie," he murmured, and that was enough for me. I rocketed forward, capturing him in a hard, fast, demanding kiss.

His mouth was open to me, and I tasted him, drawing him in, savoring him. He broke the kiss suddenly, gasping, and I arched back to look at his face. His eyes met mine, and I saw myself. My need and my desire. I saw years of pent-up passion, and in that moment I felt wholly vindicated—at least until the moment the shadow passed between us.

"Oh, Jesus, Angie," he said as he looked away. And in that instant the world around me shattered like glass.

"Evan," I said, but what I meant was "Please."

It didn't matter. He'd been with me—right there—but now he was pulling back. Frantic, I reached out, grabbing his collar and holding him in place. "I want this," I said. "I want to finish what we started last night. What you said. Don't you see? I'm still not running."

Once again, his eyes met mine, and this time there was no passion. Only regret and bald determination. "I know you're not." He closed his hand gently over mine, then loosened my grip. "But you should."

He drew in a heavy breath, then took my shoulders and rolled me onto my back. I lay there, numb, as he sat up on the side of the bed. His back was straight as a board. His shoulders were squared. I had the impression I was looking at a soldier about to go into battle. Reluctant, but determined.

I understood what he was doing—what I didn't get was why.

"Evan." My voice was barely a whisper, as if volume might push him out the door. "We both want it. I do, and I know you do, too."

He stood up, then turned to look at me. I dragged the covers up to my neck, needing to keep at least part of me hidden. I'd already exposed too much of myself to him.

"Don't you?" I pleaded when he said nothing. My voice was laced with a note of insecurity, and I hated myself for it. I watched the expressions shift across his face like clouds upon the wind, and fear slashed through me. "You're not seriously going to stand there and tell me I'm wrong? I felt it, Evan. I felt *you*."

His expression was flat, but his eyes were like a storm when they met mine. "I have done and will do a lot of things that you would probably find reprehensible. But I will never, *never,* lie to you."

I shook my head, confused and wary.

"Last night—what happened in the alley." He shook his head. "It was a mistake," he said, and with that single word, I understood everything. Whatever he'd seen in me—whatever he'd wanted—I'd managed to destroy it. He might have lost control last night, but in the end, I *was* dragonbait—some weak female who needed rescuing. But it wasn't a princess that Evan Black wanted. It never had been.

"A mistake," I repeated dully. I thought of the way I'd felt in his arms. The way he'd kept the nightmares at bay.

Yeah, maybe that was a mistake. Because he'd given me peace—and I damn sure didn't deserve it.

"You're a fucking idiot. You know that, right?"

I gaped at Flynn over the coffee I was sipping to nurse my raging headache. "What the hell?"

I'd called Kat first for cupcakes and sympathy, but she'd had to go into the coffee shop to cover someone else's shift. I'd ended up at Flynn's, figuring that if anyone could cheer me up it would be him. So far, I was less than impressed with his technique. "When you said I should come over, I thought it was so you could make me feel better."

"That was before I knew the full story. And that you plan to just let the guy walk. Like I said. Fucking. Idiot."

"Let him walk? He practically sprinted." I ran my fingers through my hair. "He doesn't want me. And I sure as hell shouldn't want him."

He added some Tabasco to the Bloody Mary he was mixing, then slid it onto the counter in front of me.

I raised my steaming coffee mug. "Headache."

"Trust me. This'll knock it out a hell of a lot better than coffee."

I rolled my eyes. Flynn held a firm belief in the healing powers of vodka. But despite my doubts, I sipped the drink—and had to acknowledge that it was pretty damn good.

I was sitting at the breakfast bar that was attached to the kitchen island. For the eight months we'd lived together, that had been my usual weekend perch. I'm not exactly competent in the kitchen, but Flynn can make anything taste good. At that moment, he was scrambling eggs, making hash browns, and frying up sausage patties, and the kitchen smelled like heaven.

He moved between the island and the stove with casual efficiency dressed in gray sweatpants and a John Barleycorn saloon T-shirt. He was damn good-looking, with deep-set eyes and a swoop of hair that fell over his brow, though he constantly pushed it out of the way. His obsession with jogging and biking kept him in shape, giving him a tight ass and the kind of biceps that made even the tallest woman feel petite. He could cook—which in my book was a plus—and I happened to know that he was a lot of fun in bed.

He flipped two sausage patties, then turned to me, his eyes narrowed. "What?"

I held up my hands in a gesture of innocence.

"You have that look. What's on your mind?"

"I don't have a look," I countered.

"I've known you forever. Trust me when I say you have a look."

"There is no look. But if there was a look it would be one of confusion."

"And you're confused because . . . ?"

"I'm just wondering how you're justified in giving relationship advice. I'm pretty sure you've gone out on a first date with every woman in Chicago, but somehow that whole second date thing eludes you."

"I'm highly selective," he said. He pulled himself up to sit on the granite counter. "This isn't an exercise in dramatic irony, is it? You're not going to blurt out that even though you've been pining after Evan all these years, now you realize it was really me you wanted all along?"

"Don't flatter yourself," I said. "And I think your potatoes are burning."

"Like hell they are," he said, but he slid off the counter and turned down the heat, then started filling a plate for each of us.

I absolutely loved Flynn to death, but I wasn't in love with him any more than he was in love with me, and I never had been. Of course, that hadn't stopped me from sleeping with him all those years ago. He'd been angry at his father. I'd been angry at the world. He'd stolen the keys to his dad's Harley, and we'd rocketed down Sheridan Road all the way to Wisconsin.

I didn't remember which one of us initiated it. I only knew that he'd wanted to get laid, and I'd wanted the release. More than that, I'd wanted to get my first time over with. I wanted to make the fantasy that Evan would be my first go away. Because if I could put an end to that, maybe I could put an end to it all.

It hadn't worked. Thankfully, our experiment in sexual healing hadn't messed up our friendship. It had been weird for about a week. Then we'd gotten drunk on the beach, confessed that even though it had been fun and felt nice, neither one of us wanted a repeat performance, and continued on the way we'd been going. Only now I had the added benefit of being able to talk to him about sex stuff. Considering he came at the whole dating and girl thing from the perspective of a straight male, that was a pretty handy perk.

"Let's back up to this idiot thing," I said as he slid a plate in front of me. "Pretend you're a guy—"

He cocked his head, cupped his balls, and lifted a brow.

I rolled my eyes. "Pretend you're a guy who's just walked away from a woman he's attracted to."

"We're not playing this game, Ang. He didn't walk away because you melted down when some assholes with knives came after you. He walked away because your fucking uncle made him fucking promise."

"He damn sure managed to get over the promise in the alley before the assholes showed up."

"He was thinking with his cock."

"And he wasn't when he went down on me?"

He opened his mouth to retort, then shrugged. "Score one for the little lady."

I reveled in my victory, even though it was the purely Pyrrhic kind. And, frankly, the reason didn't exactly matter. I'd thought for a shining moment that I'd get the man I'd always fantasized about, and then it had all gone to hell.

Honestly, I should have expected that.

"And you know what?" Flynn said, waving a spatula in my direction. "If he's so worked up about keeping promises, he needs to keep the one he made to you."

I had no idea what he was talking about, a fact that must have shown on my face, because Flynn just shook his head in exasperation.

"What do you think happened on that dance floor? In that alley? Not to mention your bed."

"Not enough," I muttered grumpily.

He lifted his Bloody Mary in salute. "True, but I was going to say that it was a promise, too, right? He was promising you one hell of a good time, and then he went and cut you off. Do girls get blue balls?"

"Yes," I said flatly.

He snorted. "Well, I know guys do, and he must have a serious pair. I mean, shit, the guy got you off, had you right there naked, and still didn't fuck you. Do you have any idea how much self-control that takes? The guy's freaking Hercules."

At that, I laughed outright. I'd known coming here was a good idea. Already, I felt better. "Maybe he's just not attracted to me," I said, forcing myself not to grin.

"Now you're just fishing for compliments."

The smile I'd tried to suppress blossomed. "Well, duh. I'm not sleeping with you, remember? What good are you to me if you don't lavish me with positive affirmations?"

"Good point." He shoveled in the last of his eggs, then slid off the stool to go scrape the dregs from the pan to his plate. "You're an exceptionally gorgeous woman with astounding acrobatic abilities in the sack. You have good taste in movies, terrible taste in candy, and you make a damn good Manhattan, thanks to my incredible teaching, of course."

"Thank you," I said graciously. "You're wrong about Twizzlers. But I love you anyway."

"As you should. But as for Evan Black . . ." He trailed off, shaking his head regretfully. "He's an asshole who doesn't keep his promises."

"No, he's not," I said.

Flynn burst out laughing. "Oh, man. You really do have it bad."

I sighed. Because I did. I really did.

Flynn took the last bite of his sausage, then glanced at my mostly untouched plate.

"I'm eating," I said, shoveling a huge forkful of hash browns into my mouth. "Where are we going this week?" I asked, thumbing my nose at etiquette and talking with my mouth full.

Our weekly museum jaunts had started last May on the very day that we'd moved in together after I'd graduated from Northwestern. Before that, I'd lived on campus and Flynn had kept his tiny bedroom in the groundskeeper's quarters that came with his father's job on the massive Kenilworth estate just a few blocks from my uncle Jahn.

Flynn's father, who rarely left his world of flowers and trees and shrubs, had taken the train into the city the day we moved into the apartment. He'd looked around the room, nodded approval, then pulled his son into a bear hug. I'm pretty sure there were tears in his eyes.

I'd felt a knot of jealousy curve in my belly. The neighborhood was safe and affluent to satisfy my parents' concerns, but we'd taken the cheapest one bedroom we could find. We'd both wanted to pay our own way, and my starting salary at HJH&A wasn't exactly impressive. Not that Flynn was doing much better between tending bar and working as a flight attendant. But we figured that we'd make do with me in the bedroom and Flynn in the living room—and the Oak Street Beach just a short bike ride away.

While the setup might have made Flynn's dad proud, it had only frustrated my father, who made it more than clear that he'd happily buy me a condo if I would just say the word.

I remained silent.

Pops, as Flynn's father liked to be called, had taken us out to breakfast, then led us to the Red Line. We'd asked no questions, just gone with him until we reached the stop at Roosevelt. Then he walked us to the museum campus, bought a hot dog from a vendor, and pointed to the Field Museum of Natural History. "Whenever you two have a day off," he said. "Here, there," he added, indicating the aquarium. "The Art Institute, one of those boat rides that shows you all the buildings. You explore. You learn. You see the world that you're part of and you live in it. You understand me?" He poked Flynn in the chest. "That goes double for you. The opportunities you have flying all over the country. All over the world." He sniffed, then pulled out a handkerchief and blew his nose loudly. "If only your mother could see you."

Flynn glanced at me, his expression a little amused and a little embarrassed. But I liked the idea of living in the world. Especially since I sometimes feared that I'd forgotten how to do that.

Now Flynn started the dishwasher before we headed toward the door. "Let's do the aquarium this week."

"How about the Art Institute?"

"We went there last week."

I shrugged.

He eyed me sideways. "If you already knew where you wanted to go, why'd you ask me?"

"An overabundance of politeness?"

"Let me guess. The windows."

I took his hand and smiled happily. "See how well you know me?"

I feel about the Chagall windows the way some people feel about Notre Dame or the National Cathedral or Westminster Abbey. There is something about the experience of looking at that stained glass, with the oddly fractured images, so many of which seem to have been caught mid-flight, that makes my soul want to soar.

I'd discovered them by accident one day when I'd gotten turned around trying to find the café, and I'd stood there, no longer hungry, and just watched the light move across the vibrant, vital blue.

I knew that Flynn didn't get my fascination. Monet, Rembrandt, even Ivan Albright's dark and brooding images were the things that captured his imagination. But to his credit he stood by my side, watching me as much as I was watching the windows.

"You know you're not going to find an answer in the glass," he said after we'd been standing there for well over half an hour.

"I might," I countered. I turned to look at him. "Maybe I already have."

"Yeah? What are you going to do?"

I shrugged, not sure how to put into words all the thoughts that had been bouncing around in my head as I'd stood there in my private meditation. The blue sky. The images that floated through an eternity, soaring but never falling. Evan's voice telling me to let go. To fly.

And my own fears holding me back.

But when you got right down to it, what did I have to lose?

"I'm going to go for it," I finally said, boiling all my thoughts down to their utmost simplicity.

"Well, look at you. Angelina's getting her groove."

"Don't be an ass."

"I'm not. Seriously. I'm proud of you. The guy wants you. You've wanted him since forever. So make your move. Tell him that he's an idiot for keeping a promise to a dead man. All he's doing is punishing you and giving himself blue balls. And if he sticks to his guns then he's an idiot and doesn't deserve you anyway."

"Exactly."

He hooked his arm through mine. "Come on. We'll hit American Modern on our way up to three, then I'll buy you a glass of wine at Terzo Piano."

"We just had breakfast."

"And your point is?"

I had to concede I didn't have one. After all, it was past noon and even though it was a Thursday, neither one of us was working today.

Besides, a little afternoon buzz might give me just the courage I needed.

nine

Before my weekly museum jaunts with Flynn, I used to come regularly to the Art Institute with Jahn. He'd loved the place as much as I did, so much so that he'd donated both art and money to the museum through the Jahn Foundation, a nonprofit organization that he'd founded and that he personally ran. It was his passion—finding artists who needed funding or institutions that needed cash in order to acquire or restore a masterpiece or an ancient manuscript—and on more than one occasion I'd ended up in Jahn's office late into the evening, listening as he discussed his plans and choices with me. It wasn't officially part of my job, but those hours were always the highlight of my workday.

As Flynn and I wandered through all our favorite galleries, I couldn't fight the wave of melancholy knowing that I'd never do this with Jahn again. But this time it was mixed with a bit of pride, too, because I knew that Jahn's generosity had made some of these exhibits—and others like them all across the world—possible. And when you got down to it, that was pretty cool.

We'd made it past the iconic *American Gothic* and had moved on to Ivan Albright's rather creepy *The Door* when my phone started singing "I'm Just a Bill" from *Schoolhouse Rock*. I grinned at Flynn, then snatched it up, turning away from the strange, disturbing image before me. "Daddy!" I kept my voice low and took a few steps back from the painting. "Are you back in the States?"

"Not only are we back in the U.S., we're in Chicago."

"Really? Where? Are you at the condo?"

They're here? Flynn mouthed.

"Not at the condo," my dad said as I nodded to Flynn. "Your mother insisted on a hotel. Too many memories."

"What hotel?"

"The Drake. We're only staying the night, though. I need to be back in D.C. by noon tomorrow."

"Tomorrow?" I frowned, wondering if I'd somehow gotten my dates mixed up. "We're meeting the attorney tomorrow to go over Uncle Jahn's will. Aren't you coming?"

"I'm not a beneficiary."

"Oh." I couldn't imagine why Jahn wouldn't have included his brother in his will. Technically they were half-brothers, but my dad had been three when Jahn was born, and they'd always been close. "Oh," I repeated stupidly.

"Your mother made a reservation at the Palm Court for tea. We'll see you here at three?"

"I'll be there." I loved high tea, and The Drake was one of my favorite places in Chicago. Most of all, though, I just wanted to see my mom and dad.

I ended the call, then caught up with Flynn. He'd moved on to another painting, equally unsettling. A woman, Ida, slavishly dressed, her skin lumpy and discolored, her face drawn and sad. I looked at it and the other paintings nearby, each done in a similar style that showed all the ugly underpinnings of life. All the nastiness.

That's what I didn't like about the Albright images, of course. They made me remember that sometime, when I least expected it, someone was going to see all the way through my layers to my dirty little secrets, too.

I shuddered. "Come on," I said to Flynn. "Let's get out of here."

We skipped the drink—I didn't have time if I was going to make it to The Drake by three. "You want to come with?" I asked, certain my parents wouldn't mind.

"Tea and tiny sandwiches and prissy harp music? Not to mention your parents grilling me about why I didn't bother with the college thing? No, thank you. Besides, if you're booked for the rest of the day, I may see if I can pick up the afternoon shift at the pub."

I nodded, feeling a little guilty. Now that I'd moved out, I knew that money was tight. "Have you found a roommate? I know Kat's been thinking about moving into the city."

"I think you're about the only one I'd be willing to share a one-bedroom apartment with," he said.

"Are you going to have to move?" Now I really did feel guilty.

"Nope. I've got it worked out."

I paused as we reached the main lobby. "Really?"

"What? I don't look like a guy who knows how to make a buck?"

"Did you get a raise?"

He grinned. "You're looking at a man with green flowing in."

"Good for you," I said, taking that as a yes.

We hurried outside, blinking in the sunlight, and Flynn hailed a taxi for me. I gave him a hug, double-checked that he didn't want a lift at least as far as the hotel, and then gave the driver my destination.

He pulled out into the Michigan Avenue traffic and I settled back. The Magnificent Mile stretched out ahead of us, and I sighed, half-wishing I could tell the driver to just drive, drive, drive until I was certain that I'd stop stumbling over every bump in my life.

I loved The Drake and I loved my parents, but I knew damn well that seeing them was going to bring everything back.

Each day since Jahn died was getting a little easier. But then I'd turn a corner and it would be hard again. I'd catch the scent of his cologne. Or hear his name unexpectedly.

Or maybe I'd see the tears in my mother's eyes.

I closed my own eyes and drew in a calming breath. This was one of those corners, and I needed to steel myself to get past it. To be strong for my parents, who'd always been strong for me.

The outside of The Drake has a sort of art deco vibe that I love. I could imagine girls in flapper dresses hanging out in the Roaring Twenties, much to the delight of the stuffy businessmen who were secretly thrilled to see so much leg and so much cleavage.

But while the outside got my imagination humming, it was the inside of The Drake that took my breath away. It didn't scream elegance. It simply *was* elegant. A massive staircase leading up to a beautiful floral arrangement that was flanked on either side by stunning chandeliers. That was all you could see until you climbed those stairs and entered the fairyland.

I did that now, pausing at the top of the stairs to turn and face the magnificence of the Palm Court. My parents had first brought Grace and me here when I was seven and she was ten, and I'd been certain that we must secretly be royalty. The entire room glowed white, from the drapes on the columns to the upholstered chairs to the massive wash of flowers that seemed to bloom out of the fountain that was the centerpiece of the room.

I took a moment to push down my memories, then headed toward the hostess stand. "I'm meeting my parents," I said, even as my mother rose from a table behind the fountain and waved at me.

"The senator's table. Of course. I'll take you."

I followed, amused. He might have been elected by California voters, but even in Illinois, my father was The Senator.

"Sweetheart, you look tired." My mom engulfed me in a tight hug, then stood back and examined every inch of me.

I shrugged, feeling seven all over again as I smoothed my sundress and straightened the sweater I'd worn to ward off the museum chill. "I'm okay," I said. "Just not sleeping that great. The funeral and all."

I still remembered the look of horrified impotence in my mother's eyes when I'd told her about my nightmares after Gracie's death. I couldn't stand knowing that I was adding to what was already a terrible burden, and so the next time she'd asked, I'd lied and told her that the bad dreams had been a passing thing. Her relief had been palpable, and sacrificing the comfort of my mom's hugs and soothing words had been a small price to pay to see that burden, however small, lifted from her shoulders.

"Where's Daddy?" I asked in an effort to change the subject.

"We ran into the president of Trycor Transportation." She nodded across the room, where my father stood by a table chatting amiably with a silver-haired man and two young girls who were obviously his daughters. "He'll be back in a minute. In the meantime, you and I can order."

Our table was far enough from the fountain and the harpist that we could easily hear each other. We ordered high tea and Earl Grey for all three of us, and then Mom dived into all the mundane life stuff. I settled back, comfortable with the warm familiarity of the conversation.

"How is Flynn?" she asked. I gave her a rundown of his flight and bartending schedule, and she made maternal *tsk-tsk* noises. "Tell him he needs to seriously consider going to college. He's too bright to simply ignore his education."

I bit back a smile, remembering why Flynn had chosen not to join me at The Drake. "I'll tell him."

"And why don't you and I take a trip home soon? We'll take some time, get a bit of relaxing in. Maybe even drive up the coast and go shopping."

"La Jolla?" I asked, knowing that had to be what my mom meant by home. Though the Washington lifestyle had fit both her and my father like a glove, they hadn't moved there full-time. "I'd love it," I said truthfully. "But I've been away from work for more than a week now, and things are going to be crazy when I get back."

"I'm sure we can work it out," she said dismissively, as if whatever issues I might have at work weren't even worth bother-ing about. She lifted an arm, her smile bright. "Here comes Daddy."

I stood up and folded myself in my father's arms, and the comfort I found there was enough to make me forget my moth-er's weirdness.

To my parents' credit, we didn't talk about Uncle Jahn or the funeral or the will. They seemed to innately know that I needed space. That I just needed *them,* and so we talked about Mom's fund-raising and the various charitable organizations she worked with and the most recent legislation that Daddy was pushing and how well his new aide was working out.

As we'd been talking, the waitstaff had come with our tea and food, and now I took the final scone, slathering its sugared top with clotted cream before taking a not-very-ladylike bite.

As I did, my mom and dad exchanged a glance.

"What?" I said, afraid I was about to get called out for bad manners. "Did I do something?"

"I mentioned my new aide," my father said. "That reminded me of something I wanted to talk to you about."

"Reminded," I repeated. I wiped my mouth and took a sip of tea, then sat back and studied my father. He was not the kind of man who needed to be reminded of anything, and I realized with sudden insight that whatever he was about to say was the reason they'd come to Chicago in the first place. "Okay. I'm listening."

"Do you remember Congressman Winslow?"

I shook my head slowly. "No."

For the briefest of moments, my dad looked irritated. "Well, he remembers you. He's serving his second term in Washington now, but before that he was in Sacramento with me. And every year he was one of the faculty at the legislative summer camp that your sister used to go to. He was even her mentor when she did the youth ambassador program."

"Oh." I nodded as if this all made sense. But from what I could tell so far, it was my sister the congressman remembered, and not me. "So what is the congressman up to?"

"Quite a bit, actually. He's definitely a man to watch on the Hill. But most recently, he's hired himself a new legislative aide." He grinned at me, but I just shook my head, confused. "*You*, Angie." He leaned over and captured me in a hug, then released me so that my mom could repeat the process from my other side.

"Wait. Me?" I asked, when the hugs and kisses were over. "How can I be his aide? I've never even met him."

"It took some maneuvering," my dad said. "But he's also a Northwestern grad, and knows just how competitive your poli sci degree is. And I don't think it hurt that you beat out his GPA by a hair, too."

"It's exactly the kind of position you want, sweetie," my mom said.

I nodded automatically. The truth was, I didn't have a clue what I really wanted; I'd never let myself think too long about it. But they were right. It *was* what I'd worked toward. It was what I'd gone to college for.

Most important, it was what Gracie had wanted.

"It's the perfect position for a young woman starting out," my father said.

"It sounds great, Daddy. But I'm not sure if it would be right to leave Chicago so soon after Uncle Jahn's death."

His face tightened. "You do what you have to do, of course. But you should know that there's a lot of opportunity for growth. A congressman who's not only on the public's radar, but has the ear of the White House, too. I promise you, baby, your climb will track his—and your mother and I will be beside you all the way."

My father reached out and took my hand, and if I didn't know him better I would have sworn his eyes got misty. "I love you, Angelina," he said, and my heart twisted both because I knew it was true, and because of what he had left unspoken: *You're all I have left.*

I turned down my father's offer to have his hired driver give me a lift home. I'd told him I wanted to do some shopping, but mostly I just wanted to be alone. To walk and to think.

I'd wanted to tell my dad that I wasn't ready to move to Washington. That even though public relations wasn't my thing, there were parts of my current job I found fascinating. And wasn't that what being in your twenties was about? Exploring all those options?

But then I thought of Gracie, who'd probably known in utero that politics was her calling. I could still remember the long conversations she'd have with Daddy at the kitchen table, while I'd nod seriously and pretend to understand, trying desperately to think of one clever thing that would make my dad look at me with the same light that he'd shined on Grace.

Then she'd died, and it had broken my heart to think that the light inside my dad would die with her. Except it hadn't faded, because I'd saved it. Maybe I couldn't save Gracie. Maybe I couldn't bring her back. But I'd signed up for student council. I'd joined the debate team. I'd completed a summer internship in Sacramento. I'd gone to Northwestern to major in political science.

And I'd kept that light inside my dad alive.

That was a small price to pay for not following my own dreams, right? Especially when I didn't know what those dreams were in the first place.

I was walking fast down Michigan Avenue, my feet moving in time with my churning thoughts. I dodged tourists and buskers and forced myself to focus on the faces of passing strangers and the overpriced clothes that filled the shop windows. Anything to turn off my thoughts.

It wasn't working, and so I walked even faster, so that all my mental energy was bound up by speed and the need to watch where I was going so I didn't mow down another pedestrian. I needed to get out of my own head. To erase all thoughts of the way Evan bailed on me and the way my father was navigating a path through my life.

A familiar antsy feeling—edgy and raw—pressed hard against me. I told myself that I could handle this. I didn't need a rush; I just needed to get home. Avoid the stores, keep my focus, and don't do anything stupid.

By the time I reached the condo lobby, my hair was a frizzy mess, my muscles ached, I felt sticky with sweat, and my stomach was actually rumbling. So much for the staying power of scones and tiny sandwiches. But at least I'd sort of pulled myself together.

Peterson was in the foyer when I stepped off the elevator and into the penthouse. "Mr. Warner is waiting for you on the patio. Shall I make the two of you an early dinner?"

I shook my head, feeling at loose ends all over again. My stomach twisted in knots, and eating was the last thing on my mind. "How long has he been here?"

"About an hour. I told him I wasn't sure when you'd be back, but he asked to wait. He said he had some reading to catch up on and would enjoy sitting on the patio. I hope that isn't a problem."

"It's fine," I lied. And then, though I really just wanted to turn around and leave again, I steeled myself and headed for the spiral staircase that led up and to the outside. I pushed through the glass door, then paused. I'd just walked home, so I already knew the weather was crisp and clear. But up here, it seemed even more so. From where I stood, I could see part of the lake through the glass barrier, and the sun was making the surface sparkle and the white sailboats shine. Had it only been last night that I'd looked out upon a field of stars with Evan's voice in my ear promising to take me there?

I closed my eyes, taking a deep breath and forcing myself to shake off the memory before I turned to the left and walked to the covered area. I found Kevin on a wrought-iron love seat near the outdoor kitchen area. He had a document in his hand, a folio open beside him, and his laptop on the coffee table. A glass of white wine sat next to the computer, and I had to frown; Kevin didn't usually drink during working hours.

"Hey," I said, going to the little fridge and grabbing myself a Diet Coke before sitting in the chair opposite him. He didn't look up from the document he was reading. I crossed my legs and sat back, then popped the top on my drink. The sound of the carbonation bursting free was like a small explosion and made me jump—and that only pissed me off. I felt edgy and uncomfortable, and considering I lived here and he didn't, my discomfort was all the more annoying.

"Kevin?" I said, working hard to keep my voice light. "What are you doing here?"

He set the paper aside, then slowly turned his attention to me. His expression resembled a disapproving parent, and I had to force myself not to fidget in my seat as I thought of my detour last night. "I came by a few hours ago. I wanted to see how you were."

"Oh." I took a sip of Diet Coke. "You could have just called."

"I did. Twice, actually. Considering your state of mind last night, I was concerned when you didn't answer."

"Twice?" For the first time it occurred to me to look at my phone, and I fished it out of my purse. The Do Not Disturb feature I'd turned on last night only allows calls from my parents and work to ring through, and I'd forgotten to turn off the app.

I checked the screen and saw three missed calls. Two from Kevin and one from Kat.

There was nothing from Evan.

"I was at the Art Institute this morning," I told Kevin. "With Flynn. Then I met my parents at The Drake for tea." I shrugged as if this were no big deal. Then again, it *was* no big deal. We weren't married. We weren't engaged. We weren't even dating exclusively. And I'd made him no promises when I'd left last night.

Not that those justifications quelled the guilty discomfort that was twisting like a serpent in my gut.

Kevin regarded me silently for a moment. "I see," he finally said, and despite that ridiculous roiling guilt, my temper flared.

"What exactly do you see? Did I commit some horrible transgression at the Art Institute? Or maybe by dining at The Drake?"

"Is there something I should know about?" he asked, his tone of complete calm grating on my nerves like sandpaper. "Something between you and Flynn, maybe?"

"Of course not," I said automatically, and it was only when the words were out of my mouth that it occurred to me that I should have lied. If I wanted to break up with Kevin, faking a relationship between Flynn and me would be the perfect way to do it.

Mentally, I rolled my eyes, disgusted with myself. What was I, in junior high?

"Then maybe it's something between you and Evan Black," he continued. The transition was smooth, but I heard the sharpness in his voice. And when I looked at his face, I saw both anger and hurt.

"What the hell are you talking about?" I asked, but the righteous indignation I'd wanted to infuse into my voice didn't quite make it past the guilt.

"Dammit, Angie. If you'd really wanted to go out, I would have taken you. But the Poodle Dog Lounge?"

"Wait. You *followed* me?" Anger had me leaping to my feet.

"If you want someone to lie to a federal agent, you need to pay them more than forty bucks."

"You son of a bitch." I started pacing, a blur of fury and motion. "You goddamned son of a bitch!"

My rage didn't even faze him. "I was worried about you. Apparently I had reason to be." He picked up his wineglass and swallowed what was left, the only sign that he wasn't as icy calm as he looked. "Evan Black is not someone you can trust, Angie. I thought I made that clear last night. A guy like that is interested only in himself."

I'd been pacing the small area between the tiny kitchenette and the coffee table. Now I came to a halt in front of him. "Really?" I said, lacing my voice with as much sarcasm as I could manage. "Because last night I needed to cut loose a little, and Evan was there for me. Funny that I didn't see you there at all."

He leaned forward, putting his head in his hands, then dragging his fingers through his short hair. "Dammit, Angie," he said. He lifted his face to look at me, and my anger faded under the genuine hurt I saw there. "How do you think it makes me feel when you leave me to get what you need?"

I sank back into my chair, suddenly exhausted. My anger had fizzled, but now I just felt hollow, all the more so because even though we were talking about what I'd needed last night, all he could focus on was himself. About me making him feel better for not being the person who'd been there to assuage my grief. "I don't want to do this now."

"We're so right in so many ways," he continued, deaf to my protest. "Jesus, Angie. I just want you to talk to me. I just want you to tell me what you need."

"I thought I did."

He drew in a slow breath, then let it out carefully. "Okay. Fair enough." He stood up and walked around the table to stand behind my chair, his hands on my shoulders. "I should have listened. I should have taken you out. I'll do better, I'll try harder." He bent and kissed the top of my head. "I want us to work."

He was barely pressing on my shoulders, and yet it felt as if he was trying to shove me into a tube that didn't quite fit, and suddenly I knew that if I didn't do something he'd eventually wear me down. I'd slide through that tube and what would come out the other end would look like me, but it wouldn't really be me at all anymore.

"Kevin," I said softly. "We need to talk."

"Okay." He moved around the chair to face me.

"You should sit."

His eyes narrowed slightly, but he didn't argue, and as he seated himself on the couch again, I drew in a breath for courage.

What I should have done was tell him that it was over. That he wanted this to work, but I didn't. Instead, I took the coward's way out. I did what all princesses do and ran straight into daddy's arms.

"I'm leaving," I said. "I'm moving to Washington."

"Washington," he repeated.

"I've got a job as a legislative aide," I explained. "And that's not going to leave any time to think about a relationship. I'm sorry, Kevin," I said as I stood up to punctuate the point. "I'm sorry, but this just isn't going to work."

ten

Alan Parker had been my uncle's attorney for as long as I could remember. He was an ancient man with a corner office in a prestigious law firm that also handled all the corporate business for HJH&A.

I arrived at the office harried, sticky with sweat, and a full ten minutes late because I'd broken the heel on my shoe, and the elevator ride back up to the penthouse and then down again had taken far longer than I'd expected. I probably should have taken a taxi, but I'd wanted the walk and had assumed that I could make up the time.

I'd assumed wrong, and when the receptionist led me through the halls toward the conference room, I felt positively gross. My blouse was sticking to my back beneath my summer sweater and I was certain my thick hair had frizzed out.

I took solace in the fact that I would be only one among what would surely be dozens of beneficiaries, and that in the crowded conference room no one would pay me any attention at all.

But when I arrived, there was only one other person in the room. *Evan.*

He stood as I entered, looking as cool and polished as I looked rumpled and miserable. Then he nodded politely and sat down again. I saw no hint of the man on the dance floor. For that matter, I saw no hint of the man who'd made me cocoa and held me close. I didn't even see the man who had walked away.

I didn't know this Evan, and I told myself I was glad. My announcement to Kevin that I was moving to Washington may have been a knee-jerk reaction, but apparently it had been the right one. And I was struck with the urge to announce to Evan that I was leaving and that I was damn happy about it, thank you very much.

Before I had the chance, Alan came in, flanked by two younger attorneys whose faces, hair, and posture were at least as polished as their suits.

I took a seat opposite Evan as Alan and his associates settled in at the head of the table. I kept my eyes on the attorneys, determined not to glance Evan's way. "Are we still waiting on the rest?"

"No," he said. "All the beneficiaries are present."

"Oh."

The female associate scribbled a note, then smiled at me with unnaturally white teeth. "A great deal of your uncle's property was in trust and passes outside of probate."

I nodded as if I understood what that meant.

Alan cleared his throat. "As you both know, Howard Jahn amassed an extensive collection of art and artifacts in addition to his cash, securities, and real property holdings."

Considering I lived in the condo—which was practically a museum—I knew it well.

"Not long before his death, Mr. Jahn did a major overhaul regarding his estate. He added extensively to the trust for the benefit of the Jahn Foundation. Everything from cash down to the smallest coin in his collection. So extensively, in fact, that only three bequests remain to be distributed through his will. We are here today to address those items." He cleared his throat, opened the folder in front of him, and began reading.

"To my good friend Evan Black, I leave my six-shot, nickel-plated, dual-action Colt revolver, which once belonged to Al Capone himself, in the hopes that he will remember to always watch his back and to take nothing for granted."

I bit back an ironic grin. I knew that Evan had always admired the gun, which Jahn had kept mounted in a shadow box in his study. But if Kevin was right about Evan's extracurricular activities, then that made the bequest all the more appropriate.

Evan looked amused as well, but sobered when Alan added that Uncle Jahn also left him a letter. "He presented it to me the day he revised his will, and asked that I give it to you contemporaneously with the bequest."

"Am I the only one to receive a letter?" Evan asked, and though he didn't say, I was certain that he was wondering about Cole and Tyler, both of whom were conspicuous by their absence.

Alan shook his head. "No. I was entrusted with several. Shall we move on?"

Evan nodded.

"To my beloved niece—"

"Wait."

We both looked at Evan.

"Shouldn't you finish the bequests to me?"

Alan pushed his glasses up on his nose. "I have, Mr. Black. As I explained, Mr. Jahn significantly overhauled his trust, his will, and his bequests just a few weeks ago."

"I see," Evan said, though it was clear that he didn't. Alan regarded him for a moment, then nodded as if in satisfaction, and turned back to me.

"To my beloved niece, Angelina Raine, sometimes referred to as Angie or Lina, I leave my penthouse condo—including the adjacent servant's quarters—as well as all furnishings and property remaining in my estate." Alan looked up at me. "You should understand that most items of value within the condo are included in the trust. What is referred to here are the more simple household items such as furniture, pots, pans, bath towels. He also created a trust to cover Peterson's salary—as well as a one-time bonus—along with the annual property taxes and monthly maintenance fees. I'll be administering that trust for you, but the condo will be in your name. If you choose to rent it or sell it, you are fully empowered to do so, though if you do part with the property, the maintenance trust will be folded into the foundation, less a severance package for Peterson."

"Oh." My head was swimming. "Okay."

"In addition to the property and contents thereof, your uncle left you one specific bequest of personal property. Though it is located in the condo and not part of the trust, he was very clear that he wanted there to be no dispute as to his wish that this item go to you." He rattled the papers again, then cleared his throat. "Also to my beloved Lina, I leave my facsimile copy of Leonardo da Vinci's Creature Notebook, as I have come to realize that she will undoubtedly understand and appreciate the true value of this item and my bequest."

"Lina?" I murmured. Why the hell had he referred to me as Lina?

But no one heard my soft query, as it was buried under Evan's very loud outburst.

"Are you fucking kidding me?" He was on his feet, more animated than I'd seen him all morning. "He left the Da Vinci notebook to Angie?"

"What the hell is your problem?" I snapped. "He knew I loved that piece. Why shouldn't he leave it to me?"

Evan ignored me entirely, his full attention focused on Alan, his expression so intense that I half wondered why the attorney didn't toss down the folder and run for his life.

"When?" Evan growled.

"I—I'm sorry?"

I watched as Evan took three deep breaths, gathering himself with obvious effort. "When did Howard revise his will?"

With a start, I realized that I was five steps behind everyone else. Evan wasn't upset because I was getting the notebook. He was upset because until Jahn changed the will, *he'd* been getting the notebook.

Alan glanced at his associates, both of whom started rapidly flipping through documents. "About a month ago," the guy finally said. "On April third."

"I see," Evan said, though from the curious way he eyed me—the first time he'd looked directly at me all day—I could tell that he didn't see at all.

I, however, thought that I did, and I drew in a sharp breath. That was the day Jahn bailed me out of jail. The day I'd told him the truth about Gracie.

Which begged the question of why my confession had prompted him to leave me such a strange—albeit wonderful—bequest. Was it his way of telling me he trusted me? That no matter what I'd done he didn't think of me as an irresponsible twit? Or maybe—

"Ms. Raine!"

I jerked my head up, realizing that Alan had been trying to get my attention. "Sorry," I said. "I was just thinking."

Alan nodded and continued, but Evan's eyes stayed on me, his brow furrowed as he openly studied me. I wished that I had the balls to boldly return his stare, but I didn't. Instead, I dipped my head and doodled on the pad of paper that the firm had thoughtfully placed at every seat in the conference room.

The rest of the meeting was about signing documents and transferring titles, and I moved through it like a zombie. Or, more accurately, like a celebrity, signing my name blindly where I was told to sign and then turning to the next piece of paper that someone shoved in front of me.

Finally, we were done and allowed to leave. I hurried ahead, wanting to catch the elevator by myself, and not wanting to walk next to Evan in the circle of conspicuous silence.

It didn't work. He was at my side by the time the elevator car arrived, and when I got on, so did he. The silence was thick and uncomfortable, but I thought I'd be able to tough it out. I mean, how long could a ride down to the lobby take, anyway? Besides, he was standing all the way on the other side of the car, his hands on the bar, his head slightly down. He looked like a man deep in thought, and I assumed he'd stay that way until the doors opened and I could bolt.

I assumed wrong.

We'd barely started the descent when he pushed away from the bar and came over to where I was standing by the control panel. He wore a business suit, and the way he moved exuded power and confidence, and even though I just wanted to escape I couldn't deny that my knees felt a little wobbly and my pulse had started skittering.

He leaned in, and an electric jolt shot through me, sparked by his proximity. I clenched my jaw, angry with my body for reacting to this man when I was mentally giving him the finger.

I thought he was going to touch me, but instead he reached over my shoulder and pushed the button to stop the elevator.

We jerked to a halt, and I stumbled, thrusting my hand out to steady myself. My palm landed flat on his chest, and the shock of our contact ricocheted through me. I jerked my hand back, but it was too late. I'd felt it. That awareness. That need. That zing. *Oh, dear god, I was in so much trouble.*

I forced myself to stand up straight. "What the hell do you think—"

He silenced me with a finger to my lips and a shake of his head. He took a step toward me, and I swear I heard Klaxons. He was so close we were practically touching, and the air between us was hot and thick. My hands were behind me on the handrail, and I gripped it tighter, afraid that if I let go I would reach out and touch him again. That I'd close this distance and demand that he kiss me. That he finish what we'd started.

For one brief, shining, magical moment, I thought that was what he had in mind. His head dipped toward mine, his lips coming close to my ear. "Why?" he said. "Why the hell did Jahn leave it to you?"

"What?" I jerked back, embarrassed and confused. And, at the same time, I realized that he hadn't leaned close to me to flirt, but to be heard. The Klaxons were real—he'd triggered the alarm when he'd stopped the elevator.

A tinny voice suddenly filled the car. "Sir? Ma'am? What's the problem?"

Evan tilted his head up toward the ceiling vent where, presumably, a security camera was recording our little drama. "Turn off the damn alarm," he said.

"I need to know if there's a problem. Ma'am, is this man threatening you?"

I realized what it must look like from the security guard's perspective. "No," I said. "I'm okay."

For a moment, there was just the sound of the alarm. Then the guard's voice came back on, tight and authoritative. "Sir, you need to put the elevator in motion."

"In a damn minute," Evan said. "Turn off the fucking alarm."

"Sir—" But Evan just reached over and flipped the switch that controlled the intercom.

A moment later, the alarm quit howling. Then the elevator started moving again, and I wasn't sure if I should be relieved or amused.

I settled on amused. "Guess they have an override button," I said, unable to help my grin.

"Fuck it," Evan said, and although I couldn't be certain, I thought he was biting back a grin, too.

The display showed that we were passing the thirty-second floor. Evan reached over and pressed the button for thirty. A moment later, the elevator stopped and the doors slid open. I didn't have a clue what he was doing, at least not until he took my arm and tugged me out of the car with him.

The elevator bank was empty, bordered on the left by the glass doors of a law firm and on the right by solid wood doors with tiny gold letters. Presumably a small business. Neither place looked busy today.

"We're going to talk," Evan said. "Without building security listening in, and without sound effects."

"Yeah," I said. "I figured that out on my own." I crossed my arms over my chest. "So talk."

"I want to know why he left it to you."

"I don't know."

"Bullshit. I saw your face."

Since I couldn't argue with that, I shifted course. "Why do you care, anyway?"

"I have my reasons."

"Yeah? Well, I'm sure Jahn had his, too." I dragged a hand through my hair, which was a mistake, as it reminded me of how grungy I felt. Which was not a happy thought, considering Evan was standing right there looking, as always, as sexy as sin.

"You know what?" I finally said. "It doesn't matter. He's gone. And as far as I can tell, you're gone, too." I cocked my head as if just remembering something. "Oh, did I say gone? Not really the best choice of words, since you shouldn't have even been in my life in the first place. After all, it was just one big mistake. Right?"

He said nothing, but I saw the way his jaw tightened, as if he were digging in, preparing to stand his ground.

I felt tears prick my eyes and hated myself for it. "Damn you, Evan Black." I leaned over to push the elevator call button, but he grabbed my hand, stopping me.

I looked down at where he held my wrist. "Careful, I might break." I met his eyes. "That's what you think I am, right? Some fragile porcelain princess? That you'd shock me with all those things you said? That you'd break me if we went too far?"

"Angie." The regret in his voice curled through me, and I clutched tighter to my anger, holding it close to give me strength.

"No, don't even. You saw the way I melted down, and after you went too far comforting me, you ran for your goddamn life. Well, you know what, Evan, you're an idiot. You can't break me. I'm already broken." What I didn't say was that I was afraid that he was the only one who could put me back together. He was certainly the only one who'd ever made me feel whole.

"You think I see you as fragile? You think I don't want you? Do you have any idea how hard it was to sit in that room just now and not touch you? It was hard enough before the other night, but Jesus, to come as close as we did, and then back it off? It's like trying to turn the goddamn *Titanic,* and I feel like I've crashed into a fucking iceberg."

I gaped at him, my heart pounding, my skin prickling. He was saying things I thought I wanted to hear, but I was afraid to hope, and so I only stood there, silently begging him to continue.

"Do you want to hear me say that I look at you and I go weak? That I want to taste you and touch you? That I want to break you and see you shatter beneath me? Dammit, Angie, is that what you want to hear?"

Yes, dear God, yes.

I was screaming the words inside my head, but outside I was too shocked, too amazed, too damn aroused to say anything at all. It didn't matter. As always, Evan understood me.

His face softened, the vibrancy fading to a passionate glow. "I'm telling you now, because we both need to hear it. I want you, Angelina. I've wanted you since the first moment I saw you. Wanted your fire, and that haunted look in your eyes. Wanted you to look at me the way that you do. For years, I've wanted to lose myself in you. Wanted to break you open and see the woman inside."

"You could," I whispered, though I'm not sure how I managed to find my voice. "I think you're the only one who could shatter me."

"Maybe." He reached out as if to touch me, but his hand only stroked the air above my skin, as if he was warming himself in my heat, or as if he was afraid that if he lowered his hand those few millimeters to actually make contact, that we would both burst into flames right then.

He may not have touched me, but he might as well have, and when he pulled his hand away, I heard myself whimper.

Slowly, he thrust his hands into his pockets. "I can live with the things I've done," he said. "After all, I can't be anyone other than the man I am—the man walking the path I made. But we all have a code, baby. And how can I break my own code and still live with myself?"

I realized I was shaking my head in protest. "Fuck your code," I said, but I spoke gently, my tone in sharp contrast to my words. And then, emboldened, I leaned forward and brushed my lips over his mouth.

I heard his moan. I felt his hands close over my shoulders. I felt the hard knot of passion growing in my belly, the sweet tingling sensation growing between my thighs.

And then, more keenly, I felt him gently push me away.

"Don't do this," he said. "Don't tempt me."

"Maybe I want to tempt you."

"I'm not the man you want."

"You are," I said earnestly.

"Maybe. But I'm not the man you need."

I flinched, because he was so very wrong. He just might have been the only man I needed.

"How do you know what I need?" I demanded. "Because you made a promise to a dead man?"

I saw him wince, and I pounced, sensing weakness. "Do you think I don't understand why you're turning away from me? I loved him, too, but he's not here. And even if he were, he's not in charge of us."

I waited for Evan to say something. To pull me in his arms. To tell me I was an idiot. To just plain turn and walk away from me.

But he said nothing. He did nothing.

And my temper flared.

"You know what? Fuck you, Evan Black."

I reached over and pushed the button to call the elevator. This time, he didn't stop me.

"Fuck you," I repeated.

I stood, vibrating with anger as I waited. Finally, the doors opened, and I started to step onto the car. I stopped when his fingers closed around my upper arm.

I didn't turn.

"It's for the best," he said, his voice so low I could barely hear him. "Your uncle was right. I'm not a safe bet."

I waited one beat, then another. Then I shook my arm free, stepped onto the elevator, and didn't look back.

eleven

I needed to get lost. Needed to get free. My head was swimming with everything that was going on around me—Jahn, my parents, Kevin. And Evan. At the center of it all, there was always Evan. His proximity. His desire. His heat.

His rejection.

I felt as if my mind—hell, as if my *life*—was trying to tune in to a particular frequency and all it could find was static. As if I was bouncing around lost in the stratosphere with no rope, no guide, to bring me back down to where I belonged.

I was anxious and frantic and needy and confused. I needed release even as much as I needed an anchor. I needed to appease the demons. I needed—

Oh, hell, I didn't know what I needed. But I knew that whatever it was, adrenaline would soothe it. If I could just manufacture that wild rush of sensation, then maybe all this static in my head would go away. Maybe I could get clear. Maybe I could think.

Because I damn sure wasn't thinking right then. Not as I barreled down the streets, pushing past other pedestrians, ignoring crossing signals, and letting my feet eat up the pavement.

And I wasn't thinking when I wandered into department stores. When I let my fingers trail idly over blouses, over jeans, over purses, and samples of cologne.

But as I wandered—as my mind started to focus on the ways that I could manufacture that singular sensation that would restore my clarity and help me find my center—that was when my surroundings took focus. That was when I started to realize where I was and what I could do.

What I *needed* to do if I wanted to get clear.

Department store.

Jewelry.

Do it.

I felt the tingle in my palms and the quickening beat of my heart.

It would be so easy. So fast, so clean.

So perfect.

I mean, sure. Maybe I'd messed up before. But that didn't mean this would go wrong. This time, maybe everything would come together. Maybe this time, the rush would be enough to pull me through. Hell, maybe it would even last until I got to Washington.

And then—well, then, I'd just have to learn to keep myself in check. Because I'd be a different girl then. A different me. A new Angie altogether.

Just do it.

I sucked in air, willing myself to take it down a notch. I was just a girl. Just a shopper. I was just looking around, just letting my fingers dance over the countertops, the displays. I picked up a pair of earrings, then held them up as I inspected my image in the mirror.

I put them back, unimpressed.

I picked up a pair of sunglasses and returned them, too, equally unimpressed.

I was alone, unobserved, and when I picked up the bracelets, then moved to casually drop them into my purse, I was certain that no one would see me.

Don't.

The voice in my head was bold and assertive, but I wasn't even certain I'd heard it.

Goddammit, don't.

I sucked in air, then saw a saleswoman in the shoe department glance my way. I froze, suddenly terrified, then dropped the bracelets back on the display table. There was an exit just twenty or so yards away, and I willed my feet to move me in that direction, because I needed to get clear before I collapsed.

Because I was absolutely certain that the collapse was coming.

It was about the hardest thing I'd ever done, but I managed to make it out of the store before my legs gave out. I sank to the ground, my back to the cool stone façade, my tailored linen slacks probably getting ruined on the filthy sidewalk.

Tourists and locals hurried by me, some ignoring me completely, others glancing warily in my direction. I barely saw them through the blur of tears and the red haze of confusion and loss and regret.

Maybe I'd managed to get my shit together in there, yes, but I wouldn't exactly call it a victory. I was a mess. A horrible, raging, fucked up mess. And all I could think about was the way Evan had held me. The way he'd soothed me. The way he'd kept the nightmares at bay. And, more, the way I was certain he would keep all my demons at bay. The ones that haunted my nights as well as the ones that crept up on me during the days.

He was what I craved. More, he was what I needed.

But I couldn't have him. And that one simple truth would end up breaking me.

It took a few hours to pull myself together, and I spent the time wandering aimlessly down the Magnificent Mile and the intersecting streets. Even then, I still didn't feel clear. I needed to get it out, to talk about what was churning around inside of me. I needed familiarity and forward motion.

Naturally, I called Kat.

I didn't confess to almost stealing the bracelets, but I did tell her that I was a mess—and that it was Evan who'd gotten me there. Evan and my father and Kevin, too. The whole nasty business that was bubbling up into a big, molten, explosive mess.

And, in true BFF fashion, she'd known exactly what to do—a girls' night in.

We'd made cupcakes, licked the mixing bowl, drank beer, and talked about nonsense, all of which had brought me down to the level of feeling human. And maybe even slightly centered.

Now we were kicked back in Jahn's media room, fresh beers in our hands and a plate of warm cupcakes between us. Kat had control of the remote because my uncle's entertainment system baffled me, and she'd been scrolling through iTunes, looking for something to rent. Now she put the remote in the cupholder and shifted to face me more directly, every bit of her body language shouting that we were about to move from general comfort to a Serious Conversation.

"'Not a safe bet'?" Kat said, repeating what I'd told her about Evan's parting comment. "What the hell is that supposed to mean?"

"Beats me," I said, which wasn't entirely accurate. I'd juxtaposed Evan's words against Kevin's accusations, and it hadn't taken a massive mental leap to reach the conclusion that Kevin must be right. Evan, Cole, and Tyler were into something. I just didn't know what.

"Oh, come on," Kat said. "You've known him for forever."

"Hardly," I said. "I met him when I was sixteen."

"Like I said. Forever. You must have some idea of why he'd say that about himself."

"Fine," I said. "I've been around him forever. I've been in lust with him forever. But 'being around' and 'being in lust' don't translate into knowing his deep dark secrets, you know? I mean, I don't even know where he lives."

"Seriously? What about Cole? Do you know anything about him?"

I glanced sideways at her, but she just shrugged.

"Not really," I said. "Not about any of them. They were friends with Jahn, not me. I was still in high school when we met, and I was only in Chicago for a few weeks each summer. I mostly hung out with a sketch pad and pretended to draw when Evan and Cole and Tyler came over. And if I did talk, it wasn't exactly a conversation full of deep emotional resonance. I mean, we talked about school or movies or whatever Jahn was cooking on the grill, you know?"

"Yeah, but then you went to college and somewhere along the way he got a little hot for you. Which means this has to have been bubbling along for a while, right?"

All things considered, I had to agree that she was probably right. Somewhere along the way, Evan had become as hot for me as I was for him. "Yeah, but I was totally clueless," I told her. "Even though I was living full-time near the city, I think I saw the guys even less once I started Northwestern. I wasn't living with Jahn and my school schedule was nuts. I saw them on a few weekends, but it wasn't like a regular thing."

She sighed. "It's so romantic," she said, with an affected lilt to her voice. "You were like completely blacked out ships passing in the night."

I rolled my eyes. "I know some stuff. I know he likes his steaks medium rare because that's how he made them when we grilled out. And I know he likes opera because he went with Jahn a few times. And some Finnish heavy metal band because he and Cole were psyched to get tickets. But I don't have a clue what toothpaste he uses, what his favorite class was in college, what his first pet was named, or if he committed a felony last week."

"A felony?"

I waved the word away as if it meant nothing. I had yet to tell Kat about Kevin's allegations. I'm not sure why I was so reticent, but I think it was because I'd begun to believe them.

The truth was, Evan could very well have dark secrets that were completely hidden from me. After all, when you got right down to it, except for bits of trivia picked up in Jahn's living room and backyard, I didn't know a whole lot more about him than anyone else in Chicago.

He might not have been as much of a public figure as my dad, but his position and charitable donations had made him a local celebrity, and I'd devoured every article written about him. All of them talked about his tragic past. How his father had died in a fire that had also injured his little sister, Melissa. How Evan had worked his ass off during high school to help his mother make ends meet and to cover the medical bills, taking any and every job he could find and thereby honing the job skills and tenacity that served him well during his entrepreneurial climb.

But none of that meant that I understood why he'd call himself a bad bet.

"Does it really matter?" Kat said when I told her as much. "It's not like you're the kind of girl who wants a safe bet, anyway. What?" she asked innocently when I crossed my arms and raised my brow. "I'm just saying that you like a little excitement in your life. Nothing wrong with that."

"It doesn't matter anyway. I'm not going to be around long enough for anything to come of it."

Her brows puckered. I'd told her about my plan to move to Washington, and to say she was less than enthusiastic would be an understatement. "You're really sure about this?"

"It's what I went to school for."

"That's not an answer."

I sighed and snagged one of the cupcakes. I dragged my finger through the frosting, then licked it off as I considered what to say. That's the problem with having a friend who understands you. Sometimes they understand you too well.

"Yes," I said. "I'm sure. It's a good job in a field I understand. I grew up in politics. I have the degree." *It will make my parents happy.* Only I didn't say that last part. Instead, I shrugged. "It makes sense. I mean, not everyone can know exactly what they want to be when they grow up. Some of us fall into careers by default."

Kat took a long swallow from her Heineken. "Oh, I don't have a career plan. Just a goal."

"Rich," we said together, and then laughed.

"So how's that working out for you so far?" I asked.

"Apparently the road to riches isn't paved with coffee filters. At least not unless you're the dude who invented Starbucks. But I have some irons in the fire."

"Really? Tell me."

She waved it off. "Nothing to talk about. Just some stuff my dad's putting together."

I frowned, but didn't say anything. From what she'd told me of her dad, he was hardly someone to emulate. Then again, the guy did have a house in Winnetka and a condo in Palm Beach, so maybe he knew his stuff.

"You need to totally do him," Kat said.

"Excuse me?" I wrinkled my nose, then realized she was still talking about Evan. "I think he put the brakes on that plan."

"Just once or you'll regret it. Besides, your uncle only said he wasn't the guy for you, right? Not that you couldn't fuck him. After all, it's not like you're marrying him."

I took a sip of my beer. "You have a very convoluted way of thinking," I told her. "I like it."

She laughed. "Years of dedicated practice. And I know you."

"What's that supposed to mean?"

She shrugged. "Just that you get off on the thrill. He's put on the brakes? Big deal. That just makes him more of a challenge. And a lot more interesting challenge than snagging a couple of earrings."

I leaned back in my seat. "I don't do that anymore," I said, purposefully staring at the white movie screen instead of Kat because I didn't want her to see the truth in my eyes. Didn't want her to see how close I'd come just a few hours ago. "I told you." I hadn't told her why. Hadn't told her about the arrest. For one, I hadn't wanted to get into it. For another, I'd been damned embarrassed at getting caught. But most important, Jahn had moved heaven and earth to get my record clear, because I was so freaked out about my transgression soiling my dad's pristine reputation and ruining his shot at the vice presidency.

Which means I wasn't about to tell anyone. Not even my best girlfriend.

More than that, the fact that I'd come so close today only underscored just how much of a wreck I was.

I thought of Evan. Of the peace I'd felt in his arms. Of the way I'd slept through the night with no nightmares nipping at my heels.

I so desperately wanted to be soothed like that again. I was centered right now, but I was balancing on a fence, and it would take only the slightest push to send me tumbling over.

I wanted the man. Needed him, even. And that only made the pain of his rejection that much keener.

Beside me, Kat was oblivious to my mental meanderings.

Even so, she'd reached pretty much the same conclusion. "The point is that you'd get off on the thrill of having a guy like Evan Black in your bed."

"I would," I admitted, because I could hardly deny it. But that didn't mean I was going to chase him.

I leaned toward her, sliding into gossip mode, both to distract her and because I wanted her reaction. "Kevin says the FBI is watching Evan. Tyler and Cole, too."

Kat shifted in her seat, obviously intrigued. "Really? Do you think it's true? I bet it is. They all have that bad boy look about them." The corner of her mouth curved up. "Especially Cole."

"You are *so* not subtle, you know."

"What? He's hot."

"Can't argue with that. Hell, they all are."

"But are they criminal masterminds?" Her voice was laced with intrigue.

"Maybe. I don't know." I shrugged. "Probably not."

"Oh, I bet they are," she said. "Most of the time, the cops get it right. They just don't always get the bad guys. Of course, that depends on how you define 'bad guy.'" She leaned back in her seat, looking almost smug.

I frowned, the idea that Evan might end up behind bars was undeniably disturbing. But at the same time, the idea that he was cool enough and smart enough to avoid that net . . . well, I couldn't deny that just thinking about it got my blood pumping. Like playing chicken on the train tracks or surfing on the roof of a car. Or even like snagging a pair of crappy earrings from Neiman Marcus.

She laughed. "Oh, man, the look on your face. You are so busted."

I grimaced, but I didn't deny.

"At any rate," Kat continued, "all of this is beside the point."

"I've completely forgotten what the point is."

"The point is that you have to go for it. If you're really moving to Washington—and I know the way you are with your dad, so I'm not even going to try to talk you out of it—then you need to go for it."

"Go for it, as in what?" I asked, even though I knew damn well what she meant—and was only a hairbreadth away from agreeing.

"Take a chance, Angie. You don't have to be in Washington for a few more weeks, right? So work your magic and get Evan in your bed. If you don't do it once, you're going to regret it forever."

She was right. Not only would I regret it, but I wasn't sure that I could get through the next few weeks. That I could keep myself pulled together as I moved through the condo that had once been so full of Jahn's laughter and conversation. As I packed to move to a city I didn't want to live in for a job I wasn't sure I'd even like, but that I knew Gracie would have loved.

The nightmares would return in full force. Hell, I could already feel them poking at me, like jabs from behind a dark curtain.

Could I take three weeks of this without needing to break free?

I could if I was in Evan's arms—I was certain of it.

Without him, though . . .

Without him, I was terrified of simply crashing.

But that wasn't the only reason that Kat's proposal enticed me. The truth was, I simply wanted the man. Wanted him, and was certain that he wanted me, too.

I remembered the way I'd felt when he'd stood close to me in the elevator, the way the air had vibrated between us. The scent of him. The presence of him.

And then I remembered the way he'd shut me down. The way he'd shut us both down.

I shook my head. "I don't know. . . ."

"What's not to know? It's not like you're going to get arrested—though you may end up on a surveillance tape."

"Oh, like that's an enticement?"

She ignored my half-assed protest. "And since he's already said no once, if he says it again, you're in the exact same place. And if he says yes, you're golden, right? I mean, honestly, Angie, what have you got to lose?"

I remembered the feel of his hands upon me in the alley, the way my body had fired and opened to him.

I remembered the smell of cocoa when he handed me the mug, and how the soft glow in his eyes had warmed me even more than the liquid. I remembered the way I'd come awake the next morning, clear and crisp and nightmare free.

What did I have to lose?

That was easy—*nothing*.

Nothing, that is, except my heart.

It turns out that the whole "go after Evan Black" plan was a little more complicated than I'd anticipated, primarily because I had no idea how to get in touch with him other than through his office. I'd done that, leaving a message with his assistant through the automated voice mail system. Since I didn't immediately get a call back—and I fully expected him to ignore the message—I decided to scour the entire condo in the hopes of finding his personal cell number. Then I'd cross my fingers and hope he'd answer.

Too bad for me, I found diddly-squat. Not one single number for Evan, Cole, or Tyler. I did find the mother lode of family photo albums in the bottom drawer of Jahn's bedside table, and I spent two solid hours sitting on his bed and thumbing through them, soaking up the memories and feeling melancholy.

Most of the pictures were of people I vaguely recognized but didn't know by name. Grandparents who'd passed away before I was born and third cousins I'd met only at various graduations, weddings, and funerals. But two of the albums focused on my little corner of the family. There were pictures of me and Gracie at the Kenilworth house. Me and Gracie on a sailboat in the middle of the lake. Me and Gracie at Disneyland.

My mom and dad were in all of the pictures that featured me and Gracie, but there were earlier pictures, too. Pictures without either of us that looked old enough to be from before even Gracie was born. My mom was in all of those photos, my dad in very few. In some, Jahn stood beside my mother, his arm around her as she leaned against him, smiling and radiant.

I wondered if my father was the one behind the camera, but I had a strange feeling that he wasn't. Instead, I had the feeling that I was a voyeur. That I'd stumbled on something I wasn't supposed to know about.

Feeling melancholy, I closed the albums, put them back in the drawer, and made a mental note to mail them to my mom.

I poked around a bit more in Jahn's bedroom and found a battered address book that included Evan's name, but when I dialed, I heard only the message that the number had been disconnected. I would have called the office and talked to Jahn's secretary, but it was Saturday, and this hardly seemed like the kind of thing I should bother her at home for.

I was about to ditch the whole thing and give Flynn or Kat a call, when I realized there was one more place I could check. I reached for my phone, searched the Internet for Destiny, and dialed.

"Destiny," a woman's voice crooned. "Where your fantasy is our pleasure."

"Um, yeah. Hi."

"How can I help you?" She sounded perfectly polished while I sounded like an idiot.

"I'm looking for Evan Black. Could you tell me if he's there right now?"

"I'm sorry, we don't expect Mr. Black for another hour. Can I have him return the call?"

"Oh. Um, no. Thanks, but I'll just call back."

I stabbed my thumb on the button to end the call, feeling a bit like I'd just done espionage. I did, however, now have a plan.

I glanced down at myself and realized I was still wearing yoga pants and the Northwestern T-shirt I'd bought my freshman year. Not exactly appropriate attire for a strip club. Then again, I had no idea what one wore to a so-called gentleman's club, and though I'd had the chance to find out in college, I'd managed to completely blow that opportunity.

My roommate sophomore year had thought it would be a hoot for a group of us to check out a strip club, and she'd set her sights on Destiny, which she'd heard was the biggest, nicest, least sleazy strip club in the area.

I'd been desperately curious, not only because I knew the knights owned the place, but also because I was dying to know what went on inside a club like that. Were the women completely nude? How exactly did a lap dance work? And were there really private rooms where guys went for a three-martini lunch and a blow job?

And, though I hadn't shared this little tidbit with my friends, I also wanted the kindling to fuel my imagination. Because even though I didn't really know what went on inside a gentleman's club, I'd read enough and seen enough movies and TV to know that at the very least there would be girls doing sexy dances and getting guys hot. Teasing and titillating and being rewarded with bills in their G-strings and the high of adrenaline.

I told myself I only wanted to go and watch and stoke my own fantasies. But it's not easy to lie to yourself, and the truth was I didn't want the fantasy, I wanted the rush, and I was afraid that with enough coaxing and enough liquor, I might give in if my friends pushed me up on that stage, expecting me to squeal and blush and rush away. I might surprise them with how much I enjoyed gyrating to the music. With how much it turned me on to know that all those men's eyes were on me, but they weren't allowed to touch.

The whole idea got my juices flowing just a little too much, and in the end I backed out. I claimed that I had a paper to write. But really, I was simply determined not to do anything to risk my reputation as a girl who had her shit together and played by the rules.

Tonight, though, I was tossing those rules aside. And that opened the door to a lot of interesting possibilities.

I mean, if nothing else, it was time to have a little fun with my wardrobe.

twelve

I ended up dressing in a sheer, white short-sleeved blouse over a blood-red bra. I paired it with a black circle skirt that hit mid-thigh, sexy and flirty and—if I do say so myself—totally hot.

I finished the outfit with strappy black sandals with four-inch heels and a small red purse to tie the whole thing together. I'd spent more time than I liked to admit debating about my wild, thick hair—always my nemesis—and ended up piling it on top of my head and letting a few tendrils hang down in what I hoped was a provocative manner.

Finally, I'd kept my makeup simple, highlighting my lips in red and my eyes in a smoky gray.

I stood in front of the full-length mirror and assessed the result of my efforts. I needed to be prepared. Confident. Sexy.

I wanted him to look at me and get hard. I wanted him to look at me and regret walking away.

Most of all, I wanted him to look at me like he didn't even see the clothes I was wearing, and then I wanted this outfit that I'd so carefully selected to be wrinkled on the floor, tossed negligently there as Evan pulled me down into his bed.

I drew in a breath, struck a pose, and decided that if this outfit didn't do the trick, nothing would.

I considered having Peterson ring for Jahn's driver—as hard as it was for me to remember, those services were mine now—but decided that I needed to be more confident. A driver would wait for me, after all, but I didn't want to have any way home other than in Evan's car.

I took a taxi, then settled back for the ride toward Midway airport and the club. I stayed lost in my thoughts for most of the trip, but when we turned off the Stevenson Expressway, I tuned in. We headed down the tollway for a while, passing various neighborhoods, before turning off into a light industrial area.

I'm not sure what I was expecting—gaudy neon signs and naked women, maybe?—but when the driver finally stopped in front of the massive building, I had to admit I was impressed. It was the size of a large warehouse. There were no windows facing the street, and the entire building was surrounded by ample parking. Even at just past three on a Saturday, most of the parking slots were full.

The sign was low-key and classy. A black monolith with the name—Destiny—written boldly in red so that it stood out against the black. Though the sign looked like stone, I could see immediately that it was not, because the lower portion was an LED screen flashing the various specials throughout the week. Today, I saw, was "Six Dollar Saturday," which I presumed referred to the cover charge.

On the whole, the place looked unassuming and fit in just fine with the area, which boasted a few office complexes, a delivery company, a fire station, and a convenience store.

The driver pulled up in front of the door, then turned in his seat to face me. "This the place?"

"Hell yes," I said.

I paid him, slid out of the car, and marched myself to the front door. I didn't pause, because that would be like showing weakness. Instead I just reached out for the brass handle and tugged the door open. And then, despite the fact that it was bright and sunny outside, I stepped into the dim, casino-like interior with the same awe as one might experience crossing over into a whole new dimension.

It took a moment for my eyes to adjust to the change in lighting. All I could see was the dark entry area and the bright lights filtering in through frosted glass doors, along with the twisting cords of colored neon that curved upon the black walls, subtly hinting at the lushness of the female form. To my right, there was a polished reception desk that looked almost like what you might see at a classy hotel. A woman with glistening blond hair stood behind it wearing a tight T-shirt that emphasized her bra-less breasts as well as the word plastered across her chest: *Destiny*.

Two video cameras were displayed prominently in the area, their red lights glowing steadily as if to underscore the message printed neatly on a sign that hung on the door that led from this reception area to the main part of the club: *For the safety of our employees, these premises are under 24-hour video surveillance.*

Muffled music filtered in from the main area, but for the most part, this little room served as a transition between the mundane world outside and the promise of what lay beyond those frosted doors.

"Six-dollar cover," the blonde said. "Unless you'd like to enter the wet T-shirt contest." She glanced at the clock. "It'll be in the champagne room in just under an hour."

I glanced down at my barely B-cup boobs. "What's the champagne room?"

"It's totally awesome. There's an additional cover, but you get all the champagne you want while you're in there. And, of course, for the wet T-shirt contest, we can't just spray the girls with water. Where's the fun in that?" She laughed, obviously delighted with the idea. I grinned, too, sucked in by her infectious attitude.

"I think I'll pass," I said, even though it was a little tempting. "The truth is, I'm looking for someone."

"Oh."

The room seemed suddenly chilly and I hurried to explain. "No, no. I'm not an angry girlfriend trying to track down my guy. Nothing like that. I'm looking for Evan Black."

She leaned down and pulled a sheaf of papers from somewhere behind the counter. "Job application?"

I laughed. "No."

"Oh." Her brows lifted and she did a quick up-and-down scan, her eyes covering me from head to toe, and I could see the curiosity in her eyes. "Is he expecting you?" Her corporate-polite voice now held a hint of ice.

"No," I said. "I just thought I'd drop by." I almost blurted out that I was a friend, but at the last second I clamped my mouth shut. Hadn't I come here with the intent of becoming exactly what she imagined me to be?

I cleared my throat. "So, um, is he around?"

Her plastic smile was so tight I thought her cheeks might crack. "He's not on the premises at the moment, but—"

The frosted glass door burst open, cutting off her words, and Cole strode through, all power and poise, fire and energy. "You want to tell me what the hell you're doing here?"

I bristled. "Excuse me?"

He glanced sideways toward the blonde. "Take a break."

She nodded, eyes wide, and slipped out through a door that was camouflaged in the velvety blackness of the wall behind her.

"This isn't the place for you," Cole said, all of his attention on me.

"No?" I crossed my arms over my chest and mentally dug in my heels. "Because I'm feeling right at home."

He moved closer to me, emotions storming across his face. "Dammit, Angelina."

I forced myself not to cower as he approached. Instead, I held my ground, telling myself that I knew this man well. That even though he'd grown up around gangs—that even though he could snap me in two without breaking a sweat—that he absolutely did not intimidate me. On the contrary, I knew that Cole would always watch out for me.

"I mean it," I said. "I'm not leaving until I get some answers."

"Answers?" He cocked his head, his eyes narrowing as he examined me. "And what exactly is the question?"

"Evan," I said simply.

"What about him?"

I sighed in exasperation. This felt a little bit too much like junior high. "I want to know how to find him, for one thing. And since I don't have another address, this was my best option."

"And why exactly do you want to find him?"

I almost told him it was none of his damn business, but I was tired of being contentious. "Come on, Cole," I said wearily. "He owes me something. And I don't think that Evan's the kind of guy who squelches on his debts."

"Something?" Cole said, and I was grateful for the dim light that kept my blush from showing.

After a moment, I nodded and his grin grew wide. I had the feeling he knew exactly what kind of debt Evan owed me. "Well, look at little Dragonbait, all grown up. You win. Come on in." He cocked his head toward the frosted glass doors.

I exhaled in relief and followed. Considering the understated entry, I'd expected the main room to be nice, but I wasn't expecting it to be so big or so shiny. The room was huge, with the same cavernous feel of the casinos I'd visited with college friends on jaunts to both Vegas and Atlantic City. Instead of blackjack tables, there were individually lit raised dance floors—I counted six—scattered around the room. Each featured a pole, and each pole featured a girl. There was a bar around the edge of the platform, and men lined the barstools, some standing long enough to tuck a bill into the sequined nothingness that the dancers wore. And nothingness was pretty much it. Though some wore bikinis and some wore G-strings, some were entirely naked but for a garter belt around a thigh, the purpose of which was clearly to serve as a tip-collection device.

For those guests who didn't want such an up-close-and-personal view, there were round tables surrounded by four comfy chairs scattered throughout the room. A long bar with three scantily clad waitresses took up the far side of the room, and I saw the doors to private rooms as well. I figured one must be the champagne room, and I couldn't help but wonder what the theme was for the others.

The main area was primarily illuminated by the glow of the dancers' spotlights, which meant that the corners were much dimmer. I'm pretty sure that if I'd stood there peering into the dark, I would have seen one of those lap dances that I was so curious about.

Honestly, I was tempted to do just that.

On the whole, it was a nice place. Not the Palm Court, but classy in its own way. And the girls were pretty. Not too skinny or used up. They had curves and moves and they looked like they were genuinely enjoying their work. As I followed Cole to the far side of the main room, I didn't see any touching that they didn't somehow consent to. I did see one guy get a little rowdy, but a bouncer who looked like he used to play professional football descended on him like a tick and politely but firmly showed him the door.

Finally, Cole stopped at one of the tables, signaled to a waitress, then pulled out a chair for me. "So what do you think?"

"It's a nice place," I said honestly. "Classier than I would have guessed."

"You thought we'd lean more toward skanky?"

"No, I—" I cut myself off when I saw his shit-eating grin. "Dammit, Cole. Don't tease me. I'm not exactly in my element here."

He chuckled. "You sure the hell aren't, baby girl."

I sat, still taking it all in—and thinking about my words, and the lie hidden within them. Because even though I'd never been any place like this before, the truth was I found the whole environment rather intoxicating. I looked at the girls doing their moves around the pole, and I could imagine myself up there. All eyes on me. My leg hooked around that hard length of steel, and all the while that I was shimmying against the pole, it was Evan that I imagined I was touching.

I swallowed, looking down at the tabletop until I was certain that my face revealed nothing. I looked up just as the waitress arrived. She wore a top made of gauzy scarves crisscrossed over her breasts. An equally transparent scarf was tied around her waist in what resembled a bathing suit cover with no bathing suit beneath it. She slid a drink in front of Cole and a glass of red wine in front of me. "Shiraz," she said. "I hope that's okay?"

"Perfect. How did you—"

"Beth knows everything," Cole said.

Beth smiled. "I even know that the liquor delivery is here. Since Mr. Sharp already left—"

"Yeah, yeah. Have Frankie check the invoice. Tell him I'll be there in a minute."

She nodded and hurried toward the far side of the room.

I leaned back in my chair. "So what's the deal? You three work out of your downtown office during the week and come here for a little R&R on the weekends?"

"Fuck that," he said. "Evan's the one with the hard-on for a high rise. Tyler and me? We go in when we have to, but we work mostly out of the back."

I cocked my head. "So this isn't Evan's kind of place?"

Cole's eyes narrowed, but I just smiled innocently. "I didn't say that, baby girl. But our Evan's a man of many vices—and many virtues. I guess that makes him multifaceted."

"I guess it does."

Cole swallowed the rest of his drink, then thrust his legs out as he leaned back in his chair. "You gonna tell me why you're here? What exactly does Evan owe you?"

"Cole, I love you to death, but you're completely fucked if you think I'm telling you my personal business."

He laughed. "You have more of your uncle in you than any of us gave you credit for."

"I mean it. All I want to do is see Evan. When's he going to get here?"

"I just wanna help, baby girl. And I get that there's some shit between you and Evan right now. He told me what happened."

"About the Da Vinci?" I asked, because I couldn't imagine that Evan would have told his friend what went down in the alley.

It may have been my imagination, but I thought Cole sat up straighter. "The Da Vinci? You mean the Creature Notebook? What about it?"

I frowned, wondering why Cole was so keyed up about the notebook. Then again, Evan had been in a snit about it, too. "Jahn left it to me, and that didn't make Evan a happy camper." I peered at his face. "Or you, either, I'm guessing. But this is all news to you, which means it's not what Evan told you about. So what did he say?"

For a moment I had the impression that he was going to force us to stay on the topic of ancient manuscripts. But then he seemed to change his mind. He shrugged casually. "The alley."

I'm not sure what he saw on my face, but it made him laugh. "The Poodle on Wednesday, my fine establishment tonight. You're certainly expanding your horizons, Dragonbait."

I'd never until that moment fully understood what it meant to get your feathers ruffled. But mine were very ruffly indeed. "Fine," I said snippily. "You win. I am expanding my horizons, and I want Evan to expand them even further. I want him to finish what he started. And I came here to convince him that he should."

I finished my speech, tossed back the rest of my wine, and glared at him, daring him to say anything that might set me off again.

If he was shocked by my words, he didn't show it. He just leaned back in his seat and studied me. It was an interesting tableau. Cole's eyes on me, his face carved in question. Half-naked women serving drinks behind him. Even more naked women dancing on platforms all around us.

I'd dropped down into Wonderland, and all I needed was someone to hand me the bottle labeled *Drink Me*.

About the time that I was certain he wasn't going to respond at all, he spoke. "It's a losing battle, sweetheart. No way is Evan going against your uncle's wishes. Especially since we all know that Jahn was right."

"I don't know it."

For the first time, his expression turned brotherly. "You'd end up getting hurt, Angie. And that's the last thing any of us want. Shit." He ran his hand over his buzz-cut hair. "Honestly, it's a damn good thing that Evan's the one with the hard-on for you," he said, as my body started to melt simply from the spoken acknowledgment that not only was Evan attracted to me, but he'd told his friends as much.

"Not that you're not adorable," Cole continued with a grin. "But you're not my type."

"What do you mean it's a good thing?" I asked warily.

"Evan has the most self-control of any of us, and the highest capacity for self-deprivation. You're sweet, Angie, and Evan doesn't do sweet. And if he thinks that something he's doing will hurt someone he cares about, then he simply doesn't do it. And that's that. Trust me, Angie. Whatever debt you think he owes you from that alley, it's going to remain unpaid."

"Sweet," I repeated. "He thinks I'm sweet?" My head was swimming. After everything he said to me about taking flight. About wanting to tie me down and fuck me silly?

After the way his tongue had teased my clit? After the way he'd made me come?

After all that, he thinks I'm *sweet*?

"Aren't you?" Cole asked, and I could hear the laughter in his voice.

Instead of answering, I signaled for Beth, calling for her to bring me a flight of tequila shots. She arrived with three, and I tossed them back while Cole watched.

"Trying to prove something?" he asked.

"Not a damn thing. I just prefer tequila over wine. What?" I asked innocently. "You didn't know that?" I pressed my finger to my chin. "Hmm. Maybe you three don't know me as well as you think."

"Angie—" There was censure in his voice, but I cut him off.

"No. I told you once I wasn't dragonbait, and I meant it. You haven't got a clue what will and will not hurt me, so don't sit there acting all smug and pretend like you really believe that you three are in cahoots with Jahn to keep me safe. Because that's bullshit." I glared at him. "And don't make assumptions about what I want or need."

Sweet.

The word grated on me, which was ironic since I'd been playing the role for almost eight years. But it wasn't sweet that I wanted Evan to see. More, I'd believed that he'd seen under my sugary coating to the gooey center inside. Wild and tasty and very high in calories.

Apparently I'd been wrong.

Apparently I'd just have to fix that.

Unfortunately, I wasn't sure how.

Cole reached over the table and put his hand atop mine. "I'm going to go take care of that liquor delivery, and then I'm going to drive you home. We can talk on the way."

"I'm not going anywhere. I'm waiting here for Evan, and I don't particularly feel like talking."

"Fine. I'm still going to go take care of that delivery. And you may want to wait here, but last I checked, I own the place and you don't. So I'll be driving you home and you can just bitch about it."

"Cole—"

"Don't *Cole* me. As for the scintillating conversation, we can talk about music. We can talk about movies. Hell, we can talk about that damned Da Vinci notebook. But I'm making sure you get home safe, so you wait for me here, okay?"

I nodded, too defeated to argue. Evan hadn't yet arrived, and I could hardly dig my heels in if Cole was determined to get me out of there.

In other words, I was screwed. And at the moment, I had no plan B.

He headed toward the back where a guy, presumably Frankie, was holding up a clipboard and some paper.

I sat and stewed and looked around. Some of the nearby men turned to look at me, but no one approached, and I assumed that was because I'd been sitting with Cole. That was fine; I had no interest in these men. No real interest in what was going on in this room. There was lust, true. Lust and heat and attraction. Not sparks, though. Not electricity. This room was about sex and titillation, and while I didn't have a problem with that, it wasn't what I wanted.

What I wanted was Evan. The power. The explosion.

I wanted to experience what I'd felt in his arms, and I wanted him to take me where he'd promised we'd go.

And damn it all, it was pissing me off that I wasn't able to get what I wanted.

And then—like a dream—there he was. *Evan.*

I actually blinked twice, in fact, afraid that I was only imagining him. Because how on earth could my fervent wishes have conjured him?

But it was true. He was real and solid and despite the dim light, I could see the hard angles of his face and the dark fire of his eyes. He was staring right at me—and he didn't look happy.

Well, shit.

I started to stand—then sat down again when he turned away and moved toward one of the darkened corners, crooking his finger at a petite redhead who followed him with the kind of sexual confidence I was trying desperately to conjure.

I knew I shouldn't, but I couldn't help myself. I stood up and moved across the room, then settled down at a table closer to that corner.

I was looking at him from an angle, unable to see the expression on his face, but not really needing to. I could see the redhead just fine. The sultry expression as she slowly moved to straddle him. The way she bit her lip when he put his hands on her hips. She dipped down, teasing his crotch, brushing against him with the tiny bit of material that covered her sex. Then she rose and leaned forward, her breasts brushing his chest, her face rapturous.

I watched, and I seethed.

At the same time, though, I was strangely fascinated. I wanted to be that woman. I wanted to writhe upon him, to turn him on, to feel him grow hard beneath me. I wanted to be the one making him crazy. Me, and no one else.

Certainly not that little twit of a redhead.

I stood, not certain what I intended to do, but knowing damn well that I had nothing to lose. I tugged a fifty dollar bill from my wallet, then marched toward them. Evan didn't even look up when the girl turned to me.

I handed her the bill. "Go."

She glanced at Evan, who nodded just once.

The girl scurried away, and I reveled in my tiny victory.

I circled the chair until I was standing right in front of him. "You shouldn't be here," he said, but I only leaned forward and pressed a finger to his lips.

"Don't," I said.

"Don't what?"

But I just shook my head, said a silent thank-you that my circle skirt had enough material to hide a multitude of sins, and settled myself on his lap. Or, more accurately, *over* his lap, because while my knees were pressed into the soft leather of the overstuffed armchair, there was no actual contact going on except for the slight brushing of my knees against the outside of his thighs.

It didn't matter. I was already wet, my sex hot, my panties clinging to me. The bit of cool air that sneaked in under the loose folds of material did little to quell the fire inside me.

I leaned forward, using my hand on the back of the chair over his shoulder to balance myself. My eyes were locked on his, and he was looking straight at me, too.

"Don't what?" he repeated. His voice was low, his eyes never leaving mine.

"Don't put on a show trying to make me think you don't want me."

He didn't flinch; he didn't move. "Maybe I don't."

I leaned closer. Slowly. Seductively. "Bullshit."

His face stayed exactly the same. And yet I could see the smile growing inside of him.

And as my own smile bloomed, I lowered myself until there

was nothing separating us but the satin of my panties and the cotton of his slacks. I held on to the chair, moving my hips forward and back, letting the friction drive me a little crazy. "Did you think I'd run?" I asked, keeping my voice low. "Did you think I'd be shocked watching that woman do these things to you?" I leaned forward and ran my tongue over the curve of his ear. "I wasn't. I didn't even see her. Do you know why?"

"Why?" he asked, the single syllable more of a growl than a word.

"Because as far as I was concerned there was no other woman. It was me on your lap," I said as I rocked my hips. "Me touching you. Me making you hard."

I slid my hand down between our bodies and pressed my hand over his erection.

And as I watched the heat flare in his eyes, I reveled in a sense of smug satisfaction. Because I knew that, no matter what, I'd won this round.

thirteen

"This isn't happening, Angie," he said, blowing away my sense of victory like so much dandelion fluff.

"You're wrong," I said.

"I'm very rarely wrong."

"You're smug, too. I like that in a man." I shifted forward so that my lips brushed his ear as I spoke. "I just want to fuck," I said, and felt my lips curve into a smile as his cock stiffened in response to my raw—but very honest—words. "I'm not asking for a wedding ring. I'm not asking for forever. I'm not asking for any commitment at all. Hell, I'm not even asking for a date. I only want this," I said as I stroked him. "I only want to finish what we started."

"It's not a good idea," he said, and I heard the tight note of control in his voice.

"I think it's one of the best ideas I've ever had," I murmured.

"What was it you said when you ran out of the condo? About how you made a promise to my uncle? You're so damn worried about keeping your promises. Well, you know what, Evan? You made one to me, too. Maybe not in words, but . . ." I trailed off, letting my body language finish that sentence as I shifted on his lap, feeling wild. Feeling reckless. He was right—we shouldn't. And yet how could I stop when this was what I'd wanted for so damn long? When I needed it so desperately?

I brushed my lips over his. I felt powerful, certain victory was near, and I didn't intend to relinquish an inch.

I pulled back, my eyes locked on his. "I want what you promised me."

"Dammit, Angie . . ."

"You say you're a bad bet?" I pressed, determined to cut off all protests. "I don't care. Not everyone goes to Vegas to win. Some just go to have fun."

"I like to win." His rough voice sent shivers over me.

"Then I'm your prize. No," I said, pressing my finger to his lips before he could say another word. "I want to go wild with you, Evan. I want to fly with you. One time. Can't we both take the risk one time?"

"It's reckless," he said, as his hand slid up my back to cup my neck.

"Maybe."

"You'll regret it," he murmured as his other hand stroked my exposed thigh.

My breath was ragged. "I won't."

"It won't be gentle. If I let go, I'm not going to hold back."

"I'm not asking you to." Triumph swelled through me as I swallowed. My breasts were painfully tight and my sex throbbed, demanding everything he was promising. "Don't you get it? I want it all. I want to fly."

"Fly?" he said as that hand moved higher and higher, each millimeter setting off a flurry of sparks that ricocheted through me. There was no hesitation left in his voice, just passion and a power so vibrant that I knew without a doubt that any control I'd thought I had was now buried under the strength of this man.

"How high do you want to go?" His finger eased up to trace the edge of my panties. "This high?" he asked as he slipped his finger under the elastic and stroked my baby-soft skin.

I couldn't help the little moan that escaped my lips as I lost myself in the pleasure of his touch.

"Oh, baby," he murmured, as he stroked me, his fingers teasing and exploring. "But you haven't answered me. You want to fly"—he thrust a finger deep inside me, and I bit back a cry as my body tightened around him, silently begging for more—"you need to tell me how high."

But I couldn't tell him anything. I could only feel, could only exist in that moment. That power I'd felt only moments before had completely faded. I was as weak as a kitten and completely at his mercy.

I shifted, lifting myself up a bit to give him better access and, yes, to silently beg for more.

He flashed a self-satisfied smile, then added another finger. He was deep inside me, the soft pad at the base of his thumb teasing my clit as his fingers filled me. I was desperately wet, my hips moving in rhythm with his thrusts. I was need and desire personified. He had reduced me completely.

"I'm going to take you to the heavens, Angie. And I'm going to be your tether to this earth when you explode."

I whimpered, then shifted on his lap. Somewhere in my mind reason shouted that I needed to get free before I came right there, but at the same time I didn't want this to ever end.

He leaned forward and captured my mouth in a kiss, his hand on my neck holding me in place while he deepened it, his tongue mimicking the movement of his fingers inside me. I was lost, floating, shimmering with sensation. And when he pulled away, I moaned in protest of the loss.

Reality returned to me for the briefest of moments, and I glanced around, realizing just how public we were. The corner was dark and we were alone, but there were waitresses walking by and dancers on the platforms and somewhere, though I didn't see him, was Cole.

"Evan," I began, but his soft "No" cut me off.

"You started this," he said with a grin that held both mischief and mastery. "Stay still and no one will know." He was stroking me as he spoke, his fingers sliding from my cunt to my tight and sensitive clit. I squeezed my eyes shut, so aroused it was almost painful. I felt on fire, every inch of me sizzling. But then it shifted as all that feeling, all that electricity, all that pleasure, gathered like a storm.

He'd taken charge of my body, of my senses. There was no pleasure without his touch, no passion without his caress. It was all culminating in that one point, every bit of sensation inside me, building up, ready to rocket through me.

Ready to explode.

I almost cried out when the orgasm shot through me, but I managed to bite it back. He held me as I burst into a wash of stars, until I finally collapsed against him, my body shuddering from the force of the pleasure he'd brought to me.

My breath came in gasps and though I wanted to see his face, I didn't want to move. My head was on his chest, his hand upon my back. He had completely destroyed me.

For one brief, shining moment, I'd held the upper hand. But he'd deftly turned the tables, and I'd never been so happy to have been so soundly and thoroughly defeated.

"I told you," he said, leaning in close and whispering in my ear, "I like control. You want to fly with me tonight, Angie? Those are the terms."

I lifted my head to meet his eyes and saw my own passion reflected back at me. "Tonight?" I teased. "You want more?"

I'd caught him off guard, and he laughed, the sound rich and genuine. "Baby, we haven't even gotten started."

"I—oh."

"Let's get the hell out of here."

I nodded blindly. All I knew was that I wanted more. I wanted the man—and I wanted to see just where he would take me.

He carefully adjusted my panties and skirt—his ministrations sending little electric shocks of pleasure zinging through me. I felt a tug of satisfaction when he also adjusted himself. I had a feeling it wasn't particularly comfortable to walk with an erection, and I felt a swell of feminine pride for being the one who got him in such dire straits.

He took my hand and led me toward the back, pausing now and then to chat with some of the waiters, the dancers, the bartenders. All very normal. All very businesslike. And I thought I would scream in frustration every time he delayed for even a second.

Finally we moved through the employee area, passing dressing rooms, a conference room, several offices, and the kitchen on our way to the back door. He pushed it open, letting in a swath of sunlight that temporarily blinded me. As we started to step outside, I saw Cole emerge from one of the offices. I had no doubt that he saw us, too. Nor did I have any doubt about the deep frown I saw etched across his face.

Not that I had long to think about Cole's disapproval. The bright afternoon sun erased everything from my mind but the pleasure of the moment, and when we arrived at Evan's car, I laughed outright in joy.

"You have a convertible."

He looked offended. "Not just a convertible. It's a 1962 Thunderbird convertible. This thing's a classic."

"It's fabulous," I said, and meant it. It was a vibrant blue with sleek lines. Most important, the top was down. He held the door open for me, and I had to smile at the gentlemanly nature of the action in stark contrast to the very ungentlemanly way he'd had his fingers up my panties in public only moments before.

Evan Black was an exercise in contradictions, even more than I'd known. But, then again, so was I.

I slid into the car and settled back in the warm leather seat. Even before he started the engine, I imagined the thrum of speed and the wind whipping through my hair.

"There should be a scarf in the glove compartment if you want one," he said, as if reading my mind. He'd fired the engine and was waiting to make a left turn out of the parking lot.

"Not on your life," I countered, though I did open the compartment and peer inside. Sure enough, there were a variety of colored scarves. "For your harem?" I teased, fighting a knot of jealousy. Honestly, the man was gorgeous, eligible, and single. Just because I'd never seen him bring a date to Jahn's gatherings didn't mean there wasn't a gaggle of women waiting in the wings for him. I mean, that redhead had looked pretty cozy on his lap.

The thought didn't sit well with me at all.

"I have a lot of things," Evan said, as he accelerated. "A harem isn't one of them."

I didn't answer, but as I settled back to enjoy the ride, I was smiling.

Traffic was a bitch, so it took almost forty-five minutes to reach Lake Shore Drive and Uncle Jahn's—or rather, my—condo.

Evan handled the car with the same gentle yet firm touch with which he'd handled me, and the Thunderbird was at least as responsive. Now he had his hand draped loosely over the steering wheel and the other on my thigh, where it had been for most of the journey. It was just resting there, his thumb making idle back-and-forth motions that seemed unconscious, but I knew were purposefully designed to drive me crazy.

Honestly, I no longer gave a fig about the wind in my hair and the sun on my shoulders. With each mile, each foot, each inch that we drew closer to the condo, all I wanted was to climb out of the damn car and slide into Evan's arms. The anticipation was killing me, and despite the fact that during the drive he'd touched me in only the most casual of ways, my body was primed—the rhythm of the engine, the vibrations of the road, and the presence of the man keeping me blissfully on edge.

When the condo was only one block ahead, rising in the distance like some fantastical phallic monolith, Evan turned to me. "Shall we just take off?" he asked. "Cruise all the way up Sheridan Road. Continue through Wisconsin and keep going until we cross over into Canada?"

Hell no. I wanted to scream the words. To rail at him for even thinking of teasing me like that. But I'd lost too many points in this game already, and so I leaned my head back, casually closed my eyes, and lifted a negligent shoulder. "Whatever you want," I said. I opened my eyes long enough to look at him. "You're in control, right?"

He chuckled, then kept his foot on the accelerator as we breezed past the condo. I bit back a curse, not quite believing that he was calling my bluff. Then he glanced sideways, met my eyes, and hit the brakes.

"Evan!"

"Forget Canada," he said, twisting the wheel into a sharp left turn and then speeding back toward the building. There was heat in his eyes as he pulled up to the valet stand. "I want you naked."

"*Oh.*"

As the valet opened the car door for me, Evan popped the trunk and pulled out a leather briefcase. He tossed the keys to the valet, then took my elbow and led me inside. I knew the building intimately—I lived there, after all—but right then everything seemed bright and shiny and new. The doorman more regal, the concierge more friendly. The polished stone walls glowed, and the steel doors of the elevator gleamed in invitation. I was looking at the world differently now, anticipating something wonderful. Anticipating Evan.

There was no one else in the elevator bank, and we had the car to ourselves. As soon as we stepped on, he moved closer to me, pressing his palms against the wooden paneling as he caged me with his body. "Do you remember the alley?"

It was only the controlled sensuality of his voice that kept me from laughing. Did I remember it? How could I forget?

But I said none of that. I only nodded.

"Do you remember what I said I wanted to do to you?"

Suddenly shy, I didn't quite meet his eyes. But I nodded. Every single word was burned into my memory.

"Tell me."

My stomach twisted with nerves, but the rest of me tingled simply from the promise of what was to come. "What?"

He leaned forward, and I felt his lips brush against my ear as he spoke, the contact sending shivers rushing through me to pool between my legs. "Tell me what I said to you. Tell me what I want to do."

"I—" I wanted to protest, but one look at his face nixed that plan. I looked quickly away. When I spoke, my voice was so low I wasn't certain he could even hear me. "You said you wanted to strip me bare. That you wanted my breasts in your hands and my nipples tight between your fingers." As if in response to my words, my nipples tightened and my breasts felt suddenly needy.

He reached up and loosened the clip that held my hair. It tumbled to my shoulders and he ran his fingers through it, lifting it, then leaning even closer to graze his lips over my bare neck. I shuddered, certain I was going to come undone right at that very moment.

"I'm impressed," he murmured. "What else?"

"You—you said you wanted to spank me. To tie me up." My breath was ragged and I gathered my courage, then pulled away enough that I could see his eyes reflecting back every bit of heat that was coursing through me. "You said you wanted to make me come."

His eyes seemed to go even darker with my words, but his face remained unchanged, as if any reaction would trigger an explosion. For a moment, we only stared at each other, the air between us vibrating, my entire existence hinging on the need for his touch.

His voice was raw when he finally spoke. "I did say all that. And I want a hell of a lot more that I didn't say." He traced a fingertip along my jawline. "You said you wanted it, too." He paused, the moment hanging heavy between us. "Is it still what you want?"

I nodded as the elevator car shuddered to a stop.

"Say it."

I opened my mouth to speak, but it was too dry. I swallowed and tried again. "Yes," I said as the doors slid open. "Oh, god, yes."

He took my hand and led me off the elevator, but paused before opening the door to the condo. For a moment, he just looked at me. So long, in fact, that I began to feel uncomfortable.

"What?"

"All this time," he said, but didn't continue.

I shook my head, not understanding.

"All this time, all these years." His brow furrowed as he studied my face, as if I were a puzzle to be solved. "I've thought there was something about you. Something I couldn't put my finger on."

"You see me," I said simply. "I think you've always seen me."

His smile was slow, gentle, and sweetly sexy. "Why would I want to look anywhere else?"

I felt my cheeks bloom with delight at the compliment. Then I followed him inside, feeling suddenly awkward. Like a teenager on a first date.

Evan, apparently, didn't feel that way at all. He crossed the foyer toward the intercom panel as if he owned the place, then pressed the button to locate Peterson. "Ms. Raine and I would like the condo to ourselves for a while, Peterson. Take the rest of tonight and tomorrow off."

"Certainly, sir."

I gaped at Evan, not sure if I should be irritated that he was bossing around my butler or excited about the prospect of another twenty-four hours.

I settled on embarrassment when I realized that Evan had pretty much drawn Peterson a picture of what was going on up here. "Subtle, much?" I grumbled.

He only laughed. "Trust me, I can be very discreet when the occasion calls for it. Right now, though, you're mine. And I don't care who knows it."

"Oh." I swallowed, those first date nerves firing up again. "So, do you want a glass of wine?"

"No," he said simply. "I already told you what I want. I want you naked."

Beneath the red lace of my bra, my nipples tightened. "I—oh."

He nodded toward the bedroom. "On the bed. On your back. I'll be along soon. Unless you'd rather I leave," he added, when I didn't move.

Slowly, I shook my head. And then, in the thick silence, I turned and started toward the bedroom.

I moved slowly, part of me wondering why I was so tentative. This was exactly what I'd wanted—and more. A man to take control. To not ask, but to tell. To not hesitate, but to act.

No, I corrected. Not a man. *Evan.*

There had only ever been Evan.

I still couldn't quite believe he was here—and since I damn sure didn't want him to go away, I did as I'd been told, gathering my courage and then unzipping my skirt. I considered folding it neatly, but I liked the recklessness that came from leaving it in a puddle on the floor, topped by my very damp panties.

I kicked my shoes aside and then moved to the bed, still in my shirt and bra. The air conditioner was blowing, and the breeze from the vent above me tickled my skin, and made me hyperaware of just how overheated I was.

Slowly, I unfastened the buttons of my blouse, letting my fingers drift over the swell of my breasts. I found the clasp on my bra and unfastened it as well. I closed my eyes, savoring the moment. All my wildness, all my adventures, and yet I'd never done anything like this before. I wanted it—dear god, I wanted it—but I couldn't ignore the ripples of nerves or the tiny beads of sweat at the back of my neck and under my arms.

I drew in a deep breath for courage, then shimmied out of the blouse and tossed it carelessly over the side of the bed. And then, before I could think too much about it, I tugged off the bra and left it draped over the headboard, as if I'd tossed it there in a flurry of undressing.

And then that was it. I was naked.

I was naked, and I was alone. And I was all kinds of nervous.

I sat on my knees on the bed, since that seemed to be the most modest way to sit. Then I remembered that he'd wanted me on my back. I considered staying on my knees anyway, but I could still hear his toss-away comment about leaving.

Okay, then. On my back it was.

I stretched out, my legs so tight together they might have been superglued. I tried keeping my arms at my sides, but only managed that for about sixteen seconds before crossing them over my chest.

I wanted to be a vixen, really I did. I wanted to stretch out and enjoy the feel of the satin duvet on my naked skin. I wanted to spread my legs. To prop myself up when he entered the room, then beckon him in with a crook of my finger and a come-hither smile.

Unfortunately, my fantasies hadn't quite caught up to my reality. And my reality was all tied up with my nerves.

"You're stunning," he said from the doorway.

I lifted my head enough to see him leaning casually against the door frame with a glass of red wine in his hand. He wasn't smiling. Instead, he was looking at me with such intense longing that it was no longer nerves I felt, but arousal.

I licked my lips and managed a smile. "I thought you didn't want wine."

He didn't answer. Instead he took one step into the room, and in that singular moment it became his room as much as mine. Just by virtue of being there, he controlled it. Dominated it. It struck me suddenly that this was a man who could have anything he wanted anytime he wanted it. But he was here, tonight, with me.

The corner of his mouth curved up, and I entertained myself with the thought that he could read my mind. More likely, though, he was simply pleased with how well I'd followed instructions.

"I wanted the wine," he said. "But I want you more." He took a sip as he let his gaze trail slowly over me. If vision were a caress, then there would be no part of me that he didn't stroke throughout the course of that long, slow inspection. I was hot. Needy. And, yes, I was ready.

"Put your head back," he said gently, "and close your eyes." And though I hated losing sight of him, I complied.

"Your breasts are perfect," he murmured. "Don't hide them. Put your hands to your sides."

My arms were still crossed over my chest, and now I slowly moved my arms to my sides. As I did, I reminded myself that I wanted this—and I did, I really did. But at the same time, I couldn't help but wish that it wasn't the afternoon, and the sun wasn't streaming in through the floor-to-ceiling windows. I felt exposed—which, of course, was exactly what Evan wanted me to feel.

"Spread your legs, baby."

"Evan." I said nothing else, but there was no missing the protest in my tone.

"Spread your legs."

I squeezed my eyes more tightly shut and did as he ordered. At first, the air cooled my overheated sex. But that faded quickly. My inner thighs seemed as hot as embers, and I was suddenly acutely aware of how open I was. How wet I was. How terribly, wonderfully, deliciously exposed I was. My muscles clenched as if in anticipation, and my clit was a hard, demanding nub.

"Oh, baby," he said. "You look good enough to eat."

"Why don't you?" I whispered, shocked that I could not only form words, but that I would utter such provocative and demanding ones.

He chuckled. "Patience."

I whimpered, absolutely certain that if I didn't do something to release some of the pressure bubbling up inside me, I was going to explode.

"Do you want to be touched?" he asked. His voice was closer now, and I realized that he'd stepped farther into the room.

"Yes."

"Do you want a fingertip stroking you? Playing with your clit while your orgasm builds? Teasing your nipples into tight buds?"

The muscles of my sex throbbed in response to his words, and I heard the smile in his voice when he said, "I thought so, baby. Go ahead, then. Touch yourself."

"What?" I couldn't possibly have heard him right.

"Caress your leg, then slide your fingers up to heaven." The amusement in his voice didn't overshadow the tone of command.

I hesitated only briefly, then slowly did as he said. My touch was feather light and just as enticing, and I stroked down my leg, then slowly trailed my fingers up my inner thigh. A string of electric sparks, like a kickline of fireflies, seemed to follow my touch. I kept my eyes closed. Not because he'd commanded it, and not even because of embarrassment. But because it helped me to see—and what I was looking at was Evan's hands stroking my body.

"Oh, Angie," he said, as I trailed one fingertip over the soft skin between my thigh and my sex. His voice sounded wrecked, even painful, and I couldn't help but smile as I imagined his erection straining against his slacks.

"Stroke yourself," he said. "Tease your cunt. Do you feel how wet you are?"

"Yes," I breathed.

"Imagine those fingers are mine—"

"I am."

He groaned before continuing to speak. "And imagine that I'm playing with you. That I'm sliding my finger deep inside you. That I'm teasing your clit. Stroking it, finding that perfect rhythm."

My hand moved in time with his words, and I spread my legs wider as the pressure inside me built. I was imagining it was his touch, yes, but at the same time I couldn't deny the thrill of knowing that he wasn't the one touching me. That he was only watching. And that seeing the way I touched myself was making him hard.

"Please," I said, because I was so very close now. "Please, I want you touching me."

"I want that, too," he said. "But right now I'm enjoying this particular view. And from the way your pretty pink cunt is glistening, I think you're enjoying it, too."

I bit my lower lip, both in silent protest and in agreement.

"So tell me, Angie. Are you enjoying it?" His smooth voice was like an oral seduction.

I nodded. Right then, I couldn't manage words.

"You like me looking at you?"

"Yes," I said, though I'm not sure I actually managed a word.

"Does it make you hot, knowing I can see just how aroused you are?"

"Yes," I said, my fingers continuing their dance.

"Come for me, baby." His command was low and full of heat, and as his words washed over me, the orgasm building inside me unfolded, filling me up and growing and growing until it had no choice but to burst free. "I want to watch you explode and know that I took you there without even having to touch you."

As if he'd commanded it, my body seized up and then shattered. My climax ripped through me in time with his words, destroying me so thoroughly I wasn't quite sure I could ever get myself back together again.

When I finally lay there, calm but breathing hard, Evan was sitting beside me, his hands caressing me, his touch more like worship than exploration. "You're amazing," he said, then closed his mouth over mine and took me in a kiss so deep and consuming it almost had me coming again.

I tried unsuccessfully to silence the drumlike pounding of my heart so that I could speak when his mouth left mine and he sat up again. But my pulse wouldn't settle. I'd never experienced anything like what he'd just given me, and all I wanted was more. All I wanted was everything.

"Please," I managed to say.

"Please what?"

"I—I want the rest. I want everything you promised."

"Do you?"

I started to sit up, but he shook his head, a gentle hand keeping me on my back. "There's something I need to know," he said. "Do you wear pantyhose or stockings? Maybe tights in the winter?"

The question baffled me. "Um, yeah."

"Where?"

"In the dresser. Left side, middle drawer." It was only after he'd eased off the bed and was opening the drawer that I realized what he intended to do.

"Evan, I'm not sure that's such a—"

"I'm sure," he said, and I had to nod. For now, at least, that was good enough for me.

He held two pairs of winter tights in his hands as he moved around to the foot of the bed. Gently, he lifted my left leg. I closed my eyes as he did, letting myself surrender to the sensuality of the moment. The way he slid my leg toward the edge of the bed, leaving me scissored and even more exposed. The way the knobby cotton felt as he encircled my ankle with one foot of the tights. He pulled it tight, then tested the knot by slipping a finger between the material and my skin.

"Does that feel okay?"

I opened my eyes to look at him, and was so overwhelmed by the intensity with which he was looking back at me, that I could manage only a single, simple nod.

His eyes crinkled with his smile, and he took the tights and pulled on them until all the slack was taken up and my foot was almost brushing the edge of the bed. Then he knelt down and disappeared from view. If it weren't for the persistent tugging on my leg, I would have had no idea what he was doing. As it was, I realized that he was using the tights like a length of rope, and he was tying me down to the bed frame.

He repeated the process with the other leg until I was trussed up and spread wide. Completely open to him. Utterly at his mercy.

I bit my lower lip, grateful that my hands were free. I trusted

Evan, I did. But the thought of being that exposed, that vulnerable . . .

Well, it was both exhilarating and unnerving.

Then he moved back to the dresser and withdrew another pair of tights.

I didn't even have to ask. I knew. "Hands," I said.

"Above your head," he confirmed.

I complied, taking only enough time to draw in a ragged breath before doing so. He bound my wrists together and then somehow managed to restrain them so that there was no way I could pull my arms down to cover my body.

"I want to touch you," I said in mild protest.

"And I very much want you to. But later. Hush now," he said when I opened my mouth to reply, then silenced me with a kiss.

It was, I thought later, that kiss that had launched me into space. Because it started the chain reaction. It was long and deep and had the effect of melting me, making me soft and malleable, my body little more than a repository for sensation. And then he exploited that state by slowly—painfully slowly—trailing a line of kisses down my neck and over my collarbone.

When he reached my breast, he closed his mouth over me and drew me in, scraping his teeth lightly over my nipple, then using his tongue to drive me absolutely crazy as his fingers traced lazy designs up and down my other breast.

Every touch seemed magnified. Every lick more intimate, every caress more sensual. It was as if by tying me up he'd flipped a switch in me, and since I couldn't maneuver my body in order to absorb or deflect sensations, I had to adapt to completely and wholly experience them.

I moaned in both pleasure and anticipation when his mouth abandoned my breast to spread kisses down my belly.

"Oh, god, Evan," I whispered, writhing as much as was possible against my bonds.

He murmured an unintelligible reply against my skin, and

then his lips were grazing the top of my pubic bone, and then straight down—no slow build, no tease upon my inner thighs—just a full-on assault on my senses as his tongue flicked over my clit on his way down, down, down.

I arched up, pleasure coursing through me, as he thrust his tongue into me with at least as much power and skill as his fingers had worked upon me earlier. His hands were on my hips to hold me in place, and his mouth closed over me, tasting and teasing, his tongue laving me. And his own groans of pleasure only made the waves inside me build faster.

"Do you have any idea how incredible you taste? How much you have exceeded every fantasy, every expectation?"

But I didn't care about sweet words right then. "Please," I begged, my hips bucking with insistence. "Please, don't stop."

"Never," he said, and pressed his mouth once again to my slick cunt.

He played me, nipping and licking and sucking. And with every touch and every stroke I could feel the waiting orgasm building like a swell of waves growing before a storm. Higher and higher until there was nowhere else to go, and I went soaring off into the night sky, then crashed down like so much froth upon the shore.

"Oh, god," I said, because I couldn't seem to manage anything more articulate. "Oh, god, oh, god."

He slid up my body and held me, but kept his hand cupped around my sex, his finger idly stroking me. I didn't know if he was purposefully trying to keep me on edge, but I didn't care. Right then, he could do any damn thing to me he wanted.

"That was amazing," I said, turning my head to receive his gentle kiss. "But you haven't—I mean, it was very lovely for me a million times over, but aren't you a little bit—"

"Frustrated?"

"Well, yeah."

"Very," he said. He pulled his hand away from my sex, then

made me shiver as he traced lazy patterns around my inner thigh where my panty line would be. "But this was about you."

"Oh." I considered that. "I like the way you think."

He laughed.

"So will you untie me now?"

"Sweetheart," he said in a voice so laden with promise it almost made me come again, "I'm not even close to done with you."

fourteen

I woke in pitch-black, sweetly relaxed and completely sated. Evan had made me come twice more with mouth and hands, focusing so keenly on my pleasure that everything else faded away. Reason. Rationality. The whole damn world.

What he hadn't done, though, was what he'd promised—he hadn't fucked me. He'd focused entirely on me, making me exquisitely aware of my body, of each millimeter of my skin, of every nerve that had the power to send sweet pleasure twisting through me. He'd used me up, and when I was finally limp and lost, warm and sleepy, he'd gently untied me, pulled me close, and held me as I drifted off.

Now though . . .

Well, now I was awake. And I wanted the pleasure of watching him come. I wanted the feel of him moving inside me—and when I slid across the bed to find him, I had to fight down the sharp stab of fear I felt at realizing he wasn't there.

"Evan?" I sat up, telling myself that gone didn't mean *gone*. He could be in the bathroom. He could be on the phone. He could be anywhere.

But I wanted him beside me.

I sat up, then padded into the bathroom. He wasn't there, so I grabbed my robe off the hook behind the door, wrapped the terry cloth tight around me, and headed out into the hallway to look for him.

I found him in the darkened living room. He'd pulled on his slacks, but remained shirtless. The only illumination in the room came from the glass and chrome case that held the copy of Da Vinci's Creature Notebook. I stood across the room, lost in the shadows, and watched as he stood over it, looking down at the pages, with the soft light from below making his face and the intricate vine tattoo glow in a way that seemed almost magical.

I stayed perfectly still. The moment seemed strangely private. After all, until very recently, Evan had believed that notebook would be his, and I couldn't help but wonder if in some small way he was angry at me. The thought troubled me enough that I took a step toward him. "Evan?"

He looked up at me, but I wasn't sure that he saw me. He seemed far away, lost deep in thought. Then his expression cleared and he smiled, holding out his hand in an invitation that I eagerly accepted. "Hello, beautiful. You look rested."

I tilted my head up to receive his kiss. "You, sir, wore me out. But in the best possible way."

His dimple flashed, the charm of it contrasting with the wicked gleam of the scar across his eyebrow. "I'm very glad to hear it. Are you hungry?"

"Mostly for you," I said. I expected him to laugh and was disappointed when the smile that touched his lips seemed forced and didn't reach his eyes.

I cleared my throat. "The truth is, I'm starving."

The moment I said it, I had to acknowledge that it was true. I couldn't remember the last time I'd eaten.

"Unless there's a grill, I'm a terrible cook," he confessed. "How are your culinary skills?"

"Worse than yours," I admitted. "I'm not allowed near a grill unless I dial ahead and put the nearest fire station on notice."

"Apparently we won't be having soufflés as our late night snack."

"How does a frozen bagel with cream cheese sound?"

"Can you operate a toaster?" he asked.

"I can not only work a toaster," I bragged, "I can even manage a pot of coffee. French roast," I added. "That's your favorite, right?"

"Sweetheart," he said, with a smile that soothed all my worries, "you've just made my evening."

I managed to pull together a feast of toasted bagels, cream cheese, strawberry jam, and fresh blueberries in heavy cream. We sat at the cafe-style table in the breakfast area and as we ate in companionable silence, I glanced around this kitchen that was now mine. Even here, fine art decorated the walls. Alan had told me that a crew would be coming soon to crate it up and move it to the foundation's storage facility, and I couldn't help the pulse of sadness at the knowledge that these lovely canvases would be hidden away, lost in some sort of warehouse until whoever ran the foundation found a home for them.

"What's the matter?" Evan said, and I looked up to see that he was peering at me over the rim of his coffee cup, his brow furrowed as if he was pondering some knotty problem.

I gathered myself and used my knife to smear jam on top of my cream cheese. "Nothing. Just thinking."

"Deep thoughts, apparently."

I laughed. "I don't know how deep," I said. "Just melancholy."

He reached out and brushed his fingers over my hand that still held the knife. "Tell me."

"I was just thinking about all this," I said, glancing pointedly at all the art that filled the room. "Jahn used to tell me about his plans for the foundation. About how he was operating it only on a shoestring, but that when he died he wanted to see it blossom." My words were very matter-of-fact, but inside I was all twisted up. The thing I'd shared most with my uncle was our love of art, and the knowledge that all these wonderful paintings were going to go away only made the pain from Jahn's loss that much more brutal. I sucked in a breath and let it out slowly, willing myself not to cry. "I knew this was coming—the transfer to the foundation, I mean. But I never expected it to happen so soon."

"I know." The words were simple, yet held so much meaning. He *did* know. He'd loved Jahn, too. They'd connected just as Jahn and I had, and I wondered if it was art that they'd shared, or something else entirely.

I took a sip of my coffee. "Why did you stick around? After you finished Jahn's seminar class, I mean."

He leaned back in his chair. "Complaining?"

"Hardly. No, I was just thinking about connections. Jahn was my uncle, but that's just an accident of birth, you know? It was the art that really drew us together. I guess I was wondering what it was for you."

"I enjoy art," he said, "but no, it's not my passion. Not the way it is for Cole. And art wasn't your uncle's first passion, either," he said.

"You don't think so? What was? Business?"

He didn't answer immediately. Instead, he got up and moved to the counter to pour fresh coffee. There was nothing awkward about his movements, but I had the impression that he was measuring his words.

Finally, he turned back to me with an enigmatic smile. "Your uncle liked to win."

"I know. I mean it pissed him off so much when Neely acquired the Creature Notebook that he went to a hell of a lot of trouble to commission a copy."

"True enough," Evan said, but there was something in his voice that made me think that he wasn't talking to me so much as acknowledging a private joke. Or maybe he was just trying to hide his irritation. Under the circumstances, it was probably indelicate of me to mention the notebook.

"I'm sorry," I said.

As always, he understood what I meant. "Why do you think he changed his will? He knew I wanted it. And the time we spoke of it, he was very clear that he wanted me to have it."

"I don't know," I said honestly. "He never mentioned it to me at all. Not as a bequest, anyway. But he knew I loved it and that it was my favorite of all his pieces. And I think—" I hesitated, then rushed recklessly on. "I think he wanted me to know that he trusted me and that he loved me."

Evan was watching me intently. "Something happened. Something about the time that he changed his will. What?"

I glanced down at the table. "I fucked up. Jahn helped me out." I lifted my head to look at Evan, and realized he was a little blurry. I blinked, and was mortified when I felt a tear snake down my cheek. "Shit," I said as I brushed it away. "I just—I felt bad. I think the notebook was Jahn's way of telling me it was all okay."

"Angie—"

He was reaching for me, but I pushed back from the table and stood up, determined to get this conversation back on track. As in, not about me or my secrets. "So why you?" I said brightly.

"What do you mean?"

"Why was he going to leave it to you? Wouldn't it make more sense to leave it to Cole?" I'd turned to the coffeepot as I spoke, but I caught a sharp movement in my peripheral vision, as if my words had jolted him.

"Why do you say that?" His voice was low and measured, and I had absolutely no idea what button I had pushed.

"Just because art is Cole's thing. I mean, he did that whole internship in Rome, and he teaches classes at that community center." I shrugged. "I dunno. It just made sense."

"I suppose it does," Evan said.

"So why did you want it?"

He focused on spreading cream cheese on the second half of his bagel, and for a moment I wasn't sure he was going to answer. Then he said, "Because the notebook means something. It represents something huge."

"The missing dragon shield, you mean? Or something more?" The story was that as a youth, Da Vinci had painted a fabulous dragon on a shield. It was so incredible that his father had not sold it to the original buyer, and it had disappeared into history. But I didn't think that Evan was talking about a lost artifact.

"It's a reflection of how Da Vinci looked at the world. He saw things that weren't there. He looked beneath the surface. He looked at the world the way it really was, and it didn't scare him."

I stared at him in unabashed amazement.

"What?" he asked.

"It's just—I can't believe you said that. It's exactly what I love about that notebook. About most of Da Vinci's work, actually."

The corner of his mouth curved up for just a moment before his features settled back into an expression of bland indifference.

I frowned. "Evan?"

"I want to buy the notebook from you, Angie."

"You what?" Surely I hadn't heard him right.

"I want the notebook. I need it. To be honest, I need it more than you do." His voice was calm, like a businessman in the midst of negotiations.

I wasn't calm at all. "Are you fucking kidding me? I just told you how much it means to me."

"And it's served its purpose. Whatever message Jahn was sending you, he delivered it. Giving me the notebook doesn't change a thing."

"It changes everything," I said. And then—with the same shock as an unexpected slap in the face—I understood.

"Oh, shit." With a jolt, I pushed back from the table, the screech of the chair against the tile underscoring the horror I felt. "You son of a bitch," I shouted. "You fucking bastard! Is that why you changed your mind? Why you gave in at Destiny? Why you came here tonight? So you could try to seduce the damn notebook away from me?"

His face reflected shock, but I had no way of knowing if it was a reaction to my accusation or to being found out. And I was on too much of a roll to stop now.

"Well, fuck you, Evan Black. It's *mine*." I wanted to slap his face, but instead I grabbed my coffee cup and hurled it across the room. It shattered on the floor, sending dregs of coffee to splatter on the gray tiles and neutral beige walls.

I gasped, then turned to run from the room. I wanted to throw myself onto the bed and cry. I wanted to kick Evan Black in the balls. I wanted to race out of this building that right now felt so damn confining and just get lost.

I wanted to escape myself, but there was nowhere else to go and no one else to be.

And I couldn't do any of that anyway, because Evan caught my arm and jerked me violently back to him. Then he clutched my other arm, as well. He held me there, his hands tight on my upper arms, as I battled down the urge to spit in his face.

"No," he said. And then more forcefully, "Goddammit, Angie, *no*."

I tried to shake free, but he held me tight. My arms, I was certain, would be bruised by morning.

"That is not why I'm here." The ferocity in his voice slashed over me. "I'm here because I want you, dammit. Not because I want something from you."

I wanted to believe it—I so desperately wanted to believe it—and yet how could I? I shook my head. "Bullshit, Evan. You promised my uncle that you wouldn't do this. And you were damn sure willing to keep that promise—until you realized that I inherited the notebook." I saw him flinch and knew that I'd struck a sound blow. "Kevin was right," I said. "You're only interested in yourself."

"Do not—*do not*—bring that bastard into this conversation."

"I'm not even going to have this conversation," I said wearily. "Just get the hell out."

"No."

"Excuse me?"

"I'm not going anywhere. Not until you listen to me."

"I said to get out. I'm not kidding. Do you know how many panic buttons are hidden in this apartment? If you think I won't push one—"

He tightened his grip on my arms, and I remembered the man I'd seen in the alley. The man who had so efficiently and ruthlessly pressed a knife to another man's throat.

The truth was, unless he let me, I couldn't push any button at all. I couldn't run. I couldn't call for help. I could do nothing but submit. And though I knew that empirically I should be afraid, I wasn't. I was pissed off, sure, but I wasn't afraid of this man. Not even a little.

"Push them all," he said gently. "Kick me out, scream for Peterson. Do whatever the hell you have to. But listen to me first."

I glared at him.

"Please," he said, but it was his tone more than the plea that melted me.

"All right," I whispered. "Talk."

He released my arms, then took a step backward. "I need to show you something. Come with me."

I followed, feeling lost and defeated and just wanting to get this over with. In the living room, he went to the briefcase he'd dropped beside the couch. He bent down, opened it, and pulled out a letter. "Recognize it?"

I shook my head. "Should I?"

"Alan gave it to me. It's the letter Jahn left for me."

"Oh." I wanted to ask what the hell that letter had to do with anything, but I kept my mouth shut. Obviously that's where we were heading, and Evan was going to get there in his own sweet time.

He handed it to me. "Read it."

I took it tentatively, feeling strangely vulnerable.

It took me a second to get the letter out of the envelope. My hands were actually shaking. I didn't yet know what Jahn had said in this note, but I knew that it was important. And, somehow, it affected me.

I unfolded the paper and read the words written in Jahn's familiar scrawl: *I had my reasons.*

I read it again, then looked up at Evan. "What does that mean?"

He ran a hand through his hair. "It means he's not holding me to my promise to stay away from you. What I don't understand is why."

His words seemed to ricochet through my mind. "But— wait. Where does it say that? How do you know?"

"I know," Evan said.

"How?" I repeated.

He turned so that his back was to me and moved toward the wall of windows and the gray of the lake and sky. "Because that's what it has to mean."

I shook my head in confusion. "I don't get this at all."

He turned to me, capturing me in the wild gray of his eyes.

"That's what it has to mean, because anything else is unacceptable. I was fine until I touched you, Angie. Fine until we crossed that line. But now that I've felt your skin against mine—now that I've tasted you—there is no way I can keep that promise. So that is what Jahn's note has to mean. It's a Get Out of Jail Free card, sweetheart. And I took it—took you—because I wanted you. It has nothing to do with the goddamn notebook."

"*Oh.*"

I sank down to sit on the couch as I tried to organize my thoughts. At the moment, I didn't exist as a rational being. I was only emotion, and that emotion was joy.

Joy, yes. But confusion, too. "But at Destiny—you put me off. I mean, not only did you put me off, but you put on that whole show with that redhead."

I heard the jealousy in my voice, and from the way the corner of his lip twitched, I knew he heard it, too. "I don't get involved with the girls at the club," he said, as my body sagged with relief.

"Never?"

"I believe I've mentioned that I have a code. And not sleeping with my employees is high up on my list."

"Does that little redhead realize that?" I asked cattily, then immediately wished I could pull back my words when Evan chuckled.

"Careful," he said. "Green isn't your best color."

"Dammit, Evan, I—"

"Hush." He moved to sit beside me, then gently stroked my cheek before tucking my hair behind my ear. "Christy was putting on a show. For your benefit, actually, though she's done it before. Sometimes I find it beneficial for colleagues to have a certain impression of me."

"And she knows it's all a show?"

"She does," he said, then gently kissed the tip of my nose. "And so does Maria."

"Who's Maria?"

"Her lover."

"Oh." I grinned. "Oh," I repeated as what he said sank in. But then I thought about it more, and had to press. "I still don't understand why you did that. The whole show to turn me off. All the fighting to push me away. You'd read the letter by then. You had your Get Out of Jail Free card."

"I know," he said. He took my hand and idly traced my fingers with his. "I'm still a bad bet, Angie, and for all the same reasons."

"You haven't told me those reasons."

"No. I haven't. And I don't intend to."

I eyed him, certain that I knew. This was all tied up with Kevin's allegations. He was involved in some sort of criminal shit, and I'd be lying if I didn't admit I was curious—and intrigued. There was sweet temptation in the danger, and I licked my lips, wondering if I should press the point. If I should ask him what he was mixed up in. If I should press for details about his crimes, both now and five years ago. But I kept my mouth shut. That kind of talk might push him away—and I was selfish enough not to want to go there. I wanted the reality of the man in my bed, and the fantasy of his wild and dangerous side was just an added perk.

"If you're such a bad bet," I said instead, "then why did you give in at all?"

He brushed his lips over mine. "You said it yourself. No commitment, no future. Just you and me and this one weekend. Dammit, Angie, do you have any idea how long I've fought the urge to touch you? For that matter, do you have any idea how close I came to breaking my word after that damned alley? I meant what I said—you're my goddamned Kryptonite, and you have totally destroyed all my defenses."

His words crashed over me, tempting me even as he tethered me. Didn't I already know this was a man I could let go with—a man who unleashed a wildness in me that didn't involve fast cars or petty theft? With Evan, I felt free to be Lina again, even though Angie was the woman I needed to be. The woman I was going to have to be starting in three short weeks. Once I stepped into the world of politics, I needed to be squeaky clean because anything else could cost my father his career, not to mention his reputation.

This was my last chance. To let go. To fly. To have this man that I craved.

Just you and me and this one weekend.

It sounded so perfect. So tempting.

And too damn short.

I took a deep breath, trying to organize my thoughts. Because the truth was, I wanted more than this one night with Evan. I wanted a connection. I wanted the time we had left to be real and solid and shining.

I needed him, and I trusted him, but I was afraid that my earlier frenzied accusation about him trying to snatch the Creature Notebook had left a shadow looming between us. And the only way I could think of to banish that dark, was to explain exactly why Jahn had given the notebook to me in the first place.

"Earlier this year," I began. "When they rushed Jahn into surgery, he didn't wake up when they expected him to—nothing seemed to go right. It was horrible."

"I remember."

"I was a wreck."

"I remember that, too," he said, and I nodded agreement. Evan and Tyler and Cole had spent at least as much time at the hospital as I had, and I'd been grateful whenever our visits had overlapped because I'd soaked up their strength and claimed it for my own.

"I can't recall any of the details of those days. They're a blur. But the moment that they said he crossed the line—that he was okay—I had to get out of there. I had to just go, you know? Because all of that fear and worry that I'd been holding inside while I paced the hospital and waited was poisoning me. I had to get it out. And I—well, I kind of stole a diamond bracelet."

His scarred brow lifted. "All right," he said. "You have my attention."

"I got away with it, or so I thought. But it turns out there were security cameras. It took them over a month, but they caught me."

I shuddered, remembering how mortified I'd been when the cops had confronted me in the condo lobby on April Fool's Day. Jahn had been home from the hospital about a week, but he hadn't yet been cleared to go back to the office. I'd been on my way back from an ice-cream run, and they'd taken me away. "I spent the night in jail, and the next day I told Jahn everything—including why I did it."

"Why did you?"

"To feel that rush," I said, looking right at his eyes. "Sometimes, when I needed to let go, when everything just got to be too much for me—well, sometimes that's what I would do."

"I get it," Evan said, and I knew that he needed no further explanation. "So you were in jail," he continued. "What did Jahn do?"

"He moved heaven and earth for me without ever leaving his condo. I think you could probably interview the arresting officers now, and even they'd swear they have no knowledge of me. This is a big year for my dad, what with the talk of him being on the short list to run as VP. That kind of scandal would not have been good."

"And then he changed his will," Evan said, seeing exactly where I was going with this.

"He did," I said. "He left me the notebook. Me, not you. And I think it was his way of telling me that no matter how badly I fucked up, that he still believed in me. That he still trusted and respected me." I shrugged. "I loved that notebook, and he knew it. I guess the bottom line is that I think the bequest was his way of saying that he loved me."

Evan nodded slowly. "Why are you telling me this now?"

I hesitated, taking a moment to draw courage. "Because I wanted you to understand why I'm not going to give it to you. And because—"

"Why?"

"Because I want three weeks," I announced boldly. "And I thought you deserved the truth before I said so."

"What are you talking about?" He was watching me intently, and there was a small crease above his nose, as if he was concentrating on a particularly knotty problem. That, apparently, would be me.

I sucked in a breath. "I'm moving to Washington. My dad got me a job as a legislative aide. That's why I went to Destiny." My cheeks flamed, which was ridiculous considering all we'd done together in the last few hours. "I wanted to have you. Just once, like I said. I wanted to finish what we started. More than that, I wanted the way you make me feel."

"But?" There was an edge to his voice that I couldn't quite identify.

"But once wasn't enough. Now I want more," I said firmly. "You asked me how high? Well, that's my answer. As high as you can take me before I leave. And who knows—maybe we'll get each other out of our systems."

I was breathing hard, watching him. And, dammit, just thinking about what I was suggesting had turned me on. My nipples were tight behind the terry cloth of the robe, and I was suddenly aware of the heat at the juncture of my thighs.

"No," he said.

I looked up sharply, prepared to protest, but didn't have the chance before he continued.

"No," he repeated. "I don't think you'll ever be out of my system. But as for how high I can take you . . ."

I held my breath as he reached out, trailing a finger down the neckline of the robe.

"We've already gone pretty damn far," he whispered. Slowly, he reached out and tugged loose the tie of the robe, then spread the top open, revealing my shoulders and breasts. "But have we gone far enough?" he asked. He brushed the pad of his thumb over my already erect nipple. "You're right, baby. I can take you one hell of a lot further." He took his thumb off my breast and drew it along my lower lip, then thrust it gently into my mouth. I opened for him, sucking and tasting, my eyes closed as I simply reveled in it.

I wanted it—god, how I wanted it. Wanted to go completely and totally wild with him. And yet the tightness in my chest was growing. A bone-deep trepidation. Because the more I realized that this was really happening, the more my old fears bubbled up.

Part of me screamed that I was the one that started this, so I needed to just keep my damn mouth shut. But I couldn't help it. All my doubts—all my fears—were once again rising to the surface.

"Evan . . ." I trailed off, determined not to go there.

"What?"

"Nothing. Never mind. Just me being stupid." But I didn't quite look at his eyes.

"Hey," he said. "Tell me."

"It's just . . . It's just that I go a little wild and do these things sometimes," I said slowly, feeling foolish since I was the one who'd said I wanted these three weeks, so what was I doing now backing off?

"I mean, I want this—I want you. But . . ." I went silent, thinking of Grace who'd died because I'd run off to play wild child one night. Thinking of my night in jail that had come so close to destroying my dad's good name. Hell, even thinking of Evan who'd been attacked in an alley. Because that tied back to me letting go, too.

"Oh, hell. I guess I'm afraid we'd be tempting fate," I said lamely. "Besides, you're not a safe bet, remember?"

"No," he said.

"No?" I repeated, confused.

"No. No thinking, no rationalizing, and absolutely no saying no. I'm a man who gets what he wants, sweetheart, even if I have to take it. So that's what I'm doing. Consider it my present to you. Hell, consider it a going-away present."

"A present," I repeated dumbly.

"One hell of a kick-ass gift," he said firmly. "I'm the one taking responsibility. You're not diving into the rush, I'm pulling you in with me. You're not going wild, I'm just taking you along for the ride. No," he repeated when I opened my mouth to protest. He pressed a soft finger to my lips. "This isn't a subject for debate. It isn't a question. For the next three weeks, we're taking that fall together—all you have to do is surrender."

"That's just semantics," I said, but I couldn't help the flutter of bliss that was growing in my belly. *A gift.* Maybe. Just maybe . . .

"It's not just semantics," he said firmly. "It's a shift in how we look at the world."

I licked my lips, so very tempted.

"Come on, Angie. Fall with me."

I drew in a breath, held his eyes, and made the leap. "You called me Lina on the roof the other day," I said softly. I felt suddenly, unreasonably exposed, and I crossed my arms over my chest.

"Did I? I suppose I thought it suited you." He stroked his palms down my bare shoulders. "Do you like it?"

I hesitated. I should back off. I should say no; I should be Angie. "Yes," I whispered as he closed his fingers over mine. "I liked it."

"Me, too." He stood up, then held out a hand for me. "Come

here, Lina," he said, gently pulling me to my feet. The robe hung open, and he pushed it off my arms, leaving me naked.

I fought the urge to bend down for the robe, but honestly, it didn't take much effort. I wanted to be naked with this man. I wanted to be wild with him. I wanted to be Lina.

I could do this; I could take these three weeks. Because surely with Evan keeping me tethered, nothing would go horribly wrong.

"Come with me," he said, then led me to the bedroom. He sat on the edge of the bed, then guided me on, as well.

I knelt on the mattress, sitting back on my ankles. Then I cocked my head and regarded him playfully. "I'm not sure Lina is quite as compliant as Angie."

His smile was slow and held a touch of victory. "Is that a fact?"

"Mmm."

"Well, what would Lina do?" he asked.

"She'd be bold," I said, as I moved closer. "If she wanted something from a man, she'd just take it." I reached down, and stroked his cock through his slacks, then sucked in air as I felt it turn to steel in response to my touch. "Or maybe she'd just drive him wild," I said, as I slid my hand slowly up and down. "Take him to the edge and then push him over, knowing that she was the one who made him fall."

"*Lina.*" He drew in a noisy breath. He reached out for me, but I shook my head.

"No. Lay back. Lina can be very bossy."

His dimple flashed as he slid down to stretch out on the bed. "That's it," I said as my fingers worked the button and then the zipper. "Lift your ass," I ordered, then tugged his pants down along with his underwear. Once I got him free of the slacks, I got back on the bed, then returned my attention to his cock as I moved to straddle him.

His eyes were opaque with pleasure, and when I dipped my head and ran my tongue over the very tip of his penis, I felt him tremble beneath me. I basked in a glow of feminine pride, knowing that it was my touch that was driving him crazy. That I was making him hard.

I didn't waver in the attention I was paying to his cock, but I did relax my thighs, so that I was sitting on his leg instead of perched above it, and I undulated my body in time with my ministrations to his cock, teasing my clit with each delicious motion and stoking the fire that was already raging inside me.

"Jesus, baby," he said, as I licked his shaft all the way down to where I cupped his balls and then back up to the tip. His body was rigid and tight, as if readying for the explosion that I intended to give him.

I opened my mouth and drew him in. Just the tip at first, because I wanted to make him desperate. Hell, I wanted to make him beg. Then I went deeper, relishing the way his body tightened and letting his groans of pleasure wash over me. I've never felt particularly skilled where giving head is concerned, but right then I felt powerful. Hell, I felt perfect.

"Lina," he groaned. "Shit, Lina, you feel fucking amazing."

He was so damn close—but I had other plans for that gorgeous cock, and I slowly withdrew my mouth, then eased my body up. Now, I did more than just straddle a thigh. Instead, I straddled his hips, and in slow, careful moves designed to drive us both crazy, I let the tip of his cock stroke my slick cunt.

I was so damn ready, and this was torturing me as much as it was him. But as I moved—as I denied myself the pleasure of slamming my body down hard and impaling myself on him, of having him fill me in one glorious, deep thrust—I understood how he had survived so far without actually fucking me. Because this anticipation was just as exciting as the act itself, and if I were a stronger person I could have teased him forever, and with the greatest of pleasure.

But I wasn't that strong.

What had Cole called it? Evan's capacity for self-deprivation? Well, I didn't have it. I wanted him. Needed him. Had to have him right then, because my senses were on overload and the only thing that could keep me from imploding was the feel of this man inside me.

Fuck it. I couldn't wait another second, and I thrust downward, crying out as my body stretched wide to accommodate him. I rose up, then slammed down again, leaning back so I could hold on to his legs even as he reached up and grasped my hips, forcing me to go deeper, harder, faster.

He was close. I could tell by the way that tension was building in his body as we moved together, and I arched back, moaning with pleasure at the way he filled me—and then squealing in surprise and delight as he grabbed me tight and rolled us over, tumbling me onto my back with our bodies still joined.

"Evan!"

His kiss was hard and demanding and very effectively shut me up. "You didn't wait for me to get a condom."

"I'm on the pill," I said. "And I assumed you were clean."

"I am," he said.

"So that's why you stopped?"

He laughed. "Baby, I'm still inside you. Is that stopping?"

"No, but—"

He pressed his finger over my lips. "I seem to recall mentioning to you that I like being in control."

"Oh. Right. You might have said that," I admitted, squirming beneath him. "I think you liked letting me take over for a while, too."

"Careful. That's the kind of thing a woman can get punished for."

"Is that so?" I asked playfully.

"Hell yes," he said, returning my smile with one of his own, and then staying perfectly still.

He was still hard inside me, and yet he wasn't moving. I groaned in protest and tried to shift my hips in silent demand. But I couldn't do much; he'd trapped me good and tight.

I was beginning to understand what he meant by "punishment."

He grinned knowingly. "Frustrated, Lina?"

"Even if I were, I wouldn't admit it."

He laughed outright, and the sound delighted me. "How do you do that?" I asked.

"How do I do this?" he asked, moving slowly inside me.

"Oh, thank god. Finally," I said, arching up to silently urge him to thrust deeper. "But what I meant was, how do you send this melange of emotions coursing through me?" I had to concentrate on getting the words out. "You take me to the edge, you make me feel like I'm the manifestation of sensual pleasure. And then you turn it on its head and make me laugh out loud." I paused for just a heartbeat. "I don't remember ever having so much fun in bed."

He slid up my body and kissed me gently. "Me either. Of course," he added, his tone sharpening a bit as he traced his fingertip over my naked breasts, "as I believe we've already established, we've barely scratched the surface of what I can make you feel." As he spoke, he rubbed his thumb and forefinger over my nipple, the friction making the nub even tighter. He squeezed his fingers tighter, intensifying the pleasure—and the pain.

"Oh, really?" I concentrated on his fingers, on that pinching sensation that hurt a little, but at the same time felt remarkably wow, as if everything I wanted to feel had been captured and held there for me to experience. I remembered his words in the alley—the way he'd wanted to pinch my nipples. To spank my ass.

I felt the muscles of my sex clench around him, already anticipating the new onslaught of sensations to come.

From the way he smiled at me, I could tell he'd felt my body's response—and understood exactly what it meant.

"My Lina wants something," he said.

I licked my lips and turned my head slightly so that I wasn't looking at him dead-on. "I was just thinking about what you said. About how taking control was the kind of thing you might punish me for."

"Were you? That's an interesting direction for your thoughts. Would you like to elaborate? Maybe be more specific?"

I slanted my eyes at him. "You made me promises."

"Did I? You may have to refresh my memory."

He released my nipple, then trailed his finger down, lower and lower to where our bodies were joined. He moved inside me languidly, and as he did, he slipped his finger over my clit, making me bite down on my lower lip as my breath came in painful, wonderful jolts.

He took his finger away, stopped his thrusting, and looked down at me, his expression smug.

"Bastard," I muttered.

"What do you want, Lina?"

"I want—I mean, I've never been—oh, fuck it. I want you to spank me."

"Why?"

"Because I've been naughty," I murmured, because I was certain that's what he expected me to say. "Because I need to be punished," I added, turning my head away because I knew it was true.

"Good girl," he said as he began to slowly move inside of me. I felt the pressure building and closed my eyes, wanting to get lost on the cresting waves. "No. Look at me."

Reluctantly, I opened my eyes.

"It was a good answer, but it wasn't the right one." He kept up the motion, that delicious friction building with such slow intensity that it took all of my effort to focus on his words. "I don't know what you think you've done, but it's not important. Because it's not about punishment, at least not with me. The control, the bondage, the spanking, even the pain—it's all a road, Lina. A road that leads to pleasure. It's acceleration before flight. The priming of the pump. The buildup to climax."

He traced his fingertip over my nipple, then over my lips, then gently slid his finger inside my mouth as I sucked, the digit mimicking the thrusts of his cock.

"Call it whatever the hell you want," he continued. "But I promise you that pleasure is the goal. I'm not interested in hurting you. I'm not interested in punishing you. I'm only interested in pleasing you."

He slid his finger out of my mouth, and I took that as permission to speak. "You do," I whispered.

"It's going to be rough, baby, but I promise it will feel good. But I can't have you any other way. Not after wanting you for so damn long. And not now that I know you're going away. I need to know that you've surrendered to me."

"I have. I will." Hell, right then I'd do or say anything just to feel him moving inside me some more.

He didn't, though. Instead, he slid out of me, and I actually whimpered with disappointment.

He laughed, then held out his hands for me, helping me up until I was kneeling on the bed in front of him. "I want to know that until the day you leave this city, I have claimed you for my own. Now tell me that you want it, too."

"I do," I said. "I want it."

He slid off the bed and stood facing me. Then he made a circular motion with his finger. "Turn around. Bend over. Palms flat on the bed."

I opened my mouth to ask why, realized that was an idiotic question, and complied. I heard his low intake of breath, then his soft, "Oh, baby." And then I felt the sharp sting of his palm against my rear, followed by the pressure of his palm rubbing away the prickles of heat that had bloomed from the contact. "Say it like you mean it," he said, and now there was nothing soft about his voice.

"I want it," I repeated, then squeezed my eyes closed as another spank caught me across the ass. His blows were hard, and though they stung—though I'd even go so far as to say they hurt—I understood what he meant about the pleasure. My breasts felt heavy, my nipples tight, my sex tingling and wet. I wanted more—hell, I wanted everything.

He rubbed my ass in firm, slow circles as he leaned in close. "What do you want, Lina? Do you want me to stop? Or do you want me to keep going?"

"Keep going," I said, close to whimpering just from the thought that he might stop. "Please, do it."

He answered with another sharp smack. "Tell me again what it is you want?"

"I want you to spank me." *I want you to fuck me.*

"Tell me what you want." Another spank. I flinched, spreading my legs just a little. My ass was on fire, and oh, dear god, so was the rest of me. I wanted him inside me, and I was very quickly reaching the point where begging would be involved. "Tell me," he repeated, his words followed by another spank.

"*You.* I want you, Evan. I've always wanted you." I squeezed my eyes shut, afraid I'd revealed too much. But Evan just moaned in satisfaction, as if my words had been as sweet to him now as my mouth on his cock had been earlier.

"I have to have you now, Lina. I can't last another second of not being inside you."

I tried to say yes, but it wasn't necessary. I tried to turn over, but he wouldn't let me. His hands were on my hips, and he tugged me back so that my knees were closer to the edge of the bed. I felt his cock rub against me, sliding against my desire-slick sex. I spread my legs in silent need, arching up in both invitation and demand. In another moment I would have found my voice and begged, but I didn't have to, because he used his grip on my hips to pull me toward him even as he thrust forward.

He entered me in one long, deep stroke, and I cried out from the combination of pleasure and pain. He was ripping me apart with every thrust, shattering me, breaking me. He was utterly destroying me, and yet nothing had ever felt so perfect as the sensation of this man inside me. With each thrust he took me higher. With each soft moan he brought us closer.

He leaned over me, his hips moving in a steady rhythm. I worked in tandem with him, and when our bodies were in sync, he released my hips. At first I mourned the loss of contact. Then I realized that he'd reached underneath us, one hand going to stroke my clit and the other clutching tight to my breast as he slammed into me over and over and deeper and deeper until I finally spiraled off into the heavens with Evan holding on tight.

I was still soaring, my vision barely returning, when his orgasm rocked us both. He exploded inside me, holding me tight as he released himself into me.

"Evan." I said his name like a prayer.

He held me like that for a moment, his body draped over mine, one arm around me and the other keeping him balanced over me. I felt him grow soft inside me and I felt the gentle kisses he trailed down my spine.

"Lina," he murmured, but the sound was so soft I wasn't entirely sure that he'd meant for me to hear it.

Finally, he pulled out, then gathered me into his arms as if I weighed no more than a kitten. Then he brushed a kiss over my lips.

I was sleepy now, completely drained, and I clung to him as

he took me into the bathroom and cleaned us both up. Then he carried me back to the bed, got in beside me, and pulled me close.

I closed my eyes, and his soft "You're wonderful" was the last thing I heard before I slipped over to sleep.

fifteen

"I don't have nightmares when you're with me," I whispered, as I woke in Evan's arms to the soft pre-dawn glow filling the sky outside the windows.

"I'm glad." He stretched, coming easily awake. His fingers stroked my hair. "I don't like that you've ever had them at all. I wish I could erase them. They're not real, you know. They're survival guilt, baby. I get that you miss your sister, and I understand that the way she was taken from you was damned horrific, but you don't have to feel guilty for being alive."

"I don't," I said, my voice hoarse. "Not because I'm alive." I sucked in air. "It's because she shouldn't have even been out of the house that night."

I spoke in a whisper, my voice so low I wasn't actually certain I was making sound. I'd never told this to anyone but Jahn. And though part of me screamed that I needed to keep this to myself—that I shouldn't build bridges when I was just going to burn them in three weeks—the truth was that I felt safe and warm with Evan. And, more important, I knew that he was strong enough to hold whatever load I piled onto him.

"I'd been sneaking out a lot," I continued. "Meeting friends to get drunk and smoke cigarettes and do idiot shit, you know? And Grace had been covering for me even while she tried to get me to stop. But I didn't. She was always so perfect. The brilliant and beautiful oldest daughter, and I was such a fuckup, and I told her she needed to mind her own business."

"But that night she followed you?"

"And that was the night they took her." My voice broke on a sob. "I didn't see it. I didn't even know she'd followed me until the next morning when she wasn't in her room and then they found her body and no one could understand why she'd snuck out of the house. Except for me. I understood." I met his eyes, sure that mine were filled with guilt and shame. "I never told anyone."

"It wouldn't have made a difference." He stroked my hair. "It's not your fault," he said softly. "The universe is a fucked up bitch, and she doesn't play by the rules."

"I stopped, you know. That very day I stopped sneaking out and acting wild and cutting loose. I turned myself completely around."

"Did you?" he asked. "Yourself? Or your behavior?"

I didn't answer, but he was dead on the money, and I think he knew it. Nothing inside me had really changed. I'd just locked it up tight.

He sat up, then pulled me onto his lap. I leaned in close to him and sighed. I didn't like playing true confessions, but at the same time it felt good to have shared my secrets. Or, rather, it felt good to share them with Evan.

"I'm an absolute wreck, you know," I said. "I think you must be a saint for putting up with me."

His low chuckle thrummed through my chest. "Hardly. And you're not a wreck."

"Oh, I am." I sighed and closed my eyes. "You say you've wanted me for so long, but I don't think you're seeing the person you think you're seeing."

"No? You told me before that I see you."

"Wishful thinking, maybe," I said.

"No." The word was strong and simple and held a world of understanding. "You were right. I see you. I do. I see what you are."

"What am I?" I asked, hating how small and insecure my voice sounded, but I had to know. Had to hear.

"Beautiful, vibrant, smart. You're selfless. You're empathetic. And though you may not always be correct, you always do what you think is right. And," he added with a mischievous grin. "It turns out that you're quite talented in bed."

At that, I laughed out loud.

"I see you," he repeated. "I see the core of you, Lina. The heart. And I damn sure hope that's what you see in me, too, because my top coat may be shiny and bright, but underneath that you're going to find a lot of tarnish."

"And beneath the tarnish?"

"Much shinier," he said. "But very hard to get to. Except for Tyler and Cole, Jahn is probably the only one who ever has."

I sat up straight so that I could see his face better. "That's sad," I said, but even as I spoke, I realized that his words could apply to me, too. How many people had I truly let in? Honestly, except for Jahn, I could think of none. Not even Kat. Not even Flynn.

"What about your mom and your sister?"

He nodded slowly. "Yes. To a degree. But they're not around. They moved away years ago. I hardly ever see them anymore."

"I'm sorry." I regretted bringing it up. I remembered now that the various articles I'd read had talked about the fact that he'd worked his ass off to move them out of Chicago so they could make a better life elsewhere. He'd remained behind, running the businesses that had earned the money to finance their move.

"It must have been hard," I said. "Growing up the way you did. Your father's death, and then having to shoulder so much when you were so young."

His smile was humorless. "Just how many articles have you read about me?"

I shrugged. "All of them, I think."

As I'd hoped, he laughed.

"Fiction writers aren't the only ones who spin stories, Lina," he said.

"It's not true? The way you took care of your mom and your sister?"

His expression was both harsh and wistful. "I did—and will always do—whatever is in my power to protect my family. I will take any risk, I will make any sacrifice, I will do whatever it takes to turn the odds to my favor. And I will never regret a single choice I made where those two women are concerned."

The passion in his words reverberated through me, and I couldn't help but picture a young Evan carrying such a huge burden. That he'd not only survived but thrived was just one more bit of proof that this man was exceptional.

"The universe is fucked up," I whispered, remembering the words he'd spoken to me—and wondering what risks he'd taken, what sacrifices he'd made, and how, exactly, he'd shifted the odds in his favor.

"Yes," he said harshly. "It is." He met my eyes. "Don't ever be naive, Lina. Whatever you've read—whatever you think you know—keep in mind that the press coverage about me doesn't even come close to the truth."

I frowned, knowing this was an opportunity. I'd told him about Gracie; if I asked, he just might tell me the truth. About what happened after his father died. About all those secrets Jahn had mentioned. About all the things that Kevin had hinted at.

And yet I didn't ask. I didn't say one single word.

I'm not entirely sure why I held back. All I knew was that the sexy, dark, dangerous man I'd fantasized about was finally in my bed, and would be for the next three weeks. Did I want to risk that high by bringing reality into the mix?

I didn't, and so I stayed silent, gently stroking my hand over his. His knuckles had healed quite a bit, but they were still red, the skin obviously tender. "There was trouble with one of the women who works at Destiny," he said, though I hadn't even lifted a brow in question. "I had a little chat with the man causing the trouble. Now there's no more trouble."

I thought of what went down in the alley and could easily imagine him protecting the girls. I hoped the man's face looked one hell of a lot worse than Evan's knuckles.

I kissed the corner of his mouth. "I'm glad."

He met my eyes and held them, and the moment had the quality of a salute. As if he not only approved of my words, but I'd passed some sort of test. He smiled, just a little, then he laid his head back and closed his eyes. I settled against him. Even though it was still ridiculously early, I knew that sleep would elude me. I wasn't yet awake, but at the same time I was full of energy.

I let my fingers explore his body, stroking his chest, easing up his arm. The vibrant green of the vine tattoo popped in the dim light, and I traced its outline with my fingertip, feeling relaxed and lazy and so very comfortable with this man. "Does it mean something?"

He turned his head toward me, his eyes barely open.

"It's a reminder," he said. "Let's just say it keeps me focused."

I waited for him to say more, but he just turned his head back and closed his eyes again.

I thought of what Jahn had said so many years ago—about how Evan had secrets. His own, and those he keeps for others.

I might have guessed at some of his secrets, but as I looked at Evan, resting peacefully beside me, I had to acknowledge that I didn't really know the man at all.

But, damn me, I wanted to. I so very desperately wanted to.

I woke again a few hours later to the incredible scent of coffee and the even more incredible man smiling down at me.

"Hey," he said, passing me the mug. "Drink up. Get dressed. We need to get going."

I blinked at him. "Going? Where?"

"Do you trust me?"

"Yes," I said, without hesitation.

"Then you'll see when we get there."

I took a long sip of coffee and felt life returning. "Do I have time for a shower?"

"A quick one," he said.

"Do I have time for a shower with you?"

He laughed. "That wouldn't be quick." He leaned over and kissed me, long and deep and so scrumptious it curled through me, setting me just a little bit on fire. *Yeah,* I thought. *It wouldn't be quick at all.* "Now go," he said, taking the mug and then tugging the sheet off me as I squealed and scrambled out of bed.

He patted my ass as I hurried by, and I paused long enough to shoot him a saucy grin. "Naked and soapy," I said. "But I guess you're going to miss it all."

"Vixen," he said, then laughed.

When Uncle Jahn had remodeled the penthouse, he'd wanted every guest to feel as much at home as Jahn himself did. And to that end, he'd focused on making each of the four guest suites as stunning as possible. Each had a bedroom that was beyond gigantic with a full wall of windows with a view of either the lake or the city. The bedroom abutted an adjacent sitting area com-

plete with decadent furniture, a wet bar, and the most important of all essentials: the coffee station.

But it was in the bathrooms that Jahn's generosity really
shined. Unlike most homes in which only the master suite had a
bathroom with bells and whistles, in Jahn's condo, every guest
was treated as royalty, too. And the bathroom that had become
mine when I'd moved in and selected my suite was absolutely my
most favorite room in the entire penthouse.

The walls were a combination of dark teak and white marble
with pinkish veins that gave the room a classical yet slightly
funky feel. The shower stall was bigger than the entire bathroom in the apartment I'd shared with Flynn and had a line of
showerheads from floor to ceiling, and two other lines arching
out for almost 360-degree coverage. Teak benches lined two
walls of the stall, and except for the glass door and one glass
wall, the walls were made up of that marble I loved so much.

The glass wall looked in on the sauna that was positioned
beside the shower, and next to that was a steam room. Adding
to the spalike theme, there was a giant whirlpool tub, an entertainment center with the television hidden behind the huge mirror, and a beverage center, complete with a carbonated water
dispenser and a wine fridge.

When you also considered the dressing-room-style closet—
which would comfortably house a family of five—the bathroom
crossed the line from freaking awesome to fan-fucking-tastic.

The only thing that would make it better was if Evan was
with me, but if time was an issue, I had to concede that it was
probably for the best that he'd declined my offer.

Still . . . he was on my mind as I turned on the ceiling-
mounted rain-shower head, then brushed my teeth while I
waited for the water temperature to adjust. He was even more in
my thoughts when I stepped into the warm, wet spray.

I tilted my face up, letting the water run over my skin and
soak my hair. There was a shampoo dispenser in the wall, and I

put some into my hand, then rubbed it over my head. My hair was thick enough that it took a while to soap it up well, and even longer to thoroughly rinse it. I closed my eyes and let the water fall onto my face and then sluice down my body in warm trails.

I didn't hear him come in, but even before he touched me I knew he was there. Maybe it was a shift in the ambient noise. Maybe there was a change in the light. Or maybe I was just attuned to his presence, connected to him now as I'd never been to anyone before.

All I know is that I felt no surprise when he pressed up behind me, his erection teasing my rear as his hands cupped my breasts.

Neither of us said a word, but I leaned back as he stroked me, his strong hands playing with my breasts, his fingers teasing my nipples. He trailed one hand down my belly to find me slick and wet and ready. His fingers stroked me, filling me, and finding my sensitive clit, and I gasped as he brushed his finger over it, sending ripples of warmth coursing through me.

His fingers played with me, moving slowly and sensually in teasing strokes designed to drive me wild, and he kept it up with minute attention until I knew that it was a good thing he was holding me upright, because my legs felt so weak I knew I would collapse if he even thought about letting go.

I was so close to release that I actually whimpered when he pulled his hand away, but he wasn't done with me. He moved me forward, bending me at the waist and putting my hands on the wall. Still, he said nothing, and I smiled as I stood there, my hands on the warm stone, my rear pressed up against him. He stroked my back, his hands sliding down either side of me until he reached my hips. He used his knee to ease my legs slightly wider, and then—as I closed my eyes in sweet anticipation—he slid his cock deep into me.

I was so wet, so damn ready, that he entered easily, my muscles contracting to draw him in farther, as if he were part of me. As if in the short time since he'd last been inside me I'd lost a part of myself. His thrusts were deep and powerful and demanding, and I could feel his body tense as he got closer and closer.

I took one hand off the wall, then slid it between my legs, finding my clit and stroking it faster and faster in time with his thrusts. Water sluiced over us, but I felt none of it. All I could feel was my hand upon my clit and Evan's cock inside me. I was reduced to nothing but the sensation of sex, of coming release, of the electricity that now concentrated between my legs like a single vibrant point that was growing and throbbing and threatening to burst free, as if there was no way that so much pleasure could be held enclosed in anything smaller than the universe.

And then Evan was coming, his hands tight on my hips as he tugged me even closer, our bodies slapping wildly together as he emptied himself inside me, taking me to my own release as that vibrant point exploded out, making my entire body sing and tingle, all the way to my toes and my fingertips.

I pressed both hands against the wall again, gasping and spent. I wasn't certain I could ever move again. Then Evan pulled out of me and he turned me around and I moved obediently, draping my arms around his neck and pressing my head to his chest as he used a washcloth to gently soap me up and then adjusted the rest of the showerheads to rinse us both completely.

"I thought you said we'd be late," I murmured when he was done ministering to me.

"I imagine we will," he said. He kissed me so soundly that my body fired all over again. "It was worth it."

Yeah, I thought as I clung tight to him, *it was.*

I still felt boneless when we emerged from the shower moments later. I sank down beside him on the upholstered bench, my head leaning against his shoulder. "You've melted me," I said, though there wasn't a hint of complaint in my voice.

"You managed to destroy me pretty completely, too," he said. "Should we blow off my surprise?"

"Is it a good surprise?"

"The best," he said.

"Then no." With effort, I forced myself to stand, then held out a hand to help him rise. "But I warn you. My standards are high. If it's not the best, there will be consequences."

"I'll keep that in mind," he said seriously.

Since he wouldn't tell me where we were going, getting dressed was a bit of a challenge. But he swore that the flirty dress and sandals I picked out were perfect. I pulled my hair back into a ponytail with a few loose tendrils framing my face, then swiped on some mascara and lip gloss and called myself ready.

"Perfect," he said, returning to my bedroom after leaving to change clothes himself. He wore jeans and loafers now, with a casual jacket over a simple white T-shirt.

"You couldn't possibly have had an entire outfit in your briefcase."

"No. In my suite."

"You have a suite? If I'd realized, I wouldn't have let you share mine last night."

"Don't even joke about kicking me out of your bed. And yeah, Cole and Tyler and I crashed here quite a bit. Jahn gave us each a drawer."

"A drawer," I teased. "That's serious."

"It was," he said. "The man was like a father to me."

I might have been playing, but I could tell that Evan was serious. "What about your own dad? I mean, you were old enough when he died. Surely you remember him."

"I remember him," he said, his words like ice. "He was a goddamn bastard."

"I'm sorry," I said, knowing my words were inadequate. The press had painted a picture of a happy family struck by tragedy.

Now I tried to revise my perception to picture a broken family that had been even more destroyed with the death of Evan's father. A man who, from what I was guessing, hadn't exactly been around for his wife or kids.

I tried to imagine not having my dad, and the thought left a huge hollow spot in my gut.

I went to him and took his hand, then rose up to brush a kiss over his lips. "In that case," I said, "I'm even more glad you had Jahn."

We headed out, and to my surprise, Evan stopped the elevator on the lobby level instead of descending all the way to the parking garage.

"No car?"

"It's reasonably close. We'll take a taxi."

"Close," I said, running various options through my head.

"Don't even try. I'll only be disappointed if you manage to guess."

I laughed. "Fair enough," I said as a taxi pulled up in response to the call light. Evan stepped off the curb to open the door for me, then walked around and got in on the opposite side.

"One thing I forgot to mention," he said, as he settled in beside me. "I'd like you to put this on." He reached into his pocket and pulled out a black sleep mask with an elastic strap.

I peered at it dubiously. "Seriously?"

He just looked at me, not answering.

"Evan!"

"Hey, if you don't want to . . ." He trailed off, then leaned forward and told the taxi driver to take us back to the condo.

I goggled at him. "What are you doing?"

"Rules are rules."

"Fine," I said, snatching it out of his hands. I slid the mask on over my eyes. And in the moment before the world disappeared from sight, I was pretty sure that I caught the driver's smirk in the rearview mirror.

"Better?" I asked.

"Much," Evan said.

"And you're not going to even give me a clue?"

"Not even," he said.

"I know this area pretty well. I could probably count stops and turns. I've watched enough espionage thrillers to know how that works."

He laughed. "Good point." He sat silent for a moment, and then I felt him drape something across my lap. "You look a little cold," he said. "Let me warm you up."

I started to tell him that my legs weren't cold, but in that same instant I felt his hand upon my thigh. I realized as he gently stroked my skin—easing his fingers higher and higher toward the mid-thigh hemline of my dress—that he hadn't put the jacket there to keep me warm, but to give us privacy.

He eased the hem higher, and it was all I could do not to whimper. I felt on fire, my thighs craving more of his touch, my sex so sensitive that even the slight rubbing of my panties against my flesh in time with the movement of the car was making me hot. And, so help me, the fact that I was blindfolded and we were in the back of a taxi, not four feet away from some anonymous driver, made the whole thing that much more arousing.

"Evan," I said, because we should stop even though I didn't want to. Even though I wanted this rush. This heat.

"Hmm?"

"What are you doing?"

"Distracting you so you can't count turns," he said, even as his finger slipped under the tiny strip of material that made up the thong part of my teeny-tiny panties.

"Oh." My breath was a gasp, the word forced out even as he slid his finger inside me. "Oh, well, um, okay."

He chuckled. "Just relax, sweetheart. We're close."

"Yes," I said, because he was right. I was close, so damn close, but he was keeping me on the edge, slipping his finger in and out, making me wetter and wetter, playing and teasing and trailing a soft fingertip all over my sex, between my legs, on the soft skin between my cunt and my thighs. But though his touch fired my senses and made me crave more, it was more that he denied me.

He was deliberately avoiding my clit, and I had no way of complaining. I couldn't say a word—I couldn't even shift my hips and writhe in silent demand—unless I wanted to advertise what was going on to the driver. And, yeah, he might already be clued in, but since I was blindfolded I was happy to live in the fantasy that he was completely oblivious.

Which meant I had to sit there, perfectly still, as Evan's fingertips played me as skillfully as an instrument. As my body warmed. As every inch of my skin became so sensitive that every tiny hair seemed to send sparks shooting through me.

By the time the taxi finally pulled up in front of our mystery destination, I was taut and ready and totally primed.

I didn't know where we were going, but I really hoped that getting naked was next on the agenda.

"I don't think he bought your excuse about the cold," I said, as I stood blindfolded on what I assumed was a sidewalk. "It's in the seventies this morning and he didn't even have the AC on."

Evan's arm held on to my elbow as he guided me forward. "You may be right. But I wanted what I wanted, and that was you."

"Hmm," I said, adding a hint of censure to my tone.

"Don't tell me you didn't enjoy it."

I frowned. "I take the Fifth."

He burst out laughing. "Fair enough. But I know the truth. You told me, remember? You're a woman who likes to let go. Who likes the rush. Who needs it."

I wanted desperately to peel the blindfold off and look at him. "I do," I said. "But it also scares me."

"That was the point, Lina. You were with me. You can do anything with me." He leaned in close, his lips brushing my ear. "Anything. Because I will always be there. I will always catch you if you fall."

I didn't know what to say. He'd managed to twist the moment around completely. From a casual sexual encounter in a taxi to a moment of pure intimacy.

"Evan," I said, turning blindly toward him and finding his face. I pulled him toward me for a kiss, deep and long and sweet.

When I pulled back, he gently stroked my cheek. "What was that for?"

"Wherever you're taking me, whatever we're doing, I know it's going to be amazing. And just in case you have me so distracted later I forget to say it, I wanted to say thank you now."

"You're welcome." He took my hand. "Are you ready to go inside?"

I nodded and let him lead the way.

"Distracted, huh?" he said as we entered a very air-conditioned room. "I can't imagine how you think I might distract you."

I grinned, absolutely delighted with the man, with the morning, with the whole damn world.

I knew better than to ask where we were. There was stone, not carpet, beneath my feet, and the space had an echo when we walked. It felt empty, too, and I assumed it was some sort of lobby. My assumption was confirmed when I heard the ding of an elevator. A moment later, we stepped onto one. And ascended, higher and higher and higher still.

"About that flying thing," I said. "If you're thinking about hang gliding off the roof of one of the sky-rises, then I think I'm going to have to exercise my veto power."

"That's tomorrow's agenda," he said. "Today's Sunday. I figured something less active would be appropriate."

I wanted to scream with frustration because I had absolutely no idea what he had up his sleeve, but I also didn't want to give him the satisfaction. So I stayed calm, cool, and collected. And kept my curiosity soundly buried.

Finally, the elevator slid to a smooth stop. The doors opened, and I heard a few people moving around, but not too many. I heard the clattering of dishes and—happily—I caught the scent of coffee.

"Know where we are?"

"One of the clubs? A breakfast buffet?" Uncle Jahn belonged to the Metropolitan Club and had taken me and Flynn there for drinks and appetizers to celebrate Flynn's first trip as a flight attendant.

"Not a bad guess," he said. "But no."

"Well, I give up."

"That's okay. You don't have long to wait now."

I'd been walking carefully, his hand on my elbow, and now he had me turn just slightly. The floor beneath us changed texture, and I heard the scrape of a chair.

"Here you go," he said, helping me sit. He stood behind me, his hands on my shoulders. He bent over, and his breath rippled my hair as he asked, so very gently, "Are you ready?"

"I think so." I didn't have a clue what I was supposed to be ready for, and he clearly expected me to be astounded. For a moment I feared that my reaction would disappoint him, but the fear faded quickly. If anyone knew how to overwhelm, it was Evan. "Yes," I said more firmly. "I'm ready."

"Close your eyes."

I did, effectively blocking out the tiny bits of light that had crept in under the mask. His fingers brushed my hair as he gripped the elastic and pulled the mask up and off my face. "All right," he said softly. "Open."

I did, and then gasped in awe and wonder. "Evan—oh my god."

I have no memory of moving, but I must have, because now

I was standing, and all of Chicago was spread out beneath and around me, and my heart was pounding because we were suspended above the city and all I could think was that there was no place more perfect that he could have brought me. "It's the Skydeck," I said. "You brought me to the Ledge."

"I did," he said, moving to stand beside me. I'd gone to the edge, and now my hands were pressed to the glass, but I wasn't looking out, I was looking down, watching the world falling away beneath our feet as we stood in this clear box that hung from the side of the Willis Tower.

"Are you ready for breakfast?"

"What?" I asked foolishly.

He took my shoulder and gently turned me around. I saw the chair where I'd originally been sitting next to a white cloth-covered table topped with dishes and a shiny silver coffeepot.

For a moment I frowned. "Breakfast? I've wanted to come here for breakfast since I learned they served, but I thought it was closed on Sundays."

"It is," Evan said. "I arranged catering for a private party."

"A party?" I asked, lifting a brow.

"A very small party," he said. "Will you join me for breakfast on this lovely Sunday morning, Ms. Raine?" he asked, holding out his hand and drawing me toward him.

"Yes, Mr. Black. I'd be delighted."

He held my chair out, and as I sat, I looked down at the city again. The world seemed to swirl around me, making me both dizzy and excited, making my heart swell and soar. But no matter what, I knew that I wouldn't go crashing down to earth. I was safe here. Safe on this ledge, and safe with Evan.

"Thank you," I said. "This is incredible. More than incredible, in fact. It's perfect."

"I told you I'd make you fly," he said.

"Yes," I agreed. "You did."

* * *

Esther Martin swooped into my cubicle, her smile as wide as her eyes were sad. She crossed the small space in one stride, arms outstretched, and folded me into the kind of genuinely emotional hug that most women of Esther's money and breeding usually eschewed.

"We've missed you," she said, releasing me. "Are you doing okay?"

I nodded. "Yeah, I miss him. But I'm doing okay."

"Oh, honey. We all miss him." She stood back so that she could look me up and down. "You look good. You got some sun."

I nodded. "I spent most of yesterday outside." I shrugged a little. "It was nice."

Nice, in fact, was an understatement. After a breakfast among the clouds, Evan and I spent the day like petals on the wind, soft and lazy and with no purpose other than to move and to explore the city. After breakfast on the Ledge, we'd walked from the Willis Tower all the way down the Magnificent Mile to the Oak Street Beach. I'd expected him to balk when I'd suggested it, because most people don't share my love of simply walking around big cities, soaking up the vibe and absorbing the energy. But Evan didn't complain, despite the fact that we walked about three miles even before our adventure truly started.

I pointed out my favorite haunts along the way, including the funky water tower. The real one, not the mall, though as far as shopping went, I fully approved of the multistoried shopping complex.

"It's a castle in the middle of the city," I'd said, tugging Evan to a stop and pointing at the building that had miraculously survived the Chicago Fire. I dragged him inside, ignoring his mock protests, and we stood with our hands pressed against the Plexiglas as we peered down at the tubes and equipment before going into the adjacent tourist center.

"Can I help you or answer any questions?" the clerk asked as we entered. And Evan, with a straight face, told him we were tourists with only thirty-six hours to spend in town, and we needed to figure out how to do everything.

The clerk, bless him, actually had some decent suggestions, and we left with a handful of brochures and a plan that started with bike rentals from the stands that dotted the city. Then we continued on to the beach, leaving the bikes parked as we walked barefoot in the sand.

"I don't have a favorite part of Chicago," I'd said. "But if I did, this might be it. How cool is it that we're in the middle of a continent and walking along a sandy beach?"

We'd gathered rocks to toss back into the water, drank beer at a beach-hut style restaurant, and watched an old man search for treasure with a metal detector. Then we'd backtracked to The Drake hotel and bought two cheap backpacks from the gift store downstairs. After that, we took our rented bikes and cruised along the lakefront and zipped through the parks, finally ending up at the famous Bean sculpture. We'd made faces at ourselves in the curved reflective surface and held hands while we walked underneath and peered up into the interior that seemed to me like the vortex of a black hole.

"Where to next?" he'd asked. "Wait, let me guess. The Art Institute?"

I paused beside my rented bike and grinned, delighted that he knew me so well. "Where else? After all, it's in keeping with today's theme."

"We have a theme?"

I moved toward him and took his hands in mine, then lifted myself on tiptoes to kiss him. "Art makes me feel like I'm soaring—and that's how I've felt all day with you. Hanging over the city at breakfast, walking hand in hand. And now, just looking in your eyes."

"Careful," he said, with a tease in his voice. "You'll make me blush."

I laughed aloud. "That, I'd like to see."

We left our bikes at the kiosk and continued strolling through Millennium Park toward the Art Institute. "Have you ever been to Europe?" I asked.

"A few times," he said.

"I haven't. I've always wanted to, though. I want to see the Louvre and the Sistine Chapel. I want to stand there and feel the power of what those men left behind because it's important and it's enduring and—" I cut myself off with a shake of my head.

"What?" he asked.

"Nothing. Never mind."

He reached for my hand and gave me a little tug.

"Nothing, really. Just random stupid thoughts."

"Those are the best kind for a Sunday afternoon stroll."

"Fine," I said, shaking my head in mock exasperation. "I was thinking about my dad. I love him, I do. But there's no passion in politics. There never has been for me. I did the work and I earned the degree, but it never got inside me, you know? Because it's not creation, it's consumption. Politics is all about taking what others created and divvying it up."

"And yet you're leaving for Washington."

I looked away, shrugging. "It's an excellent opportunity."

"It is," he said.

My eyes snapped to him. "But?"

"I just wonder if it's an excellent opportunity for you."

I didn't answer. I'd told Evan once that he truly saw me, but only now did I realize what that meant, and I wasn't sure I liked it. It was one thing for him to know what I wanted in bed. It was something else entirely for him to see so clearly inside of me.

At the time, I'd made a point of brushing his words away like so many gnats. Trivial and meaningless. No big deal at all.

And, because I didn't want to talk about art or politics or anything that even hinted at what I might want to do with my life, I suggested that we forget about the museum and take a cab to the Lincoln Park Zoo. It had been the perfect solution. We'd left the subject of my work and passions behind and spent the rest of the day walking hand in hand, buying soft-serve ice cream and soda to ward off the heat, then snapping pictures of the animals with our phones and texting them to each other.

It was silly. It was fun. It was just what I'd needed.

And after a dinner alfresco at a small Italian restaurant, we'd returned to the condo. During the drive, I'd fantasized about wild sexual escapades. About bound wrists and spanking and all sorts of new delights forged in Evan's erotic imagination. The thought had fired me, making me tingly with anticipation. But when we'd reached the apartment, the remainder of the evening didn't go as I'd planned at all. Instead, we'd made love lazily in the shower, then taken a bottle of wine up to the patio. We'd sat on the love seat, my head on his lap, his fingers stroking my hair, and talked about our day and our lives and everything and nothing.

It was, I think, the most romantic and sensual day of my life. And though I'd originally been drawn to Evan's wild side, I couldn't help but fear that somehow, someway, this sweet romanticism was the part of him that was truly dangerous to me.

Now I stood in my tiny cubicle with the memory clutched tight around me. I didn't want to let it go, much less share it with Esther, for fear that talking about it would lessen its vibrancy in my mind.

Instead, I just smiled, told her I was refreshed, and asked where she wanted to begin. "I'm sorry I've been gone so long. I'm guessing things have been piling up?"

"Now you're just being silly. Jahn needed you, and we've managed to muddle on." She pulled out my chair and sat on it, leaving me to lean against the desktop. "To be honest, things slowed down while he was sick. As callous as it sounds, we wanted to keep a low profile. Too much exposure might remind people, and then investors might get nervous."

"And now it's time to regroup," I said, essentially telling her that I understood. Howard Jahn Holdings & Acquisitions was in the business of buying and selling businesses, and although Jahn had hired some of the best and the brightest to go out in the world and evaluate all sorts of opportunities, Jahn was still the face of the company. His death was going to change things—no doubt about that. And I didn't fault the PR department for wanting to publicly downplay his infirmity. Now that he'd passed on, though, there was no avoiding reality.

"It is," she said. "But I think we're well covered. I actually wanted to talk to you about shifting your job responsibilities over to the foundation. Things are heating up over there."

"Because of the transfers?"

She nodded, then settled in to explain more fully. "Our goal is to grow the assets and income of the Jahn Foundation," Esther said, "and use that increased revenue to start a consistent program of distributions. Education, preservation, and restoration. Your uncle's interests centered on youth, art, and history. There are too many children who don't have access to the education they deserve, and too many exceptional documents and canvases that won't survive the decade, much less another millennium."

"I agree," I said, though I'm sure I sounded wary. If I was hearing her right, she was asking me to work for the foundation. And that, frankly, would be my dream job.

And then reality hit me. So hard, in fact, that I actually stumbled a bit, and was grateful that I was leaning up against the counter. "Esther," I said dully. "I'm sure whatever you have in mind would be wonderful. But I'm moving. I'm going to Washington," I explained, even as she gaped at me with wide, disbelieving eyes. "I'm going to work on the Hill."

"Oh." For a moment, she looked blank. Then her face bloomed. "But, sweetie, that's wonderful! Your uncle would be so proud of you."

"Would he?" I asked, hoping I didn't sound as desperate as I felt.

If she noticed anything odd in my tone, she didn't call me out on it. "My goodness, yes. He adored his brother as much as he admired him. To know that you're following your dad into politics would have thrilled him."

"I'm glad of that," I said sincerely.

"Of course, I'd hoped—but never mind. I'm just chattering on. And this isn't about me. I'm very proud of you, Angelina."

"Thanks."

"Well, this changes things." She flipped open her folio on my workspace and started sorting through papers. "We'll just plan to keep you in PR for the rest of your tenure. So why don't we head into the conference room and we can brainstorm a bit about consumer confidence."

I followed her, and we spent the next two hours talking about ways to keep HJH&A at the forefront of shareholders' minds, without freaking anyone out with the unavoidable fact that Howard Jahn would not be returning to the helm. Honestly, I'm not sure of the details we discussed; I was too busy thinking about lost opportunities.

I only fully tuned in, for that matter, when Esther sighed, closed her folio, and said, "I think that's enough for today. Though there is one more thing I'd like to ask you to do. It involves the foundation, though, so if you want to decline, I understand. But since you've had social contact with so many of Mr. Jahn's friends . . ."

"What is it?"

She explained that the one official act of the foundation since Jahn's death was to announce an upcoming fund-raiser and kick-off party. "We want to start this new phase in the life of the foundation with a bang. Tie it in a tasteful way to Jahn's passing. It is, after all, his legacy."

"How can I help?"

"We need to find a venue in which to host the function. To be honest, we've already been contacted by several local businesses and philanthropists interested in participating. It's going to be tricky. As soon as we pick one to host, we risk insulting the ones we decline—"

"—and losing their future charitable contributions," I said. "I get it."

"It's a job that requires diplomacy," Esther said, with a barely suppressed grin. "It seems to me a young woman with a burgeoning political career would be able to negotiate those land mines brilliantly."

"Or fail miserably and then escape to Washington?"

She laughed. "That, too."

I had to laugh as well. At least she was honest. And, frankly, the politics of society notwithstanding, it sounded like more fun than writing upbeat press releases for investors.

"Okay," I said. "I'm in."

"Excellent." She gathered her papers as my cell phone began to ring. "I'm going to get out of here so you can get that. And," she added, pointing a red lacquered nail at me, "so that I'm long gone by the time you change your mind."

I rolled my eyes and snatched up my phone, my heart doing a little butterfly flutter when I saw that it was from the number that Evan had given me over the weekend. "Hey," I said. "You called at the perfect time."

"I planned it that way, of course."

"Would I sound too desperate if I told you that anytime would be the perfect time?"

"If it's me that you're desperate for, I have no objections."

I giggled—god help me, I actually giggled. "Well, then. You've found me out. What's up?"

"Tonight. My place. Seven."

"All right," I said. "But I don't have a clue where you live."

"I'll send a car. To the condo or to your office?"

"Condo," I said. "A woman needs to freshen up before a date."

"Does she? Well then, I look forward to enjoying the results of her efforts."

"Yeah," I said. "I bet you do."

When I hung up, I was smiling. Maybe I was leaving town for a job I didn't really want, but at least for right now, I had it pretty damn good.

sixteen

"Here? Seriously?" I peered out the window of the Lexus that Evan had sent for me. We'd just turned into the entrance of Burnham Harbor, and now we were maneuvering our way through the slips. "I thought you were taking me to Mr. Black's house."

The driver, who'd introduced himself to me as Red, met my eyes in the rearview mirror. "I am, Ms. Raine."

"Yeah? He lives on a boat?" I had to admit it seemed pretty Evan-like. I mean, the guy constantly surprised me. And, honestly, it was pretty freaking cool. It added to the illusion that he could fly away at any moment—and that he could take me with him wherever he went.

I settled back in my seat, grinning, and watched as we passed slip after slip. I played a game with myself, trying to guess which boat was his, but each time we reached a boat that looked truly spectacular, Red just kept on driving. I was starting to think that Red had turned onto the wrong section and was just too proud to admit it, when we reached the very end.

Evan's boat was anchored in the very last slip, and as I stepped out of the Lexus I saw Evan on the deck wearing cargo shorts and a polo-style shirt. His hair was wind-tossed, and he looked like he'd spent most of the day on the water. For all I knew, maybe he had.

"Ahoy," I called, and he grinned like a boy, full of eagerness and life. "You have a houseboat."

"Your powers of observation are truly spectacular." He hurried toward the ramp that was set up for easy access and met me halfway. I'd boldly brought a backpack with a change of clothes, a toothbrush, and some makeup, and he took it off my shoulder. And although it may have been my imagination, I think he not only correctly guessed what I'd brought, but that he wholeheartedly approved.

It's a wonder I didn't trip walking up the ramp as I was so busy ogling the boat. It was massive, all white, and formed in sleek lines and curves that gave it a futuristic feel. I didn't know much about boats, but I knew it was huge. And I knew that it must have cost a fortune.

"So what made you decide to live on a houseboat?" I asked, once I'd reached the deck. I had to admit that even from the small peek I'd had so far, I could see the appeal. The deck was both spacious and well-appointed, with furniture designed for dining or lounging, fishing or swimming. Hell, it even had a hot tub.

"It was a whim," he said. "I'm not prone to them—I tend to plan out my moves in both my business and my personal life."

"Do you? What do you have planned for me?"

"A great many things," he said. "I promise you won't be disappointed."

"Oh." I swallowed, suddenly feeling very warm.

"To be fair, though," he continued, returning to the topic of the boat, "while this is technically a houseboat since I live on it, most people would call it a yacht." He shrugged. "I don't call it either. She's *His Girl Friday* to me."

I laughed, delighted. "I love it."

He inclined his head. "I'm glad you approve."

"But you still haven't told me why."

"I suppose the thought of living on a boat played to my fantasies of being a pirate. Of taking off whenever I want. And, of course, it has all the essential compartments for smuggling my ill-gotten gains."

"Well, of course," I said lightly, even though I was wondering if he meant it. "Who'd bother with a houseboat that wasn't well-equipped?"

"I knew you'd understand."

He cocked his head toward the stern. Or maybe it was starboard? I never could keep anything nautical straight in my head. At any rate, I followed him through a wooden door into a stunning salon that resembled a high-end condo's living room. That opened onto a dining area, and beyond that I assumed there was some sort of cockpit area, but I didn't see that because Evan led me down a small staircase to the next level that consisted of only one giant stateroom. The realization didn't sit well with me, primarily because it conjured up thoughts of all the women he'd undoubtedly entertained there—women who didn't come for platonic visits in which they slept in their own room. I mean, "Come back to my place" is a time-tested pickup line. But how much better must it be if the line is "Come back to my boat"?

"What's wrong?" he asked. "You look pensive."

"It's an ugly rumor," I countered. "I never think unless I can help it."

He kissed my nose. "Or maybe you think too much."

I frowned. Because with that, I was in total agreement.

Fortunately, his phone rang, distracting him from figuring

out what I'd been thinking about. He glanced at the display, then looked at me. "Sorry. I need to take this. There are bathing suits in the top left drawer. Why don't you put one on and join me back on deck?"

"Sure," I said, though inside I was cursing. Apparently, I'd been right. And not only did he bring women here, he brought so many that he provided clothing.

"Hey," he said as he took the call and left the room. "Talk to me."

And then he was gone and I was alone in the stateroom with another woman's bathing suit. Except that when I started to rummage through the drawer, I discovered that they all still had tags. I glanced toward the door, as if he was still there. As if I could somehow conjure him and, in doing so, I would understand all of his mysteries.

Since the drawer was spacious, I took the liberty of taking my clothes out of my bag and putting them inside. I picked an emerald green bikini, changed, and headed back up to the salon. He wasn't there, and so I continued on toward the deck in search of him.

He was still on the phone when I arrived, standing with his back to me as he faced the expanse of the lake. "Come on, man. You know me better than that, and I'm sure as hell not going to leave you hanging. Yeah, I'm thinking two years across the board. But we need to take care of all this California bullshit now. I know it's a mess, but it's going to get messier if the rumors are true and they're coming our way. Yeah, well, we need to be sure."

He laughed. "You're such an ass. Okay, fine. Hit me with the rest of it."

I heard his low whistle. "Neely's a prick, but you're right. This could develop into a problem. Cole's good, but—yeah, I know. It's not the kind of thing I should joke about. Let me plot out some options, and get back to you on this. As for all the other—what? No. You know damn well, the more volatile, the sooner I want out. Shit yeah, I'm becoming risk averse in my old age. As soon as you get close to thirty, your whole perspective changes."

He chuckled, then said a soft, "Fuck you, and don't give me grief. We've already talked about my reasons. I can't risk fucking things up for her."

I frowned, feeling like a voyeur even as I tried to make sense of the one-sided conversation. I don't think he realized I'd come on deck, and I sure as hell didn't know who "her" was. The word seemed to hang above his head, pulsing red in some giant cartoon bubble. I didn't want to be jealous—this thing between us was, by definition, a temporary arrangement. But while my head might know that, the rest of me was turning a jealous green as verdant as my suit.

Well, fuck.

I missed some of his conversation while I was off being jealous in my head, and the next thing I knew he was beside me. "I didn't hear you come up."

"I'm very light on my feet," I quipped.

"Are you?" he asked, then pulled me to him, my right hand in his left, and his right at my back, as if we were about to waltz.

Whatever angst I'd been feeling vanished. "Evan!"

He moved on the deck, leading me and—since I can barely ballroom dance with music, much less without—I had to give him points for avoiding my decidedly *not* light feet.

"I didn't mean to eavesdrop," I said. "But what's up with Neely?"

"Neely?"

I laughed. "Yeah, you remember him? The guy who got the real Creature Notebook. You mentioned him on the phone just now. Like I said, I didn't mean to eavesdrop, but his name kind of popped for me. Is it about the Da Vinci?"

"What could it have to do with the Da Vinci?" he asked,

which was a good point. Before I could concede that, though, he spun me around, then dipped me with a flourish. I laughed, enjoying this lighthearted side of him. Then he pulled me up and kissed me, and my bubbly mood shifted on a dime to something much more intense. I opened my mouth, my body firing immediately just as it always did around Evan. Foreplay might be fun, but I damn sure didn't need it. One touch, one look, and I was aroused. As if I was a lock and he was the only key that fit. As if we were two halves of a treasure map.

As if I'd been waiting for him my whole life.

I pulled away, suddenly confused.

"Lina?"

I heard the concern in his voice and forced myself to smile at him. "Sorry. I think I got a little light-headed when you dipped me."

"Sit," he said, leading me to a lounge chair. "I'll go get you some water."

He was gone before I could protest, and I was left on the deck, feeling guilty about my lie. Because the truth was, the more I got to know Evan, the more the fantasy I'd spun since I was a teenager was being shoved out by the reality of the man.

Reality.

There was a funny word.

I thought of the secrets that Jahn had said that Evan held. I thought of the allegations that Kevin had made. I thought of the dark flashes I'd seen in the alley and about Evan's own cryptic comments about being a bad bet. All those elements had played to my fantasy of a dangerous bad boy staying one step ahead of the law.

Now, though. Now I wanted more than the fantasy. I wanted to see the reality of the man.

I'd shined a light on the dark things that I kept hidden, and now I hoped that he would do the same.

"Hey," he said, hurrying back onto the deck. He had a sparkling water with lime, and as he handed it to me, he knelt beside me, his free hand going to my forehead.

I couldn't help but laugh. "I felt dizzy," I protested. "Not feverish."

"Maybe I'm just looking for an excuse to touch you," he said.

My mouth curved into a smile. "You don't need an excuse."

"No? I'm very glad to hear that." He glanced back toward the stairs leading below. "Can I entice you with baked Brie?"

"Um, yeah. I love Brie," I said honestly.

"I know. Jahn used to make a point of buying it before you came each summer."

"And you remember that?" I was grinning like an idiot.

"I remember a lot of things. Green beans wrapped in bacon. Baked potato with no butter but tons of sour cream. And steaks medium rare."

I narrowed my eyes. "I thought you couldn't cook."

"For you, I'm making the effort."

I held out my hands and let him pull me to my feet. I caught him in a kiss—slow and wet and sensual. "Should I feel special, or do you cook for all the women you bring to your boat?" I was teasing—well, mostly—but his response was one-hundred-percent serious.

"I've never brought a woman to the boat."

"Oh." I trembled a little in his arms, warmed by the way he was looking at me. As if he never wanted to look away. And suddenly, I was lost. I didn't fully understand the effect he had on me, on my body. All I knew was that I could never have enough of him. "Evan." His name felt ripped from me. "God, Evan, I want the Brie—I do. But right now, all I really want is for you to fuck me."

His mouth curved in a slow, sexy smile, and all I could think in that moment was that it was my smile. Right now, for however long it lasted, this man was all mine. Every hard, delicious inch of him.

Slowly, he traced his finger over the top band of the bikini bottoms. I bit my lower lip, my belly tightening and my skin prickling as I anticipated that finger dipping inside the band, then sliding lower and lower until—

He pulled his hand away, grinning when I looked accusingly at him. "Patience is a virtue, Lina. And anticipation is one hell of an aphrodisiac."

"Maybe," I said sulkily. "But in case you hadn't noticed, I don't need an aphrodisiac with you."

"That's very good to know." He stepped closer to me, then let his gaze rake over me. I tried not to react, but damn me, my breasts felt heavier, my nipples tighter. And when he let his gaze linger at the junction of my thighs, my cunt tightened in response to an unfulfilled demand—because the bastard really wasn't touching me. "I should keep you perpetually like this," he said, his voice low and smooth. "All hot and wet and wanting me."

I swallowed, and I swear it was all I could do not to slide my own fingers down inside the damn bathing suit. "That's how I always am," I said, because he already knew it, and because there was no reason to hide anything from this man.

"I'm very glad to hear it," he said. "Especially since I feel the same way. You make me burn, Lina."

He brushed his fingertips over my shoulder, then trailed them lazily down my arm, making me shiver. And then, just as my eyes started to flutter shut, he pulled his hand away.

I blinked at him, wanting more, but he just shook his head. "I think that's enough for now," he said, his voice cocky.

"You're an asshole, Evan Black. You know that, right?"

"Believe me, sweetheart, I've been called worse." He gave me a gentle tug. "Come on. I should start dinner."

"Maybe I should wait here. The lounge chair is pretty comfortable. I could finish what you started."

"Oh, no you don't." He took my hand and tugged me close. "I want you frustrated, baby. No touching. Your cunt belongs to me. Your orgasm belongs to me. I want every ripple of pleasure that courses through your body to come from me. Do you understand?"

I nodded, feeling suddenly a little unstable, and not because of the rocking of the boat. And I had to admit that although I might be sexually frustrated at that moment, there was no denying that the promise in his words made it all worthwhile.

I grabbed a terry-cloth cover-up from the arm of a lounge chair and followed him to the kitchen, though he wasted no time telling me that it was called a galley. True to his word, there was Brie, and he set it out along with a selection of crackers and fruit that we nibbled on as he went about making dinner, cutting the ends off the green beans, testing the potatoes in the oven, seasoning the steaks.

I watched him in silence, wondering about all the facets of Evan Black, both seen and unseen.

I wanted to know everything, and before I could talk myself out of it, I asked the question that was most on my mind. "Evan," I said. "Why do you say you're not a safe bet?"

He looked up from where he was uncorking a bottle of wine. "There are a lot of reasons," he said, and I heard the hint of caution in his voice.

"I'd like to know."

"Are you giving up on the idea of going to Washington?"

"What?" I shook my head, confused. "No. Why would you think so?"

He held my eyes for a long moment, and though I tried to figure out what he was thinking, I found no clue in his expression. "Never mind," he said. "It doesn't matter."

I took the glass of wine he handed me, then took a sip. I

considered dropping the whole thing. He was right, after all. I wasn't staying. In three weeks, I'd be gone. So what did it matter if I never dug beneath that tarnish to see the man hidden inside?

Except it did matter. I wasn't entirely sure why, but it mattered a lot.

"Is it because of the kind of business you're in?"

"You mean the strip club?"

"I mean whatever you do that makes you not a safe bet."

He leaned back against the counter and took a sip of his own wine, his eyes never leaving my face. "I think I know a certain FBI agent who's been putting ideas into your head."

I licked my lips, suddenly unsure that I should have opened this door. "Listen, never mind. I don't want to spoil dinner."

"I haven't even put the steaks on yet. We have time." He put his wineglass down and crossed the galley so that he was opposite me across the bar. "What did Kevin say?"

I considered avoiding the question, but knew Evan well enough to know that he'd press. "He said that the FBI was watching you. That you're into all sorts of shit. He wasn't specific."

"And you believe him." There was no emotion in his voice. No anger. No nothing. Just a question, spoken in a monotone.

"I didn't say that. All I want to know is why you'd tell me that you're not a safe bet."

"Because it's the truth," he said.

"Evan . . ."

"What?" His tone had barely changed, but somehow it was harsher now. "You want me to fill up your glass and tell you a bedtime story? Something that excites you? Something that makes you feel close to the kind of guy who can make you feel wild?"

I looked away, because that was what had started all of this, but now I wanted so much more.

"Something fast-paced, right? Maybe the story of a kid

whose family went to shit when he was still in high school? Who turned to doing whatever the hell he could to make a buck in order to keep his family from having to live on the streets. Drugs. Stolen merchandise. Stolen cars. Whatever he could think of. And maybe this story's a tragedy, do you think?"

He was speaking fast, but every word was measured. As for me, I was holding my breath, taking in every word, understanding that he was giving me a view of the inside of Evan Black, and I was doing my damnedest to see the truth behind the tale he was spinning.

"Maybe he gets arrested and sent to one of those teen work camps. The whole scared-straight bullshit. But let's not write a typical ending. Let's not have it really work. Let's touch on some irony. Let's have our boy meet some other kids. Two others, and they become tight. But scared straight? Not hardly."

Cole. Tyler.

I remembered Jahn telling me that the three had met at some camp when they were teens. Holy shit.

"And then when the three got smart," he said, leaving the kitchen area and circling the bar, "they learned how to dodge the system. How to take risks. How to do whatever they needed to do to get by, because they all three knew that the universe doesn't play fair." He was right in front of me, all heat and power and control. "And if the universe doesn't play by the rules, then why the fuck should they?"

"They shouldn't," I said as my pulse pounded in my ears.

He stroked my bare arms as I stood there feeling exposed despite the fact that I'd slipped the short-sleeved cover-up on over the tiny bathing suit. "You don't want a safe bet, Lina," he said, his voice low. "Do you?"

"No."

"You want a man who lives on the edge. That's the kind of thing that gets you hot, isn't it?" His fingers toyed with the white zipper pull at the base of my throat.

"Yes," I admitted as he pushed the cover-up off my shoulders. It fell to the floor in a puddle of white terry cloth. Evan's palms caressed my arms, sliding up and down, and it wasn't mere friction that sent the heat coursing through me.

"You want a man who likes to fly," he said, tracing his fingertip over the curve of my breasts along the outline of my bikini top.

My breath became ragged. My skin felt prickly. And behind that tiny scrap of material, my nipples were painfully hard.

"You want a little bit of danger." His finger slipped under the material to flick my nipple, making me gasp. "You want to know that the man in your bed doesn't play by the rules." That same finger trailed down my belly to the band of my bikini bottom.

I shifted my stance, spreading my legs a bit, and feeling my cheeks heat when I heard his soft, knowing chuckle.

"Tell me I'm right," he demanded, though he already knew it was true.

"You're right," I said.

"Tell me you want me to fuck you."

"I do." I felt the charge through me, like I was touching a live wire. I closed my eyes. "I want you, Evan. I want you to fuck me."

"Take off the top," he said.

I opened my eyes and found him looking not at my breasts, but at my face. Our eyes locked, and I swallowed, the force of the emotion I saw in his eyes making me weak. I reached back, then untied the string between my shoulder blades. Then I reached higher and brushed my hair aside before tugging at the bow that was the only thing now holding the top in place. I let it fall, then stood there in front of him, my breasts bare and heavy, my nipples hard and tight and practically begging for his touch.

He moved closer, then pressed his thumb against his mouth,

making it wet before rubbing it slowly over my sensitive nipple. I felt the shock of his touch all the way through me, making me squirm as liquid pleasure pooled between my legs, warm and enticing.

He reached out, cupping my breasts in his palms, then bent to suckle me, so slowly and thoroughly that I had to grasp the back of a stool for fear that I would collapse to the ground.

When he pulled back, I felt the chill of the air on my damp breasts and saw his soft smile of satisfaction. I dragged my teeth over my lower lip, wondering where he would touch me next.

I wasn't surprised when he told me to drop my bikini bottom. I did without hesitation, and I saw the heat flare in his eyes. I saw, too, the bulge at the front of his shorts.

He knelt in front of me, then ran his fingertip down my pubis. I was bare, every fold visible and swollen with desire. I was sensitive—so damned sensitive, and when he bent close and blew a soft stream of air across my clit, I thought I would come right then.

"That's my girl," he said. "I love looking at you." He leaned closer, then slowly licked me along my slit all the way up to my belly button, the sensation so surprising and erotic that I cried out, unable to hold back either the sound or the shimmers of pleasure that shook my body.

He stood, and I wanted to scream with protest. I wanted more. I wanted his tongue on me, his fingers stroking me, his cock inside me. I wanted it all right then, all at once. I wanted to be so overwhelmed with sensation that I lost myself, and floated away in a haze that was only Evan.

But he wasn't moving that fast. He was doling out pleasure, and as much as I wanted the assault, I had to admit that this was fine, too.

He held out his hand for me, then led me toward the stairs. "Where are we going?"

"The deck," he said, and though I considered protesting—

what if there were other people around?—I held my tongue. I was pretty sure we were alone. And even if we weren't, I couldn't deny the excitement that came from the possibility of being watched.

"It's time for dessert."

"Oh." I decided not to ask what had happened to dinner. "What's for dessert?"

"You are," he said, with an enigmatic grin.

We arrived on the deck and he walked me to one of the large, padded lounge chairs. The sun had finished its descent and now the lake was dark.

"Lay down," he said, and I complied, looking up at the night sky, the stars hidden behind the gray sheen of the city's glow.

He ran his finger down the length of my body, slowing as he slipped between my legs, cupping my heat and then sliding two fingers deep inside me. I spread my legs wider, wanting more of him, knowing I was wet enough that I could take more, that he could stretch me as wide as he wanted.

But he didn't. Instead, he moved away, smiled down at me, and returned below.

I remained on the lounge, frustrated.

And then, when he didn't return right away, I slipped my own hand between my legs, slowly circling my clit, wanting to take the edge off the pressure building inside me.

"Naughty," Evan said, his voice soft from where he stood on the far side of the deck. "That's for me to touch, and me only."

"I—"

"I'm very proprietary about what belongs to me," he said. "But we'll worry about your punishment later. Right now, I have a treat."

He moved closer, and I could see that he was holding a bowl full of strawberries. There was a can tucked under his arm, too, and it took me a second to recognize it as whipped cream.

I laughed, then stopped when he pressed a fingertip to my

lips. Then he took a strawberry and fed it to me. It was ripe and delicious, and I sighed with satisfaction.

"Now close your eyes," he said. "And maybe I'll give you a few more."

I bit back a grin, but complied. Then I heard the shaking of the can. Then the aerosol sound of the cream being dispensed.

And then I felt the cool, soft, wet chill on my breast. Then down my belly. Then all the way to my sex.

"Oh, god, Evan. Holy fuck, that feels good. Strange. Good."

"I'm very glad to hear it. Now open your eyes but don't move."

I obeyed and felt every tiny sensation as he took a single strawberry, then rubbed it over my cream-covered breast before popping it in his mouth. He took another, then another. And all the while it was all I could do to lay still.

"I've made a bit of a mess," he said, with a devilish grin. "I better clean it up." He bent his mouth to my breast, and I gasped and squirmed as he licked every bit of cream up, driving me just a little bit crazy in the process.

And then he used a berry to follow the trail down my belly.

My stomach muscles twitched as he moved lower and lower. My sex throbbed. I was so hot that I was certain the cream had melted into a liquid goo. But he wasn't inclined to hurry. His tongue laved me all over, lapping up the cream, moaning with pleasure as he swallowed and tasted, nipped and sucked.

In front of me, the skyline rose, the buildings lit like jewels against the night sky. I felt much like those buildings, as if I was lit from within, only a few pinpricks of illumination escaping from wherever his tongue had seen fit to tease me.

He was teasing lower and lower until finally there was just the triangle of my sex. Then my slick folds, a combination of my own arousal and the froth of cream.

His tongue stroked me, deeply and efficiently, as if it was his obligation to get every last bit of cream. And with each lave of his tongue, I felt the orgasm building inside me, tighter and tighter and tighter, until finally I soared even higher than the skyline and burned at least as bright as the lights in the sky.

"Wow," I said, when I came back to earth. "I like your dessert."

I eyed him hungrily, noting his erection beneath his shorts before tilting my head up to meet his eyes. "Got any more cream?" I asked, then made a show of licking my lips. "Because if you do, I know exactly what kind of treat I want."

His laugh reverberated through me. "Sweetheart," he said as he unbuttoned his shorts. "You can have as much as you want."

seventeen

I spent the next few nights on the boat with him, popping into the condo only to reassure Peterson I was alive and get fresh clothes. Most nights we spent on the boat, making love under the stars, relaxing on the deck with wine, or snuggling in the stateroom and watching everything from *The Terminator* to *The Hangover* to *The Untouchables*. We settled into a comfortable familiarity that I loved, and the only time I felt unhappy or insecure at all was when I remembered that this was all going to end—and that the end was coming soon.

"Evan," I'd say, and he would know, just from the tone of my voice. He'd pull me into his arms and kiss me and tell me that the only thing that mattered was the moment. And as he made love to me, slowly and sweetly, I tried hard—so hard—to believe him.

Sometimes, I even came close.

Not that we were complete shut-ins. I joined him one night at a reception for all the students in the art class that Cole taught at a community center right on the edge of Wrigleyville. The center's walls were now studded with everything from still lifes to graffiti-like murals to delicate pencil sketches. And Cole was making the rounds like a proud parent, with Evan looking almost as proud as his friend.

"So what do you think, baby girl?" Cole asked, pulling me into a hug.

"I'm impressed," I said. "And your students look like they're having a great time." It was true. The students, who ranged in age from twelve to eighty, were making the rounds like celebrities. As far as I could tell, Cole's reception was the highlight of their year. "Where's Tyler?" I asked, realizing that I hadn't seen his face among the crowd.

"California," Evan said.

I remembered the phone call I'd overheard on the boat. "Trouble?"

"Nothing he can't handle." He took my arm. "We're going to go find a drink," he said to Cole. "Good job, man."

"Thanks, buddy."

I glanced around the cavernous room as he led me to the bar. "Maybe I should do something like this for the foundation's fund-raiser," I said. "Instead of picking a host, I could just have it on neutral territory."

"Who's vying for the honor?" Evan asked, as we waited for the bartender to make our drinks.

"Who isn't? And the moment I pick someone, I've basically said fuck you to all the others. I'm not sure I want to piss off the Who's Who of Chicago. There's Thomas Claymore. Reginald Berry. I mean, the list just goes on and on. Even Victor Neely is on it, and you know how much I love him." I made a sour face.

"Sweetheart, I feel just the same."

"I have to admit he's not high on my list of potentials. Not only could Jahn not stand him, but the prick isn't even offering to donate any of his collection to the foundation. Apparently he's already finalized arrangements to donate his manuscript collection to a museum in Belgium. And I think he's negotiating with the British Museum about some of his paintings." I peered at Evan's face. "What's wrong?"

"I'd heard rumors; I didn't realize the Belgium deal was in the can."

"You're thinking of the Creature Notebook, aren't you?"

His mouth curved up in a humorless smile as he took his Scotch from the bartender and handed me my wine. "How well you know me."

"Yeah, well, I was thinking of it, too. I'd love to get the original notebook for the foundation. I even asked Esther to approach him about it."

"You did? What did he say?"

"No go. I wasn't terribly surprised. He paid a shitload to keep that notebook out of Jahn's private collection, and I don't see him willingly donating it now."

"I don't, either," Evan said. His brow was furrowed, as if he was considering a thorny business problem.

"What is it?"

"I just don't like the guy." He glanced around the room, and I saw him lock onto Cole. "I need to run something by Cole. Will you be okay by yourself for a moment?"

I laughed. "I'm the daughter of the man who's going to be the next vice presidential candidate," I said. "Trust me when I say that I can fake my way through any party on the planet."

He kissed my cheek. "In that case, I'll be back in a minute."

As I watched him walk away, I couldn't help but wonder what was so urgent that he needed to discuss it with Cole right then—and why the Creature Notebook had reminded him.

Not that I had long to think about it. Cole had done the reception up right for his students, and had invited more than a few of Chicago's elite, and I soon found myself chatting with Thomas Claymore, who—under the guise of polite chitchat—made his bid to host the foundation's gala.

I listened politely, then managed to extricate myself, talking first with a young woman who was one of Cole's students and then with a short man in a perfectly tailored suit who held out his hand in greeting.

"Ms. Raine," he said, his face bland. "So glad to see you here."

"Thank you," I said. "I'm sorry, I didn't catch your name."

"Larry," he said, still holding my hand.

I started to gently tug my hand free, but Larry tightened his grip. I frowned, assuming he was one of those men who just never quite managed the art of the handshake. But then his fingers tightened even more, and before he spoke, I felt the hairs on the back of my neck prickle in warning.

"Tell your boyfriend and his buddies to back off," he said, without any particular menace in his voice. And it was his pleasant tone that made the conversation that much creepier. "Tell them that if they don't, there's going to be trouble. More trouble. Tell them that's a promise. You understand?"

"I—" I wanted to play it cool. To toss some brilliant comeback at him. To show that I wasn't scared at all. But it wasn't true, and I wasn't that much of an actress. So all I did was gape at him, my mouth open like some frantic, hooked fish.

He stared at my face, his previously bland features now turning menacing. "Yeah, I think you do."

Then he yanked his hand free, tipped his head, and disappeared into the crowd. I stood there, my blood so chilled I felt frozen to the spot. *Evan.* I willed myself to move. I needed to find Evan. I needed to warn him. To point this guy Larry out to him. To ask him what the hell was going on. *Move, dammit, move.*

I did. One step, then another.

And then one more until motion felt normal again.

But it wasn't Evan I found when I finally made it across the room. It was Kevin.

I forced a smile. "Hello. I didn't realize you were here."

"Angie," he said. "I've missed you."

I smiled again, feeling awkward, because I didn't say the expected reply—that I missed him, too.

But I didn't. I didn't miss him at all. And the truth was, I wished he'd just move on.

Unfortunately, Kevin was not in tune with what I wanted. That, of course, had been one of our problems all along.

"So who was that you were just talking to?" he asked.

That prickly, fearful feeling returned. "I—I'm not sure. Just some guy."

"I thought perhaps you knew him," Kevin said, in the kind of voice that suggested he knew exactly who Larry was—and why Larry'd come here. "He seemed very intense." He took a step closer to me. "I almost came over to ask if I could help you. Should I have? Did you need help, Angie?"

I forced myself to meet his eyes. Forced myself to mask the fear.

I could only hope that I succeeded. "No, it was fine. Just some guy." I lifted a shoulder in a shrug. "I think you're reading too much into things, Kevin."

"Am I?" His mouth curved down in a frown. "I don't know." He paused long enough that I actually thought he was going to say goodbye. But it wasn't my day for good luck.

"Looks like things have gotten serious between you and Black."

I said nothing, but inside I was terrified. Because I could read between the lines easily enough. Larry was bad news. Someone from the life that Evan kept hidden. And Kevin worked for the FBI.

"I thought you were moving to Washington," he pressed.

"I am," I said warily—was he really letting me off the hook that easily? "My mom is planning a wardrobe shopping spree as soon as I get to town. And my dad emailed listings for about a billion possible condos."

I was smiling like an idiot, and I was damn sure that I was trying too hard.

"So what's this with Black?" he asked, destroying my fantasy that he'd dropped the subject. "Just one of those good girl/bad boy flings?"

"What the hell, Kevin?" I'd intended my tone to sound sharp—the perfect *fuck off* exit point for this conversation. But instead, it came out tired and a little wary.

"I still care about you. More, I worry about you."

I held up a hand. "This isn't a conversation we're having." I had to move. Had to get out of there. But when I started to walk away, he grabbed my arm. I shook it free. "Jesus, Kev—"

"If you don't get out, I don't know that I'll be able to pull you out."

"I don't know what you're talking about," I snapped. Not exactly a lie, but not the truth, either.

"You know," he said. "Because I already told you, and I told you more than I should. He's bad news, Angie. And so are Cole August and Tyler Sharp. Stay away from them."

My heart was pounding so hard that I could barely hear my own words through the thrumming in my ears. "You know what, Kevin? I'd like to say it was a pleasure running into you, but that would be a huge lie. Now if you'll excuse me, I'm going to go find my date."

Except I didn't go find Evan. I moved out of the main room into one of the smaller adjoining rooms, then leaned against the wall, closed my eyes, and concentrated on breathing as I tried to get my shit together.

What the hell was wrong with me?

I'd known almost from the beginning that the stuff Kevin

said about Evan was probably true. That there was illegal shit going on in the background. And, hell, hadn't Evan almost—*almost*—even confessed as much to me? And, damn me, hadn't the possibility made me hot? The possibility that Evan was pulling one over on the FBI made him larger than life. Exciting. Sensual. Thrilling.

But now—

Now with worms like Larry approaching me and Kevin hounding me—

Oh, god, now it all felt too real. Too scary.

I remembered the twisting, nausea-inducing fear when I'd been arrested. No, not fear. *Terror.* The knowledge that everything I'd worked for and loved could be ripped away from me in an instant, pulled out from under me and replaced with bars and a cold floor and the eyes of the world looking hard at me and knowing that I screwed up.

I didn't want that for Evan—not for any of the knights.

Even more, I didn't want it for me. Didn't want the risk of being forced to testify. To sit in a small room with questions tossed at me. And didn't want the risk that someone I loved would be yanked away from me.

Loved.

I squeezed my eyes tight, pushing the thought away. Breathing deep. Trying desperately to keep myself from coming completely undone.

A soft tap on the door frame had me almost jumping out of my skin. I opened my eyes and whipped my head around to face Evan.

"What's wrong?"

I managed a thin smile. "That obvious?"

He moved to my side. "I know you."

"So does some guy named Larry." I watched him as I spoke, saw the tension run through him. "He gave me a message. I'm supposed to tell you to back off." I sucked in a breath. "Will you tell me who he is?"

He said nothing for a minute, then he lifted his hand, displaying his knuckles. "I mentioned him before," he said. "He's one of the assholes who was messing with the girls."

"Oh." I thought about that, then decided not to press for more. Whatever was going on under the surface, Evan already knew about it. And I didn't see even a hint of fear in his eyes. I did, however, see a spark of anger as he reached out and gently stroked my cheek.

"He scared you."

"He was creepy," I admitted. "But I'm okay now." I looked in his eyes and realized it was true. As corny as it sounded, I was okay now because Evan was beside me.

"I saw you talking to Kevin."

"Lucky me."

"Everything okay there, too?"

I nodded. What was I going to say? That I'd realized I was terrified for Evan and, oh, by the way, I might be falling in love with him, too? I settled for, "Yeah. Everything's fine. He saw me talking to Larry, too."

I met his eyes, and though he only nodded, I knew he understood my unspoken message: *Be careful. Please, please be careful.*

"What else did he say?"

"He said that he missed me."

"I see." I saw the vulnerability in his eyes, and I had to bite back a gasp as a sudden realization shook me. Evan might be everything that Kevin accused him of. He might be dangerous as hell. But right then, I had the power to hurt him.

I reached out and brushed my thumb over his lip. "I told him that I didn't miss him at all," I said.

He held my eyes for what felt like eternity. I saw relief there. And I saw what I wanted to believe was love.

After a moment, he blinked. "I need to take care of something," he said gently, and though I didn't ask, I had a feeling that Larry was the reason for this change in plans. "It shouldn't take long. Wait for me at the boat?"

My smile felt watery. "I think I'll go home instead," I said. I wanted to be on familiar ground with my thoughts.

Evan eyed me cautiously. "You're sure everything is okay?"

I leaned close and kissed him hard and slow and deep. "Everything's fine. My dad emailed over a bunch of pictures of condos. I should look at them, you know."

His expression hardened. "Sure. He's probably expecting your reply."

"Come over later?"

"As soon as I can."

"Good," I said.

"I'll have Red take you home. I'll ride with Cole."

The drive only took a few minutes, and I was up the elevator, in the condo, and pouring a glass of wine in less than an hour. There was a message from Evan on my phone, and I realized he must have called in the short span of time when I had no service in the elevator.

"Change of plans. I have to fly to Indiana to take care of a few things, but I'll be back tomorrow. Have a good day at work. I'll be thinking of you."

I carried my wine to bed and repeated his words in my head. I'd be thinking of him, too. About him. About threats and crimes and the FBI. About Washington.

And, yes. About flying.

I stayed awake as long as I could, fighting sleep. For the last few days, there'd been no nightmares. But tonight, without Evan beside me, I knew that they would come again. Salt-water-scented dreams punctuated by the hollow screams of my sister. Dreams that reached out and grabbed me from sleep, so pernicious that they even followed me to work the next day where I sat, bleary-eyed at my desk, and tried to focus on Kat's voice, tinny and thin over the phone.

"Kevin's a prick," she was saying. "He's just flashing his badge around so he can feel like a badass."

"Maybe. I don't know." I'd told her about Kevin, but not about Larry. "But I don't want to think about Kevin at all." I sighed. "I still haven't heard from Evan today. I need a distraction. Want to grab a drink? Flynn's working tonight. We could go harass him at the bar."

"Sounds like fun. See you there around eight?"

"Perfect."

I left a message for Flynn as soon as I got home from work telling him to expect us that evening. And then, since I had a couple of hours to kill before I changed and headed to the saloon, I decided to take a sketchpad and a glass of wine and head up to the patio.

I was sketching Evan's face from memory when the intercom on the bar buzzed, followed by Peterson's cultured voice. "Mr. Black is here. May I send him up?"

I pushed the button to reply. "He's here? Or he's on the phone?"

"He's standing right in front of me."

My pulse quickened. "Send him up." I stood and started pacing. I was so damn eager that I felt like a fool. He'd been gone less than twenty-four hours, and I felt like he'd been away for a year.

In other words, I had it bad.

In other words, in about a week, I was going to be royally screwed.

Dangerous. Yeah. Evan Black was as dangerous as they came.

I heard him push open the door, and I sprinted in that direction, only to skid to a stop when he emerged, looking relaxed and windblown and sexy as hell.

I wanted to stand there and soak in the wonder of him. I wanted this moment, when it was just the two of us, and no secrets and no threats.

Then he held out his arms and I collapsed into them, overwhelmed by the sudden, inescapable feeling that this was like coming home.

Except it was only an illusion.

I knew the surface of his secrets, but only what he'd revealed to me and only as an allegory. And while I'd been telling myself that was okay since I was leaving—that it was for the best, even—the truth was I wanted more. I wanted so much more.

Because I'd realized that it wasn't the fantasy I'd spun about Evan Black that gave me that thrill I craved so much—it was the man himself. His presence, his humor, his tenderness. Even his secrets.

And all I wanted in that moment was to know him. To really and truly know him.

"What is it?" he asked, stepping back to take a good, long look at my face.

I half-laughed. What was it I'd said? That he saw me? Apparently, I'd been dead on the money with that one. There was no keeping things hidden from this man.

I wanted to beg him to tell me his secrets, but I was desperately afraid that if I asked he would say no. And I didn't want to face that, not right then. Not when he'd just walked through my door.

And so I kept my own secret, hiding my real needs behind a false smile. "It's nothing," I said. "Just that I didn't expect you tonight, and I already have plans with Kat and Flynn at the pub. But I can break them."

"Don't do that. I'll go with you. Cole wanted to grab a drink tonight anyway. I'll tell him to meet us."

"Yeah?" I couldn't help my smile. It felt so nice—so *normal*—to be planning an evening out with friends. "What about Tyler?"

"Tyler thinks that you and I are a bad idea."

I nodded, my chest feeling unwelcomely tight. I loved Tyler like a brother and hated this feeling that I was disappointing him somehow. "But Cole doesn't?" He sure as hell hadn't been the picture of support at Destiny.

The corner of Evan's mouth quirked up. "He thinks we're a bad idea, too. But he also knows you're leaving soon. He said we might as well get each other out of our systems while we have the chance."

"I see." My stomach felt like it was filled with rocks. "Well. There you go. I always knew Cole was a smart guy." My smile felt wobbly. "A fling before Washington. Almost sounds like the name of a really bad movie."

I tried to force a grin, but Evan's expression was entirely humorless. He reached out and gently stroked my jawline. "It won't ever happen, you know. It's not possible that you would ever be out of my system. You could walk away right now, and even if I never saw you again, I would always hold you tight inside me."

The rocks dissolved, and I felt lighter than air. I couldn't seem to form a proper response, but when I lifted myself up on my toes and pressed my lips to his, I think he understood. His mouth tasted like mint, and though it had only been one night, I missed him like crazy. I didn't even want to think about how I was going to survive in Washington. If nothing else, I supposed Congressman Winslow was about to get himself the best damn employee ever, because I was going to dive so deep into my work that I didn't have time or energy to think of anything else, not even the man I was falling in love with.

I trembled in his arms, finally acknowledging the thought I'd tried to ignore at the art exhibition. I'd fallen for Evan Black years ago. But I'd fallen in love within the last few days. When I had to leave, it would be a different kind of fall altogether.

"Hey," he said, breaking our kiss and then dipping his head

to brush his lips over the tip of my nose. "Tell me what you're thinking."

"That I want you inside me," I said.

He glanced at his watch, then back up at me. His smile was slow and sensual and completely melted me. "What time are we supposed to be at the pub?"

"Do you care if we're late?"

"Hell no," he said.

"Then it doesn't matter." I pressed against him. "We should go down to the bedroom."

"We should," he agreed.

"I don't want to move."

"Then don't."

"I want it hard," I said. "No talk, no niceties. Just you inside me five minutes ago."

"Jesus, Lina," he growled, then scooped me up so that my legs were around his waist. We were only a few feet from the kitchen area, and he plunked me down on the countertop, yanking my skirt up in the process, then ripping his jeans open so fast I was surprised the buttons didn't pop. I spread my legs, wanting him, unable to wait even another second, and then reached down to try to fumble out of my panties.

"No," he said, and as I tilted my head up in question, he reached out and tugged the crotch of my panties roughly to one side. He thrust two fingers inside me, so hard and fast and deep that I cried out, and then he moved in between my legs, his cock positioned now where his fingers used to be. I was already soaked, but as soon as I looked down at where our bodies were joined—at the way he was moving inside me and the way my body was drawing him in—I got even wetter still.

"Harder," I demanded as he pistoned against me, his hands on my hips holding me in place even as I leaned back, bracing myself with my hands on the counter. "Yes, please, *more*." I'd lost the ability to form a coherent thought. I was need only. I was desire.

And then—faster than I could ever remember coming in my life—I burst into a wild flurry of molecules, everything I was melting into everything that was Evan.

"Baby." He sighed, his body still trembling against mine as I clung to him.

After a moment, I pulled reluctantly away. "I should probably change before we go."

"No," he said, as he reached for some napkins and cleaned us both up. "Keep the skirt and the panties on."

"Really?"

"I like it," he said. "I like knowing you're freshly fucked. That just a few minutes ago your legs were wide and I was deep inside you. I like you sitting there in your little work outfit looking all proper, and knowing that I'm the reason your panties are damp. It reminds me that you're mine. At least for a few more days."

"I am yours," I said. *I always will be.*

I didn't say the last part aloud, but he knew it. How could he not? Hadn't I learned that Evan Black knew me better than anyone?

"I'm serious," Kat said, holding up her third beer. "I think the two of you should go skydiving."

I glanced at Evan, who was clearly amused by my very drunk friend.

"And why would we want to do that?" Evan asked.

"Well," Kat said, leaning across the table with a very serious expression. "In case you hadn't noticed, our little Angie is a bit of a thrillseeker."

"No," Evan said, his voice laced with mock surprise.

"It's true." Kat nodded a few times too many, as if she was

trying to mimic a bobblehead doll. "And you need to make sure that she gets it out of her system, because once she moves to D.C., she's going to be boring as shit. *Daddy issues,*" she added, in a mock whisper. "It's true. Honest."

"What's true is that you are taking a taxi home," I said, forcing myself to smile and sound lighthearted when I really wanted to strangle my friend. My move was barreling down on me, and I didn't want to be reminded of it, thank you very much. Even more, I didn't want Evan reminded of it.

"Are you suggesting I'm drunk?"

"Not suggesting at all. Flat-out stating."

"Drunk or not," Evan said, "I think your friend has a great idea. Shall I arrange for a skydiving session?"

"Don't you dare."

"And here I thought you wanted to fly."

Beneath the table, I cupped my hand over his cock and smiled sweetly. "That's what I have you for," I said. My voice was a tease, but I meant every word.

In the interest of public decorum, I started to move my hand away, but he pressed his hand over mine, holding my palm firmly in place. He met my eyes, his amused, and I couldn't help but grin.

"The lady makes a good point," Evan said, and I had to laugh. I wasn't the only one who got off on the thrill.

"She has *so* got you wrapped around her little finger," Kat said.

"She does," Evan agreed cheerfully, and Kat flashed me a brilliant, approving smile.

"So where's Cole?" I asked as Kat signaled to a waitress for another round of drinks. "It's almost eight-thirty."

"I've texted him twice," Evan said. "No answer."

We'd arrived only ten minutes late thanks to Evan's ability to maneuver the Thunderbird at incredibly fast and unsafe speeds. But there'd been no need to hurry. Cole was still MIA, and Flynn had gotten stuck covering another shift, and so the hour he'd planned to take off to hang with us now had him behind the bar working his ass off. And when he wasn't running around mixing drinks, he was occupied by a woman who looked to be in her early forties, and who kept calling him over to talk to her.

Kat had noticed her first and pointed her out to me. Now we'd both been eyeing the action, trying to figure out who she was to Flynn. I guessed she was no one—just a woman looking to get laid by the cute bartender. Probably recently divorced. Probably had a crappy day at work.

"I think she's looking to fool around while her husband's out of town," Kat said when we'd gone to the ladies' room together.

"I hope not. The last thing Flynn needs is a pissed-off husband poking around."

Whoever she was, she was keeping Flynn busy. He'd only made it to our table once, and that was just to introduce himself to Evan. I was hopeful that by the time Cole showed up, the second bartender would have made it in to work, and Flynn could take a break.

"There he is," Evan said, looking toward the entrance. Then he pushed back his chair and stood. "Something's wrong."

Since I was a head shorter than Evan, I couldn't see Cole's approach until I stood as well. The moment I did, I knew that Evan was right. Cole was like a storm of muscle moving toward us, his expression thunderous. Even his usually kind eyes flashed with fury that he wasn't bothering to conceal.

"What the fuck?" Evan asked, obviously as baffled as I was.

Cole cast one look my way. "Sorry, baby girl. I need him for a few." He pointed at Evan. "We've got a problem."

"What's going on?" I asked, but Cole was already walking away, and Evan was moving fast behind him, his phone out and at his ear.

"What the fuck?" Kat said.

"Business stuff, I guess. Evan said there was some shit going down with one of their California ventures." I tried to sound nonchalant, but I was worried and Larry's warning and Kevin's voice were ringing in my ears.

They'd been gone about five minutes when Flynn came over and sat down at our table. "Where'd they go?"

"Parking lot, I think." I looked over and saw that the cougar was gone. "Lose your friend?"

"Fuck her," Flynn said.

Kat laughed. "That's what we thought you had planned. What happened?"

"It's like a negotiation," Flynn said. "We couldn't come to terms."

"More business shit," I said, then swallowed the last sip of my cabernet as Flynn and Kat laughed. "Another round?"

"Hell, yes," Flynn said, as he signaled for one of the waitresses. "I'm off work for a full thirty-six hours."

I'd finished two more glasses of wine and was feeling the effects of it by the time Evan came back. Cole wasn't with him, and I watched the disappointment play across Kat's face, becoming all the more pronounced when Evan refused to explain why Cole was blowing us off. "Work stuff," he said, which was hardly a satisfactory explanation.

What was worse was the way he was distracted for the rest of the evening. He was nice to my friends, saying the right stuff, laughing at their jokes, buying rounds of drinks. But he felt absent somehow. I put up with it until we left, but in the car I demanded answers. "What's going on, Evan?"

"Business," he said. He stopped at an intersection, and shot me a sideways look. "It'll blow over."

"So what's the trouble?"

"Problems," he said. "At Destiny."

I licked my lips, remembering his red, raw knuckles. "That guy? Larry? Are the girls okay?"

He focused on the road. "They're fine. It's being dealt with."

I could tell he was getting irritated, but I pressed on anyway. "So is this a legitimate business thing? Or should I be worried that the FBI is going to swoop down on you?"

He yanked the wheel to the left even as he slammed on the brakes. I squealed, the sound of my voice matching the sound of the tires as he careened into a parking lot and killed the engine. "What the fuck, Lina?"

I gaped at him.

"Seriously," he demanded. "What the fuck?"

I shook my head. "What's going on, Evan? Did Cole hit you on the head? Because your mood has turned on a dime here, and I don't know what's going on, but you're taking it out on me."

"Are you staying?"

"Staying?" I repeated, because I was completely confused now.

"Are you staying in Chicago, or are you heading off to Washington in just over a week?"

"I—" I licked my lips. "I just want to close this distance, Evan. Cole burst in and you ran off with him, and when you came back, it was like you were lost behind a wall. And I get that. There's stuff you can't talk about—stuff we both know about but that we've been avoiding, and it's my fault, too, because I've been skirting around the edge, as well." I sucked in a breath, not sure if my pounding pulse was because of my words or the lingering result of his reckless driving. "I don't want evasions anymore. I don't want stories or allegories or what-ifs. I want you, Evan. I want the real you."

I was spilling out my heart to him, watching his face, searching for softness, for acceptance, for relief.

Instead, all I saw were hard lines and angles. I saw regret, too, and it sent cold prickles of fear through me.

He turned away, his attention focused on some point outside the windshield. "I want that, too," he finally said.

I exhaled in relief and waited for him to say more. To tell me the truth. To finally let me see what was underneath the knight's armor.

But that wasn't what he said.

"Are you staying in Chicago?" he repeated, this time speaking very slowly and very clearly. "Or are you heading off to Washington in a week?"

"Dammit, Evan," I shouted, losing all patience now. "Why do you keep asking me that?"

He continued to face forward, but his voice had the same edge that I was feeling. "Answer the question."

"I—yes," I snapped. "You know I have a job. And in a few days, I'll even have a place to live."

He put the car back into gear and pulled out onto the street. I sat frozen, certain that we'd just crossed some line in the sand that I hadn't even realized he'd drawn. When we reached my condo, he passed the valet stand and pulled to the curb. He sat silently, and it took me a second to realize he was waiting for me to get out.

"What the fuck, Evan?"

"You're not being true to yourself, Lina," he said, turning to face me. "Don't expect more from me than you're willing to give yourself."

eighteen

You're not being true to yourself.

For the rest of the night and into the next day, his words ran through my head over and over, like some horrible children's ditty that had turned into a pernicious earworm.

You're not being true to yourself.

At first I was pissed. I paced and I drank and I managed not to throw things, but only because I liked all the things that were in Jahn's condo, and I'd already sacrificed one coffee cup to Evan Black.

So I worked off my anger by burning calories, stalking wildly around the condo, muttering to myself like a madwoman and making up some pretty damn fine curses in the process.

You're not being true to yourself.

Then I sat. And I tried to watch television in order to drown out the annoying little voice that kept popping into my head, telling me that he was right.

But the voice was too loud and I couldn't concentrate. Not on CNN, not on streaming episodes of *Buffy*. Not even on the fine figure of Gordon Ramsay cursing out all those little chef wannabes.

You're not being true to yourself.

Goddamn Evan Black.

He was right.

He was right, but I was scared to change. I'd been living my life under someone else's terms for so long that I wasn't sure I knew how to do anything else. For that matter, I wasn't sure I knew how to be me.

Dear god, I'd made a mess of it. My parents hadn't lost just one daughter, they'd lost two. Because they didn't even know Angelina, not anymore. I'd been trying so hard to be Gracie for them that I'd completely buried their youngest daughter.

You're not being true to yourself.

Yeah, wasn't that the understatement of the year? And it had only taken falling in love to make me finally see it.

"Ms. Raine?"

I was on the patio, standing by the glass barrier, looking out over the lake, though I wasn't really seeing it. Now I turned in response to Peterson's voice. "Yes?"

"Can I bring you anything? You should eat some lunch."

"I'm not hungry."

"You didn't have breakfast." He paused. "Is there something I can help you with, perhaps?"

"No." He couldn't help me, and I was having one hell of a time helping myself. For that matter, I was having a hell of a time getting my head on straight.

I knew what I wanted—I wanted to stay. I wanted Evan. I wanted to work for the foundation.

I wanted to be true to myself. But I was scared of stepping off the path I'd paved for myself. And I was terrified of disappointing my parents.

There was only one person I knew who could help me. Only one person who could hold me tight and keep me firmly safe while I took the kind of risk that I was thinking about taking.

I needed to jump—and I knew with absolute certainty that I could only do that if Evan was beside me.

"Peterson," I called, turning around and catching him before he moved efficiently back inside. "Wait. There is something you can do for me."

"Whatever you need, Ms. Raine."

"I need a car."

The driver took me to Evan's downtown office first, but unless his secretary was covering for him, he wasn't there.

I tried the boat next, and didn't find him there, either.

"Shall I take you back home, miss?"

"No," I said sharply. I pulled out my cell phone and almost dialed. But I didn't want to give him the opportunity to tell me to stay away. "We're going to Destiny," I said, then settled back for the ride.

I hoped like hell he was there, because if he wasn't, I was all out of ideas. And while I had reached the point of begging Cole for help, I really didn't want to go that route unless it was absolutely necessary.

I didn't see Evan's car as we drove up, but I also didn't have a full view of the rear parking lot. I thanked the driver and, since I was all about the power of positive thinking, I told him not to wait. Then I stepped inside, paid my cover—this time to a petite brunette—and pushed through the doors into the main room.

It looked just the same as it had before. The girls were still dancing. The men were still watching. Everything seemed exactly the same as the last time I'd been here. The only thing that had changed was me.

"I know you."

I glanced up to see a familiar blonde in a tiny miniskirt and nothing else.

It took me a second, but I finally recognized her as the girl who'd worked the entrance my last time here. "Hi," I said. "I'm looking for Evan."

"Again?"

"Excuse me?"

She shrugged. "He's in a meeting right now," the girl said, and I silently cheered. At least he was somewhere on the premises.

"I'll just wait at the bar." I headed in that direction, then took a seat. The girl plopped down beside me.

"Um, is that okay?"

Instead of answering, she looked me up and down. "So you're the flavor of the month."

I blinked at her. "Excuse me?"

"It's just that he fucks a lot of women. None of us, of course. Rules and all that shit. But he brings them here. Gets them all hot, you know?"

I didn't say a word.

"Anyway, the point is it never lasts. I mean, I'm not telling you anything you didn't already know, am I? He was up front, right? About the fact that you're just a temporary thing."

I swear there were giant rocks just sitting in my stomach. "Is there some reason we're having this conversation?" It was surreal. I was sitting on a barstool talking about sleeping with Evan to a woman whose breasts were only inches from my face. What the fuck was wrong with that picture?

She shrugged. "Consider me a walking, talking public service announcement. Because if he didn't tell you, then you should know. Because there's only one woman for Evan. He may burn through a dozen pussies, but in the end, she's the one he goes back to, every goddamn time. I mean, hell, he's even got her tattooed on his arm."

"He's got—wait. What?"

"Ivy," the blonde said. "That tattoo on his arm. It's for his girl. What? You didn't know?"

"I knew," I said, sliding off the stool. "And I know that I need to go talk to him now."

She didn't try to stop me as I went through the same door that Evan had taken me through the last time I was here. I remembered seeing offices back there, and since I didn't have a better idea, I assumed that he was in one of them.

I pushed through, found no one on the other side to stop me, and kept on going.

Ivy. What the hell? I thought of the tattoo on his arm. I'd even asked him about it, and he hadn't told me that it referred to a woman.

Shit.

And did that mean that Evan was lying to me—or was the blond bitch the liar?

I knew the answer I wanted. I even knew the answer I believed.

I just wasn't sure if what I believed was true.

I heard voices from behind the closed conference room door, and I paused, my head cocked as I tried to discern if Evan's voice was among them.

Then the door jerked open—Evan was right there—and I jumped so high I almost bumped my head on the ceiling.

"Lina?"

"Holy fucking crap, Evan," I shouted, more because I was embarrassed at getting caught than because I was actually scared.

Behind him, I saw Tyler and Cole at a conference table that

was covered with blueprints and technical drawings and all sorts of sketches.

They all three looked frazzled. And none of them looked happy to see me.

"What are you doing here?" Evan said.

I swallowed, feeling like I'd been tossed into the middle of the school play, but no one had told me my lines. This wasn't the way I'd imagined this. In the story in my head, I'd gone to him, confessed that he was right, and then folded myself into his arms.

Now I wondered if he'd even missed me at all.

Now I wondered about Ivy.

"I made a mistake," I said, forcing the words out past the tears in my throat. "I'm sorry. I shouldn't have come."

I caught a flash of worry in his eyes, but I didn't have time to think about it. I turned and ran toward the back door, then pushed through it and out into the bright afternoon sun.

Immediately, I knew I'd screwed up. The building was huge, and if I was going to get to the street, I had to go all the way around it. "Shit," I snapped, even though I was the only one to hear it. I dug into my purse for my phone as I started to circle the building. I'd call a taxi. I'd call Peterson. I'd do something to get the fuck out of there, because I couldn't stay. But I also couldn't really move, because the tears had started to flow, and the world was blurry, and all I wanted to do was sit down on the asphalt and cry until everything stopped hurting.

"Baby."

Evan's arms went around me, strong and firm, and though I wanted to shake them off, I let him hold me as I sank down to the curb where the sidewalk met the parking lot.

"Sweetheart, what are you doing here?"

I pulled away from him, but then I had to hug myself, because as soon as his arms were no longer around me, I felt lost again.

"Lina? Jesus, Angie, talk to me. You're starting to scare me."

I sucked in a deep, stuttering breath, pushed my hair off my face, and turned to face him. "Who is she?" I demanded, forcing my voice to stay steady. "Who is Ivy?"

His eyes widened, and he said very slowly and very carefully—as if I was a bomb that might go off at any moment—"Why do you want to know?"

I told myself I wasn't going to scream. That I was going to be rational. That I trusted him and I wasn't going to be one of those women who flew off the handle in a fit of jealous rage.

I told myself that, but I was having one hell of a hard time implementing it.

I reached out and touched his arm. It was hidden by his shirt sleeve, but I could almost feel the tattoo burning into me. "I need to know that you weren't just playing me, Evan. I mean—I guess if you were, then it was my own damn fault. I'm the one who said I wanted this to be temporary, right? I'm the one who said three weeks."

I pushed up off the curb and turned to look at him. I felt the tears trickle down my face, but I wasn't sobbing anymore. I was a wreck, but at least I was a wreck with some semblance of control.

"But then you asked if I was staying, and I guess I thought—I mean, maybe I hoped—"

"What?" he asked.

It was just one word, but he said it with such soft hope that it gave me courage.

"I came here because you're right. Because I'm not being true to myself. I want art, not politics. Beauty, not bills and bartering. And so I came here to tell you that. Because, because—" I shook my head, not yet ready to put everything into words. "But maybe I presumed too much. Because I didn't know about her. I didn't know about—"

"Ivy," he said, and I had to close my eyes to block the pain of that one simple word.

His hands closed over my shoulders. "Look at me," he said.

I hesitated, then slowly opened my eyes. I saw warmth in his face. Warmth and desire and what looked remarkably like happiness. I think I may have even seen love.

And then, without warning or pretense, he leaned in and kissed me so gently it almost made me cry again.

"Come on," he said after he pulled away. He twined his fingers in mine and started to walk toward his car.

"Where are we going?"

"I have a few things to tell you," he said. "I think we'll start with Ivy."

The car ride was quiet, primarily because Evan wasn't saying a damn thing and neither was I. He seemed content to wait. I was afraid to break the silence in case I was wrong and it hadn't been happiness I'd seen in his eyes. And if he was taking me to meet the girlfriend he had secreted away in a tower, then I didn't want to know about it until the last possible second.

Mostly, though, I was willing to just surrender. I'd worked myself into a frenzy over something I was beginning to believe was a misunderstanding. And I'd twisted my own life and future around because of guilt and fear. I needed to learn to step back— and Evan was the only one I trusted.

I hoped like hell I wasn't wrong.

But when we reached Evanston, I couldn't stand it any longer. "How much farther?"

"Five minutes."

I swallowed, then nodded. "Okay," I said, and was irritated by the way my voice broke. I glanced sideways at him. "Don't break my heart."

"Never," he said, with such firm certainty that an errant tear escaped down my cheek.

I brushed it away, annoyed at myself for being an emotional mess.

We were in a neighborhood near Northwestern now, and he pulled onto a side street and then up to the gate of a stunning mansion with a beautiful manicured lawn. "We're here," he said, as he keyed in a gate code. The gate swung open and he pulled up toward the house, and as the driveway angled around, I caught sight of a pool, a tennis court, and a guesthouse on the property.

"Where are we?" I asked.

"My house," he said, and then killed the engine.

"Yours?" I wasn't expecting that. "But the houseboat . . . ?"

"I prefer to stay there." He opened his door and got out of the car. "Come on."

I took a deep breath and followed him, not at all sure what to expect but certain of only one thing. If I tried to guess, I would undoubtedly be wrong.

The front door had a keypad lock and he punched in the code and then stepped inside. I followed, then looked around in silent awe at the beautiful interior. I'd grown up in a fabulous home, and the condo I now lived in was stunning. But the interior of Evan's home was an absolutely perfect mix of beauty and comfort. It reflected money and taste along with an ultimate sense of home. It felt cozy and inviting. And that just made it more odd to me that he didn't want to actually live there full-time.

"It's me!" he called, his volume surprising me. "Who's home?"

A moment later, a large woman in black drawstring pants and a scrub-style top came in from an adjoining room with a dish towel in her hands. "Mr. Evan! Why didn't you call? I would have held dinner for you."

"Don't worry, Ava. I'll fix us something later." He indicated me. "This is Angelina Raine. She'll be staying the night."

Before I could react to that news, Ava took my hand and was clutching it warmly. "How wonderful! We've heard so much about you."

I glanced at Evan in surprise. "Thank you. I appreciate you putting up with us on such short notice."

She waved the words away, and I thought she was going to say something else, but the pounding of feet on the floor above us caught all of our attention. The pounding was followed by a woman's voice calling, "Evan! Evan!"

Ivy, I assumed, but there was something odd about the voice that I couldn't quite put my finger on.

And then there she was hurrying down the stairs with the same excitement as a child expecting presents. Her hair was long and unkempt, and it was hanging in such a way as to cover her face. She wore a pink sweatshirt with a giant purple heart on it and Converse tennis shoes. She skidded to a stop in front of us and pushed her hair back out of her face—and when she did, I had to force myself not to gasp.

The woman's face was so scarred that it was almost unrecognizable as female. She had only half of her nose, her eyebrows were completely missing, and her mouth was twisted now in a strange contortion of a smile. That contortion, however, was filled with so much joy at the sight of Evan that it seemed to light her up from the inside, and made tears sting my eyes. After stopping for just a second, she launched herself into his arms crying, "I missed you! What did you bring me? What did you bring me?"

"Something very cool," he said, reaching into his pocket. He pulled out his wallet, opened it, and took out a two-dollar bill. "Do you know what this is?" he asked, handing it to her.

She studied it intently. "Money."

He laughed. "Well, yeah. But how much?"

Her scarred eyes widened just a little. "Two! Wow! I've never seen that before! Is it real? Will it buy Twizzlers?"

"It is and it will."

"Thank you!" She threw her arms around his neck. "I love you! I miss you!"

"I love you and miss you, too. And guess what else I brought you," he said as she released her grip. He nodded toward me. "A new friend."

She turned to me and smiled wide, revealing remarkably perfect teeth. "Hi! You're pretty!"

I had to laugh. "Thank you," I said. "So are you," I added, and was rewarded with her vibrant smile. "And I love Twizzlers, too."

"Really? Wow! How old are you?" she asked.

"Almost twenty-four," I said.

"No kidding?" she asked, as if that was the most amazing thing in the world. "I'm twenty! That's a two and a zero because it's two groups of ten—right, Evan?"

"Absolutely perfect. This is Angelina," he added, indicating me. "Lina, I'd like to introduce you to my sister. This is Melissa Ivy Black."

nineteen

We spent the next few hours in the backyard with Ivy alternating between tossing a Frisbee, playing in a sandbox, and answering knock-knock jokes. I didn't ask Evan any more questions—I wouldn't have known where to start. And I knew now that he'd tell me in his own way in his own time.

"Ivy!" Ava called from the kitchen. "Time for your medicine and bed."

"Can I watch *SpongeBob*?" she asked Evan.

"If Ava says so," he answered, standing. "Come on, we'll walk you in." He took her hand, and when she reached out her other one for me, I took it, as well. It was as scarred as the rest of her, and I had the horrible feeling that if we peeled off that layer of clothes, her whole body would be scar tissue. The thought made me unbelievably sad.

Ivy, however, was as happy and bouncy as a child. "Will you be here tomorrow?" she asked me.

I glanced at Evan.

"We'll be here for breakfast," he said. "Then I have to get back to work."

"You work too much," she said.

He laughed. "I'm trying to fix that. As soon as I do, I'll have more time to spend with you."

"Yay!" She clapped her hands and then ran ahead into the kitchen after Ava.

"She's wonderful," I said when she was gone.

"She's basically six," he said with affection. "Which means that although she was wonderful tonight, tomorrow morning when we leave we'll probably see a full-blown tantrum."

He reached out for my hand, then smiled when I took it. "Nobody knows about her," he said. "Nobody except Tyler and Cole."

"And Jahn?"

Evan nodded.

I remembered what he'd said about not trusting easily, and I understood in that moment the extent of the gift he was giving me. Not just his trust, but the chance to fully see this man.

"I thought your mom and sister lived in another state."

"And I worked damn hard to make sure the entire world thought that."

"Why?"

We'd reached the back porch steps and he sat down, then scooted over to make room for me. "To keep her safe," he said. "There are risks to what I do. And sometimes the blowback is on your family."

"You're talking the criminal stuff," I said boldly.

"I am," he said. "And yes, I'll tell you. But first I want to know how you found out about Ivy. Not Kevin?"

"No," I said quickly, understanding his fear. "It was one of the girls at work. A blonde. She was working the front that first time I came."

"Donna," he said. "She's something of a bitch, and she's been trying to get into my bed for over a year."

"I thought you didn't sleep with the girls."

"I don't," he said. "And neither do Cole or Tyler. Tyler had a thing once with one of the waitresses right after we bought the place. It didn't end well." He turned to face me. "Just so we're crystal clear on this, I've gone out with a lot of women, and I've fucked a lot of women. But it never meant anything more than a good time and someone to have a meal with. Do you understand what I'm saying?"

I licked my lips, trying to slow the rapid patter of my heartbeat. "I'm not sure. I don't want to guess and be wrong."

His smile was warm. "I mean that there's never been another woman. It's always been you, Lina. Even before I realized it, you were always there inside me."

I closed my eyes and drew in a breath, realizing that I felt relaxed now for the first time since Cole had come into the pub and dragged Evan to the parking lot. "I've missed you," I said. "You've been right beside me for hours now, but I've missed you all the same."

"I've missed you, too." He stood and then tugged me to my feet.

"Will you tell me what happened to her?"

"Yeah," he said as he led me inside and upstairs. "I'll tell you everything."

The bedroom that he took me to was small, with a double bed, a desk, and very little else. "This was my room growing up," he said. "I never bothered to do much to it, but I crash here when I visit."

"Who has the master?"

"No one right now. My mother passed away about a year ago, and Ivy and I haven't spent much time in there."

"I'm sorry," I said.

"Thanks." He stretched out on the bed, propped up on his elbow. I sat beside him, cross-legged, with my elbows propped on my knees. "The story starts and ends with Ivy, which is why I wanted you to meet her. You've read about the fire?"

"Sure. Every article talks about it. I'm sorry about your father."

"You don't need to be sorry for him," Evan said harshly. "But Ivy . . ." He trailed off, then drew in a deep breath as if gathering his thoughts. Or maybe his courage.

"It's okay," I said. "If you don't want to talk about it, I understand."

He reached out and put his hand on my knee, and that one simple touch felt as intimate as all the times we'd made love. "I want you to know," he said. "She was six, and because she has an autoimmune disease, they were limited in the amount of reconstructive surgery they could do—her body kept rejecting it. She inhaled a lot of smoke, too. For that matter, she was clinically dead for well over a minute before they revived her. The result was brain damage, and the manifestation is that she's going to stay six for a very long time. She may grow a little bit more mentally, but nine is about the best-case scenario. To be honest, I'm not seeing it, and neither are her tutors. But I love her, and no matter what happens, I'll take care of her."

"It was an electrical fire, right?"

"That's the story my mother and I spread."

I frowned. "What do you mean?"

"I mean that my fucking father decided to kill himself and almost took Ivy along with him."

I stared at him, horrified.

He sat up, then scooted back so that he was leaning against

the headboard. He was no longer touching me. One hand was above his head, clutching tight to one of the brass bars that made up the bed frame. The other was idly twisting the spread into a knot. I don't think he was aware of either.

"He was in banking. Made a fortune and then when he lost it all he was too much of a coward to try to dig himself back out. So he killed himself. Went to the guesthouse and took a bottle of sleeping pills. But he had a cigarette and managed to set the bedspread on fire. Ivy used to sneak into the guesthouse to play, and she was in there."

"My god." I couldn't even imagine how scared that poor little girl had been. "Does she remember?"

"Not much, thank god."

"And your mother?"

"She was a mess. She'd never worked a day in her life, and it turned out that my brilliant father had borrowed against his life insurance so that we were left with absolutely nothing except a bunch of debt and a shit-ton of medical bills."

"The articles hinted that your mom had a trust fund, and that helped keep you guys afloat." I looked at his face. "Oh, crap. You made that part up, too."

"He didn't leave us shit, but I needed a story. I didn't want people looking too hard at what I was doing."

"So what *were* you doing?" I asked, though I was pretty sure I could guess. Maybe not the specifics, but enough to know he wasn't working minimum wage in fast food.

"My sister pretty much lived in the hospital, and my mom fell into an alcoholic haze. I was fifteen, and I'd been your typical, spoiled, rich kid asshole. I had too much money, bought alcohol illegally, and smoked pot behind the school with my friends. I could either stay a disconnected asshole or I could get my shit together and become the man of the family. I chose the second."

"But most fifteen-year-olds work at McDonald's. And that wasn't going to pay the bills."

"No," he said. "It wasn't."

"And since the universe doesn't play fair . . ." I began, remembering what he'd told me.

"I didn't have to play fair, either."

"Go on." I scooted closer to him and rested my palm gently on his leg. "I want to know how you survived."

"Need and adrenaline," he said, then grinned. "And every time I did something dangerous and came out okay on the other side, I felt like I'd put one over on the universe and was that much stronger for it. I started taking chances to get a thrill and to get money. I did everything imaginable. Jacking cars, dealing drugs. Hell, I even got a bit of a reputation as a cat burglar—not that anyone ever found out it was me doing the sneaking around."

"It didn't scare you?"

"Just the opposite." His grin was boyish. "I like the rush, too."

He told me more and more. About how high school turned out to be the best possible place, because he could research anything and everything and taught himself how to boost cars and disable alarm systems. He even dabbled in counterfeiting. And all the while he was keeping detailed records, figuring out which endeavors brought in the most money so that he could most efficiently take care of his mom and sister.

"I screwed up senior year, though. I got hooked up with the wrong crowd—folks who weren't nearly as careful as I was."

"Did you get arrested?"

"And convicted."

"Really?" I grabbed a pillow and hugged it to my chest. My heart was pounding against my rib cage in memory of my own arrest, and I couldn't believe he was talking so calmly about a conviction. "You weren't scared to death?"

"It wasn't a pleasure ride, if that's what you mean. But it did change my life."

He had ended up in a juvenile pilot program and was shipped off to a scared-straight camp where he met Cole and Tyler. "The lessons of the camp didn't really stick," he said. "But the friendship did."

"In other words, three of the most upstanding businessmen in Chicago aren't that upstanding, after all."

"I'd say that was accurate," he acknowledged with a grin. "Not as much for me anymore. I've been selling off my share of our more shady enterprises to Cole and Tyler. And I've been legitimizing my own operations. To be honest, I've reached the point where I get just as much of a rush from negotiating a hard bargain with a competitor as I do from stealing his assets when he's not looking. Maybe more."

"Why?"

"Why is there a rush?"

"Why are you going straight?"

"You met her," he said. "Ivy."

I nodded, but I still didn't understand. "Why now?"

"Because my mother died. When she was alive, I knew that Ivy would always have family. But now that she's gone, I want to guarantee that I'm not going to be serving time in a minimum security cell when she needs me."

"But even if you get clean, they can still arrest you."

He laughed. "Thanks for the reality check."

I cringed. "Sorry. It's just that I remember what it was like when they put me in that cell. And the idea of having you arrested freaks me out."

He reached for my hand. "It freaks me out, too. That's the point. That's why I want out."

"Evan—" His name felt delicious. The world felt delicious. And, yeah, I was still a little bit scared for him, but so long as he was really getting out . . .

"What are you thinking?" he asked, and I realized my brow was furrowed.

"Just that if you're getting out, then you probably are safe. I mean, if everything you've done was white-collar, they probably don't care about stuff that's old news, right? And eventually the statute of limitations will run out. Won't it? I mean that's all we're talking about, right? White-collar stuff?"

He nodded.

"So what do you do? Or, I guess I should ask, what *did* you do?"

"We started out with petty stuff, but we expanded into everything from smuggling to money laundering to backroom gambling. No drugs—that's our line in the sand. And, once we hooked up with your uncle, we went a bit more high class. He introduced us to the world of art. Including the underworld of art."

"Wait. Wait, back up. What? Uncle Jahn?" I couldn't quite believe what he was saying. "Uncle Jahn was tied up with you three?"

"The other way around, baby. Your uncle was our mentor, and pretty much the smartest man I know. That class he taught? He used it as a front. It was a legit class, but if he was working with someone, he'd slide them into the class to establish a reason to be seen together. It worked beautifully, and no one was ever the wiser."

"How long was he doing it?" I asked. I realized that I'd slid off the bed and was pacing the length of the small room.

"About eight years on the classes, but decades with the smuggling and forgeries and everything else. From what he told us, he started dabbling in art theft when he was about thirteen."

"Holy shit." There was a chair tucked in under a small desk. I pulled it out and flopped down onto it.

How could I have not known this man that I'd loved so well? Then I remembered what he'd said about his wives leaving him. *Secrets.* "Holy shit," I repeated. My uncle had lived a shadow life that even the people who were seemingly the closest to him knew nothing about. The thought made me sad. Especially since I'd kept so many secrets, too.

"So how close are you to getting out from under all this?" I asked. I wanted him out. I wanted him done. And I'm not sure if it made me a bad person, but I didn't want him out because of any moral qualms against his criminal past. No, I wanted him out because I knew that Kevin had painted a bull's-eye on him, and I wanted to deflect that attention.

"Close," he said, and I breathed a little easier. "You've already heard a bit about the problems at Destiny."

"Larry," I said, then shivered. "But I don't know the details. Just that it's something to do with the girls, right?"

He nodded. "Some used to be prostitutes—don't worry, we don't run that shit. And Destiny's a legit operation, though we do use the facility to launder money."

I lifted a brow. "In that case, I have to question your definition of legit."

"Point taken. At any rate, that's stopping. I don't want to give up my ownership interest and Cole and Tyler don't want to go completely clean. So the money-laundering operation is moving."

"To where?"

"I don't know," he said. "And I intend to make certain they know better than to ever tell me."

"You are serious."

"I am." He looked hard at me. "I'm highly motivated."

"I believe you. And I'm glad." I would still worry about Cole and Tyler, but there was no denying that my primary concern was Evan.

"Anyway, none of the girls turn tricks anymore, and part of their compensation is tuition if they want to go back to school. That has a tendency to piss off their former pimps." He held up his hand, where the raw knuckles had now completely healed. "We have bouncers and security staff, but sometimes it's easier to deal with a problem yourself. That was part of our little crisis the other day, too. When Cole pulled me out of the pub."

I just shook my head, still trying to process it all.

"What?" he said, reaching for me. "What are you thinking?"

"What am I thinking?" I leaned forward and took his hand, then let him pull me out of the chair and back onto the bed. "I'm thinking that I'm worried about you because the FBI is watching. And I'm thinking that not many men could plant the seeds of an empire at fifteen. And not many would break that empire down in order to make sure that somebody else is safe." I stroked his face. "You're an amazing man, Evan Black."

He began to trace the outline of my collar with his finger. "There's another reason that I'm breaking that empire down."

"You mean other than Ivy."

"I do," he said.

"What is it?"

"A beautiful woman," he said, with so much heat in his eyes I thought it might burn right through me.

"Really? Tell me about her."

"She's exceptional, and she makes me want to be a better man." I wore a thin cotton button-down, and now he started to work on those buttons. "I once said that I was a bad bet. She makes me want to change that. She makes me want a future." He slipped the shirt off my shoulders. "She makes me want," he whispered.

I trembled as his fingers unfastened the front clasp of my bra. "Want what?"

"Everything," he said, and then bent to close his mouth over my breast. I arched up to meet him, relishing his touches. But I wanted more—I wanted him, and I reached down, fumbling with his fly, then shoving his jeans down over his hips.

"Take them off," I begged. "Please. I want to feel your skin against mine."

He didn't argue, and while he peeled off his jeans and shirt, I extricated myself from the rest of my clothes, too.

He slid over me, his body hard against my soft curves, making me feel decadent and feminine. "I want to go slow," I said. "But no foreplay. Not tonight. I want you inside me. I want to feel you moving inside me until neither one of us can stand it. Please, Evan. I want to push the limit, and I don't want it to end."

"Oh, baby," he said, as I spread my legs and lifted my knees so that he could thrust into me slow and deep. "That's it," he said as I hooked my ankles together at the small of his back, my legs tensing in time with his thrusts, slow and languid, then faster, then slow again as he got closer.

He was holding back for me, and the knowledge that he was keeping his own pleasure in check in order to satisfy me was that much more erotic.

"Faster," I whispered. "Harder."

He didn't hesitate, thrusting hard inside me as my body clenched tight around him, as if determined to keep him with me forever. His hands were on my hips, and we were moving together in a joint rhythm that seemed both calm and frenzied even as it grew and grew until finally I couldn't take it any longer and I cried out his name even as the world seemed to shatter around me.

I was dissolving—I wasn't anything but sensation—and yet he was still able to hold me, and he thrust inside, deeper and harder until I felt him explode, his orgasm shadowing mine, twining with it to draw us both together as our bodies, sensitive and primed, shook and convulsed and drew every last drop of pleasure out of this moment that we shared.

I gasped, finally falling back down to earth, safe now in the arms of this man. This dangerous man who had made love to me so wildly and yet so tenderly. "Evan," I murmured.

"What?" he asked, and I opened my eyes to see him smiling down at me.

"I was just thinking how safe you make me feel. It's a little ironic under the circumstances."

"I don't think so," he said, his expression more serious than I'd ever seen it. "I'll do whatever it takes to keep you safe, Lina. You need to know that."

"I do," I said, then rose up to brush my lips over his. I settled back. "I'm so happy it feels almost criminal."

He rolled his eyes, and I laughed out loud.

"You never told me the second thing," I said, suddenly remembering.

"The what?"

"You said there were two things you had to extricate yourself from. Before your criminal present could become your criminal past. You told me about the stuff still going on at Destiny, but you didn't tell me the other."

"No, I guess I didn't."

"So what is it?"

"There's just this one job that we thought was over and done with, but something's come up lately. Something that could come back and bite us on the ass."

"Can you fix it?" I asked, suddenly worried.

"I've been trying. I keep getting stymied."

"Why?" I asked, and the simple answer hit me with the force of a slap.

"You."

twenty

"You want to explain to me what the hell you're talking about?" I was off the bed and reaching for my shirt.

Evan was sitting up, still naked, and at the moment I wasn't happy about the distraction. "Baby, calm down."

"Calm down? You just said that I'm the reason you can't go completely clean. This is as calm as it gets."

He stared at me, and I felt my adrenaline drop down a notch.

"Okay," I said. "Maybe I'm a little calmer." I crammed my arms through my sleeves and dropped back onto the bed. "I'm listening."

"The Creature Notebook."

I cocked a brow. "If you tell me that you only fucked me to try to get your hands on that thing, we are going to have a serious problem, Evan Black."

"I'm tempted to say that just because I think you'd be damn

fun to fuck when you're all riled up. But no. The fact is that even though I should have figured a way to screw you out of the notebook or to romance it away from you or to just flat-out steal it, I couldn't do it."

"Why not?"

"Because it's you. And because Jahn gave it to you. And because it means so much to you."

I frowned, trying to stay one step ahead of him. "But the fact that you didn't take it from me is causing you a problem."

"Pretty much."

"Explain," I demanded.

"It's complicated," he said.

"Then simplify it."

"Fine," he said. "Your uncle wanted the Creature Notebook. Neely got it instead. So Jahn had Cole create a forgery."

"Cole?" I repeated.

"Do you want to let me finish?"

I held my hands up in surrender.

"We switched the original with the forgery. Which means that the original is in your living room, and Neely's about to donate a forgery to a museum in Belgium."

"Cole seriously created a forgery? The quality of that work must be exceptional." I was legitimately impressed. I mean, I'd spent some time studying forgeries, and that was no small feat.

"Focus for me, babe," Evan said. "This was no big deal while Neely kept the notebook in his private gallery. But it's about to go to a museum. It's going to be poked and prodded and analyzed. And while I think Cole is pretty damn talented, the odds are good that the forgery will be discovered. And if it is—"

"—then it will come back to Cole," I finished. "Yeah, I get it."

"No, you don't," Evan said. "Because it won't just come back to Cole. It'll come back to Jahn. It will ruin his business, his reputation, and the foundation. Not to mention biting me and Tyler on the ass, too."

"So what do you want to do?"

"We want your notebook," he said simply. "And then we'll just switch them back."

"All right," I said. "How can I help?"

He shook his head. "I told you. By giving us the notebook."

"And then?"

"No," he said. "No way. That is exactly the kind of thing that your uncle didn't want you to do. That is exactly the kind of shit he wanted you away from."

"I don't think so," I said. I crawled on the bed toward him and pressed my hand to his chest. "I think he wanted me in on it."

Evan cocked his head, and I could tell from his expression that he was trying to decide if I was bullshitting him. "Why do you think that?"

"Because of the timing of his will," I said. "Because of the note he left you," I added. "And because he left me the facsimile copy. Not the original."

Evan's eyes narrowed, and I knew I had his attention. "You think he was giving you his blessing with that note," I said, "but I think it was more than that. I think the note and the bequest together were his way of saying we'd make a good team."

"Keep going," Evan said. I started to lean back and take my hand off his chest, but he pulled me back, then gently shook his head. "Stay," he said. "And talk."

I moved to his side and took his hand. "Don't you get it? Jahn knew me better than anyone—and now that you've told me what he was into, I'm even more certain that I'm right about this. He expected us to work together. He wanted us to."

"Maybe," Evan conceded.

"And there's an even bigger reason to agree to let me help."

"What's that?"

"Because if this really is the last thing keeping you from being fully legitimate—from getting out of that damned FBI spotlight—then I want to help. It matters to me, Evan. It matters a lot. Please. Please don't say no."

"Baby," he said, lifting my fingertips to his lips. "Could I ever say no to you?"

"No fucking way," Cole said. "I mean, no offense, baby girl, but no fucking way."

I was sitting beside Evan on the leather couch. Now I took his hand, searching for solidarity, and was rewarded when he squeezed back. We were back in my condo, Evan and I having spent the morning having breakfast with Ivy and then playing four rounds of Candy Land. Evan had called the others from the road and told them to meet us. That we had a lot to talk about.

"Yes fucking way," I said, making Cole roll his eyes. "And guess what? I moved the manuscript to a safe deposit box at HJH&A this morning. So unless I'm part of this, there isn't going to be any *this*. Get it?"

Tyler looked at Evan. "What the fuck?"

"What are you looking at me for? Jahn left her the manuscript, not me. Unless you expect me to tie her down, I can't really keep her from moving it." He turned to me with a devious grin. "Then again, that wouldn't have been such a bad plan."

I smacked him even as Tyler groaned.

"Jesus, Evan. She's like my little sister. Can we not go there?"

Evan and I both laughed, but Evan nodded with gentlemanly agreement. "*We* cannot go there," he agreed, looking firmly at Tyler and Cole. Then he cocked his head deliberately toward me. "Whether we go there is another question altogether."

Tyler rolled his eyes, but Cole just laughed.

"Come on, guys," I said, feeling a bit like they'd reverted back to their formative high school years. "This isn't negotiable. Evan's already tried to talk me out of it and he failed. He and I are doing this thing. The only reason you two are here with us is to decide if you're going to be in on it, as well." I flashed a sweet smile. "Get it?"

Tyler shot a glance toward Evan. "You sure you want her? She's a downright pain in the ass."

I bit back a grin. Tyler, at least, had come over to my way of thinking.

"I want her," Evan said. "On this job, and after."

"Big one-eighty for you, my man," Cole said. "Weren't you the one trying to stay the hell away so you wouldn't sully her with your tainted soul?"

Evan shot him the finger.

"Maybe he likes me sullied," I said, and they all three burst out laughing. "Look," I added, before Tyler and Cole could add anything to the mix, "I know you're just looking out for me, but nothing is going to go wrong. I'm going to do whatever it takes to pull this off. So don't look at me like I'm a liability. I'm not. I'm your best goddamn asset, because I can get around your biggest problem. I can get you access to the forgery."

I glanced over at Evan, who was looking at me with pride, then back to Cole and Tyler. After a second, Tyler folded his arms across his chest and leaned back in his chair with his legs out in front of him. "I'm not saying yes, but I'll listen to what you have to say."

As far as I was concerned, that really was a yes. I had no intention of giving them the notebook if I wasn't in on the job. But I wanted them on board with having me on the team. If they were afraid I'd screw it up, then they'd be sloppy. We all would. And then it wouldn't be a rush I'd be feeling, but full-fledged fear.

"Okay," I said, standing up and feeling as nervous as if I were auditioning for the lead in the school play. "Evan ran me through what you guys already talked about this morning. I know that Neely keeps the manuscript in a case in the private gallery on the top floor of his Winnetka house. I know that the case is locked with a regular, old-fashioned key so that we can't rely on hacking an electronic lock. And I know that other than the lock, the case doesn't have any additional security. So if we can get it open and switch the manuscripts, we're golden."

I looked at them all to see if I'd forgotten anything. Cole nodded at me to continue.

"It's the gallery itself that's the problem. The Creature Notebook is only one of dozens of valuable artifacts that Neely owns, and he keeps them all locked up tight in a nearly impenetrable gallery."

"It wouldn't be impenetrable if we had more time," Tyler said. "I've got the blueprints and technical specs. I know I could figure a way past his security system."

"But we don't have time," Evan said. "The transfer is scheduled for two weeks from now. A job of that magnitude would need at least three months of planning."

"So what we need is a way to get Neely to turn off security for us," I said. "And I have it."

"I'm listening," Cole said.

"Tomorrow morning, Neely is going to get a call from Esther Martin at the Jahn Foundation, telling him that we have a new and exciting plan for the gala. Because we've had so much interest from so many of Jahn's friends, we've decided to make it a traveling event. We'll have six locations with six specialty foods. The foundation will provide luxury coaches to move the guests from stop to stop. We want him to be first on the list with cocktails and artisan cheeses."

"I'm impressed," Tyler said. "Keep going."

I relished the little flutter of pride, along with the way Evan squeezed my hand reassuringly. "We can't wait to do the switch at the actual event, since that's after the donations are shipped off to Belgium. So we're going to arrange a walk-through. Esther is going to tell him that I—her assistant—will be contacting him to arrange a time to come view the space to make sure it's big enough for the expected crowds, to take photos for insurance purposes, and all the rest of it. All of that's true. What Esther and Neely won't know is that we'll use that walk-through to do the switch. We get the facsimile notebook back, the foundation gets an awesome event, and everyone is happy."

"And this was your idea?" Tyler asked, looking at me, his expression unreadable.

"Um, yeah."

Tyler looked to Cole, who nodded. Then he looked back at me. "Damn good work, kid. Seriously, that's damn good work."

I felt the smile bloom on my face.

"I told you," Evan said. "She's an asset. Now let's focus on some of the details."

"The lock, for one," Cole said. "We're not going to have much time. Picking it isn't going to work."

"No," Evan agreed. He looked at Tyler. "We need the key."

Tyler smiled, wide and devilish. "I'm guessing there's a woman involved?"

"You're guessing right. Neely keeps the key in his bedside table. Renee is the maid who works that room. I've got details for you," he added, pulling an envelope from his briefcase and passing it to Tyler. "Sweep her off her feet and do it fast. Get imprints and we'll get a copy made."

"I love my job," Tyler said with such a wicked grin I had to laugh.

"And how are we doing the switch?" Cole asked. "Angie's been brilliant so far, but that's a little too much to ask of her."

"Which is why you'll be doing it," Evan said. "And we're all going in."

"Not buying it," Tyler said. "Why the hell would we all be there?"

"Because BAS Security is going to donate its services to the foundation for the gala," I said, referring to the company that

Evan had told me about. The three of them owned it—Black, August, Sharp—and for the most part, its operation was legitimate. But when the guys needed any sort of surveillance or hacking into an electronic system, they used the BAS resources. "It makes sense," I continued. "Everyone knows how close you all were to Jahn. It's the perfect cover. And it gets you into Neely's security room."

"We'll set it up so that for the duration of the event their security cams are feeding to our handhelds. And when we upload the software to accomplish that, we'll loop the security feed for thirty seconds. We can only manage thirty, though," Evan said, looking at Cole. "Enough time?"

"If I'm all clear for those thirty," he said.

"You will be. Angie will be on Neely, keeping him occupied talking cocktails. Tyler will be between Neely and Cole, adding additional cover as needed. Cole, you just have to make the switch. Get the notebook in and on the right page. Get the facsimile back out and stowed in your bag. And that's it. We're done. We're safe. And so is Jahn's reputation." He looked at all three of us in turn. "Any questions?"

There were none.

"Let us know when the walk-through is confirmed," Tyler said. He glanced at his watch, then stood up. "I'd love to stay, but I have a date with a maid."

"I'll get you set up to make the imprint," Cole said, then turned to me. "As for you, for god's sake, get the manuscript back."

I grinned, then slid open the drawer in the living room coffee table. I reached in, then pulled out the manuscript, now safe in a clear archival box. "I may have told you guys one tiny little fib," I said, and was relieved when they all three laughed.

We followed them to the door.

"Coming with?" Tyler asked Evan.

"Hell no," Evan said, pulling me close. "She did good. I'm going to stay here and make sure she feels fully appreciated."

I felt my cheeks burn, but Tyler and Cole both just grinned.

"And how exactly are you going to show your appreciation?" I asked, as soon as we were in the condo alone.

"I thought I would fuck you," he said.

"Oh. I—good plan."

"But not right away," he continued, his voice rough. "First I have to make sure you want it."

I licked my lips. I already wanted it, but I kept my mouth shut. I wanted to hear exactly what he had in mind.

"I'm going to tie you up, Lina. I'm going to tie your wrists together and use a single cord to bind them in place. Do you know why I want a single cord instead of stretching your arms wide?"

I shook my head, and shifted my weight from one foot to the other, trying to ease the building pressure between my legs.

"So I can have you on your back and close my mouth over your breasts. So I can kiss you and suckle you and trail kisses all the way down to your sweet, slick cunt."

I swallowed. I think I may have moaned.

"And then I can flip you over, pivoting your body on that one point, and I can spank your ass until you beg me to fuck you, and then I can sink deep into you from behind, filling you until you think you can't take any more, and then going even deeper." He leaned closer, then nipped playfully at my earlobe before whispering. "So tell me, sweetheart. Does that sound like a good way to show my appreciation?"

"Yes," I said, my voice breathy with desire. My cunt was already throbbing, and my nipples were painfully tight behind the tank I wore. "Yes, please."

"Then what are we waiting for?" he asked, as he took my hand, then bent to pick up his briefcase.

I expected him to lead me to the bedroom, but he headed for the spiral staircase. "Evan?"

"Hush," he said, and I fell back into silence, trusting that whatever he had planned would be something I wanted.

When we reached the patio, he led me to the edge. Each pane of glass was held in place between iron bars topped with a decorative finial. "Here," he said, moving a potted plant to give me room. "Take off your clothes."

I met his eyes, wanting to be as bold as he was. Needing him to know just how much I wanted this, too. This moment. This man. And, yes, the adventure to come.

With slow deliberation, I stripped off my shirt, my fingers brushing over my skin before letting it drop to the ground. I removed my bra next, but not before trailing my fingers lightly over the swell of my breasts above the line of the cups.

I licked my lips and kept my eyes on Evan's face. He looked like a man keeping himself in check, and when I glanced down and saw that his hands were clenched at his sides, I couldn't help but feel immense satisfaction knowing how much he was having to fight simply so he wouldn't reach out and touch me. Not yet, anyway.

I moved next to the bra clasp, unfastening it slowly, then using both hands to push the cups off my breasts. I shrugged out of the straps, but didn't let it fall to the ground. Instead, I let it dangle by a strap over one crooked forefinger.

"Jesus, Lina," he said.

I just smiled, thoroughly enjoying myself as I flipped it to him, satisfied when he caught it and held it tight in his hand. I rubbed my own hands over my breasts, then closed my eyes and gently gave my nipples a tug as I imagined it was Evan's hands upon me, not mine. A sizzling cord of desire shot from my breasts down to my cunt, now hot and wet with desire.

I heard a moan and knew it came from me. I'd intended to get him all worked up—to turn the tables and hold control in my hands. Yet here I was, desperate for his touch. So hot I would probably come if he just leaned forward and whispered in my ear.

So much for my grand plan.

Then again, I had no complaints about the way this was working out. He looked just as desperate as I felt, and with a smug smile of satisfaction, I moved on to my jeans, slowly working open the fly, one button at a time. They were skinny jeans, and since I wasn't actually skinny, I had to do a serious shimmy to get out of them, and I took the opportunity to put on a little show for Evan's benefit.

I was already in bare feet, and I finally worked the jeans all the way down and toed them off, then stood in front of him in just my thong—a particularly sexy pair as I'd started paying attention to my undies since Evan had come into my life—and my bed.

I met and held his eyes, then slid my finger under the thong's band and started to tug the panties down.

"No," he said, his firm word halting my hand. "That's for me." He moved closer, the air between us humming as it always did when we were together. "Arms up," he said, "and stand here."

I complied, and he let out a low, slow whisper. "Good god, Lina. Do you have any idea how beautiful you are?"

"I only care about how beautiful I am to you."

"Very," he said. "Exceptionally." He bent over to tug something from his briefcase, and when he stood, I saw that it was a strand of rope. He fastened it around my wrists, then wrapped that around the finial above me. "I'm not binding your legs," he said. "But I expect you to keep your feet where I tell you."

I nodded. "All right."

"Wider," he said, and I spread my legs wider. "Beautiful." He slid his hand down my pubic bone, gliding over the scrap of material that was now my only piece of clothing.

"Keep your feet where they are," he ordered. "Don't move until I tell you to."

I nodded, then closed my eyes as he stepped closer, his fingers stroking my body. Teasing me with light caresses. Playing with my breasts, with my lips, with my fingers. And then stroking my inner thighs, the sensation so wildly erotic that I had no choice but to squirm—and had to force myself not to let my feet move.

"Turn around," he said, and I complied. "Keep your eyes open. I want you to look at the city while I touch you. I want you to see just how high we are as I make you soar." He pressed up behind me, and though he was still in slacks, I could feel his erection against my lower back. Then his hand stroking down— and then the violent rip as he yanked the panties off me.

My immediate reaction was to draw my arms down and cover myself, but I couldn't. I was tied to the finial. Naked and bound, with Evan behind me, whispering in my ear. "Do you know what this is about?" he said. "Why I want you like this? What I want to do and why I want to do it?"

"I—tell me."

"Control," he said. "You did amazing today. You had a plan, you got what you wanted. You turned the tables on Cole and Tyler. And in some ways even on me." He bent closer, so that his lips brushed the back of my ear when he spoke. "That's fine for the world, baby. But when we're alone, you're mine. If you take control it's because I give it to you. Do you understand?"

I nodded. I was breathless at his words. My pulse kicking up, my cunt throbbing. This was it; this was what I wanted. To surrender to pleasure. To surrender to a man that I trusted and to know with absolute, unerring certainty that he would satisfy me.

"We're a unit," he said. "A team. You need the rush, and I'm desperate to give it to you. You want to surrender, and I am here to catch you."

I gasped, the clarity of his words surprising me. "How did you know?"

"I see you, Lina. I've always seen you."

"Will you—"

"What?"

"Never mind." I'd been going to ask if he would touch me. But I knew that he would, and as I waited, my nipples peaked and my cunt throbbed. I was wet and wanting and the building need was delicious. The explosion, when it came, would knock me into the heavens.

He was behind me, but I heard the rustle of clothes as he stripped. Then I felt the tease of his erection against my rear. His hands curved over the globes of my rear, and his fingers slipped down, then eased inside me before sliding back up, wet with my own desire, to press against the tight muscle of my ass.

"Evan . . ."

"Shhh."

He moved away, and a moment later I felt that pressure there again, only this time it wasn't his finger. Something hard and lubed, and Evan's voice was telling me to relax, to trust him, to surrender, and I breathed deep and let him slide the thing inside me. "Have you ever had a plug before?"

"No."

"It will feel amazing when I fuck you. And pretty damn intense when I spank you, too."

I closed my eyes and bent over in unconscious invitation.

Evan's gentle laughter brushed over me. "You like that," he said, as I felt my cheeks heat with a blush.

"I like everything you do to me," I said, because it was the truth, and I didn't want him to hold back. Not now. Not ever.

"Bend over more," he said. "As far as you can with your hands tied."

I complied, then held my breath as something hard and flat smacked my rear once, then again, then one more time before Evan stopped and pressed his hands to my flesh, rubbing at the sting, soothing it, turning the pain into pleasure, and the pleasure into the intensity of a need made all the more piquant by the addition of the plug, which, with each spank, seemed to tease me that much more.

"Oh, baby," he said. "I don't want to stop."

"Then don't."

"I have to. I can't wait. I have to have you. You're pink and wet and ready, and I can see how much you want it. I do, too. I have to fuck you, Lina. I don't think I can go another minute without being inside you."

I felt dizzy from his words, only barely aware of him behind me telling me to spread my legs. My ass tingled, and that only added to the sensation as he moved closer behind me. One hand cupped my breast, then spread me wide so that he could thrust inside me, deeper and deeper as I bent over, looking down at the city lights below as Evan lost himself inside me.

He slid his hand around and teased my clit, mimicking the rhythm of his thrusts, and as I looked out over the city below—as I felt every tiny particle that made up Angelina Raine spin and buzz and fire—I knew that I was nothing more than sensation. Nothing other than the embodiment of surrender. Whatever he wanted from me, he could have, if only he would give me this sensation, this joy. This permission to surrender in absolute safety and protection.

Because there was nowhere else for me but in Evan's arms.

And as I exploded out over the Chicago lights, I knew that no matter what happened, I would always belong to this man.

The walk-through with Neely was scheduled for Saturday, and I spent that entire morning alternating between fear and excitement. I had to change shirts twice because I was sweating so much under my arms, and I finally dragged Evan into the shower and made him fuck me blind, just so that I could get what was coming off my mind.

It worked, but only until we were dressed again.

"Thank goodness the appointment's early," I said, glancing at the time on my phone. "If we had to wait until this afternoon, I don't think I could stand it." I glared at Evan. "How are you so calm, anyway?"

"Years of practice," he said. "And I only look calm. A little bit of nervous energy is good before a job. It keeps you careful."

"Then I'm the most careful person on the planet right now."

He pulled me close and kissed me deep. "It's going to go fine. Remember, you're working with a very experienced team."

"Which makes me the weak link."

"Which makes you the energetic new blood." His phone dinged, and he glanced at it. "They're in front of the building," he said. "Let's go."

We met Cole and Tyler in the BAS Security van, and drove together to Victor Neely's Winnetka house. He greeted us at the door, gushed in a too-polite, too-obsequious way over what a wonderful man my uncle was, and led us up to the gallery.

I caught Evan's eye as we climbed the stairs and saw that his reaction was the same as mine—neither one of us liked the guy, and for a second I wished we could just blow this whole thing off. After all, if this thing went as planned, he'd end up with the real Creature Notebook and we'd have a fake.

It hardly seemed fair.

We reached the gallery and stepped inside once Neely disengaged the security system. "It's a wonderful space," I said, as Evan detached himself to go with the lanky security captain who'd accompanied us to the gallery. Cole and Tyler stepped inside and started scoping out the area, asking Neely questions about size and security and claiming that all the information was for insurance purposes.

Neely answered everything without hesitating, and when I felt my phone vibrate in my pocket as per our plan, I told Neely that I'd like to discuss the placement of the food and drinks in relation to the movement of the guests. "I was thinking we could set up a cocktail station over here," I said, pulling him around toward a wall lined with framed pages from various historical manuscripts. My back was to the wall so that I was facing the interior of the gallery, and Neely was facing me, his back to Cole.

"We can keep the food and drink around the edge of the room," I said. "That should help traffic flow."

"Whatever you want," he said easily—and quickly. Too quick, actually, because it had only been twenty seconds. He was about to turn around, and if he did, he'd see Cole with his hand inside the supposedly locked case, and then we would all be screwed.

Tyler met my eyes, and in that split second, I knew that it was all on me—and even though I had no conscious thought about how to get us the hell out of this mess, I was still in motion. I took a step forward, pretended to trip, and grabbed hold of Neely's arm as I went down to the ground, losing my shoe in the process and scraping my knee on the rough wooden floor.

"I'm so sorry," I said, as he stopped his turn and immediately bent down to fuss over me. "The heels on these shoes, they're—"

"Not at all," he said. "Don't apologize, please. Are you okay?" His back was to Cole again, and I winced a little, keeping his attention on me even though more than thirty seconds had passed, but from my on-the-floor vantage point, I could no longer see what was going on.

Then Cole and Tyler were behind Neely, and Neely was helping me up, and Cole and Tyler were asking if I was okay, and everyone was heading out of the gallery, with me and Cole and Tyler thanking Neely for his time, and Neely apologizing profusely and promising to make sure that the floors weren't waxed the night of the gala so as to make it easier for women to navigate in heels.

"Oh my god," I said when we returned to the van. I threw myself into Evan's arms. "Holy shit, holy fuck, oh my god."

I was about to start the rant all over again when Evan soundly and firmly closed his mouth over mine.

The kiss was long and deep and if he was trying to calm me, he missed the mark entirely. "That was insane," I said.

"You did great," Evan said.

"Seriously," Cole said. "You saved my ass."

"Well, it's an ass worth saving," I said, and Tyler laughed.

"I'm so wired," I said, feeling jumpy and bouncy and certain I would explode if I couldn't do something to release all this nervous energy. "This is crazy," I said. "It's like I'm hopped up on gallons of caffeine. Is it always such a high, or is this extra kick from our close call?"

"It doesn't matter," Evan said. "Because this is the last time you're doing anything like this."

I laughed aloud. "True enough," I said. "I don't need to steal ancient notebooks to feel this way." I grabbed his collar and pulled him close. "I have you for that."

"Oh, hell," Tyler said. "They're at it again. Just shoot me now."

Evan flipped him the bird, then caught me in a long, slow kiss that illustrated my point. *Yeah*, I thought. *Who needs larceny when I have this man?*

"Do we want to grab some lunch?" Tyler asked, and I wanted to scream in frustration and disbelief. I mean, honestly, how could he be so calm?

"Sure," Cole said.

"No," I said. I turned and stared Evan down. "And you don't either."

"Apparently I have a prior engagement," Evan said, his voice filled with humor.

I saw Cole and Tyler's knowing smirks and I really didn't care. I intended to jump Evan Black the moment we were out of this van—and I really didn't care who knew it.

"You're sure you don't want lunch?" Evan said as soon as we

were alone on his boat. "I think I have a frozen pizza I could heat up."

"Don't you even tease me," I said. "I don't want pizza. I don't want food. I just want you. Right here. Right now."

"Right here?" he said, looking at the dining table.

"Hell yes." I unbuttoned my blouse and peeled it off, then tugged off the camisole I wore underneath. Evan was watching me, his expression amused, which only fired me up even more. *I'll show him amused.*

I unzipped my skirt and dropped it along with my panties, then hopped up onto the table.

"You are serious," he said, but the amusement that had been in his voice earlier was replaced now with heat.

"Please," I said. "I think I'm desperate."

"I think I like you desperate," he said, unfastening his jeans as he approached me. He stepped out of them, then moved between my legs. I was breathing hard, anticipating the feel of him inside me. Wanting this wild, hard moment. And, yes, wanting it now.

He dropped to his knees then, frustrating me, but only until he hooked my legs over his shoulder and then buried his tongue inside me. I cried out, my fingers twisting tight in his hair, as he licked and sucked and then—without any warning at all—he stopped and stood.

And before I had time to protest or anticipate what was coming, he was right in front of me, pulling me close, positioning his cock so that he could slam hard and fast into me.

I arched back, crying out, my body craving more. Deeper. Harder. "Yes," I cried, alternating with cries of "Harder, Evan, please, deeper. Oh, god, yes."

I pressed against him, meeting him thrust for thrust, completely wild and wanton, totally exhilarated. And when the orgasm took me away, all I could do was cling tight to this man who had made me feel everything and all at once.

He pulled back, taking me with him, and we tumbled to the carpeted ground. "We should move," I said, after we'd laid there for a moment.

"To hell with that," he said, pulling me tighter against him.

I snuggled close, my emotions close to the surface. My desire to get even closer to him palpable.

"It's the same, you know," I finally said, my voice breathy.

"What is?"

"The kind of rush I felt today at Neely's. The kind of rush I got when I shoplifted. It's the same as the way I feel when you're inside me." I propped myself up to see him better. "You make me feel alive, Evan. You make me feel like me." It was true. I could be myself with Evan. No secrets. No holding back. I'd never understood what it meant to be free until I was in his arms. "Do I make you feel that way, too?" I asked. He gave me such a gift simply by being himself, and right then I wanted more than anything to know that I did the same for him. That I could give him a gift of such profound pleasure, too.

"Do you make me feel that way?" he said. "God, Lina, don't you know? You are the biggest rush of my life. The biggest thrill. The wildest ride. You are everything I always wanted, and everything I thought I didn't deserve. You are exceptional. You are beautiful. You are mine. And I love you."

I blinked, then realized that I was crying. "Could you say that again, please?"

His grin spread wide. "I love you," he said as he slid down my body trailing kisses over bare flesh. "Would you like me to show you just how much?"

I laid back, my arms and legs wide, my body completely open to him. "Yes," I said, grinning happily. "Very much, yes."

twenty-one

We drove out to Evanston the next morning to have Sunday brunch with Ivy. I ate too much, played too hard in the sun, and spent the drive back feeling sleepy and satisfied.

"I need to take care of some things at Destiny," Evan said. "Do you mind?"

"Of course not. I can pack while you're gone. But I'm still fixing you dinner tonight, right? My plane leaves at eight in the morning, so I really want the night with you."

"You got it," he said. "Your return flight's on Wednesday?"

I nodded. I'd decided that I needed to tell my parents my decision in person. And since I felt more comfortable on familiar territory, I wanted to go this week while they were staying in our California house.

"I'll be back by seven," Evan promised as he dropped me at the condo. I changed into jeans and a T-shirt, then took a taxi to Fox & Obel and returned with two full shopping bags. More food than we needed, I was sure, but I wanted everything to be perfect.

I'd just set one of the bags down so that I could punch the elevator call button when Kevin stepped into the lobby.

"Let me get that for you," he said, picking up the bag.

"It's fine. I have it." I grabbed the bag. "What do you want, Kevin?"

"We need to talk."

"I don't think we have anything to talk about."

He pulled out his badge. "Yeah," he said. "We do."

"I—oh." A wave of fear shot through me. Did he know about Neely? Did he know about the manuscript? I worked to keep my voice steady. "What's this about?"

"Your boyfriend," he said, his voice hard. "Let's talk upstairs."

I nodded, mute, then followed him onto the elevator. In the condo, I headed straight for the kitchen, hoping to use that time to gather myself, but when I came back to the living room, I didn't feel gathered at all. I sat stiffly in a chair, stared at him, and told him to cut to the chase.

"I can nail the bastards," he said without preamble.

"Who?"

"Don't even pretend not to understand me," he said. "Evan Black, Tyler Sharp, and Cole August." He spat each name, and my heart twisted a little with each one.

"Nail them?" I asked, trying to sound a little bored and a lot confident. "For what exactly?"

"For violating the Mann Act," he said, his words chilling me.

I wanted to tell him that I didn't have a clue what the Mann Act was, but that would be a lie. My father had been on too many task forces, and he'd spent too many hours talking with my mother about using the Mann Act to combat white slavery.

"What exactly are you suggesting?" I asked icily.

"Those fuckers are transporting prostitutes. They're bringing women across state lines for the purpose of sex. And I have a feeling that once we open the door and dig a little deeper, we'll learn that it's even more insidious than that. White slavery. Drugs. All sorts of shit. They're in deep, Angie. And the longer you stay tied to them, the deeper you sink, too."

I felt light-headed, and realized that I'd been shaking my head almost from the moment he'd started talking. "Why are you telling me this?"

"Because you need to know," he said. "And because you're going to help me."

"No." I stood up. "You're wrong. There is no way Evan is tied up in something like that, and I am not going to help you harass him."

"Sit down," he said sharply.

I sat.

"I have a few witnesses who are willing to talk, but I need more."

Witnesses. The word seemed to pulse red in the air. This couldn't be true, so how could he have witnesses?

I realized he'd continued talking. "What?" I blinked at him. "Back up. What?"

"I said I need you, too. You're going to wear a wire."

"The hell I am."

"You're going to talk with your boyfriend," he continued, as if I hadn't said a word. "You're going to get him to admit to you what he's doing—and then you'll see that I'm right."

"You're not," I said. I would never believe that Jahn's knights were into that kind of shit.

Kevin kept talking as if I hadn't said a word. "And the reason that I know you're going to do this is because it all ties back to you. You're dating him, right? That has you mixed up in this mess, too. Not a good place to be, Angie. And it's definitely not a good place for your father to be," he added, the words sending a chill up my spine. "Not when he's making a bid for the vice presidency. The press gets hold of something like this, and it won't be pretty."

"You unimaginable bastard."

"I'm not the bastard. Evan is. Him and his friends." He stood up. "I'll be back tomorrow. I want your answer then. And, Angie," he said, "it had better be yes."

I stayed in the chair as he let himself out, and I was still there hours later when Evan arrived. I didn't even hear Peterson let him in. I didn't even realize he was in the condo until he sat on the edge of the coffee table in front of me.

I'd drawn a blanket around me, but even beneath the flannel, I was cold and numb.

"Are you sick?" Evan asked, leaning in to press a warm hand against my forehead.

I shook my head. "They want me to wear a wire," I said, and I watched his shoulders droop with understanding.

"Kevin," he said. "That goddamn little prick."

"He says you're into prostitution. That you're violating the Mann Act. That I have to watch you—to spy on you. And he says that if I don't, my father's going to get dragged into this."

He slid off the table to kneel in front of me, his expression gentle. "Baby," he said. "We can fix this."

I shook my head, then met his eyes. "This could destroy my dad."

He looked at me warily. "What are you doing, Lina?"

"What I have to," I said. "What I can."

"Tell me."

"I'm going to California, just like I planned. And I'm going to call Kevin on the way and tell him you dumped me and that I'm moving to Washington just like I planned. And that means that putting a wire on me wouldn't do him any good. He'll leave my father alone, and if you and the guys can get Destiny cleaned up fast enough, then I bet he'll leave you alone, too."

"Lina, shit." He ran his hands through his hair, and his eyes looked wild and desperate. I kind of envied him that. I only felt numb.

"Sweetheart, listen to me." He took my hands and squeezed them tight. "You're not being punished. This isn't a case of the bad shit happening after you go a little wild. You don't have to pay penance. We can work it out."

I leaned forward and kissed him. "I love you," I said. "And I know it's not punishment. I do, really." I pressed my palm to his cheek. "You of all people should get it."

"What are you talking about?"

"It's like what you did for your mom and Ivy. You made huge sacrifices for them, and you did it because you loved them. Well, I love you. I love my dad. And I can't live with the thought of knowing that I didn't do everything in my power to keep both of you safe."

"Dammit, Lina—"

"No." The word came out quick and firm and full of absolute conviction. "Please," I said. "My mind's made up. I know Kevin. I get him now. And he's vindictive. If I stay, he won't ever let up. You want to be safe for Ivy? You want everything you've given up to shut your operations down to actually matter? Then you have to let me do this."

He didn't say anything. He just looked at me with storm-gray eyes, so flooded with regret that I had to look away.

"I'm sorry," I said as I stood up. "I love you desperately. And that's why I have to go away."

It felt good to be back in California with my mom and my dad, but I missed Evan terribly. And every time the pain got to be too much, I just reminded myself that I'd had a reason for walking away. For Evan. For my parents. And even a little bit for me, because there was finally something that I could do for them, even if they weren't actually aware of the sacrifice I was making.

But I couldn't completely bury myself, and so I sucked up my courage, sat my parents down, and told them that I didn't want to work in Washington.

"I think it's fascinating," I said, "and I don't regret my degree or the years I spent or any of that. But it's not me."

"Then why—" my mother began, but my dad pressed his hand over hers, gently silencing her.

"I always thought politics was more your sister's fascination," he said. He spoke blandly, but I saw the comprehension in his face, and I think that may have been the first time I truly understood how well-suited for politics my father was.

"She loved everything about it," I agreed. "I like it. I think it's interesting. But I don't love it, Daddy. Not like you do. Not like Grace did."

He nodded slowly. "What do you love?"

"Art," I said, without hesitation.

He inclined his head. "I shouldn't have even had to ask that. I think you were born with a sketchpad."

"Too bad I can barely draw a stick figure."

"Nonsense," my mother said loyally. "You're very talented."

I laughed and hugged her. "I'm not," I said. "But I can see talent. I'd like to maybe manage a gallery someday. Or work in restoration. I don't know. To be honest, I'm not sure what all the options are. But I think I want to go back to school to find out." I wrinkled my nose as I held my breath, trying to gauge their reactions.

It was my mother who spoke first. "I'll talk to Candace in the morning—you remember Candace? She spent two years interning at the Louvre. If anyone knows the best schools to consider, she will."

I tried to say something, but couldn't manage to talk with my throat full of tears. Instead, I just smiled like an idiot and looked at my father. He shook his head with mock sadness. "I'm going to owe some major favors on the Hill," he said. "Congressman Winslow will never find an aide as competent as you would have been."

I threw my arms around him and hugged him.

And for the first time in almost eight years, I felt like it was truly me with my parents, and not me channeling the ghost of my sister.

"Have you considered moving back to Chicago?" my mother asked me days later as we wandered some of La Jolla's galleries. "There are several good programs there, I believe."

"There are," I said. "But I don't think so. I'm not sure I want to move back to the same city that Kevin's in."

Her brows lifted. "That young agent that your father introduced you to?"

"Don't tell Daddy, but he's kind of a jerk."

"Is he? Or did you just meet someone else?"

I grimaced. "There was a guy," I said. "It didn't work out."

"Why not?" she asked, and I kicked myself for opening that door.

"A bunch of stuff."

"Do you want to tell me?"

I shook my head. "No."

We walked in silence for a while. "Did you love him?" she asked.

I almost lied, but I couldn't do that to Evan. Even if he was no longer in my life, I couldn't lie about the way I felt about him. "Yes," I said. "Yes, I love him."

She glanced at me sideways and I expected her to launch into some sort of maternal pep talk. Instead she said, "Your father wasn't the first man I loved."

"He wasn't? Who was?"

A whisper of a smile touched her lips. "It doesn't matter. But he was exciting and bold and he made me feel like anything was possible so long as I was with him."

"I know that feeling," I said. Evan was the rush I needed in my life, that extra something that made me feel alive. And, I knew now, I was the same for him. "Do you feel that way with Daddy?"

"I love your father very much, but it's tamer," she said. "It's more of a partnership. And there's nothing wrong with that, Angie. But if you can find the passion and the partnership—" She cut herself off with a wavering smile. "These are not the kinds of things mothers are supposed to talk about. But I want you to have everything good in the world."

"So why didn't you marry him? The first man, I mean."

"He didn't want me. Or, rather, he wouldn't have me."

"Why not?"

"He was involved in some things that skirted the law. He said that was no life for me."

I stopped, turning to look in a gallery window so she couldn't see my face. *Jahn.* That's why their pictures were in those albums without my dad. Because my dad very literally wasn't in the picture when those photos were taken.

"Did you agree?" I asked softly.

"I never let myself think about it," she said, though I didn't believe her. "He thought he was saving me. That he was making some grand sacrifice to protect me. But really he was just hurting us both. And I think he regretted walking away."

I felt hollow inside. "How do you know?"

"Things he said when I saw him years later." She waved the words away. "It doesn't matter. I'll never know for certain."

But I knew, I realized. That was why he'd kept those photos. And what was it he'd told me so many years ago? *Sarah is special.*

Yes, I thought, *she is.* And although I loved my dad desperately, I couldn't help but want to weep for my mother and my uncle, and the love they never truly got to share.

I tried hard not to think about Evan, or the sacrifice I was making for him. A sacrifice that I was making without his consent. And one that I was starting to fear I would regret. But I still didn't know what choice I had. I couldn't leave him or my father to the wolves, and right then, with Kevin waiting so eagerly for any mistake, I was certain that those two men I loved would get eaten alive.

I made an effort to be more upbeat for the rest of our shopping trip, and when we returned home, laden with bags, we were both laughing about the horrible outfits we'd tried on at a local boutique.

"You should have bought the pink one," my mom said.

"Are you insane? I would have looked like a marshmallow Peep." I was about to counter that she should have bought the blue caftan-looking thing, but we'd reached the living room, and I stopped dead in my tracks. Evan was there. So was my dad and three men I didn't recognize, but who were wearing suits and looked very official.

"Um, hi. What's going on?"

"I had some business to conduct with your dad," Evan said, which made absolutely no sense to me. "But I think we're square now." He stood up and extended his hand. "Senator, it's been a pleasure."

He finished the goodbyes, then turned toward the door. "Angie, could I have a word?"

I saw the realization bloom on my mother's face, but now wasn't the time to confirm or deny. I followed him outside feeling lighter than I had in days—and at the same time angry that he'd come out here just when I was starting to get the pain under control. Because nothing had changed. There was still no possible future between us—not when my father's career hung in the balance—and seeing him only created fresh wounds.

"What the hell is going on here?" I demanded.

"It's done," he said. "The bullshit Mann Act threat—it's dead and buried."

I gaped at him. "How?"

"We cut a deal. Cole. Tyler. Me."

"A deal?" Fear and disgust twisted in my stomach, all knotted up with disbelief. "So Kevin was right? You were really—"

"Hell no," he said. "Just the opposite, in fact. There's a group working out of California and Mexico that's doing the very thing that Kevin was accusing us of—luring girls in and forcing them into prostitution. We learned about it and have been running interference, bringing the girls into our clubs, giving them legitimate jobs. We're doing nothing illegal, at least not on that front. But we've pissed off the ring—Larry's one of their flunkies—and after you told me what Kevin said, I knew they must have threatened some of the girls into making false statements. So I came out here and met with your dad—he's been on a task force to shut this kind of thing down for a few years now. And in exchange for immunity against the bogus Mann Act charges, Cole and Tyler and I are going to work with the FBI and local authorities."

"In other words, Kevin's got shit," I said. "Nothing on you, and nothing to hang over my dad. And since you and my dad are doing this task force thing together, if Kevin tries to make a stink, it'll just come off making him look bad."

He grinned. "It's easy to see you're a politician's daughter."

"But—but this is incredible." So much so that I had to lean against the hood of his rental car. "Thank you," I said. "Thank you for getting my father out of this mess."

"You're welcome, but my motive was a selfish one, too. I don't want to lose you."

"I don't want to lose you, either," I said. "I miss you so damn much."

"But you need to go in with eyes wide open. Because Kevin is going to be pissed and he just might be vindictive. I'm getting out—I already told you that. I'm cleaning up my various businesses, and if I can't clean them up, I'm dumping them. Ending them altogether or selling my share to Tyler and Cole. I've been cleaning up for a while now, ever since my mom died, and I don't think there's a stitch of evidence for him to latch on to. But that doesn't change the fact that I've done things. Things he can jump all over. He might not be able to make it stick, but he can still make life miserable for us."

He took my hand and raised my fingertips to his lips. "In other words, as long as Kevin's determined to poke around, I'm still not a safe bet."

I looked at him, thinking of the way he made me feel. Of my uncle's regret. Of my mother.

Most of all, I thought about what I wanted.

And what I wanted was this man.

"I love you, Evan. I want to go home. And I'm willing to accept whatever risk." I drew in a breath. "I don't want to ever be without you."

"And you never will be," he said, then pulled me into a long, deep kiss punctuated by that extra special Evan kick that I loved so much. "Do you want to go back to Chicago right away?" he asked.

I frowned, not sure what he was driving at. "Why? Do you want to stay in California for a while?"

"I was thinking we could take a short detour on the way back," he said. "A weekend in Italy? Or we could just go wild and spend a full week there. What do you say?"

I laughed, delighted with the man, with the world, with the whole entire universe.

"I say that sounds absolutely amazing."

epilogue

Luckily for me, Esther hadn't yet filled the director position at the foundation, and so I was able to slide seamlessly into my new job. It was a lot of work between that and my classes, but I loved it. I especially loved coming home at night to Evan.

The day that the job was official, my parents sent me flowers and Evan took me to high tea at The Drake to celebrate.

Afterward, Evan and I walked to the beach, and even though I was wearing heels and a cocktail dress and Evan was wearing dress slacks, we kicked off our shoes and walked barefoot in the sand to the water's edge.

"There's something I need to tell you," he said, looking not at me but at the lake that lay spread out in front of us.

His tone captured my attention, making me suddenly and unreasonably afraid. I stopped drawing designs in the sand with my toes and looked at him. "All right," I said, telling myself that no matter what, it would be okay. This was Evan, after all. This was the man I loved. "Tell me."

"I asked the guys to do some poking around in California. Talk to our connections in the various police departments. Ask a few questions of some of the gang leaders. We got some good intel. And when I was out there, I followed up on it."

I tensed. "Gracie," I whispered.

His fingers were still twined with mine, and now he raised our joined hand to his lips. "Jahn found them," he said. "I don't know how, but he found the three sons of bitches who killed your sister."

"Oh." My legs suddenly felt like noodles, and I held tight to Evan's hand, determined to stand. "How? When?"

"Five years ago. He never said a word, just went out to vindicate his niece. As for how, I'm not certain. But he managed it. He found them, and he killed two. The third he put in the hospital. He survived and then bragged about it to his buddies. That's how we were able to get our intel."

"I—" I drew in a breath and realized that at least a little of the burden I'd carried for close to eight years had been lifted. "Did they arrest him?"

"No," Evan said, his jaw tight.

I licked my lips. "Did you kill him?"

He faced me, his gray eyes as flat as I'd ever seen them. "No," he said. "Some gangbanger got to him six months ago." He drew in a breath. "I have never killed a man, but I went out there intending to do just that. To find that son of a bitch and to end him. Do you understand what I'm telling you?"

I nodded, feeling numb.

"I've walked away from a lot of my past. For you. For Ivy. For myself. But I have a code, and if someone comes after me or mine, I will strike back. And if it comes down to it, I will kill to protect the people I love."

"Do you think it scares me?" I asked. "You should know me

better by now. You're not a killer, Evan. You're a protector. And I've never felt more safe than when I'm with you."

"Good," he said, looking both relieved and nervous. "I needed to make sure you understood that before—"

I cocked my head, confused by the way he suddenly broke off his words. "Before what?"

"Before I ask you to marry me," he said.

"Evan!"

For a moment I thought he was joking. Then he reached into his pocket and pulled out a ring. He held it out to me even as he sank to one knee in the sand. "I love you, Angelina Raine. I want to spend the rest of my life with you. Will you marry me?"

I looked from the ring to the man holding it and realized that both were blurry, probably because I'd started crying.

I sniffled, then laughed, then slid the ring on my finger before dropping down into the sand myself and knocking him backward. I kissed him, hard and fast, this man of mine. And as we lay in the sand under the bright summer sun, I said the only thing there was left to say.

I said yes.

While Angie may have found all she ever wanted in Evan Black,
Tyler Sharp is about to bring Sloane Watson to the boiling point
in

HEATED

The next red-hot novel in J. Kenner's Most Wanted series
Coming soon from Bantam Books

Turn the page for an exclusive sneak peek!

one

Right and wrong.

Good and evil.

Black and white.

These are the parameters of the world in which we live, and anyone who tries to tell you otherwise—who argues that nothing is absolute, and that there are always shades of gray—is either a fool or is trying to con you.

At least that is what I used to believe.

But that was before I met him. Before I looked into his eyes. Before I gave him my trust.

Maybe I'm a fool. Maybe I've lost my balance and my edge. I don't know.

All I know is that from the moment I met him, everything changed. One look, and I feared that I was in trouble.

One touch, and I knew that I should run.

One kiss, and I was lost.

Now the only question is, will I find my way back to who I was? And more important, do I want to?

Nothing is ever as easy as it should be.

My dad taught me that. He served as a special agent with the FBI for twenty years before leaving that post to become the chief of police in Galveston, Texas, an island community with enough crime to keep his life interesting, and enough sunshine and warm weather to keep him happy.

During the years I was growing up, I'd watch as he spent hours, days, weeks, even months putting together a kick-ass case against some of the vilest criminals that ever walked this earth. Thousands of man hours. Hundreds of pieces of evidence. All those little ducks lined up just the way they should be—and it didn't make one bit of difference. The defense would spout some technicality, the judge would cave, and *poof,* all that work went down the drain.

Like I said, nothing is ever easy. That's the first truism upon which I base my life.

The second is a corollary: No one is who they seem.

My stepfather taught me that. He was a fresh-faced minor league baseball player that the press took a liking to. They called him the golden boy, predicted he'd make it to the majors, and did everything but genuflect when he entered a room. What they didn't report was the way he beat my mother. His hands, his fists, a broken beer bottle. Whatever was handy.

Somehow none of those hospital visits were ever reported in the local paper, and on the rare occasions when the cops showed up at our house, nothing ever came of it. Harvey Grier had the face of a prince and the smile of a homecoming king, and if his fifteen-year-old stepdaughter was calling the cops at night, it must be because she was your typical bored teenager. Certainly it couldn't be that she lived with the monster day in and day out, and had learned to see beneath his pretty boy disguise.

My stepfather is dead now. As far as I am concerned, that is a good thing. The man was good for nothing except driving that second lesson home: There are monsters hiding under the most innocent of countenances, and if you don't keep your guard up, they will bite you. And hard.

The take-away? Don't take anything for granted. And don't trust anyone.

I guess that makes me cynical. But it also makes me a damn good cop.

I sipped champagne and thought about my job and those two axioms as I leaned against one of the white draped pillars in The Drake's cloyingly elegant Palm Court restaurant. I didn't know a soul here, primarily because I'd crashed the party, and I was doing my best to blend with that pillar so that I could simply sit back and watch the world—and the people—go by. I was looking for one face in particular, because I'd come here with a plan. And I intended to stay in my little corner, holding this pillar, until I spied my mark.

I'd been standing there for an hour, and was beginning to think that I had a long night ahead. But I'd survived worse stakeouts, and I am nothing if not determined.

I'd been here once before, but tonight the familiar tables had been moved out, giving the crowd room to socialize around the elegant fountain and massive floral arrangement. As far as I could tell, the dress code for the evening was anything that had premiered during Fashion Week, and the only reason no one was pointing a finger at me and snickering was that my off-the-clearance-rack dress was so utterly pedestrian that it rendered me invisible.

The flowing strains of classical music filled the room, provided by an orchestra tucked into a corner, but no one was dancing. Instead they were mingling. Talking, laughing. It was all very proper. Very elegant. Very festive.

And I was very much out of my element.

My natural habitat is Indiana, where I'm actually a bit of a celebrity within the force as the youngest female ever to make detective with the Indianapolis Metropolitan Police Department. I'd come to Chicago because I'd been going out of my mind while I rode out a stint on medical leave, and when my roommate from college told me that her little sister had run away, I'd decided to do a little off-the-books investigation. I'd traced her as far as Chicago, then lost the trail, thus illustrating the First Truism.

Because I am just that awesome—and because I have friends in the Chicago PD and the local FBI office—the trail warmed up again reasonably quickly. I learned that she got her hands on a fake ID, though I hadn't yet nailed down the new name she was using. And I had reason to believe that she was working as a waitress at a local gentleman's club called Destiny.

Easy squeezy, right? Not so much.

I'd told my FBI friend my suspicions over coffee and he'd clued me in on some suspicions of his own. A whole laundry list of badass shit he thought was going down in that club, but that he wasn't authorized to officially pursue. And then suddenly my mission to get one runaway back to Indiana had morphed into a full-fledged, albeit off-the-books, undercover operation.

It was that whole "undercover" thing that was my current sticking point.

You'd think it would be easy for a reasonably attractive woman—that would be me—to get a job as a cocktail waitress in a Chicago-based gentleman's club, but you'd be wrong. I'd hung around the club for a few days, doing my research, figuring out what they look for in a waitress other than nice tits and a tight ass. I qualified on both fronts—and had the waitressing skills, too—but was turned down anyway. Apparently Destiny hires its girls through a pure referral system.

Like I said, nothing is ever as easy as it should be.

And that brings us to the Second Truism—no one is who they seem. The three supposedly upstanding owners of Destiny were the proof in that particular pudding. Take Evan Black, for example. This was his party that I'd crashed. A formal affair to celebrate his engagement to Angelina Raine, the daughter of vice presidential hopeful Senator Thomas Raine.

I saw him standing across the room, his arm around a stunning brunette. She was leaning against him, looking giddy with happiness, as they chatted with two other couples. It was almost like looking at a Norman Rockwell tableau. But Black wasn't the man he appeared to be.

Or what about Cole August, Black's business partner, who received so much adulation from the press and the public for the way he'd pulled himself up out of the muck of his Chicago South Side heritage to become one of the most respected and influential businessmen in the city? He might look positively drool-worthy as he stalked the far side of the room with a cellphone pressed against his ear, the very picture of the entrenched businessman.

But I happened to know that August hadn't left that shady heritage as far behind as he liked to pretend.

And then there was Tyler Sharp.

He'd been out of town for the last few weeks, so I had yet to see him in person, but I'd done my homework, and I was certain I'd recognize him the moment he entered this room. He stood just over six feet tall with a lanky, athletic build and the kind of dark blond hair that boasts flashes of gold in the summer. I knew that his business interests were wide and varied, and that he carried an American Express Black card. He owned a Corvette, but he rarely drove it, preferring his Ducati motorcycle.

Useful background info, I was sure, but it was the other aspect of his reputation that had intrigued me—Tyler Sharp had a weakness for women. He liked to fuck them, sure, but he also liked to help them. As far as criminal bad boy types went, Tyler was downright chivalrous.

I fully intended to use that to my advantage.

But, first, I had to find him.

"You look lost."

I'd been glancing toward the entrance, but now I jerked my head to the left and found myself staring at a brown-eyed blond with hair so thick and shiny she could do shampoo commercials. She held out her hand, and I took it without thinking. "I'm Kat," she said, then hooked her thumb toward Angelina Raine. "I'm the bride's best friend, which makes me the pseudo-hostess. But don't tell that one," she added, pointing toward an incredibly good-looking guy who was chatting up one of the waitresses. "Flynn thinks he has some claim on the whole best friend thing. He's a little insecure, so I let him keep his delusions."

She's chatting happily, and although I think that the eager conversation is fueled partly by the nearly empty wineglass she is waving, I can't help but smile. Yes, I was enjoying my effort to mimic a pillar, but I couldn't deny that human interaction was a good thing.

"Who are you here with?" she asked.

"I'm sorry, what? I didn't quite hear you." That was a lie, of course. I was hoping she'd had several of those glasses of wine and had forgotten the question.

"I was wondering who you came with. I think I know everyone on Lina's side of the guest list, so you must be a friend of Evan's?"

"I'm actually looking for Tyler," I said, and prided myself on my ability to tell the truth and lie all at the same time.

"He was running late, but I just saw him," she said, surprising me. I wouldn't have tossed that out so cavalierly if I'd realized he was in the building. I wanted time to watch him. To think and plan and choose my moment. Kat, however, had lifted herself up onto her tiptoes. Her fingertips were pressed against the pillar near my shoulder as she balanced herself and scoped out the crowd.

"Don't worry about it," I said. "I'm sure he has people he wants to say hi to. I'll find him in a minute. Besides, I should probably hit the ladies' room and—"

"There he is!" Her voice was triumphant, and she grinned at me as she waved to him. As I'm a good three inches shorter than Kat and was wearing flats, I had absolutely no idea if she saw him or if he was on his way over.

I took the opportunity to gather myself and plan my attack. Kat's enthusiasm may have thrown me for a loop, but there was no denying that she was doing me a favor. I needed to get close to Tyler Sharp—he was my best bet for getting inside Destiny. And if Kat had actually called him over, I couldn't get much closer than that.

I was beginning to think that he either hadn't seen her or had chosen to ignore her, when I saw the glint of gold as the light struck his hair. He wore a charcoal gray suit, and the fine lines and expensive material contrasted with the slightly mussed hair that he wore just a little too long for the corporate rule book. Now, it was tied back in a manner that highlighted the sharp angles of his cheeks and jawline.

His cerulean eyes were the perfect contrast to the golden blond hair, conjuring thoughts of sun and sand, wild days and wicked nights. All in all he had a devil-may-care look about him, and that was only accentuated by the beard stubble. My fingers twitched, and to my horror, I found myself wanting to reach out and stroke his cheek, letting the roughness there smooth away my hard edges like sandpaper.

He eased around the fountain and jockeyed through the

crowd with the kind of confidence that comes from knowing that people will move out of your way because you're just that cool.

"Tyler!" Kat called again, and I had the unreasonable urge to clamp my hand over her mouth. This was the guy I'd come here to get close to, but right then, I didn't feel prepared at all.

But I couldn't run. He'd seen us, and though he nodded to Kat, I was the one who drew his focus. His eyes met mine, and I suddenly had to reach back and grip the drape on the pillar, because the impact of that simple look had ripped through me in a way that left me weak and confused. I'd never met Tyler Sharp—had seen him only in photographs. But in that moment it felt as though I'd known him all my life.

I wasn't entirely sure I liked the feeling—or perhaps I just liked it too much.

He stopped in front of us, and I told myself to get it together. I was not the kind of woman who lost her cool around a gorgeous man. Or, at least, I hadn't been two minutes ago.

"Do I know you?" His gaze drifted over me, making my body tingle in a way that caught me off guard, but that I couldn't deny liking.

"You do now," I said firmly, determined to take back at least a modicum of control. "I'm Sloane."

"Sloane was looking for you," Kat said.

"Was she?" His eyes never left my face, and I thought for a moment that if I stepped closer, I would drown in those liquid eyes. "Funny," he said. "She's just the woman I was looking for, too."

J. KENNER (aka Julie Kenner) is the *New York Times, USA Today, Publishers Weekly, Wall Street Journal,* and #1 international bestselling author of over seventy novels, novellas, and short stories in a variety of genres.

Though known primarily for her award-winning and international bestselling erotic romances (including the Stark and Most Wanted series) that have reached as high as #2 on the *New York Times* bestseller list, Kenner has been writing full-time for over a decade in a variety of genres including paranormal and contemporary romance, "chicklit" suspense, urban fantasy, and paranormal mommy lit.

Kenner has been praised by *Publishers Weekly* as an author with a "flair for dialogue and eccentric characterizations" and by *RT Book Reviews* for having "cornered the market on sinfully attractive, dominant antiheroes and the women who swoon for him." A four-time finalist for Romance Writers of America's prestigious RITA award, Kenner took home the first RITA trophy awarded in the category of erotic romance in 2014 for her novel, *Claim Me* (book 2 of her Stark Trilogy).

Her books have sold well over a million copies and are published in over twenty countries.

jkenner.com

Facebook.com/jkennerbooks

@juliekenner.com.